Wolf Shadow's Promise

"Has it always been this way between us?"

He nodded, his head against her own, his breathing quick and shallow.

"And do you think it will be like this still, when we have been long married and are growing old together?"

He caught his breath and held it while several moments swept by, followed by a deadly silence. His hands had slowed and his body had gone suddenly rigid. Had she been at all experienced, she might have taken heed of the brusque change in him, but she had never been in love before, had never been with a man.

He should have gone while he had the chance. But he didn't. Instead he said, "It was wise of you to go your own way all those years ago. Our worlds are too far apart."

But his touch told her that his words might not be true. At once, he was holding her up, turning her around to face him. He pulled her in close, his lips above her ear, kissing it, kissing her, inhaling deeply as though memorizing the very scent of her . . .

Other **AVON ROMANCES**

KAREN KAY

WOLF SHADOW'S PROMISE

AVON BOOKS
An Imprint of HarperCollins*Publishers*

This is a work of fiction. Names, characters, places, and incidents are products of the author's imagination or are used fictitiously and are not to be construed as real. Any resemblance to actual events, locales, organizations, or persons, living or dead, is entirely coincidental.

AVON BOOKS
An Imprint of HarperCollins*Publishers*
10 East 53rd Street
New York, New York 10022-5299

Copyright © 2000 Karen Kay Elstner-Bailey
Map by Trina Elstner
ISBN: 0-380-80340-2
www.avonromance.com

First Avon Books paperback printing: July 2000

Avon Trademark Reg. U.S. Pat. Off. and in Other Countries, Marca Registrada, Hecho en U.S.A.
HarperCollins® is a trademark of HarperCollins Publishers Inc.

Printed in the U.S.A.

WCD   10 9 8 7 6 5 4 3 2 1

For Nancy Richards-Akers

Our friendship, the magic of
who and what you are,
will live forever in my heart

Acknowledgments

I would like to especially thank
the following people, without whom
I could not have written this book.

James Willard Schultz
and his book *Why Gone Those Times.*
Mr. Schultz documents the story of
Laughter, the tame wolf.
What an adventure in reading.

Chief Buffalo Child Long Lance
and his *Autobiography of a Blackfoot Indian Chief.*
Your accounting of an "I saw" Dance was thrilling.

My good friend, Maria Ferrara
of Celebrity Center International, whose
encouragement has provided great assistance for me.

And my daughter, Alyssa Howson,
my inspiration.

Note to the Reader

The following historical background will hopefully shed some light on this moment in history, one that has oft been forgotten. The time is circa 1870 and the place, the Montana Territory.

Let's go back to 1862 when gold was discovered near Bannack, Montana. This attracted floods of white men into the Montana countryside. These men were described by their contemporaries as rough, uncivilized and often criminal. As John C. Ewers noted in his book *The Blackfeet: Raiders on the Northwestern Plains* they were considered little more than "thieves and blackguards," the sort of persons who could "not be tolerated in any civilized society." With the advent of these people flooding into the country, a series of wrongs committed against the Indian people began to go unpunished, thus setting the stage for war.

To add to this, in 1863, annuities, promised to the Blackfeet by treaty with the U.S. government, never reached the Indians due to a Sioux war and the Blackfeet agent's fear of travel. Ultimately he refused to complete the journey north, and the goods were never delivered to the Indians.

At last a new agent was chosen for the Blackfeet, but he was possibly worse than the previous one. In his writings, he referred to the Indians as "degraded savages," and called them "hopeless." Under his "care" and "guardian-ship," more injustices were committed, and the Indians, who had voiced their disapproval of the white invaders, escalated their protests from capturing a few horses (a practice laudable to Indian society) to killing the white invaders.

Also, at this time, the governor of the district, Governor Edgerton, took steps to ignore the U.S. government's treaties with the Blackfeet and stated openly, "The Government will, at an early date, take steps for the extinguishment of Indian title in this territory, in order that our lands may be brought into market."

In 1865, a war between the Blackfeet and whites ensued after gold was discovered in the Sun River Valley. The whites wanted the gold; the Indians demanded that the treaties, which had given the land to them, be upheld. Also that winter the Indians helped many of these white men to survive a particularly harsh season. However, this aid was clearly forgotten when friendly Indians visited John Morgan in Sun Valley that winter. There he killed one of the Indians and hung the other three affable visitors from a nearby tree.

Now add to this, the horror of smallpox, which may have been transmitted to the Indians through contaminated blankets. This disease was carrying off the tribe's young people, and the Blackfeet began to fear for their future.

About this same time the white settler's eye began to covet not only gold, but the rich grazing land, which again had been promised to the Blackfeet by treaty. Perhaps because of the discovery of gold, or perhaps only because the white settlers screamed so hard all the way to Washington, the United States government blatantly refused to uphold the promises of the Treaty of 1868.

Hostilities grew and in 1869, two Indians, while on a peaceful errand for their agent, were shot and killed in broad daylight on the streets of Fort Benton. No action was ever taken to right this wrong.

Then the worst happened. In 1870, one of the friendly villages of Blackfeet was struck by the cavalry, an incident that is now known as the Baker massacre (see appendix), in which an entire village of women, children and old men were killed while the warriors were out of the camp, on a buffalo hunt.

While news of the massacre stirred the hearts of those in the east and incited their protests, closer to home, the white settlers in the west applauded the military's action.

It was during this time that the Indian whiskey traders began to take unprecedented advantage of the Indians' uncertainty of the future by pouring barrel upon barrel of illegal liquor into their trade. While liquor had always been a part of the trade, never had the west seen such large quantities of the "white men's water" so easily obtained. The liquor had ill effects on many in the tribe and the weak-hearted went crazy under its influence, ofttimes killing family members or friends or even freezing overnight in a drunken stupor.

In its defense, the U.S. government, witnessing the horrible effect on the Indian tribes, cracked down on the traders whom the Indians called "whisky sneakers," thus making it almost impossible to trade alcohol to the Indians south of the Canadian border.

In 1869, a new problem began when the Hudson's Bay Company ceded its vast territory north of the "medicine line" (the divide between the United States and Canada) to Canada. This effectively left no law and order in the land; no one to prevent American rascals from trading more and more liquor to the Indians. During the next four years more than a dozen forts, large and small, flew the American flag on Canadian soil.

As said by John C. Ewers in his book *The Blackfeet:*

Raiders on the Northwestern Plains, these "whiskey forts" were directly responsible for one of the bleakest time periods in Blackfoot history when easily twenty-five percent of the tribe perished, directly due to the liquor trade.

In spite of their colorful names, these American posts north of the "medicine line" were responsible for one of the darkest chapters in Blackfoot Indian history. At a time when these Indians were disturbed by the steadily growing influx of white settlers upon their Montana hunting grounds and by the United States government's refusal to honor treaties made with them, when another smallpox epidemic was carrying away large numbers of their sturdy young people, and when they were thoroughly shaken by the massacre on the Marias, it took but little more to demoralize the Blackfeet completely. That little was a ready supply of "white men's water" with which to drown their sorrows . . .

There are no complete records of the number of Indian deaths caused by "white men's water" in the period 1869–74. But the Blackfoot agent in Montana estimated that six hundred barrels of liquor were used in Blackfoot trade in 1873, and that in the six years prior to that time, 25 per cent of the members of these tribes died from the effects of liquor alone.

And so it is during this turbulent time period in American history that our story begins.

WOLF SHADOW'S
PROMISE

The Whiskey Trail

Fort Benton to Fort Hamilton, at Whoop-Up
210 miles

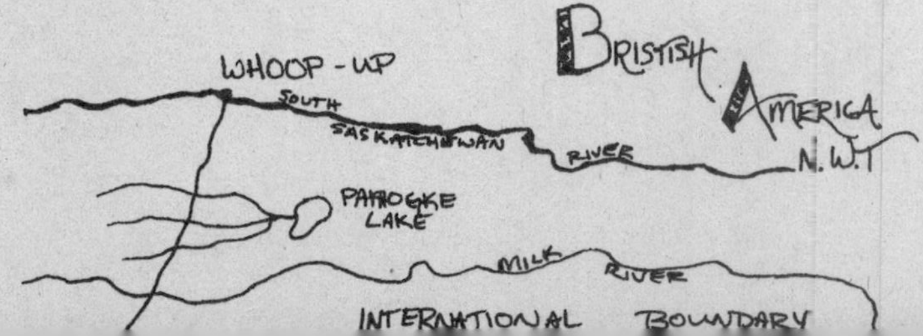

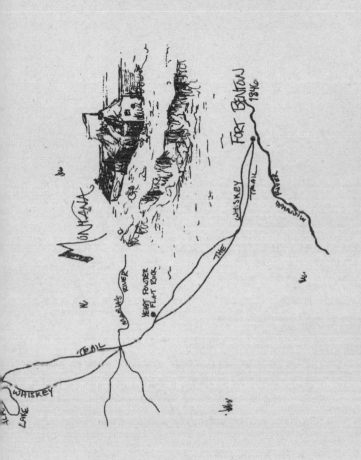

Prologue

Blackfeet Reservation, Montana
Early 1900s

"Sit down, my grandchildren, and I will tell you a story."

The youngsters, laughing and giggling, crowded in through the tepee's entryway, its canvas flap thrown back to allow access. Several women, their mothers, were at work in the sunshine, the men out tending to their livestock and horses.

Smoke from the lodge's inner fire found its way under the still colorful tepee lining, the sooty fragrance, reminiscent of an earlier time, curling its way up and out of the upper opening, the "ears" of the home. But there the similarity between this lodge and the lodges of old ended. No longer were the riches of Indian life strewn throughout the home: no tanned buffalo robes, no comfortable willow backrests, no parfleches, no spears, and certainly no rawhide shields depicting a warrior's dreams.

1

Spread out on the ground, underneath where the old man sat, lay a three-point trade blanket and several other quilts, lining the floor. These, and the single medicine bundle hanging from the inner lining, remained the only evidence of the once powerful Blackfeet confederation.

"What story are you going to tell us today, Grandfather?"

The old man smiled kindly at the pretty little girl whose dark eyes sparked with vitality, something in them reminding him of the former, wild life of the Indian; a life he had loved well. He motioned the child toward him, noting, in doing so, that the child's features mirrored the spirits of her ancestors. If only she knew.

The child flopped down next to him and he drew her closer, grinning at the small creature who sat so trustingly beside him. Then he gestured toward the other children, inviting them to sit.

It was time, he decided. Time to tell these youngsters the great stories of their fathers, stories that the missionaries and the new government agents had forbidden. Tales he hoped these youngsters would never forget.

Aa, yes, he set his head back slightly and shut his eyes. He remembered it well. It had been in an era before the white man had invaded their country so thoroughly, a brief interval before the reservation days. An age when the Indian had still roamed free.

Taking a deep breath, he began, "My children, today I will tell you a story about a great warrior, a brave man. A man who alone defied the United States army."

"Alone, Grandfather?"

"*Aa,* yes, alone . . . that is, except for a brother wolf and his—"

"A wolf?" The small voice at his side sounded awed, as well it should.

"*Aa,* yes, in those days, the wolves ranged over the

countryside in huge numbers. They were our brothers, the wolves. Now, I have heard the tales of the white man which say the wolf preyed on human beings, but such stories never came from an Indian tongue, for the wolf in this country never bothered man. *Saa,* no, the wolf was kinsman to the red man. Now listen well and I will reveal to you a time when the white man had just begun to live next to the red man . . . a day when the people's future hung delicately . . ."

Chapter 1

⟨◦◦◦◦⟩

Fort Benton on the Missouri River
1857, Northwest Territory

"Two and two equals . . . ?" The teacher slapped the ruler against the blackboard, the *wap* of the wooden stick an unspoken threat. The teacher—who, by invitation, had only recently arrived here—stood frowning, arms crossed at her waist. "Young lady," the teacher said as she took a menacing step forward and unfolded her arms, "answer me."

Still the young Indian girl standing at the head of the class didn't make a sound. Head down, she stared fixedly at her feet.

Looking at the child, who was no older than herself, Alys Clayton felt as if her own heart might break. Personally, she had never understood why the wild Indians had been brought to this school. Her mother said the whole thing was an experiment by their Indian agent, Alfred J.

4

Vaughan, to see if the Indians could be civilized, whatever that meant.

But the project was doomed to failure because Indians didn't learn from this kind of teaching.

At least that's what her mother said: that the Indians of the plains had not been brought up with the same books and stories as the white man; that the Indians had their own stories, their own way of teaching, of doing things. Indians were close to the land, were free, or at least they were supposed to be. Alys's mother had also said, and Alys agreed, that the Indians would be better off if left independent which, Alys decided, must mean "left alone."

So, if all these things were true, why was their teacher making an example of this poor child? What did it matter if the girl could or could not add the two plus two on the chalkboard? Alys knew that if she were to approach the girl and promise her four beads while giving her only three, the young girl would know the difference.

Tears streamed down the young girl's face as she endured not only the silent threat of the teacher but the sneers and scoffings of her "fellow classmates" too.

Something should be done. Such things were not right. Yet Alys felt helpless. She was only eight years old, a child herself. What good was she against a teacher—against the taunts of the others?

Oh, no. Alys caught her breath.

The teacher—an overly skinny, sickly-looking woman— had raised the ruler as though she might hit the girl, causing the youngster to put a hand over her eyes as though to shield them.

Then the worst happened. Down came the ruler, down across the Indian girl's arm.

The child didn't cry out, didn't even flinch, although she whimpered slightly as tears streamed down her face.

The teacher shouted out a few more unmentionable words. Still the young girl remained silent.

"I'll teach you to sass me, you heathen," the teacher threatened, while Alys tried to make sense of what the teacher had just said. The young girl hadn't uttered a word.

Wap! Another slap across the girl's arms. The teacher raised her arm for another blow.

It never came.

In a blur of buckskin and feathers, a young Indian boy, the same one who had been at their school for about a week, burst into the classroom, putting himself between the youngster and the teacher; in his hand, he wielded a knife.

The class went from a mass of jeers and prankish cat-calls to abrupt silence.

Where had the boy come from so suddenly? And the knife? Where had he obtained that? It was well known that the wild Indians, even the children, were relieved of their weapons upon entering the fort.

Yet there was no mistaking that knife or the boy's intent.

Good, thought Alys.

Immediately, the teacher backed up, but in doing so, she tripped over a wastebasket, losing her balance and falling into the trash can, bottom first.

Alys couldn't help herself. She laughed.

It was the only sound in an otherwise silent classroom. No one looked at her, however. Everyone appeared . . . stunned.

The teacher's face filled with color, her hands clenched over the top of the basket. "You . . . you savage. You pushed me—"

"This one," the Indian responded, pointing to himself, "has not touched you. But give me good reason to"—he waved his knife in front of her—"and I will."

The teacher muttered something deep in her throat before she uttered, "I'll have your skin for this, young man."

"Humph." The boy approached the teacher, saying, "And I will have your hair."

It took a moment for his meaning to register, but as the boy swung out his knife, taking hold of the teacher's tight bun, she screamed. *Whack!* Off came the bun, harmlessly falling into the youngster's hand.

"You savage, why, I'll . . ." In an almost superhuman effort, the teacher jumped up, out of the basket. The boy quickly grabbed hold of the Indian girl and, pulling her after him, fled toward the classroom's only window.

That was all it took for the other youngsters in the room to come alive. Insults and threats all at once reverberated through the early morning air, while the two fugitives tried to make their escape. Boys, almost all of them of mixed heritage themselves, suddenly sprung up from their chairs, leaping after the two runaways, who had by this time cleared the window.

The entire school became a mass exodus as student after student bolted out the door, out the window, chasing after the pair.

Alys, however, arose from her seat at a more leisurely pace, strolling slowly and thoughtfully toward the doorway of the tiny cabin which served as the schoolhouse. Fingering her soft auburn curls as she moved, she trudged home, concluding that school had been let out for the day.

Poor Indian kids, she mused. Wasn't it enough that the children had been taken away from their family to be "educated"? According to her mother, the townspeople weren't making it easy on these wild ones either, scolding them and making fun of them. Who would want to stay, amidst such hatred? Alys asked herself.

Her thoughts troubled, Alys left the schoolhouse and slowly trudged toward her home.

Her house, a wooden structure and one of the nicer

homes in the fort, lay situated toward the rear of the town, away from the river and isolated from most of the fort's more rambunctious activities. It was a relatively quiet spot, a location her father had personally selected before he had passed away almost four years ago.

That Alys's mother had refused to return east after her husband's passing had been the fort's greatest gossip during the first few years after his death, at least for the few white women who had come west with their husbands.

There were only two types of unmarried women on the frontier, or so it was said. Indians and the hurdy-gurdy girls. Her mother had been asked which one she was.

And it hadn't mattered that her mother had helped found this town, right alongside her father. Nor had the richness of her purse given her immunity. As it was in many small towns, there wasn't much to provide gossip, leaving Alys's mother to supply fodder for the wagging tongues, a circumstance that had effectively isolated her, and her youngster, from the community.

As Alys made her way through the fort, she wondered what her mother would say about the events of this day, knowing that it was her nature to blame the townspeople, not the Indians. Hadn't her mother often commented on the unchristian-like behavior of the few white women in this town? Hadn't she herself observed that those here, more oft times than not, made up the grievances they complained about?

Why? Alys Clayton could little understand it.

She only wished there were something she could do, some way to help. If only she knew where the two Indians were right now, she would offer them kindness and hope. Yes, she decided, with all the naivete of a young girl her age. She would be kind to them, make friends with them, show them that they could trust her.

Why, she would . . .

What was that? A glimpse of something out of the corner of her eye. Buckskin, feathers—two small arms and legs? There in the bushes? She turned to look.

A knife suddenly appeared out of nowhere, pressing close into her throat, and a hand covered her mouth as arms slipped about her waist, dragging her backward, toward that bush.

"You cry out . . . I kill you," threatened a young male voice.

Alys looked up into a set of the deepest, blackest eyes she had ever seen. She nodded.

The dusty scent of the boy's skin, the dirt on his hands assailed Alys until she thought she might gag. It wasn't that the smell was unpleasant, it was more that he held her mouth too tightly. She squirmed.

"Be still."

Two young boys flew past them, more footsteps followed, more shuffling, the pounding of boots, of adult feet striking the ground, rushing by.

Alys struggled in the boy's arms. She wanted to let him know that she was a friend, that she would help him.

It was useless, however. The boy held his hand too securely over her lips.

Gunshots in the distance caught Alys's attention, and then came more shouts and hurrying footsteps. Gunshots? Surely no one intended physical harm to these two, did they?

She had to do something. Quickly, Alys took stock of where she was. Over to her right was her home—within running distance—and beside her house was the secret place, that place known only to Alys and her mother . . .

A place that might prove to be the salvation of these two outcasts, if she could make them understand. Could she?

She had to try. Motioning toward the house, Alys

pointed at the two Indians, then flapped her hands like wings, trying to make an image of birds, flying away free. Would he understand?

The young boy followed her hand motions for a moment, then tugged at her to remain still. He looked away.

Alys tried again. Point to the house, to the Indians, a bird flying away free. Once more.

It took a few more tries, before the boy frowned, looking down at Alys, at her hands, at the house.

More voices, more footsteps coming toward them.

Alys gestured again.

With a stern frown at her, the boy loosened his grip, allowing Alys to whisper, "I know a secret way out of the fort."

Would he believe her? Did he understand she meant to help him?

Dark eyes glared into her own.

"It's at the side of my home." She motioned toward the house.

"There is nothing there, white girl; a house, a wall, no more. Do you try to trap us?"

Alys didn't say a word. And perhaps it was her silence that accounted for her redemption.

He asked, "How we escape there?"

"In our root cellar," Alys was quick to answer, "my mother's and mine, there is a hidden tunnel."

"What is this . . . root cellar?"

Alys pointed to a set of bushes that almost, but not quite, hid the wooden doors of the cellar. "There," she said. "See it? It goes down to a passage underground. It's like a cave. It leads to the hills."

She could see him hesitate, watched as indecision played across his features. At last, though, he volunteered, "You show us."

Alys nodded.

They waited until the approaching footsteps faded away. Then he prodded her forward, and she fled, as fast as her small legs would carry her, on and on toward the side of her yard, with the two Indians following close on her heels.

"Here." She pushed her way into the bushes and pulled at the doors of the cellar. They wouldn't give. She almost cried.

The Indian boy came to her rescue, tugging on the doors and hauling them up.

"Hurry." She motioned to the two of them to enter. Quickly, they did as she bid, fleeing down into the cellar, Alys coming in after them and dragging the doors shut behind her. Instantly, all was darkness inside, but it didn't bother Alys. She merely sighed in relief.

"This is trap," the boy said, his knife coming once more to Alys's neck. Maybe he didn't like the darkness, Alys considered.

"No," she insisted, unafraid. "I'll show you."

Lifting a rug on the floor, Alys uncovered a small earthen mound. Brushing the dirt away, Alys pointed to a meager trapdoor.

Pulling on the door, she glanced up toward the boy, barely able to make out his features in the darkness.

"Come," she said and dropped down to the ladder. Down and down she climbed, her two charges following.

Plunging to the stone floor of the cavern below, Alys fumbled in the dark until she found the lantern her mother always kept there. Checking first to make sure it was working properly, she lit the wick, instantly throwing a shadow of light throughout the cave. Instinctively, she took the hand of the Indian boy.

"Hold hands," she instructed and began to lead the two of them through the tunnels. The darkness of the caves, their earthy smells and coolness had never bothered Alys. They were a part of her family, a part of her.

She and her mother came here often, hunting a treasure that had been lost here long ago. Although if Alys were honest, she would admit that sometimes she sought out the comfort of the caves for pleasure alone, these caverns being a legacy to her from her father.

"If you lead us back to . . . that village, white girl, I will kill you."

"I know." Alys hesitated. "But I won't. I promise you."

He let out a snort. "The vow of a white girl."

"The word of Alys Clayton." She might not be aware of it, but Alys lifted her chin. "Not all white people are bad."

He didn't say a word, though another menacing growl escaped his throat.

Well, what did it matter anyway? She would show him. Wasn't it what her mother had always told her, that actions, not words, were important? It took an hour or so of careful travel, but she didn't falter in her step. She knew the way.

The tunnel climbed slowly, gradually, until at last, up ahead, she could see light, hear the rush of a waterfall.

Ah, the great falls, behind which lay the tunnel's entrance. This was her most favorite spot in the world, isolated, untouched and unspoiled. No one else knew of the caverns or the beauty of these cliffs either, as far as she knew, since they were hidden on all sides by the height of the hills. At least, Alys silently corrected herself, no other white man knew of them.

Alys led their party underneath the falls, out onto the rocks and into the bright sunshine, allowing the two young people to adjust their eyesight to the light before she stated, "I don't know where your people are, but I reckon you'll be able to find them from here."

The boy looked around him and inhaled a deep breath before glancing back at Alys and staring intently at her.

Then, without any expression on his face whatsoever, he murmured, "What strange manner is this? A white girl who keeps her word?"

Alys stiffened her spine before she responded, "I told you I would."

He nodded. "So you did, white girl, so you did."

The young Indian miss at his side didn't seem as devoid of human emotion as her male counterpart, however, and she came up to Alys, hugging her profusely and saying something in a very strange tongue.

The lad translated, "She says something good will come to you."

Alys nodded, smiling. Then it occurred to her. "She doesn't speak English?"

"*Saa, no*"

"So she could not even understand the teacher . . ."

The boy remained silent, though when he gazed down at Alys, he suddenly smiled, the first cheerful emotion Alys had seen on his face. The action made him look younger still, innocent, and oh, so very handsome. Alys gaped at the long dark hair that fell back from his face. The cooling breeze from the falls brought tiny droplets to his tanned skin; his dark eyes, surprisingly full of approval for her, watched her closely. Alys couldn't help herself. Gazing back, she fell instantly under his spell.

Slowly, the boy took a piece of jewelry from around his neck. A round, single white shell dangled from a chain of bleached buckskin. He drew it over Alys's head and settled it around her neck.

"*Soka'pii*, good." His right hand signed the meaning of the word in a single gesture. "Looks good on you."

With the tip of his finger, he tilted her face up toward his. "I will remember you always, young white girl, and what you have done for me and my sister."

So, thought Alys, the Indian girl was his sister. Pleased

by the realization, she said, pointing to herself, "Alys."

"Aa-lees," the young lad rolled her name smoothly over on his tongue.

She pointed to him. "And your name is?"

He shook his head. "A warrior does not repeat his own name. To do so would be dishonorable."

"But I would like to know . . ."

She was interrupted by the boy saying something to his sister, again in that strange tongue.

With a quick glance up at Alys, the Indian girl spoke, and, pointing to her brother, said, *"Ki'somm-makoyi."*

"Ki'somm-makoyi," Alys whispered. "That is your name?"

He nodded.

"What does it mean?"

"I cannot say."

"Please?"

He took a deep breath, grinned at her slightly, then said, pointing to himself, "This one is called Moon Wolf."

"Moon Wolf."

Another nod.

She smiled up at him. "Moon Wolf, I will never forget you."

He stared into her eyes, his look serious, before he volunteered, "Come with us, young Aa-lees. Come with us and I promise that when we grow older, I will take you for wife and show you great honor for what you have done for us this day."

Under any other circumstance, Alys might have chuckled, the thought absurd for one so young. Yet there was a somberness to his words that she couldn't discount.

"I cannot," she replied, her voice sounding strangely adult. "I would bring you more trouble if I went with you. No one in the fort would rest until I was found."

He inclined his head. "That is true. For a small girl, you

speak with wise tongue. But still," his chin shot up in the air, "no matter what others would do, I would honor you in this way."

His words, or perhaps something in his manner, reached out to her, its effect on her profound, and she felt herself responding to the boy, tears of appreciation, maybe even joy, coming to her eyes. She said, "I cannot. My mother would miss me too much."

He remained silent for many moments before he nodded at last. "So it will be," he uttered, "but know that, though you choose to stay behind, I will carry your image with me, here," he held his hand to his heart, "for so long as this one should live."

Alys stared. These were strong words, a powerful declaration, for a boy not much older than she, and Alys contemplated him in silence for several seconds, afraid to move lest she spoil the moment. Slowly, he brought his hand up to run his fingers over her cheek, his touch gentle; he reached up with one of his fingers to trace the path of her tears, before bringing that same finger to his own cheek. "And now," he whispered, touching his face with her own tears, "a part of you is a part of me."

He didn't wait for her to respond. All at once, he turned and fled, disappearing with his sister down the rocks and into the countryside as though they belonged to it.

Alys fingered her cheek for what seemed an eternity, letting the warmth of the sunshine wash over her and dry her face. In the distance she could hear the birds sing, while closer at hand, she could smell the perfumed scent of the grasses and wildflowers. Lightly, the wind ruffled her hair, lifting her spirit gently upward until she felt herself becoming a part of all this, a part of the natural course of things.

She would never forget this, never forget him. She couldn't.

Alys had become, in the space of a moment, infatuated:
She had fallen in love. A love that would last her a lifetime, she thought, no matter the state of her youth. And in
that instant, she knew she would never be the same.

Chapter 2

It was a grand night for a ball. Indian ladies and the few white women present danced round and round with their handsome or not so handsome gentlemen. Kerosene and lard-oil lamps brightened the ballroom, while the strains of the fiddles played out a concertina. The music, which had been taught by ear from father to son for generations, sweetened the otherwise smoky air and lent a lively atmosphere to the place. Conversation and laughter, shouting and giggling, had fallen into a dull hum, barely heard over the music.

The celebration was for Alys, a homecoming, although Alys would never have asked for such a thing. Her mother lay ill at home with what looked to be pneumonia, and Alys wished to be there, not at this party.

But she couldn't very well miss a gala thrown in her

17

honor. Not without making serious enemies. Besides, her mother had insisted that she come.

Alys glanced down at her gown, a fashionable creation with an underskirt of blue faille and an overdress of the same material in gold. With pearls in her auburn-brown tresses and blue and gold enamel jewelry accenting her attire, Alys looked out of place on the western frontier. The dress, combining the season's three different colors of blue, gold, and white, had been the height of fashion back east. But here at Fort Benton, where her counterparts wore mostly homespun dresses of calico, it lost its effect. In comparison, Alys felt overdressed and uncomfortable.

She had arrived back at the fort only yesterday, having traveled over a month on the steamboat the *Assiniboine,* one of many vessels sailing the Missouri waters between here and St. Louis. Alys had been thrilled to return and to put the long years of eastern schooling behind her.

She remembered a particular conversation she'd had with her mother five years ago. Alys had begged to remain in Montana. But her mother, who would hear none of it, had taken a firm stand and had insisted that Alys be properly educated by people with more on their minds than gold, furs, and cattle. Money had been no object, and the elder Clayton would see her daughter brought up correctly. Perhaps, her mother had also suggested, Alys might even find a young man back east.

But Alys's heart had been lost to the frontier long ago, to the land and the first people who inhabited it. This was her home, rough though it might be, and she could not remember a day passing when she hadn't yearned for her life back in Montana.

Alys wrapped her cashmere paletot, a fashionable cloak, around her shoulders and stepped outside, her blue silk slippers in evidence, but only for a moment. Perhaps, she thought, she had put in enough of a presence at the party tonight to excuse herself.

As she emerged outside, a certain gentleman, a Lieutenant Warrington, ran after her. He was handsome, young, and, she had come to realize, quite persistent. Taking hold of her sleeve, he placed her gloved hand on his arm.

"You're not leaving already, Miss Clayton, are you?"

"I'm afraid so, Lieutenant."

"But you can't do that just yet. It's not completely polite, now, is it? Not when every man here, including myself, has been waiting all night to dance with you. You must know that we've all been lovesick since the day you stepped off that steamboat."

She smiled faintly, then chuckled. "Lieutenant, how you do flatter me."

"No, ma'am. Just plain speaking. That's all. Now, surely you can't think of disappointing us, can you?"

"I am sorry, but I must," Alys replied, though she tried to lessen any possible blow from her words by bestowing the man with a kind smile.

However, instead of being discouraged, the lieutenant gave her a big grin, obviously quite heartened. "You really should stay," he coaxed. "What must I do to convince you?"

Alys scrutinized Lieutenant Warrington's set features. At any other time, she might have allowed herself to be coaxed into doing exactly as this man asked, his gift for persuasion excellent. But she couldn't give in. At least not tonight. And truly, at this moment, her attention could not have been further removed from the party and from these people.

"Thank you kindly, Lieutenant Warrington, you are most generous, indeed. But you must know that I can't stay. My mother lies ill at home, and I cannot allow her to be alone for long."

"But she's not alone, is she?" he asserted. "Doesn't that half-breed Mary stay with her at night and look after her?"

"Yes, that is true, but—"

"Then you needn't return, after all. Not yet anyway. Stay a little longer." He glanced away from her, out into the night. "Look around you, Miss Clayton, at the evening, at the multitude of stars up there"—he motioned toward the sky—"and tell me that you haven't missed your home here in Montana."

Alys grinned and shook her head. The lieutenant could certainly be determined. "Yes," she replied, "but still . . ."

The lieutenant picked a bloom from a nearby lilac bush and twirled it delicately under Alys's nose. "It must have been difficult being away for so long."

Alys nodded. "It was."

"And how did you find the east?"

"It was most . . . fashionable." She inhaled deeply, the fragrances of the night, the delicate blooms, the wildflowers, and the prairie grasses acting like an intoxication.

He chuckled softly. "Ah, it is that. It certainly is fashionable."

Alys moved a little farther away from him, from the ballroom. Sighing she realized that she'd forgotten how cool and crisp the air was here, how solid the earth felt beneath her feet, how redolent the wind. And above her, as she looked up, a million stars splashed across the sky, twinkling as though they hadn't a care.

Oh, how she had missed this, the howling serenades of the wolves so far away, yet so close; the crisp barking of coyotes, the peculiar song of the crickets. She asked the lieutenant, "Do you yearn for your own home very much?"

"Me? What? Oh, you mean the east?"

"Hmmm," Alys replied. She might have said more, but she was silenced by the more unpleasant sound of gunshots—off in the distance. Lieutenant Warrington stiffened and muttered a barely audible curse under his breath.

Uniformed men suddenly appeared from out of nowhere, rushing past them, all cursing a certain personage.

"Damn! It's the Wolf Shadow!" Lieutenant Warrington swore. "Pardon my language, ma'am."

Alys nodded, unoffended. She had grown up in this town, after all, and had become used to the crudeness of the language. She did ask, however, "The Wolf Shadow?"

"Yes, ma'am. That's what Indians call him."

"Wolf Shadow? Is that the Indian who has all the townspeople talking?"

"That's him."

More men, armed civilians, filed past them.

"I heard he's made quite a nuisance of himself here at the fort, this Wolf Shadow."

"Yes, Miss Clayton, he has."

"I also heard that no one has been able to trace him, where he comes from, where he goes. Is that correct?"

"Hmmm, maybe . . ." The lieutenant looked somewhat annoyed.

"Has he hurt anyone?"

"No, not yet anyway, though it's only a matter of time. He hurts us by these constant skirmishes, though."

"How do you mean?"

"He attacks the bull trains that pass between here and our Canadian allies. He dumps out all our supplies, causing the merchants in town to take more and more of a loss. It's why the military was dispatched here. To put an end to these raids and protect the cattlemen and merchants."

"Hmmm, I see," she said, then asked, "What is on these trains that he should attack them?"

The lieutenant drew in a steady, deep breath. "That is the mystery of it all, Miss Clayton. The trains carry no more than trade stocks for the Indians. Food and utensils, beads and blankets."

"How odd," she responded. "Why does he strike them, I wonder?"

The lieutenant shook his head. "No one knows."

She hesitated a moment. "He is Indian, isn't he?"

"Yes, he is."

"You are certain?"

"We are not sure of anything. But if he isn't Indian, someone has certainly mastered the art of Indian warfare."

"How . . . interesting. And there are no tracks, nothing to follow to give an indication as to who he is?"

"Miss Clayton, rest assured, if there were tracks to follow, I would have caught the scoundrel by now."

"Of course," she offered, "of course you would."

He sighed deeply. "I am sorry, Miss Clayton, if I sounded irritated just now, it's only that—"

"Think nothing of it."

"Thank you, Miss Clayton. This villain has been playing havoc with us." The lieutenant shifted his weight.

"You do have good scouts, don't you, lieutenant?"

He looked momentarily distracted, then without warning, he suddenly turned on her, challenging, "Do I look so incompetent, Miss Clayton, that you ply me with all these questions? Do I appear to you to be the sort of man to let a single criminal pass through my fingers?"

"Of course not," she was quick to answer, taken somewhat aback by the lieutenant's flare of anger.

He continued, "I have done and am doing all I can to catch this thief."

"I'm certain that you are." She sneaked a quick glance at the lieutenant. "But don't your scouts find his tracks? Shouldn't it be easier to find him if they could—"

"He leaves no tracks. And the Indians are afraid of him, think he has some 'medicine' that will harm them if they betray him . . . that is, all except for one drunken loafer who . . . well, never mind, Miss Clayton, I'm sure I'm boring you."

"Not in the least," she smiled, wondering at the same time if the lieutenant realized that it sounded as if this Wolf Shadow was the winner in these little tests of will.

She would have voiced her thoughts aloud, but the lieutenant muttered, "If you would excuse me, Miss Clayton, I have matters to attend to. Although," he turned to her with a strained smile, "I must admit to a desire to stand here in the moonlight with you all evening. But I am afraid that I am needed out there."

Alys nodded as she murmured, "Of course."

"I will call on you tomorrow," he said, before sauntering away, aggravation clearly marking his gait.

Alys watched the lieutenant's retreating back for several moments and wondered, not about Lieutenant Warrington's behavior but about this man called the Wolf Shadow.

Since returning to Fort Benton, Alys had heard nothing but complaints about this Wolf Shadow who, if the townspeople were to be believed, seemed to have nothing better to do than attack honest merchants and prey upon "innocent" prairie schooners. Already she had heard stories about the man, but, prone to discount gossip, she hadn't given it much consideration . . . until now.

An Indian attacking the bull trains full of supplies for his own people? How very strange.

Yet, there must be some truth to the rumors . . .

The lieutenant had just confirmed what Alys had already overheard: that this Shadow was more ghost than human. This was supposed to explain, she assumed, why no one had a defense against him.

Distractedly, Alys gazed off in the distance, the figure of Lieutenant Warrington now no more than a faint speck. More shots were fired; that, along with the flash of light and the sounds of shouting, attested to the struggle.

What did this Wolf Shadow look like? she wondered. Would he be dressed like a warrior? Or was he more half-breed?

And why was he called Wolf Shadow? Why wolf?

She took a step forward, wanting to go there, to be there, to see.

Still, she hesitated. She really shouldn't go closer, she would only be in the way, yet . . .

She took another step forward and paused. Perhaps she should just go home and see to her mother.

Yet, as the lieutenant had pointed out, her mother had hired Mary, an elderly Indian woman who stayed with her and nursed her. Alys wasn't needed, wouldn't be missed at home, at least not for some time.

Something drew her toward the fight, something . . .

Without further thought, Alys reached down, picked up the blue faille of her underskirt, and rushed to the scene of the fight, following the lieutenant's trail.

She dashed right up to the perimeters of the struggle, where the noisy din of the gunfire, the smell of gunpowder, and the occasional bursts of light reached out to her long before she could see the action. It was dark, also; much too dark.

Raising her hand to shield her eyes, she strained to see. Nothing, until all at once, she made out the figure of a man running—or was it animal?

There, under the shadowy beams of the moon, she could just make out the silhouette of a man, naked to the waist and . . . wearing a wolf headdress.

But what an uneven fight this was. The odds were impossible. One lone man and what? A dog? No . . . it was a wolf that loped alongside him.

How curious.

One man and one wolf against what? Twenty or thirty men?

Wolf Shadow appeared to be the lesser in the matter of firearms, too. Barely a shot came from the rifle he held in his hand.

Yet it didn't seem to matter. He and his canine companion put up an offense that was meticulously planned. The Shadow fought no one unless he had to, the focus of his attention centered on the bull wagons and their cargo. Slashing the merchandise, dumping the contents of jugs on the ground, the man flew from one wagon to the next, fighting off soldiers and bullets with a shield, or with pure dodging, but he attacked few people, his sights set only on the cargo.

How magnificent.

Why such destruction of supplies slated to go to the Indians? If the lieutenant were to be believed—and Alys had no reason to doubt him—the supplies contained nothing more than food and blankets. Was this Wolf Shadow daft?

Perhaps.

Yet, watching him, Alys could do little more than stare . . . and admire . . .

Strong in body, lean and tall, he could only have been described as brave and courageous, fighting under such poor odds. Yet, he did not cease his activity until he had managed to ruin every schooner full of cargo. Then, suddenly and with seeming ease, the man faded from sight, though the wolf remained behind, high up on one of the wagons, silhouetted against the moon, howling, as though it would guard the man's departure.

Bullets fired, missed.

And then nothing.

The wolf had gone, as had the man.

Amazing. Alys pinched herself. Had it been real?

Curses, all in English, rang through the air, a few more stray bullets followed, voices off in the distance ordering others to pursue the man. But what trail had he left? No one seemed to be looking, not even the few Indian scouts . . . all had turned their attention to the liquid contents of the bull train, now seeping into the dry ground.

Gradually, the men moved off. But not so Alys. She couldn't budge, feeling as immovable as a statue.

Spellbound, she could barely breathe; even then, she had to remind herself to do so. She'd never seen anything like it. Why did the man fight so determinedly? What purpose did it serve?

She forced herself to come alive, to move closer, slowing her pace to a stop as the whiff of something strong and acidic hit her nostrils. What was it? The stench of whiskey?

She took a few more steps, telling herself that it could not be.

Again . . . she sniffed the air. There was no mistaking it.

Surely the fort, the merchants, and the military were not involved in whiskey trading, were they? Not with the new laws. It was too fantastic.

It was a well-known fact that the Indians could not tolerate liquor, that fights ensued after a binge of drinking. Something terrible always happened, and the Indians themselves, when sober, grieved over what they had done. Alys had grown up listening to the tales of the fights and the deaths that had occurred because of the Indians' use of alcohol and the traders' insistence on selling it to them.

But the government had clamped down on all that. Or so she had been led to believe.

Stunned, Alys went from wagon to wagon, examining each shipment, a certain nausea beginning to build within her. Was the military aware of this? They must be. It would be impossible to miss an odor such as this. Yet if they were, why wasn't something being done?

She would find Lieutenant Warrington, she decided with

sudden vigor. And she would discover the truth, if she could. Lifting her head, she picked up the hem of her dress intending to move away, when she noticed something peculiar and dark on the bottom of her skirts. It wasn't simply the usual dirt from the street. What was it?

She bent down and removed her gloves, running her finger over the hem. It was some sort of sticky substance . . . she lifted her hand high against the moonlight. Mud? She sniffed it. No, not mud. Blood—fresh, red blood.

Whose? The soldiers'? Not unless a bullet had found the wrong target. The Wolf Shadow had fired almost no shots.

That meant it could only be . . .

Alys examined the ground.

A fresh pool of blood. How the soldiers and hired scouts had missed this she didn't know.

Alys glanced around her, barely breathing. She moved over the bloody mess until her skirts completely covered it, then she shuffled her feet in the dirt.

"Miss Clayton, what are you doing out here?"

Startled, Alys glanced up, only to find Lieutenant Warrington staring down at her. Had he seen her and what she had found? She didn't know why, but some instinct told her to hide her discovery. Pushing her glove into her hand and hiding it behind her back, she forced herself to smile brightly as she explained, "I wanted to see the Wolf Shadow for myself."

"For yourself? You, a woman?" he snorted. "My dear, this is much too dangerous a place for a lady." His voice became softer, though his tone continued to patronize. "You shouldn't be here."

Alys lifted her chin. "Why not?"

"Because," he glared at her as though she were a naughty child. "Because you are a woman. And being female, you are too weak, and unarmed. And because—"

"Lieutenant Warrington, I have just discovered something that I think you should know."

"Have you?" he asked, his manner condescending. "And what would that be, m'dear?"

The "my dear" grated on her nerves. However, she held her peace, asking only, "Did you know that the merchants in this town are sending whiskey to the Indians?"

The lieutenant had the grace to look sheepish. "Miss Clayton, I don't believe you know what you're saying."

"Don't I? Have you lost your sense of smell, Lieutenant? Here, stand still for a moment. The stench is unforgettable."

"There is a tavern around the corner. Perhaps what you smell is—"

"I know what I see right here, dripping from this wagon, from that one, too." She pointed.

The lieutenant took her arm. "You see nothing, Miss Clayton. Nothing at all. Now come, I will escort you home. You should forget about all this."

Alys did not budge; she couldn't, not without uncovering a trail of evidence. She snapped her arm away from the lieutenant. "Lieutenant Warrington, don't you understand? The merchants are trading whiskey to the Indians."

Lieutenant Warrington gave her a blank stare.

"But then, I guess you probably know that, don't you?" The lieutenant made another reach for her, which Alys deftly avoided. "If you please, I think I'll find my own way home, thank you."

"Miss Clayton, really, you are making too much of this. Liquor, in modest quantities, has always been traded to the Indians. It is nothing new."

"But I thought the government had forbidden—"

"Forbidden? And what do you know of the laws?"

"I don't know them as well as you, I am sure. But I do know enough to realize that this shipment is illegal."

"Illegal? I think not, Miss Clayton. If the merchants were doing something criminal, the military would act on it at once. Trading a little liquor is hardly illegal."

Alys's head reeled slightly. Hadn't she recently heard of new liquor laws when she had been back east? "But I thought that the government had . . . I thought the military was here to protect both the Indians and the settlers."

"And we are. We do. I can see that you don't understand."

"No, I don't. How can you protect the Indians when you allow the merchants to sell liquor to them? It's well known that liquor disrupts their culture."

"Miss Clayton . . . Alys, the Indians have no culture and I have little enough time to stand here and educate you on the business of the military. Especially when I would rather be discussing other, more pleasant things."

"Oh?" She tried to keep herself from physically recoiling.

"Yes," he suddenly grinned at her, "like the way the moonlight makes your brown hair shimmer, makes your dark eyes sparkle."

Alys felt her body go rigid under the compliment. While only a short while ago she might have delighted in hearing this man declare such devotion, right now such waxed enthusiasm sent shivers of revulsion running along her nerve endings.

She squared her shoulders. "Please, Lieutenant, we leave the point, which is the sale of liquor."

"Yes, but that's not so bad, is it?" Again, he grinned at her. "To leave the point?"

Alys took a deep breath. "I hope you don't mind if I speak my mind."

He shrugged. "By all means, do."

Alys nodded. "It seems to me, Lieutenant, that if the merchants are trading illegal liquor to the Indians, then this

Wolf Shadow is within the boundaries of the law in what he is doing and should be praised by the military, not shot at."

The lieutenant's stance became decidedly tense. He cleared his throat. "I can see that pleasantries with you will get me nowhere. You seem to be stuck on this one subject. Very well. Now, Miss Clayton . . . Alys, need I remind you that it is the Indians who are making the west rough and uncivilized? They raid, steal horses, kill women and children. Now, as I see it, my job here is to protect the townspeople from any such Indian attacks. And this, tonight, was an Indian attack."

"Upon merchandise?" she countered, her temper rising. "I hardly think so. From my position here, I didn't even see the man fire but a few shots. And as far as the raiding and stealing, aren't you forgetting the recent Baker massacre? Wasn't it the military who was doing the killing of Indian women and children then?"

The lieutenant shook his head. "What have they been teaching you back east? Leave it to those soft city folk to get the thing all wrong. Now, I think you are mistaken, Miss Clayton. That Baker raid was against warriors, that is all."

"Yes," she said, "so I heard. The warriors had left some old men and boys in that camp of women and children, while they were out on a buffalo hunt, isn't that right?"

The lieutenant's body stiffened, his hands clenched at his side, and for a moment, he looked as though he might like to strike her. At length, however, he volunteered, "I won't argue this with you any further, Miss Clayton." His words were clipped. "I can see that either your mother or the good people of the east have tainted your outlook upon the honest citizens of this town."

She pulled a face. "Somehow, I'm not convinced."

"Convinced? Of what?"

"Of that so-called honesty."

He *tsked, tsked.* "Come now, Miss Clayton. You should have more faith. You clearly don't understand the politics of the west and, truth to tell, I don't have the time to enlighten you. At least not now."

"No," she agreed, "you're right. Now, Lieutenant, if you will excuse me." She made to step around him, hoping to capture his attention, distracting his gaze from the ground and what she was certain was a trail.

He didn't watch her, however. Someone had called to him, demanding his attention, and he had already turned away from her.

Alys breathed a sigh of relief and, quickly scanning the area around her, stepped out of the light and away from the blood. She calmed slightly. She had managed to cover up the evidence fairly well.

But if there had been a pool of blood here, it made sense that there would also be a trail to follow. No wounded man would be able to keep from making one.

Trying to look as demure as possible, Alys studied the ground. She knew something about following trails, thanks to her rather unorthodox upbringing.

Luckily the tracks seemed to lead in the same direction as her home, and Alys, kicking dirt over the imprints as she went, began to follow the bloody signs, hopefully not looking too obvious in doing so.

Meanwhile, Lieutenant Warrington, having settled his business as well as he was able, came back to where he had left Alys, only to find her gone. He scanned the area in all directions, but to no avail.

He could go after her, he supposed, discover where she had gone. But he wouldn't. At least not tonight.

"Damn easterners," he murmured aloud. "They've tainted her."

And with nothing more to be said on the matter, the lieutenant trotted off in the direction of the tavern.

It was still early evening. The excitement in town had died down, the main talk of those around her, as she passed by them, being that of the ruined shipment and not of the man who had upset it. No one seemed to take much interest in her either, if they even saw her, and she relaxed. It appeared she would be allowed to complete her task without interference.

Despite her misgivings, she followed the trail left by this ephemeral creature, this Wolf Shadow, as it wound behind the fort's military barracks. Through dark alleyways, she continued to follow the trail even when it seemed the markings had almost disappeared. And whenever she found traces of the man's passage, of his blood, she covered it with dirt and straightened any nearby grass, that no one else might find it. On and on she tracked, toward the back of the fort—toward her own home.

"My home?" she mumbled under her breath.

Taken slightly aback, she kept on, the trail taking her directly to . . . her house. Could it be that the man had scaled the adobe bastion and the walls that stood at her backyard?

It would seem doubtful that a single man could accomplish such a feat, and yet, the tracks wound toward her house. She followed those imprints, barely able to believe it when they led right to her own cellar . . .

Alys glanced around her, mystified.

No one knew about the secrets of her cellar. Only her mother and herself . . . plus, she reminded herself, one small Indian boy and girl from so long ago . . . an Indian boy who would now be a man.

Alys shook herself, as though that action might clear her mind. Was it possible that this Wolf Shadow might be the boy she had once helped? Not likely. That lad, if he were wise, would have long since put as much distance as possible between himself and the fort.

Still, the thought that this Wolf Shadow might be the youth she had once known caused her heart to skip a beat.

Unwittingly, she touched her cheek.

"And now a part of you is a part of me."

She had never forgotten. Nor had she easily put aside her childish infatuation. She could even now call back to mind the image of the young Indian as he had been, his tanned body strong and lean, his dark eyes warm with kindness and respect for her.

She stood still, momentarily lost in her own thoughts. At length, she shook herself.

What utter foolishness. She had long ago put away her schoolgirl crushes, had grown up and dismissed such things as nothing more than childish dreams. Although without realizing that she did it, she even now fingered the outline of the necklace she always wore, there beneath her bodice—a single shell, suspended from a bleached white buckskin chain.

Becoming suddenly aware of what she was doing, she drew her hands to her sides and determinedly stared back toward the ground, concentrating and looking more closely for the trail. Ah, sure enough, there it was . . . heading directly to her cellar.

A wave of remorse rushed over her, perhaps for things that could have been, but the emotion was quickly replaced by anger. This was *her* cellar, these were *her* caves and caverns. No one was allowed here.

Her anger overriding her caution, Alys pulled up the cellar doors. If someone else were using her caves, she meant to find out about it.

Pushing her skirt between her legs, she climbed down into the darkness, quickly finding the rug that was sup-

posed to hide the false bottom of the floor. However, the
rug had already been pulled back, the opening of the caves
revealed. She breathed out a sigh and, bending down,
swiftly negotiated the ladder, vaulting down to the hard
rock floor of the caves, the coldness of the ground seeping
into her slippers. Complete and utter blackness engulfed
her, but such a thing meant nothing to her. She picked up
the lantern that always hung there and lit it, its flicker
splattering light across the thick, solid boulders. Shadows
appeared and disappeared on those walls, but she ignored
them. She held no fear of these caves.

These were *her* caverns. Hers and her mother's alone.

She would ensure they remained that way. Grabbing a
shovel, she proceeded cautiously.

Chapter 3

Perhaps an amateur might have been disoriented by the blackness of the caves. Not so, Alys. She followed the trail of blood easily and found that the man's path kept to the main cavern, not diverging off into some of the lesser used passages.

As she moved farther and farther into the tunnels, she calmed down somewhat and became more determined to confront the intruder. But as she did so, the coolness of the underground caverns seeped into her. Perhaps she had been unwise to come here without a warmer wrap, but it was too late now to go back.

She grimaced. The man, this Wolf Shadow, was going nowhere, not if this trail of blood held any indication of his condition. A feeling of premonition swept over her. What if this man and the boy Moon Wolf were truly one and the same and she got to him too late?

Suddenly, from out of nowhere, two golden eyes appeared in front of her. It had to be the wolf who accompanied the man. Would the animal attack? She had no time

35

to ponder the question, however, or even to feel fear. If she were running into his pet, she knew the man himself was close-by.

The animal soon gave her to understand that it meant her no harm. Instead of growling or attacking, it whined, coming up close to her, then pushing away; back toward her again. It repeated the action. In truth, it couldn't have said "follow me" plainer than if it had spoken to her. And so, she trailed after the wolf, down through a little used cavern, around a bend.

It didn't take long to find the man, collapsed as he was on the chilly floor. She realized, too, that if he weren't unconscious from the loss of blood, he soon would be from the shock of the cold, stone floor.

She approached him tenuously, shovel held high. Would he attack her, if awake? Was there still danger from the wolf?

The man remained motionless, even when she stood directly over him. Was he unconscious? Dead, maybe?

Setting the shovel and lantern down, she bent over him, one hand going to his chest, the other to what should be the pulse in his neck.

He was alive. Barely. The beat was weak.

It was amazing to her that he had negotiated the caves this far. Removing her gloves and kneeling next to him, she checked his head, his arms, his chest. No injury there, though his body was chilled. Much too cold. She would have to do something to warm him.

She couldn't tell his identity, at least not right now. He wore too much paint on his face, plus the wolf headdress hid his more prominent features.

Still looking for the injury, she made a path down his body, its instantaneous jerk telling her she was getting close. Down his hips, inward toward his upper thighs, her hand suddenly came in contact with something warm and sticky. His body convulsed.

Blood.

The injury was to his thigh, the wound still bleeding heavily. She would have to tie a tourniquet around his upper leg and then . . . she would have to remove that bullet.

She needed a doctor, that's what she needed. But who could she trust? The closest medical doctor in these parts was a week's hard ride east, to Fort Buford. Too long a trip.

True, there were people here at the fort who tended to one another when needed, but could she trust any of them with this man's secret? With her own secret of the caves?

She considered moving him into her house, but she instantly dismissed the idea. She didn't have the strength to do it, nor, if she were honest, did he. Plus, moving him right now might exacerbate his injury.

There was nothing for it. She would have to tend to him herself . . . here. She had seen a doctor take a bullet from a man once.

All she needed was a knife, fire, hot water . . . and courage.

Lifting her skirt, she tore a strip from her petticoat, which she tied around the man's thigh as well as she was able. Her progress was hampered in part by her embarrassment. Because of the location of the injury, her hand kept brushing against the strength of the man's thigh. But she had little time to consider such things.

The man's life was in danger.

There. Done. At least the tourniquet would stop the bleeding for a little while.

She would need to return to the house, throw a work wrapper over her gown, get a knife, some hot water, clean bandages, and blankets.

"Hold on there, Mister Shadow Wolf," she whispered to him. "Help is on the way."

With nothing more to be said, she hurried back through the caves to her house.

Yellow eyes guided her once again to the man. She accepted that help although she didn't require it. She knew her way.

She had needed to make two trips: one with bandages and blankets, the other with water, alcohol, and herbs.

She had thrown a calico wrap over her gown, and now, leaning over the man, she examined him gingerly. He was well-built and strong, explaining why he was still alive. Though she could not clearly identify him, it didn't matter. She had to attend to his injury, and quickly.

The first thing she had to do, after positioning a blanket under him, was strip off his clothing. Not too difficult a job, since he wore little more than a breechcloth.

However, the wound lay dangerously close to that tiny bit of clothing, causing her to remove the buckskin more cautiously and more slowly than she would have liked, having to actually cut it away in several places.

She resolutely ignored the evidence of his gender as she stripped away his clothing, but not before registering the fact that he was well equipped to please a wife, if he had one. She felt herself blush at the thought, ashamed of herself.

Firmly, she reminded herself that the man's life hung in the balance of her actions . . .

She moved his leg until the wound was easily accessible and, putting the knife to the flame of her lantern, she brought the hot point within inches of the gash.

"I'm sorry, Mister Wolf Shadow, but I have to do this if I am to save your life. That bullet must come out. This will hurt."

She thought she saw his eyes flicker for an instant as though he had heard and understood her. Then nothing.

He jerked when she applied the knife to the wound, and she heard a rapid intake of breath. So he wasn't unconscious. Too bad.

"Hold on there, mister." She brought a soft towel toward him, guiding him to place it between his teeth. "The pain can't be helped. I'm sorry."

And with little more said, she cut the knife into the wound, slicing and pushing out the bullet with such deftness, one would have thought she'd been born to doctor.

To his credit, the man didn't utter a sound, although she was more than aware of the moment he fainted. Alys thanked God that he was being spared the rest of the pain.

As two yellow eyes watched her from a distance, she placed the bullet to the side, cleaned the wound by pouring alcohol over it, and finished by positioning a poultice of herbs, echinacea, and elderberry upon it.

Next came a compress, which she applied pressure to, until the bleeding subsided. Then she wrapped the area up with soft bandages.

Her breathing coming in short puffs, she spoke to the wolf, who hadn't moved. "I've done all I can," she explained, as though the wolf sat in judgment. "There's little more to be done now except wash away the sweat and the dirt that clings to him. But that can wait. And I'm exhausted. I promise, however, that I will check his bandages in a few hours."

Glancing down at the man, she continued, "I hope you don't run a fever, Mister Wolf Shadow. Just the same, I'd better brew a dandelion tea"—she lay her head down on a pillow, which she had placed next to him, her eyelids closing almost at once—"first thing tomorrow."

*   *   *

His groaning awakened her.

She sat up and ran a hand over his forehead. He was burning up.

Quickly, she felt the temperature of the water she had hauled down into the cave. What had once been boiling was now cool. Good.

Tearing off another strip of material from her ruined petticoat, she dipped it into the water. A nice cool bath should bring his temperature down. Of course, she'd have to change the blanket under him once done, but first things first.

Removing his wolf headdress and setting it aside, she brushed cooling water over his face and hair, the black paint coming away and onto the cloth.

"Oh," she uttered, the sound barely audible. Little by little his features were revealed, his look achingly familiar. To be sure, the boy who had once infatuated her young girl's heart had certainly become a man.

"So, Mister Wolf Shadow," she spoke to him as though he might hear her, "your secret is at last unmasked. I only wonder if you will remember me and the proposal you once made to a young, impressionable girl. I, for one, have never forgotten it.

"I suspected," she continued to speak to him, "that it might be you who was terrorizing the merchants of this town when I saw your trail come into the cellar. I covered your tracks, Mister Wolf Shadow, that you might be safe, but I am uncertain if I approve of your use of my caves. It is something we will have to discuss when you awaken. And you will awaken, Mister Wolf Shadow. You will."

Of course he had known about the caves, she told herself silently. He'd probably explored them in detail by now. She wondered briefly about his sister. Was she a part of the revenge upon the town's merchants?

Somehow she doubted it. The man, or rather the boy

she had known, had carried an air about him, even as a child, which would have tolerated no interference.

She began to wash his face with delicate care, smoothing back his hair, her fingers reaching out to run over his cheeks much as he had once done to her, so long ago. It was as though she were memorizing by touch the look of him.

Oh, how she had weaved dreams around this man, or rather around the boy she had known. She realized that he was probably nothing like her fantasy warrior, and yet wasn't he one of the main reasons why she had yearned to come home? Not that she had really expected to meet up with him again.

Still . . .

She rinsed her cloth and set it to his neck. He moaned slightly.

"Miistap-aaatoo-t annomce!"

She glanced up quickly toward his face, watching as he shifted his head from side to side. What had he said?

It didn't matter.

The more important issue was, would he live?

Well, he would if she had anything to do with it.

Down each arm, she washed away the dirt and grime. Down his chest, her fingers itched to search at a more leisurely pace those masculine contours. Down further, over his hips, closer and closer to the wound, to that part of him that blatantly declared his masculinity.

Tempting as it was, she ignored it. She had no right to examine this proud man that way.

Down each leg, pulling off his moccasins and washing his feet.

Rinsing her cloth again, she brought it to his face, realizing at the same time that there would be no sleep for her tonight. Not if she were to ensure he remained cool.

Taking his hand in her own, she whispered to him,

"Don't you dare leave me. I have not gone to all this trouble only to lose you. And don't you pretend not to understand English. I remember you well, and know you comprehend what I am saying."

He muttered something else, but she couldn't make it out.

Dipping the cloth again in water, she washed the sweat from his face, preparing herself for the long night ahead.

She changed the water twice, refilling her bucket from the waterfall at the end of the tunnel and trudging it all the way back to the man. There was no alternative. She could not chance going above ground during the daylight hours. She might look suspicious carrying water in and out of her cellar.

Still, he hadn't awakened and his fever hadn't abated.

He had tossed and turned throughout the night, muttering unintelligible words, which she had ignored as best as she could. Instead, she focused on changing the poultice and the bandages, which proved difficult, considering the location of his injury.

Every time she worked over him, she was all too aware of his masculinity. It was impossible to ignore. And though she needed a break, she wouldn't take one. She wouldn't chance something happening to him in her absence.

"Someday, when you're awake, I'm going to tell you about the difficulty I had in working over you. Imagine, a young woman such as myself slaving over a nude man who looks like you do, with an injury so close to his privates."

She glanced at his face. No reaction.

"What do you think of that, Moon Wolf? Or should I call you Wolf Shadow now? I have heard that Indians change their names when they perform deeds of bravery.

And I would suspect that Wolf Shadow is now a name of distinction."

She sighed. Shortly, as soon as she was certain that he wouldn't relapse, she would go outside, pick some dandelions, and brew a good, stiff tea. That, too, should help with his fever.

She had checked on her mother last night when she had gone into the house for herbs and bandages and left a brief note. Her mother had been sleeping soundly, her breathing clear. That was good. At least Alys could stay with this stranger with a free conscience.

He moaned, twisting from side to side. She took his hand in her own and patted it before speaking softly to him. "Don't you dare leave me," she whispered. "I have waited years to be reunited with you, don't let go now.

"Will you remember me? I have never forgotten you, even when I was in school back east. Never a day went by when I wasn't thinking about Montana, about the life I had led here, nor, if I am to be honest, about you. I used to weave dreams around you, did you know that? Not that I expect you to be anything like my imaginings, but you left an impression upon me, Mister Wolf Shadow. An impression I have not been able to escape."

He quieted, and she continued, "Let me tell you about my illusions, about my knight in shining—or rather Indian—armor."

His hand tightened around hers. That had to be a good sign.

Washing his face and body from time to time, she spun her story, telling him about her silly, girlish dreams, sparing him no detail, not even her more erotic imaginings. On and on she spoke, the time flying by quickly.

Her voice hoarse, she continued to talk to him until, in

the wee hours of the morning, he suddenly opened his eyes and stared at her.

"Aa-lees," He spoke her name with fervor, then said, "*Soka'piiwa*."

She leaned toward him. What had he said? Had he recognized her? Even in his delirium?

Surely that was impossible. Still, it proved to be a turning point in his condition. He immediately broke out into a sweat, his fever falling rapidly. She washed his brow and his chest, encouraging this turn for the better.

"Come on, Mister Wolf Shadow, you will pull through this."

It was close to dawn the next day when his fitfulness turned into a sound, healing sleep. And Alys, exhausted, recognizing it for what it was, lay down beside him, her hand still clasped in his. She fell into a deep, peaceful sleep, her dreams haunted by a magnificent Indian brave named Wolf Shadow.

Chapter 4

Wolf Shadow woke with aches and pains all over his body. Mostly, however, his head throbbed and his left leg felt as though it had been torn in half.

Curious, he scooted up onto his elbows and glanced down at his leg.

What was this? A compress of white cloth bound around his thigh? He reached down and felt the peculiar object. Ouch!

Wincing, he looked quickly around him, breathing in the cool, earthy smell of the caves, trying to recall what had happened. But nothing came to mind except . . . he had tried to stop the shipment of whiskey, which had been slated to go north to his people. He had gone into the fort, under the cover of darkness, accomplished his task and then . . . nothing . . .

Had he been hit? Evidently so. The pain in his thigh was unmistakable.

But who had tended him? It had to be a white person—most likely a white woman, if this dressing were any indication, for it looked as though it had once been part of a woman's wearing apparel.

Who? It couldn't be Ma Clayton, his one and only white friend in the town of Fort Benton. She had been in bed with illness for several months and was still very sick.

Then who? He knew of no one else who had the knowledge of these caves except a young girl who . . .

It couldn't be. He hadn't seen that girl for many, many years. It had been so long ago, that he had assumed she had left this country.

He flopped back down, his attempt at sitting up and thinking proving too much for his weakened body.

He stared upward at the familiarity of the cavern's stone ceiling, realizing in doing so that there was light, here in a cave where all should be darkness. Where was the light coming from?

He glanced beside him. A white man's lantern, which sat next to his head, was the source.

What had happened? He tried to recall something . . . anything . . . but he remembered nothing . . .

He heard a noise and instantly stilled. What was that? The sound of singing? A woman singing?

It could be the rush of the waterfalls at the end of the tunnel, making him believe that . . . no, the tone, the quality of it . . . it *was* a woman's singing . . .

He heaved back up onto his forearms. Yellow eyes stared at him at a safe distance from the light.

"*Makoyi*, wolf, *poohsap-oo-t*, come here." The big animal crawled slowly forward, whining, until he was able to put his head on his master's chest. The familiar scent of the wild animal filled his nostrils, "*Tsa anistapii-waatsiksi?* What is it? You know, don't you old friend?" The wolf whimpered, placing his paws up on his master's shoulders and bringing his nose into contact with his master's face. *"Takaa/tahkaa a-waasai'ni-wa?* Who is the singer, or the crier?"

The wolf sprang up onto his feet and started off in the direction of the falls, returning to his master and nudging him slightly.

"I am not certain I have the strength to follow you, old brother."

But the wolf again sprinted off, coming back and prodding him, until Wolf Shadow had no choice but to sit up, the blanket which had partially covered him falling away.

At once, he reeled, his head spinning under the simple movement. He groaned, feeling the aches in every muscle of his body, as another problem presented itself—he urgently needed to relieve himself. But there was nothing he could do about it now. He would have to ignore the pain, the urge, and center his attention on how to rise. Carefully, he brought himself up onto his knees.

The cold hit him at once, and he glanced down at himself. There was the source: besides the bandage, he wore no clothing. Had the white woman—if it were a white woman—also undressed him? The thought was anything but comforting.

Struggling forward in a crawl, he finally reached the wall of the cave. Holding closely to it, he pushed himself up, onto his feet, pausing for a moment to see if the spinning in his head would ease. It didn't, and he began to feel as if he had recently taken a journey to the Sand Hills, where his ancestors resided, only to have been spat back out.

Groping along the wall to steady himself, he dealt with the urgency of his body before slowly proceeding toward the opening of the cave, every step a test of his strength.

Closer and closer he shambled, the sound of the singing, soft and high-pitched, becoming more and more alluring.

Despite the noise from the falls, the source was unmistakable. Definitely a woman, most likely a white woman,

since he knew of few Indian women who could speak the
English language without accent.

He managed the gradual incline toward the end of the
cave, the cold walls of the cavern acting as his cane. Closer
and closer he inched, until light began to filter into the
tunnel.

He squinted, letting his eyes adjust to the sudden brilliance of the outside world before seeking out the source
of such enchanting sound. Slowly, he pushed himself into
the opening of the cave.

Then he saw her. Weak though he was, he felt his whole
body go stiff.

This was certainly not Ma Clayton. Had this young
woman attended him? He glanced down at himself, at his
nakedness, the thought crossing his mind that he had little
to hide from her if she had been his attendant.

Unusually irritated, he moved a little closer. Who was
she? And why had she helped him? Was it possible that
she was the young girl from his past? His Alys? It seemed
highly possible.

Her voice resonated with an alluring quality, he noted,
the sound of it lilting and beautiful. Her body was pale,
smooth, rounded, and soft. Despite his weakness, he felt
his body respond to the sight before him, to her.

Her back was to him, allowing him an ample view of
her slim, rounded buttocks and long legs. Brown hair, auburn tinged with highlights, had been piled high on her
head, and he stood transfixed, able to do little more than
stare at her. Belatedly, she reached up to release her hair,
letting it shimmer down her back, before it surrendered to
the water of the falls.

He suddenly felt . . . not so ill.

She stopped singing, turned, and plunged her face into
the falling water. In that brief moment, however, he had
caught sight of something she wore around her neck. A

necklace. One he recognized as his own. A single white shell, the same necklace he had given to a young girl so very long ago.

It had to be his sweet Alys, the girl from his past. It remained only for him to look into her eyes and glimpse her spirit to confirm his suspicion.

He had never, would never forget that young girl, nor his initial impression of her. Once, long ago, he had gazed into her child-like eyes, had witnessed her spirit, and . . . had never been the same.

Had that same girl grown into this beautiful woman who unknowingly paraded before him? Or more importantly, had that same person come to his rescue yet again?

He wondered, too, if she and Ma Clayton were related, the older woman's daughter perhaps? Though Ma Clayton had befriended him, he knew little about her or her life.

The vision before him unexpectedly stepped from the falls, her flawless, nude body in full view for his curious perusal.

And, as a drop of moisture does in a ray of sun, any thought he'd had in his head fled. He stared. What man wouldn't?

His body responded to the sight of her, stiffening as though he hadn't just returned from the dead.

He felt dishonorable. If this woman had nursed him— and he believed that she had—then under no circumstances should he be watching her while she bathed.

Perhaps that was to account for the rudeness of his first words to her . . . perhaps. But he needed to say something; he would have her know that he was here, watching, staring . . . for her own protection.

He called out, "Is this the way the white woman offers herself to me?" Immediately he chided himself for his crudeness.

He heard her indrawn gasp, saw her startled gaze rise

up to meet his. *Aa,* yes, so he had been right. This was the girl from his past. He would know this person anywhere, from her soft, brown eyes and the delicate dimples in her cheeks, down to the very tips of her toes. She was a slight little thing, even full grown, and would probably come up to no more than his shoulders, yet she was well rounded and feminine in all the right places. Much too feminine.

In truth, despite the weakness of his body, he was having a difficult time curbing a sudden fire within him, the tantalizing display before him providing the fuel. And he didn't need to remind himself again that his inclinations were all out of place, that good manners dictated he show her the respect she so rightly deserved.

Yet, despite his attempt at self-control, he could not repress the urge of his body; its pure, lustful desire clearly exhibited, providing her more than a healthy view of its demand. He said, none too gently, "I assume it is you who has nursed me back from the dead?"

No expression crossed her face, her wide-eyed stare his only reply.

"I owe you my gratitude, I think," he continued on, "although . . . perhaps it would have been wiser if you had ensured my unconsciousness before you"—he gestured toward her—"bathed."

She bristled. "I did not believe there was a need. You are not supposed to be up and about, wandering through the caves. And you are welcome." To her credit, she did not try to hide herself from him, though that lack sorely tried what little rein he held over his body's strong inclination.

And so, with the conviction of censoring himself and shielding her at the same time, he took refuge behind a harsher tone of voice, baiting further, "*Aa,* yes, you did not think me able to roam. That explains why I find us both without clothes. Am I right? Was there something the matter that you could not dress me? I can only think, when I look at you, then examine myself, that it is something you . . . planned?"

Planned? Had he really said that? Irritated with himself, he tried to turn and put his back to her, but the weakness in his body would not allow it. He sank back against the wall of the cave and drew in a deep breath.

Meanwhile, her mouth had fallen open, as rightly it should. She uttered, "Planned?" He could see her eyes moving this way and that, not in fright, but rather as someone searching for something. She asserted, "I have not *planned* anything these past few days. I have been doing my best to help you."

"*Aa*, yes, help." He peered down at himself. How he wished he could hide from her. But he could not, could only think that perhaps this was the cause for his continued rudeness as he said, apparently unable to help himself, "I seem to be behaving strangely to your 'help.' But then, you can see that for yourself, can you not, having taken my clothes? Was this, too, what you wanted?"

He heard her gasp. "How dare you speak to me this way. I have done nothing to you but—"

"I dare a great deal, I think, and I am certain that later I will have to apologize. But at this moment, I am at a disadvantage, being weak, unclothed, and unable to—"

"Well, you're not supposed to be up and moving around, spying on me. What *are* you doing walking around these caves?"

He smiled, his glance, unfortunately for him, a leer. "I heard singing and became curious. And I would not have missed seeing this . . . you, the way you are . . . what man could ignore such womanly singing? I can tell you now that if it was your intention to bring me back to life, you have certainly accomplished that. At least a part of my body. I am not sure of the rest of me."

"Of all the . . . that was impertinent." She glanced at him as if waiting for an apology.

Yes, he did, and he would have to agree.

He saw her glance take in the lower half of his body, heard her gulp, delighted devilishly in the color that filled her cheeks. *Aa,* yes, though it was wrong of him to tease her the way he was, at the same time it made him feel so very much alive. And that was better, very much better than the alternative.

He almost smiled, but she had stiffened her spine, the action causing her breasts to jut forward, and he caught his breath. Had he ever seen a more beautiful woman?

She continued, "I was singing because I *was* happy, although I'm not so sure that I should be. I had thought that I was saving a great man's life. Great man, indeed. How wrong can a body be? Perhaps I should have left you to the elements . . ."

Through her tirade, he noticed that her eyes were again searching the cave, as though she were looking for something. He followed her gaze, finding it centered around his feet. He glanced down, then silently rebuked himself. Why hadn't he noticed this before? Her clothing lay in a heap next to him. She couldn't dress without approaching him.

Despite the physical torment it cost him to do it, he bent down and picked up her dress, throwing it to her. "Cover yourself," he ordered, his voice harsh, if only to mask the pain, "unless you wish me to do something that my body is urging me to do, despite its weakness."

He inwardly groaned. He was going to have to curb his tongue. Was it possible that his lack of control was because of his weakness? After all, he respected her, had thought pleasantly of her these past years. Why couldn't he simply tell her that his body's response was a quirk, that he didn't ordinarily lack for control where females were concerned?

Pride? Perhaps.

And though he knew his accusations were unfair, his implications untruthful, having started down this dangerous path, he seemed destined to continue. Besides, she needed to get into her clothing, and quickly. "You must hurry and get dressed before—"

"Hush up, do you hear me?"

She bent over, causing him to follow her every motion. Her arms reached out to retrieve the dress he had thrown to her and, without delay, she pulled it on.

He took a deep breath, unaware he had been holding it, and slumped against the cave wall.

"You are one to talk," she reprimanded him, all the while fastening her clothes. She had apparently not seen his lapse in strength. "You say that I tempt you, that I planned this, that I had something besides helping you on my mind. Yet, look at you. You, who stand before me, naked."

He didn't even glance down at himself. "I only do so because you stripped me, white woman, and I cannot find my clothes. Did you hide them from me?"

"Of course not. I had to cut your clothes away because the injury you sustained was close to your . . . ah . . . to . . . well, you can see for yourself where it is. I'll find you some clothes after I see you back to your bed."

A feeling of weakness overwhelmed him, yet he could not help baiting her further. "And did you enjoy taking my breechcloth from me, young Alys?"

"Why . . . why, you ungrateful—" Despite his waning strength, he observed that his use of her name had an impact on her. "You . . . you know who I am?"

"I suspected."

"And you remember me?"

"How could I forget the one who saved me so long ago? I have never forgotten you, though I recall that many great suns ago you rejected a proposal of mine to become my wife. Is this how you repay the honor I bestowed upon you? For if it is, young Alys, come here. We were both too young the last time we met. But I am ready to be enticed by you now."

He closed his eyes and swayed. He had meant the words to be no more than a teasing comment, but too late he realized their effect had a far more serious ring to them. Again, he silently scolded himself.

Still, all his talk had the effect of goading her. How could it not?

He watched as she stalked toward him. "I can't believe how I have fretted over you these past few days. If I'd known what an insolent, impudent oaf you've become, I wouldn't have bothered. I simply would have left you to yourself."

He knew even as she spoke that it wasn't true. She was too kind, too considerate, had been so even as a child. It was he who had pushed her into anger; he who had set into motion the outrage he now witnessed in her, causing her to say these things. But she was continuing. "What a fool I've been. Why did I bother with you? It's evident that you have no sense of gratitude. And here I thought that you were a man of honor. At least that's how I'd remembered you. If you only knew how I—"

He collapsed. He couldn't help himself, the weight of his body and, perhaps, his guilt finally being too much for him.

Whatever she had been about to say ended abruptly as she closed the distance between them. Pulling his weight onto her own, she directed him back into the caves. He noted, though, that his weakness did not prevent her from scolding him.

"Of all the stupid, idiotic things to do," she admonished. "The first thing you do upon waking is to get to your feet and waste your strength telling me what a fool I am. Well, I'll tell you true, mister Wolf Shadow, *you* are the fool."

He couldn't have agreed more.

Half-conscious though he was, her touch on his naked skin was creating urgent, pressing needs on his body, making him think of carnal pleasure, of bliss, of promises he knew his body could not fulfill, at least not in his current state of health.

He looked down at her and, still treading down the same dangerous path, commented, "If it was your intention, sweet Alys, to touch me like this, and make me think of other things we could be doing, I must tell you that I am too weak to do anything about it. At least for now. But I promise you that in a few days, I will—"

"Hush, do you hear me? You know perfectly well that I am only trying to help you."

"*Aa*, yes, I like your help very much. But then, if you look closely at me, you can probably see that for yourself."

She glanced down automatically, his laugh quickly bringing her eyes back to his half-lidded gaze. She shook her head. "Men."

He chuckled again. He couldn't help himself. It was all so ridiculous. And she did have a point. A very good point.

At length, they came to his bed, and he noticed that it was made of soft blankets and pillows, all clean and fresh. She had done much to help him, this sweet Alys. He must keep reminding himself of that, for his body had other, less than honorable cravings toward this girl who had grown into such an enticing woman.

But as he had said, he was in no condition to do anything about it . . . now.

He collapsed onto the bed of blankets, Alys following him down. He had only closed his eyes when from somewhere nearby he heard her pick up something, felt the cool touch of the white man's metal against his head.

"Do you see this? Do you feel this?" she asked, and he opened his eyes sleepily to note that she had a gun, his gun, in her hand. He yawned. And she continued, "If you so much as look like you're going to move again, mister Wolf Shadow, I will finish the job the soldiers tried to do. Do you understand me?"

Another yawn.

"Just give me a reason to pull this trigger."

"I am sure I have given you plenty already. If it is this that you wish, to take my life, by all means do it."

He heard her softly muttered oath, felt the stirring of her indrawn breath. "Now, listen here," she began, and he peeped an eye open to watch her, to admire her. "I have to leave you for a little while to go and get more clothes, for both of us. I'll bring some food, too." She glanced over toward the wolf. "Guard him, wolf. Don't let him get up again, do you understand?"

Those golden eyes stared back at her, not a whine or a howl coming from it.

"By force, if necessary."

The wolf blinked.

"Good. And you," she glared down at him, "you rest, do you hear me? Rest. Nothing more. I will be back."

"Tell your mother that I am all right. And see how she is for me. I brought more herbs for her that my 'almost mother' gathered. I put them in the cellar, on a shelf. You bring them to her now."

"You know my mother?"

Ah, so he had been right. The two women he had met in the caves were mother and daughter. He said, "For many years, I have known the woman Ma Clayton."

"Of course. You must have met in the caves. And you two get along?"

He nodded. "You take her the herbs. They will make her better."

"I will." Alys made to get up, but knelt back down beside him. "Would you look at what you've gone and done?"

He opened an eye.

"Your bandage is soaked with blood. I can't leave you now, not like this," she motioned toward his thigh. "I'd better change it before I go. I'm going to have to apply a tourniquet."

"What is a tourniquet?"

"A tight bandage which will keep your leg from bleeding."

He accepted this piece of knowledge in silence and watched as she tore a strip off a piece of clothing . . . her own undergarment . . .

He felt her soft hands, down there on his thigh. And perhaps it was only the loss of blood that kept him from disgracing himself with his body's need to display his sexual prowess yet again. He sighed, comforted that he had regained some control over his urges, and hopefully over his tongue, too.

But he was comforted too soon. Her hands kept nudging him in places best left for the eyes of one's wives, and he supposed it was bound to happen. He became all too intensely aware of her.

And then she began to talk. "Wolf Shadow, I think, despite the way you speak to me, that you might be a little happy to see me again."

"Only a little?" he countered. "Truly, I would like to see more of you, the way I had only moments ago."

"You speak to me as though you can only think of one thing, but I am not talking of that. I am speaking about the affinity one person feels for another, not . . . not . . ."

He did not answer, just grinned at her and lay his head back, shutting his eyes. "Aa, yes," he said, "I think that I have spoken too harshly and too openly to you, young

Alys. I hope you will forgive me, for I had not expected you to grow up to be so . . . female . . . and I think that you should be warned of me, of my unhonorable urges. I fear that seeing your body as I did made me think of you in a way which I should not. But know that I am glad to see my friend Little Brave Woman again."

"Little Brave Woman?"

"It is the name you are known by."

"Known? By whom?"

"By my people. It is the name that my sister and I gave to you."

"Little Brave Woman?" she repeated.

"*Aa*," he acknowledged, then almost at once fell into a light, restful sleep, with her gentle touch still down there where, had he a choice, he would never have had her go.

Well, maybe not never.

Chapter 5

Alys knew a little about herbs and about healing, having learned from an old Indian woman who had married a local trader, and from her mother, who had once told her that she had the "gift." She put that gift to work now, urging her mother to sip the dandelion tea she had just brewed.

Ma Clayton put down her cup and eyed the fresh herbs in her daughter's hands. "So you say Moon Wolf had you bring these herbs to me?"

Alys nodded, sitting down on the bed. "He said his almost mother had picked them for you."

"Then they will be good. His almost mother often doctors the people in their tribe."

"Does she? What is an almost mother?"

"I believe it is another wife of the father."

"Hmmm," Alys mumbled, fingering her mother's quilted bedspread, barely paying attention. The mere mention of Moon Wolf's name had brought back to mind a mental picture of his nude body, forever etched upon her memory.

"Why didn't he bring these herbs to me himself?"

"What? Who?"

"Moon Wolf. Why didn't he bring the herbs to me himself?"

"I think he meant to, but—" Alys glanced up swiftly. "Mama, you allow that man to come into the house?"

"Of course."

"Is that safe?"

"Now, Alys, don't tell me your eastern education has caused you to become prejudiced?"

"No, not prejudiced. It's just that . . . have you thought what would happen if he were to be caught here? What if those vigilantes—the seven—eleven—seventy-seven—should find him here? They would hang him and maybe you with him."

"I don't think they'd do too much. Don't reckon that vigilance committee would even recognize him. Naturally, I've thought about it. And you're right. I reckon it is most dangerous. But it's not likely that any harm would come from it."

"No harm? How can you say such a thing? Mama, Wolf Shadow is not your usual Indian, and I'm afraid that if that group of men caught him here . . . have you thought that we don't even know who the men are that make up that committee? What if one of them saw Wolf Shadow coming in and out of here?"

"Sh-h-h, don't say his name aloud." She motioned her daughter to lower her voice. "Do you want Mary to know all about it?"

"I thought that Mary would be a party to all this, too . . . well, if he comes here, and she is Indian—"

"No one knows that he is the Wolf Shadow except me . . . and now you. And he comes to the house only after dark, when Mary is asleep. Besides, you must have seen the way he is disguised when he appears in the fort."

"What do you mean? I saw him the other night."

"Well, then you know."

"Know what?"

"Why no one would think anything about . . ." Her mother eyed her suspiciously. She asked, "Just what happened the other night when you discovered Moon Wolf? How did you find out about him, about him being the Wolf Shadow?"

"I saw him, I followed him."

"What? How?"

"A few nights ago he upset a shipment of supplies going north into Canada."

"The whiskey trade. So, you saw him in action."

"Yes."

"Really," Ma Clayton frowned, "it's gotten so that the whiskey problem is plumb out of hand."

Alys nodded thoughtfully. "You could be right."

"Then you have seen him only as the Wolf Shadow?"

"Only? You talk about him as though there were some other person involved."

"Hmmm, I suppose I do. Tell me what else happened that night."

"Well, I watched him, and I didn't understand what he was doing until I came closer to the shipments. Then I smelled what was in the cargo and I understood. That's also when I saw that he'd been hurt, so I decided to follow his trail."

"He left a trail? That's odd. He usually covers his tracks well."

"It was a path of blood, Mama."

"Of blood? He's not—"

"No, I think he'll be fine now. For a few days, he ran

a terrible fever and I didn't know if he would pull through, but I think the worst is behind him."

"So he's recovered?"

Alys nodded.

"And that's where you've been these past few days, I would assume?"

Another nod.

"I had wondered. You were gone for so long each day and seemed in such a hurry, even when you were here." Her mother looked thoughtful. "A trail of blood, you say? Did anyone else see it, do you suppose?"

"I don't think so."

Ma Clayton seemed to settle down somewhat, though her eyes took on a faraway look. "He told me what you had done for him when you were young," she said. "I don't think he ever knew that you were my daughter, I had never mentioned you, but he told me how he'd come to know about the caves." She gave her only child a warm look. "That was a brave thing you did for him. Why did you never tell me about it?"

Alys shrugged. "I was afraid for them, the Indians and for myself, too, partly. I was too scared to say a word about it."

"I understand." Her mother took Alys's hand into her own and patted it, continuing, "I don't rightly know when the few white people in this town came to be in such a powerful grip of hate. I can still remember the first time your father and I took a look at this land—right here where this town is. We fell in love with it. There was nothing here back then, not in the fur trade days, and making friends with the Indians was a necessity if we wanted to stay alive. Why, I've thought more times than I can count that if it weren't for the caves and the legacy to you down there, I'd have left here long ago."

"To go back east?"

"East? Land sakes no, why east? I don't know anyone back there. No, I've often wondered what it would be like if I should go spend some time with the Indians. I have a hankering to see how it might feel to be free again."

"But we live in a free country now, Mama."

"In this town?"

Alys grinned. Her mother had a point. Although the country was free, here one had to toe the line with certain people, whose tongues were known to be more than a little unfriendly. That is, if one didn't want to find one's life in a shambles.

Luckily for her, her mother had never cared to cater to such people. "I never knew that about you, Mama, that you yearned to be with the Indians."

"Well, I never told you or many others about it. I wanted a better life for you. That's why I sent you east."

"Only to have me return as soon as I was able. I never really fit in back there."

"I'm sorry."

"I learned a lot, though," Alys added as an aside in the hopes that her mother might not think her efforts had been wasted.

"What's he doing now?"

"Moon Wolf?"

Her mother nodded.

"Oh," a wave of heat washed over Alys's skin and she prayed that if there were any color in her face, her mother wouldn't notice. "He's probably asleep," she offered. "I left him with the wolf to guard him. I guess I'd better get back and see how he is faring."

"Yes, you're probably right. You go on ahead, then. And treat him well. He's a right honorable young man."

"Hmmm," Alys uttered noncommittally.

"Go on, now. There's some fresh bandages in the drawer

over there and you can take him some of your father's old clothes."

Alys drew in her breath in a hiss. Had she mentioned that Moon Wolf lay naked in the caves?

"If I know him," her mother went on, as though reading Alys's thoughts, "he's probably only wearing that breech-cloth. He'll need something warmer."

"Thank you, Mama." Alys let out her breath slowly and arose, stepping quickly toward the chest of drawers. "I'll be back tonight to check on you."

"That will be fine, although you know that I have Mary to take care of me."

"I know. I'll be back tonight, anyway."

Ma Clayton looked doubtful, but Alys didn't see.

"Now look what you've gone and done," Alys scolded, coming upon the man in the caves. She eyed the bandages around his leg. "Have you been moving about some more?"

He didn't budge.

"Are you awake?"

A single eye popped open. She saw it.

"Well, your dressing is soaked with blood again, Mister Wolf Shadow."

"The wound will get better," he muttered.

"No thanks to you." Bending down toward him, she fingered the old bandage and began to strip it away. "I'm going to have to stop this bleeding, wash it again and put another poultice on it. And when I'm done with it this time, you are to stay put until I tell you that it's all right to move. Do you understand me?"

He didn't say a word, although he smiled.

She stripped the bandage away, taking care to place a blanket over his unmentionable parts and avoid them altogether. Even more carefully, she retied the tourniquet and, putting a fresh bandage to the wound, pressed on it until the bleeding subsided.

"When did you decide to return to the caves?" she asked, choosing her words and her subject with care. "I've only been away at school for five years, and I don't remember your coming back while I was still here."

"I returned four great suns ago, or four years as the white man says, when the whiskey traders started coming north."

"I see. Not until then?" She let up on the pressure and picked up a bunch of herbs, beginning the task of crushing them.

"I did not want to return to this town. It held bad memories for me."

"All bad?" She cast a shy glance at him.

He came up onto his elbows, his look humorous, yet serious all at once. "Not all." His eyes raked over her form, up and down, from the top of her dark-brown head to the tips of her slippered toes, where they peeped out from beneath the folds of her dress. He commented, "I was happy to see that the school is no longer here. It was a bad place."

She nodded. "It did not last long. A few weeks after your trouble, the teacher quit and went back east. It was just as well. I would rather have been taught by my mother anyway."

"Aa, yes," he said as he attempted to sit up straighter. "It is always better when someone close to you educates you in the ways of the world. In my village, it is one of the highest duties of an Indian parent, to teach their young. No man or woman ever becomes a parent without dedicating their life to their children. And teaching them, this is the natural way for a child to learn."

She gave him a smile. "I think that's a wonderful thing," she remarked, her tone social, "and I do agree, but please,

Mister Wolf Shadow, do not move about when you talk to me. It makes the wound bleed again. I may have to sew some stitches in it, I fear."

"*Aa,* if you must," he uttered and fell back down. "Why do you not call me Moon Wolf, or perhaps 'Indian' as the other pale-eyes call me?"

"I don't know. It seemed the right thing to do. And I'm not like all the other 'pale-eyes.'"

"*Saa,* no, you are not."

She paused, expecting him to say more, her brow pulled into a frown. But, at last, when it appeared he had finished, she asked, "Am I not supposed to call you by your name?"

He gazed upwards, toward the solid rock of their ceiling, his voice low as he said, "It is a sacred name, given to a man who helps his people, a man who is more ghost than real flesh. Or so it is said. It is not a name that others call me."

"Is it not? And what do other people call you?"

"It depends upon who is talking. To you, I would be a friend . . . although maybe, if we were to be again at the falls, you might call me your—"

"Do not say it."

He chuckled, although he relented. "I am sorry, young Alys, I should not tease you in this manner. But to answer your question, to my mother, I would be a son; to my other relatives, a brother or perhaps a cousin."

"Does no one address you by your name?"

"Good manners do not allow this. Only if a person has another's permission, is it used."

"I see. I didn't know that. I did not mean to offend you by calling you Wolf Shadow. It's only that—"

"You have my permission to address me directly as Moon Wolf or as the Wolf Shadow, if you would like. I gave that right to you many suns ago when I had my sister tell you my name."

"Thank you." She poured water on the herbs she had crushed, slowly making a paste out of them. "Would you prefer me to call you Moon Wolf?"

"*Aa*, yes, at least for now."

"I see." She became silent. At length, she asked, "Why do you do it?"

"What?"

"Why do you harass the military and the merchants of the town? Wouldn't things bode better for you personally if you kept to yourself? Then you wouldn't be shot at or—"

He rose up onto his elbows. "Do you insult me?"

She gave him a blank look.

"What is this thing that you ask of me? Are you inviting me to think only of myself? What sort of a warrior would put himself and his own needs before the welfare of his own people? Look to me closely. Do I appear to be such a man?"

"No, I only . . ." What had she meant? Was she questioning him because, in her experience, she'd known only a few people who would champion the well-being of an entire group of people before their own? Perhaps she simply didn't understand him.

"Look to yourself," he suggested.

"What do you mean?"

"Many years ago a young girl threw herself into danger when she aided two Indian children. Think well. Why did you do it?"

"That was different. You were being mistreated."

"*Aa*, yes, mistreated. Now, maybe you understand." He lay back, sending his gaze up toward the ceiling.

"Are you saying that your people are being ill-treated by our merchants?"

"*Aa*, yes, that is exactly what I am saying."

"I know that giving your people liquor is bad, but isn't

it also true that the merchants and the military are feeding your people and providing them with the necessities of life?"

"Are they?" He glanced over at her. "Yet, within the memory of my father is a time when the Indian needed no white man in order to survive. There was a time when the Indian was well cared for by the Above Ones alone, when the buffalo flourished, when my people rarely starved or wanted for anything. It is only since the white man has come here to our country that we starve. No longer do the buffalo roam the land in great quantity. No longer is the earth rich with game. All the Indian sees is that everywhere the white man goes, he leaves behind the destruction of the land and the game"—he paused—"and the Indian."

He hesitated, and Alys could think of nothing to say to fill the void.

"Also," he continued after some time, "the white man carries with him a powerful agent to help him in his destruction. And for the weaker spirits in my tribe, it is something they cannot resist—this whiskey."

"But the whiskey has been with us for many, many years. What makes it so different now? I don't recall the Indians rebelling so greatly in the past. Maybe a little, but—"

"Perhaps the damage was not so widespread in the days of our fathers." Moon Wolf scowled. "You have only been back a short time, and so it is possible that you do not realize what has been happening with my people."

"No, I don't reckon that I do."

Silence.

She prompted, "And what is happening to your people?"

He didn't answer for so long that she thought he might have drifted off to sleep. At length, however, he began, "The whiskey is killing them. And it is happening quickly."

"Killing? I have heard of the fights that come about

when the Indians drink, but isn't it going a little far to say that it is killing them?"

He didn't argue. Instead, he began to talk, his voice hushed. "It started long ago. Always in the past, from the day the white man came here, did the Indian have two choices of trade. Here in the south with the newer Big Knives—or the Americans—and up north with the French and regular traders. Then no American would cross the 'medicine line' into the north because the Queen mother and her people guarded their territory well. But now those posts are gone."

"You mean the old Hudson Bay Company?"

"That is the one. There is no one left to guard what was once a vast realm. Now the Americans and the seizers— the ones you call the soldiers—come up north to trade, but they bring with them little more than whiskey. They build forts where bad things happen and they make great profit from our tribes. The women tan and cure many hides, but the men have become so addicted to the white man's whiskey that they trade all they have for little more than a quick drink. And the more they drink, the more they need. You have already seen that some of my people are not good drunks. Always bad things happen, someone is killed."

Alys nodded. Yes, she had heard of this, witnessed a little of it.

He continued, "Before the whiskey became so important, our people would feel bad if killings happened, but now even that is gone. All they know is the craving for more and more of the liquor. And each day my people die, if not from the weakness and the sickness that the drink creates, then from the drunken fights."

She paused in her work. She hadn't known. "You say they're building forts up north?"

"*Aa*, yes, it is so. One of those forts is called Fort Whoop-Up, in the land above the medicine line. Bad things happen there. Even our women come away disgraced."

Alys became quiet, while she applied the poultice to the wound, cleaning it first, then binding the whole thing up with bandages. She asked, "And so you are trying to put a halt on the whiskey being sent north?"

"The fewer wagons that travel the 'whiskey trail,' the better."

"What is the whiskey trail?"

"It is what my people are calling the road between here and the forts in the north."

How appropriate, she thought.

She finished wrapping the wound and sat back, sending her gaze briefly toward him. "I have brought some clothing for you," she said, changing the subject. "They are clothes that my father used to wear. My mother had them in a chest in the house and has kept them all these years. She told me to bring them to you."

"*Aa,* that is good. And how is your mother?"

"She is better."

"My heart is happy to hear that."

"I will leave the clothes here for you, while I go back to the house."

He smiled and came up onto his elbows again, his eyes filled with a peculiar sort of mischief. "And where is it that I will get the strength to rise up and dress myself?"

She shot a quick look at him. "You seemed to have no trouble finding enough energy only a short while ago."

He grinned. "So it is true. But I think I used it all up when I did that." He paused significantly, his demeanor slightly cocky.

She stiffened. "If you mean to solicit my help, I will tell you now that I will not dress you."

"But look there where the injury is." His eyes twinkled with pure roguery, his face brightening.

She raised her chin, refusing to gaze where he suggested. "That is why I will not help you dress. I have already seen more of you than any woman who is not your wife has a right to see."

His expression didn't change. "I believe I am deeply offended."

"Then it will have to be so. You are lucky that the bullet didn't find you in a more vulnerable place."

He grinned. "You are right. How could I possibly pleasure a woman such as yourself then?"

"Oh!" She knew her face flushed, and she felt terribly like chuckling, it was all so absurd. "Be quiet, now," she took refuge in scolding him. "It is time for you to get some sleep. And if you don't feel like dressing, then don't. Tomorrow, even the day after, will be soon enough for that."

He seemed to take this good-naturedly enough, though he stared at her for a long, silent moment, the playfulness in his gaze turning hungry.

She offered, "I imagine you would like something to eat."

"I had not thought of it, but now that you mention it, I believe you are right."

"Very well," she said and rose to her feet. "I will go and fix some soup. I'm hungry, too. I will leave one lantern here for you and take one with me. That way you will be able to find your way out of the darkness if you need to."

"I do not mind the darkness."

"Don't you?" she asked. "Neither do I. Truth is, I have always enjoyed the solitude of the caves. I feel at home here."

He nodded. "It is good. I will wait for that food, Little Brave Woman. Do not be long."

She didn't reply. She didn't have to. Unspoken communication passed back and forth between them as though their spirits had become attuned to one another. And she was more than aware that he knew she would move boulders if she had to, just so that she could do as he asked.

But then, if their places were reversed, she knew he would do the same thing for her. Again, it was there between them. An unspoken trust.

One she knew neither of them would break. So where did that leave them?

"Don't go out too much farther," she called to Moon Wolf while she sat alongside the pool. To her left, a cascade of clear water fell about five hundred feet, into their lagoon, the falls hiding the entrance to the caves. A thin mist usually collected toward the bottom of the falls, she had often noted, as the force of the water shattered against well-worn rocks. Today was no different, and the mist practically made Moon Wolf invisible to her as he slowly tread through the water toward the falls. He didn't respond to her either, making her wonder if the roar of the water had drowned out her words. She called to him again. "Don't go too far, Moon Wolf, where I can't see you. What if you were to overexert yourself?"

She held her breath until at last, he turned around, shooting her a grin. She didn't miss the mischievous gleam in his eye, either, as he asked, "Would you come in to save me?"

"Never," she lied, shaking her head in case he couldn't hear her. "Didn't I tell you already, when you appealed to me to bring you here, that I would be only too happy to have you off my hands?"

He simply smiled at her, his look much too roguish for her own peace of mind. Darn the man. Wouldn't it be just like him to test her?

He wouldn't, would he?

"Moon Wolf, please. I can hardly see you as it is."

"Do not worry," he called to her. "I told you that I am

stronger now. There is nothing here that could possibly hurt me and I—ouch!"

She lifted her head. "Moon Wolf?"

No response.

"Moon Wolf, are you all right? Don't tease me. I can't see you."

Still no answer.

The rascal! What was wrong with him? She should never have brought him here. She knew that now. There was absolutely no controlling the man. He had entreated her, had insisted that he was well enough to endure a simple swim, but she knew differently. Nothing was simple with Moon Wolf. Still, he had promised her . . .

"Moon Wolf, answer me," she tried again. "If you don't do that, I will not bring you here again . . . Moon Wolf? . . . Darn!"

She threw down the herbal poultice she had been working over and stood up. "Moon Wolf, stop it this instant."

She heard a splash . . . far away.

"Alys, hurry, I hurt myself . . ." The rest was drowned out.

Oh, no. She didn't think further. This was real. He needed her. She plunged into the water, clothes, petticoats, and all. "Moon Wolf, where are you?"

"Over here," he answered, then nothing.

Although hampered considerably by her clothes, she swam in the general direction of his voice. And then it came to her. This water wasn't *that* deep. She put her feet down, the water settled just above her waist. "Are you in trouble?"

"I have a pain. You were right. I do not think I can make it back to the shore."

"Yes, you can." She struggled through the water toward him, counting the seconds until she spotted him. But then her heart constricted. Bent over, as though he had a cramp, his head was barely above water level. She drew a deep breath, reminding herself to remain calm. The water was not deep. She would be able to save him. She said, "Just put your feet down and stand up straight. It's not deep here."

"I cannot do it, the pain is too much. You will have to help me."

"All right," she agreed, coming right up to him and reaching out to place an arm around him. She hadn't looked into his eyes. A tactical error.

"*Aa*, Little Brave Woman," he sighed a little, humor all at once coloring the tone of his voice. "Would that you would hold me like this all through the night."

At last, she stole a look up at him, her stare shifting from concern to surprise. Without pause, she let her arm drop from around him. Blast the man. "How dare you give me a fright like that. There is absolutely nothing wrong with you, is there?" The question was spoken much like a statement.

"There is a great deal wrong with me," came his response. "Here, feel." He took her free hand to guide it toward his injury.

Oh, no, he wasn't. She twisted easily out of his embrace. "You . . . you tricked me." She splashed him.

"How can you think such a thing of me. I am injured, is it not true?"

She gave him another splash. "That is not what I meant and you know it. Look at me now. I'm all wet."

He gave her a splash right back, albeit a small one. "Does Little Brave Woman wish to have a water fight with me?"

She drenched him. "I am not fighting."

He tread toward her, showering her with water with each slow step he took. "*Aa*, yes, neither, then, am I," he said, a silly grin pulling at the corners of his mouth.

"You are, too. Now stop it this instant."

Amazingly enough, he did exactly as she ordered, although their previous exertion caused the water to remain turbulent. It lapped up onto them harmlessly, the sound of it oddly soothing. Still, he grinned at her.

And she could barely keep herself from responding in kind. In truth, a chuckle escaped her throat before she could check it.

Her laughter seemed to enchant him, however, and his look became suddenly intense. Despite the roar of the falls, a veil of silence drew around them, enclosing them as though they stood in a universe apart. She meant to say, *You are a rogue,* but all that came out was, "You are . . ."

". . . beautiful," he finished for her, his hand coming up to run his fingers over her cheek, down over her neck, down farther still, his gaze boldly dropping from her eyes, to her neck, descending slowly toward her breasts.

She could do no more than stare at him while her whole body remained inert. The man exuded danger, to be sure. She could feel it, knew she should move—swim back to shore, do anything but simply stand here. She couldn't budge.

His face came close to hers; so very, very close. And still she waited, able to do little more than draw in a few brief gasps of air, watching him in wonder, mesmerized by his slow descent toward her.

She closed her eyes a mere fraction of a second before his lips touched hers, the kiss tentative, gentle, no more than a light brush of his lips upon hers, although the feel of him, the erotic taste of him made her head feel as if it had been set to spinning. And, although outwardly she might have presented an appearance of calm as she accepted his tender gesture, in secret and within herself, she exploded. Her pulse raced, her knees trembled, and excitement dashed over her nerve endings as though they were alive with a spirit of their own, making her feel as though she needed more; much, much more.

He lifted his head, his lips still achingly close to her own, and she throbbed with the need to throw herself into his embrace. But she couldn't move, could only feel.

Surely he would kiss her again. She closed her eyes and bent forward with invitation, certain he would give her more; more of his kisses, more of the embraces she felt she so desperately needed.

But he didn't. Even though she had leaned forward so temptingly, offering her lips to him once again, he abruptly turned away from her, the sound of the water spraying against him giving her testimony to the fact. She popped her eyes open to catch his barely contained shudder and immediately pulled back from him, embarassed.

Had he found her distasteful? That thought chilled her, and she felt a blush creep up to her cheeks despite the coolness of the water.

Thankfully, he didn't appear to notice any of the questions or confusions spinning round and round in her mind. With a quick lunge forward, he called out to her, "Come, beautiful Alys. Let us see if you can beat me back to shore."

It took her a moment to gather her senses together and respond. But at last, with a quick jerk of her head, she plunged forward, her race to the shore displaying such vigor that one might have thought a simple contest such as this could erase the past few minutes. Of course, it couldn't.

That he let her win, pretending fatigue, was too sweet, and she thought she might forgive him anything, even his turning away from her. Well, almost anything.

Unfortunately, he had made a point, one she would not quickly forget. For she realized that despite her long years in the east, despite her protests that her infatuation with this man had been only a childish affair, he held her in the palm of his hand. Always had for that matter, right from the start.

It put her at a disadvantage with him, for he clearly did not feel the same way for her. Or did he?

Alys gave the man one last searching look before she came up onto her feet and waded to shore. Was it only her imagination, or did Moon Wolf, too, appear more than a little uncomfortable?

The thought brightened her mood considerably, and, turning her face away from him, she secretly smiled.

Chapter 6

As Wolf Shadow grew stronger, his teasing took on a new turn. He began touching her, his hand brushing against hers as she would hand him a bowl of soup or a cup of tea, a pat on the back if she'd done something he liked, a quick graze of his fingers on her cheek. Always when she worked over his wound he made some outrageous comment; even when she had sewn in his stitches, he had smiled at her at the same time in that oh, so seductive manner.

Not once in her childish imaginings had she ever added this sensual awareness to his untarnished image. It had never occurred to her to do so. And she was finding the real man more difficult to handle than anything she could have ever envisioned in her girlish fantasies.

She took stock of the man as he now appeared. True to his word, he had dressed himself in her father's clothing. The old buckskin pants, she had discovered, were his favorite, though Alys had needed to cut away a part of them so she could attend to his wound. He had also donned one of her father's homespun shirts, leaving it open so that she was constantly confronted with a tantalizing view of his broad chest. Such times always made her think of how he had looked without any clothing at all . . .

She jerked her thoughts away from that memory and forced herself to focus on other, safer images. His hair, for instance, which came almost to his waist. And his eyes, which were extraordinarily dark, practically black, glowing with merriment whenever he teased her and pride when he wasn't. His face was more oval than round; his cheekbones were high and prominent, his nose straight, his lips full and sensuous. His was probably the most handsome face of her acquaintance. And the interesting thing was, he seemed unaware of it.

His body was rather large, boned, but sleekly muscled, its masculine splendor a breathtaking testimony to his chosen lifestyle. And the cleft between his ribs was deeply grooved, making her wonder what it would feel like beneath her fingers.

Truth to tell, she found her hand halfway to him when she pulled it back and focused her attention on his injury, involving herself in rewrapping it.

All at once he came up onto one elbow. She sent him a quick look. Oh dear. His eyes held that glimmer of mischief that she had come to expect from him, and she tried to prepare herself for what he might have in store for her today. She wasn't long in waiting to find out.

"I have been thinking very long and hard about this and have decided that I would like to take another trip to the falls, that I might have a bath," he said, then grinned at her.

"Fine," she replied, matter-of-fact. "You know the way." She had taken to bringing him fresh water each day in which to bathe; since that one time, he had not indicated any desire to have the arrangement any other way.

He smiled at her. "Do you think I can make it on my own?"

"You'd darn well better be able to make it, for I will not accompany you there, not again."

"And why would you not?"

She gave him an exasperated look. "You know why. The last time I took you there, you tried to make me go swimming with you and I ended up drenched, rescuing you when you didn't need rescuing."

"Was that so bad? Is Little Brave Woman afraid that I might influence her and prompt her to join me again?"

She straightened up from where she had been tending his wound. "Of course," she answered, carefully masking a smile. The man needed no encouragement. "You tease me incessantly."

"You insult me, I think. What is this incessantly?"

"It is a word that means continually."

"Continually? *Aa*, you wound me deeply. You think I only tease?"

She almost allowed herself a grin, but she held it back. She was beginning to realize that she couldn't give this man an inch. She said, "Call it what you will. I will not go there with you and you know why."

"Are you saying that you think I might persuade you to swim with me?"

"A wise man."

"Then you admit that you may not be as unresponsive to me as you would like me to think?"

She didn't even deign to answer that one. She shot him an irritated glance instead.

"*Aa*, so you are telling me that you might peek at me as I take my time under the falls?"

"Now, why would I want to do that?"

"I do not know." He cast her an angelic look. "You are the one who said it."

"I said no such thing. Do not put words in my mouth that I haven't uttered, or credit me with something that only you would do."

He laughed. "Come you here, sweet Alys. I will need you to help me bandage up the wound once more."

"Fine. I will do it when you return from the falls."

"And what if I slip while I am there? I could hurt myself."

"If you're worried about it, don't go."

"And you would not concern yourself about me, even a little?"

"Not this much." Her fingers showed him the measurement of an inch.

"Too bad," he countered with a sigh. "I think it is important that I have this bath if I am to recover completely."

"I bring you water each day."

"But it is not the same thing, and you know it. Come with me."

"I know you well enough to know that you want something else from me. What is it?"

He gave her another of those guileless looks, to which she was becoming accustomed.

What was it? She planted her arms over her chest. "What?"

"I grow bored, and more intrigued with you every day. I think I would like to get to know you better."

" 'Better' meaning? . . ."

"Better. Though you come here every day, I do not know you well enough. I would like to see you swimming again, I think."

It was a strange thing, this closeness that had sprung up between them. It was a necessary thing, and probably natural, since she was nursing him, but he had never relented in his purpose. He pursued her with titillating vigor, as though she were the only woman on earth; teasing her with his odd sense of humor, tantalizing her with his body, although he never took advantage of her when she might have let him.

She said, "I suppose you would like to see me swimming in something that would be altogether unfitting?"

"Unfitting? I would like to see you without your clothes. *Aa,* yes, this I would like, very much."

She drew in her breath. "Now see here, Mister Wolf Shadow, there is little I have done to make you think that—"

"Every day, you are here with me."

"It cannot be helped. I will tell this to you once again. We are not a couple. We are not married, are no more than good friends. So set your mind to other things."

He grinned at her, not even pretending to misunderstand. "But it would be good for me."

"And bad for me."

"Very good for you. Not bad. Never bad."

"You are impossible. And I don't remember you being like this when we were young."

"*Aa,* yes, we were young, too young. But now—"

"Stop it. I am not going to go to the falls with you nor am I going swimming with you . . . not now, not in the future . . ."

"Come in, Little Brave Woman. The water is good, very, very good."

Alys turned her head away from the man, her air dismissive.

She heard his laugh and wondered what it would feel like to dunk him under that falling water. She felt certain it would bring her great relief.

She drew in a deep breath. She'd had no choice in accompanying him, of course.

She had watched him struggle toward the falls, had tried

looking away, knowing he had exaggerated each and every falter in his step. Yet in the end, she had not been able to remain a simple observer.

She had come to his rescue, had helped him through the tunnels and outside into the falls. She had even spied on him as he had undressed, much to her chagrin.

The flirt. He knew the effect he was having on her, seemed to relish in it.

"Hmmm. Feels good, this water," he called to her again. "Are you certain you will not join me?"

"I am going to the house. I will come back here later and check on you."

"What? And leave me here by myself?"

"Yes, and leave you here by yourself."

"But what will you do if I fall? What if I need you to help me return to the cave?"

"You should have thought of that before you came here."

"But I am thinking of it now. Can you really consider leaving me?"

"Very easily."

A long silence befell them, and suddenly he was in front of her, dripping water all over her, with no more than a cloth covering his unmentionable parts. She stared up at him, shivers running up and down her spine. And it wasn't from the cold: she didn't need to be told twice how this man would look without that tiny bit of cloth covering him.

He said, "If you are not going to take advantage of the water, then I will dress and follow you back through the caves. But I think you are unwise to leave the bath, and me ready to attend your every—"

"Enough. Do you hear me? You have done nothing these past few days but bait me. And what do you mean, coming here in front of me with so little clothing on?"

"I am covering myself properly."

"You call that proper? Do you think I don't know what you look like without that? . . ." She felt a deep flush creep up to her cheeks, saw a grin on his face. "How much of this do you think I can stand?"

"I do not know. A little too much in my opinion."

"I am a friend. I am trying to help you. There is nothing more to it than that. This constant flirting with me must stop. Do you understand?"

"Me?" His look was comically innocent. "Flirting? What does this word mean?"

She frowned at him. He knew exactly what it meant. "You are impossible."

"And yet I have only your good at heart."

"Humph. I'm not so certain of that either."

He smiled at her before, looking away, he suddenly frowned. "I think I am well enough to use some of my day in exercise." He stole a glimpse toward the falls. "Have you heard anything about any more whiskey schooners going north?"

"I . . . I haven't asked."

He sent her a hard look. "Would you . . . ask? I would know what is planned."

"Why? You are not well enough to do anything about it."

"I do not agree. Look you here to me. I am practically recovered."

"So much so that you have needed my help to get to your bath?"

He smirked. "That is different."

"I hardly think so."

He came down onto his knees before her, his dark eyes staring into hers, his look completely serious. "Would you please find out what you can? That is one thing I cannot do on my own. I cannot yet move about the fort with ease."

"And you are in no shape to stop any of the wagons, even if there were any."

"Still," he persisted, "I must know."

She hesitated, even while his dark eyes pleaded with her. Though she knew she might come to regret it, she found herself saying, "Very well, I will do it, this once, but only after you are fully recovered. Do you understand?"

He grinned. "And will you help me to recover?"

"Yes, I will try."

"*Aa*, it is good." He lifted one eyebrow. "And how will you help me, do you think? I have many ideas . . ."

She rolled her eyes heavenward.

"Why, Miss Clayton, it's good to see you here in town."

Alys turned around quickly, her auburn-brown curls falling around her face with the movement. And though her corn-colored silk parasol and her muslin cap should have hidden her from the identity of that voice, it was no use pretending. She recognized Lieutenant Warrington. Unconsciously she frowned.

He was not one of the people she wished to see. Not now. Not today.

He took off his hat as he approached her, his steps sounding hollow and hard against the wooden slabs of the walkway. "I have come to your home to call on you several times, but so far I have only been able to have tea with your mother and Mary. You have been away. Where do you go?"

Alys hadn't meant to, but she felt herself go rigid, both physically and mentally. Unfortunately, she did not have a ready-made answer. If she were aiding the Wolf Shadow, and she was, then Lieutenant Warrington had to be one of her staunchest opponents . . . if he were ever to find out.

Besides, there was more at stake here than her own reputation and that of her mother's. There was Moon Wolf, his life, his purpose; also her own secrets, there within the caverns . . .

She smiled faintly before she countered, "Has a young woman no privacy in this town?"

"Very little."

"Then it is something we should change, don't you think?"

He nodded, taking hold of her white-gloved hand and placing it on the sleeve of his coat. "Perhaps we should at that," he agreed. "A young woman must need her privacy. That is, if you are any example. Perhaps I can ensure it. Come, walk with me."

Alys didn't want to go anywhere with him, itched to remove her hand, but she dare not assert herself. At least not now. Not only would it be socially unacceptable but she also did not wish to draw attention to herself, to them. She forced herself to smile at him once again.

They had taken only a few steps, however, when the lieutenant leaned toward her and offered, "I have been wanting to talk to you about the other night."

"Oh? The night of the party?"

"Yes, I have been thinking about what I said to you that night, and I am afraid that I gave you entirely the wrong impression of the bull trains and the merchants."

"Did you?"

"Yes, I think that I did. I was mistaken, you see. There is no whiskey being shipped across the border into Canada. I'm sorry if I gave you false information. It has probably caused you some concern, too. I am sorry about that."

"Oh? Are you? Why, thank you, Lieutenant. How kind of you to think of me."

"Not at all, my dear. Not at all."

She paused suddenly, causing him to jerk back unexpectedly as she said, "You are forgetting one thing, however, aren't you?"

"Am I?" The grin he gave her appeared more anxious than pleasing.

"Yes. I remember what I smelled after that fight, what I saw dripping from the cargo—"

"But it is so easily explained, my dear." He patted her hand and drew her back into step with him. "What you smelled was the tavern next door. I'm entirely certain of it. One of the soldiers had accidently shot a barrel full of the hard liquor. What you saw . . . well, it was dark, after all, too dark to see clearly. I'm sure you understand."

"But I—"

"That's all there was to it, Miss Clayton. Nothing more."

She slowed her steps until the lieutenant was forced to do the same. She muttered, "I see." Although truly, she did not. Why was the lieutenant lying? Surely he must know that she was intelligent enough to figure out that he was hiding something. But who was she to draw suspicion on herself? She continued, "You could be right. I'm terribly glad that you have informed me of this. And I must say, it makes the merchants' integrity and their intentions, ah . . . clearer to me."

Amazingly enough, he seemed satisfied. "You're too pretty to set your mind to worrying about these things," he said. "You should be concerning yourself with more feminine matters."

"Should I?" Abruptly, she removed her hand from his arm. "Do you have anything in mind that would be . . . more appropriate?"

"I have no knowledge of what the female mind would consider important."

She afforded him a meager grin before she commented, "Then perhaps you shouldn't pretend to have wisdom about something you know nothing about." Though her meaning was more than a little harsh, her words were so softly spoken and so gentle that the lieutenant stopped to stare at her.

"I beg your pardon?" he asked.

She smiled. "Thank you for escorting me to the general store, Lieutenant. I have found our conversation most enlightening." And with nothing more said, no further explanation given, she fled into the comfort of the general store.

What was happening here in this town? Why was Lieutenant Warrington telling stories out of hand? And why had he made it a point to seek her out and try to mislead her? Were her opinions that important?

It seemed unlikely.

Still, the lieutenant had done nothing if not confirm her suspicions: wagons were heading north illegally and, if the lieutenant's actions were to be at all significant, whoever was doing it was in league with the military.

She sighed, feeling helpless. She'd placed herself into the middle of it by aiding Moon Wolf. Yet what choice had she had? She couldn't have allowed someone else to find him, could she?

Perhaps she should write a letter back east. If she could find a sympathetic ear? . . .

"Good morning, Miss Alys. What can I do for you today?"

Alys brought her attention back to the present and smiled kindly at the owner of the general store, a slightly plump young man whom she had known most of her life. "I have come to look at your new bolts of fabric, Mister Thompson—"

"You can still call me Bobby, Miss Alys."

She grinned up at him, remembering briefly when they had played together as children. "Fine, Bobby," she replied. "Thank you. And how have you been?"

"Oh, I reckon I can't complain none, though business hasn't been as good as it used to be. Don't have as much trade from the Indians as we did in my pa's day, but that don't make much difference since them beaver-skin hats have gone out of style."

"Hmmm. That's true," Alys replied, "but then buffalo robes are all the rage back east right now, aren't they?"

"I guess so, but even the trade in buffalo robes is dwindling. Ain't near as many buffalo in these parts as there used to be."

"Is that so?"

Bobby nodded. "We've had some lean years, but my ma says there's always been lean years, even when pa was alive."

"Yes," Alys agreed. "I think your mother is right. And how is she, your mother?"

"She's well enough."

"Hmmm," was Alys's only reply. What more could she say? Unfortunately, Bobby's mother, one of the few white women in the fort, had the reputation of being the town's worst gossip, as well as its most prejudiced resident. Her poor son might never find a wife, considering that most of the women in these parts were Indian. Alys changed the subject. "My mother tells me you have some fashionable new lengths of cloth. She said there had been a recent shipment?"

"That's true, Miss Alys, that's true," Bobby affirmed, turning around to gather up the colorful bolts of material and lay them before her. "These have come to us all the way from Boston."

"From Boston?" Alys repeated. "Indeed." She fingered a length of the muslin lovingly, while Bobby watched her with a look in his eyes not unlike adoration.

Alys grinned at him self-consciously, more than aware

that she was one of the few eligible young women in town, if one didn't consider the Indians.

"This material is beautiful," she said, quite honestly. "Do you mind if I look at all the material before I make a choice?"

"Take your time, Miss Alys, take your time."

Alys smiled. She hadn't really happened into town to look at material; she'd come here to discover, if she could, some information for Moon Wolf. But now that she was here, she was discovering that the urge to have a new dress, one that more suited this western environment, was infinitely pleasurable.

After all, though her percale walking suit had been the rage back east, she really should consider making herself another outfit, perhaps a simple one of calico.

Alys stood still for several moments as indecision played across her mind, feeling at the same time rather silly and frivolous. She had to remember her purpose.

Several days had passed—almost a week—since Moon Wolf had asked for her help. And in that time, she had debated whether to assist him or not. She had to be careful; there being so many factors to be considered.

In the end, of course, she'd had little choice. She would aid him.

The tinkle of a bell and high-pitched giggles sounded behind her and interrupted her thoughts.

She heard Bobby gasp, and she glanced up quickly to catch a red flush gradually beginning to stain the poor man's cheeks, his attention clearly centered upon someone who had just entered. Glancing behind her, Alys noted two young women, younger than herself—perhaps barely over seventeen—who stood at the entrance to the store, accompanied by Lieutenant Warrington.

Young white women? Here? What an unusual sight.

Alys had long been used to the notoriety of being the

only young and unmarried pale-faced woman in these parts—that is, except for the hurdy-gurdy girls down in Helena. Of course there were other beautiful women in town, but they were mostly of mixed blood, not that there was anything wrong with that in her opinion.

She asked Bobby, "Who are those women?"

"H-haven't you met them, Miss Alys?"

"No, I don't believe that I have."

"Th-they come from . . . one of them, the blond, is the governor's daughter, and the other is her cousin and, well, I reckon she's about the prettiest thing I've ever seen."

"But what are they doing here? At Fort Benton?"

"Her father is in town for some government meeting. Gonna be here for a while. Brought his daughter and her friend with 'im. She sure is pretty."

Alys reserved her opinion. It looked to her as though the two young ladies might be the kind of females that she could barely tolerate: spoiled, willful, and prejudiced against anyone the least bit inferior to themselves.

Clearly, however, Bobby Thompson did not agree with her. As he gazed at the two young women, Alys was reminded of a look she had once seen upon a man's face, when he thought he had seen an angel.

Bobby turned to Alys and muttered, "Excuse m-me, M-Miss Alys. I have th-the new c-cus . . . customers to attend to."

Alys gave the poor man another kindly smile. "Of course, Bobby. I'll be fine here. You go on and wait on them. Don't give me another thought."

Bobby nodded and moved away, Alys observing that even his movements had become strained. He suddenly tripped over something, a piece of matted rug, and fell clumsily to his knees, though he recovered himself quickly. Standing up and brushing off his clothes, he stepped forward to meet the girls.

Alys shook her head. Bobby's infatuation was obvious. She spared a moment to wonder at the stupidity of the male character—that is, when it came to love. There were so many other beautiful women in town. Why would Bobby fall for one who, in Alys's opinion, probably had a vicious tongue? Because of his mother and her prejudice?

Sighing, Alys decided she could be judging the women prematurely, and, resolving to leave the store and come back at a later time, she put the material down.

She heard Bobby stutter, "M-may I h-help you two be-beau . . . beautiful women?"

"We have come to look at ribbon," she heard a young, though haughty, voice reply. Alys looked around to see which one was speaking: the pretty blond. "Have you anything new?"

"Y-yes, come right this way and I will—"

"Oh, Lieutenant Warrington," it was the other young woman speaking—the redhead—"you simply must help me make my choices."

Alys turned away from the picture of the lieutenant and the girl, considering for a moment that perhaps the female mind was just as witless when it came to men.

Lieutenant Warrington, however, was doing his best to disentangle himself from the young lady. "Really, Abigail, I have more important matters to attend to than to help you with . . . ah, there you are, Miss Clayton."

Alys suddenly wished she could shrink to perhaps an inch tall. The lieutenant started to walk her way, poor little Abigail hurrying after him, keeping her arm firmly affixed to his.

". . . It had better not be the same ribbon that you showed us yesterday, Bobby," came the voice of the pretty, yet harsh blond. ". . . such inferior quality that was. I think you might have mistaken us for the more lower-class of

woman in this town. Now, please . . . do not do it again. I
will return tomorrow to see if you have any new samples.
Abigail, are you coming?"

"I . . . I think so. Lieutenant, will you leave?"

The lieutenant, however, had caught up with *her*. Alys
gulped and tried to look polite.

He reached out toward Alys, taking her arm. "Miss
Clayton, have you met Abigail Flint?"

The two women exchanged hellos, Abigail pulling on
the lieutenant's arm. "Daddy told you to accompany me,
so—"

"Oh, please," Alys waved toward the two of them, "do
stay with her, Lieutenant Warrington. I was leaving to go
home and I—"

"But there was more I wished to discuss with you."

"Was there? Perhaps you could call on me at a later
date, then."

"Say tomorrow?" he asked her.

She gave him a polite smile. "Perhaps."

"It was so very nice to meet you," said young Abigail,
who exchanged smiles with Alys. "Come, Lieutenant."

Lieutenant Warrington, having little choice, did her bid-
ding.

Alys turned away, intent on making good an escape,
when from behind her came a loud shriek. Alys whipped
around quickly, in time to catch the blond giving poor,
slightly overweight Bobby a good dressing down.

Alys's eyes widened. How dare that woman?

Ready to interrupt on Bobby's behalf, Alys had taken
no more than one step when, from outside a nearby window came the question, "When is it leaving?"

The voice had been deep, slightly husky, as though the
man were trying to whisper.

Alys froze in midstride.

She had to hear this. Much as she wanted to defend

Bobby, she could not leave this spot. Not yet.

Alys turned toward the cloth still laying on the counter and, bending back toward it, pretended interest in it.

"Day after tomorrow, Jake." *Jake?* Who was Jake? "That is, if that rascal Wolf Shadow doesn't get to it first."

Alys caught her breath. Day after tomorrow? Was she overhearing a plot to send more whiskey up north?

"Come meet me in the usual place in about an hour and we'll discuss the terms."

What place? What terms?

Did she dare follow the men? Of course she would have to if she were to assist Wolf Shadow.

From out of the corner of her eye, she watched the two men walk away and with a brief, sympathetic glance toward Bobby and the blond who was, even now, scolding him, Alys turned away.

She would make it up to Bobby later. Somehow. She promised herself this.

Chapter 7

◦━━◦◝◟◦━━◦

She watched him as he slept, his chest rising and falling in an even and unchanging rhythm. She had crept upon him, her footfalls making little noise as she had entered the caves, only to find him resting . . . a result, most likely, of his recent exertion.

Though his injury had barely healed, already Moon Wolf was testing his body, running longer and longer distances each day, hunting and carrying home his prizes despite the weakness in his body.

She bit down on her lip, her brows pulled into a frown.

Should she tell him what she had learned? About the bull wagon ready to leave in only two days' time?

He had asked her to find out what she could, and she had done it. But now that she knew, could she tell him? He would seek to stop it, of this she had no doubt.

Which left her in what position? Had she healed him only to have him risk his life again? This time he might not be so lucky, especially when he was still so weak.

Would he forgive her if she kept the knowledge to herself? Or more importantly, would he give her quarter when he at last found out? Particularly if the whiskey train got through to the north? To his people?

She doubted it.

She glanced toward his face, espying there, over to the side, his wolf headdress. Odd, it seemed to beckon her.

She set her lips together and scowled. Was there another way? Could she possibly ask one of the other Indians at the fort to take the Wolf Shadow's place? For this night and this night alone? Did she know of anyone she could trust?

She knew the answer to her question and despaired. It was too bad. With the wolf headdress hiding the more prominent features, it was doubtful anyone would know that someone else took his place . . . except Moon Wolf.

It was also too bad that she wasn't male. She would herself have pretended to be the Wolf Shadow. It would have been easy. She was already a good shot and had learned at a young age to track and care for herself. Plus, she knew these caves better than any other individual alive, besides perhaps her mother and Moon Wolf.

She glanced up, her eyes coming to alight on the large yellow ones of the wolf. The animal sat at a good distance from her, watching her carefully.

"What do you think, Wolf?" she asked the animal. "Should I find someone to impersonate him so that he can quietly regain his strength?"

No answer.

"I have two days to find someone. And that would give him at least two more days to regain his strength. Do you think he would forgive me for keeping this to myself just this once?"

The wolf blinked. Did that mean yes?

"I'll ask my mother. She knows a great many of the

Indians in the fort. I'm sure there must be one of them that I could trust. Do you think so?"

No answer came, not even a blink this time.

She arose. It didn't matter. She had to try.

She crept around Moon Wolf toward the wolf headdress. She had thought he was never going to go to bed despite the fact that she had given him a light sleeping potion earlier.

She had to work fast. There was only a certain amount of time in which to stop that whiskey train. She was already testing her luck by waiting until the wee hours of the morning, but she hadn't wanted to force an attack too soon. More military would have been on duty in the early evening, and her chance of success would have been less.

She knew the enormity of what she was attempting and hadn't told a soul of her plans, not even her mother. But she could not let Moon Wolf expend all of his strength. Not this once. Besides, she'd not been able to find another to take his place.

Oddly enough, all the Indians she had approached had expressed some sort of antagonism toward the Wolf Shadow, and she'd dared not share her secret or coax one of them into doing this.

There was nothing else for it. She would do it.

The wolf headdress would fit her as well as another. And she would wear the Indian shirt that she had purchased from one of the hang-around-the-fort Indians. It would cover up her figure completely while also allowing her freedom of movement.

She didn't dare think too closely about what this night could bring. She knew it could mean her life.

But oddly enough, she would rather it be her life than Moon Wolf's. Why she felt this way was something she had no wish to examine too closely.

"Don't look at me like that," she addressed the wolf, who stared at her from the foot of his master's bed. "You know this is the only way. I have written a letter to Washington. I even suggested they send a sheriff here to police the whiskey traffic. But that will take time, too much time, if Washington will respond at all. Besides, I thought you had agreed with me about this."

She'd had many conversations with Wolf over the past few days, finally deciding that what she was contemplating was for the best. There was simply no other way. She had even imagined that the wolf approved of her decision.

She rose, trying to gain as much familiarity with what she wore as she could. Knee-high moccasins, which she had also purchased from one of the Indians, clung to her calf muscles. A long Indian shirt hung shapeless over her form, hiding her more prominent feminine features.

Carefully, she tried on the wolf headdress. The nose and eyes of the animal covered the top of her head and, like a hat, fell forward, the shadowy reflection masking her features. The rest of the body of the headdress, long hangings of fur, fell down over her shoulders, covering the lengthy tresses of her hair.

"What do you think?" she asked of the wolf, who appeared to watch her with disapproval. "Don't look at me like that. I've told you and you alone why I have to do what I'm doing. Don't make me feel guilty now."

The earthy smell of the garments and the headdress served to increase her anxiety. Though she would carry a gun, what she was about to do was completely alien to her. Still, she had come this far. She would go the distance.

She glanced once more toward Moon Wolf, and on impulse reached around her neck and untied the necklace that she always wore. Smiling sweetly, she placed it on his chest.

If she never returned, at least he would know that she

had cared enough to turn over her prized possession.

"You will tell him what I have done," she instructed the wolf; those golden eyes, staring at her, were the animal's only response.

And with no more to be said, she turned away.

Something cold pressed against his cheek. He tried to brush it away. It wouldn't leave.

Moon Wolf groaned. "*Miistap-aaatoo-t annoma!* Go away from here."

It wouldn't stop. Again and again that slimy object pressed against him.

He brought up his hand, only to find the snout of a wolf. "*Makoyi*, Wolf, what is it that you do? Let me be."

A howl was all he received in response.

Moon Wolf opened his eyes to the darkness shrouded all around him. He reached an arm up past his head to where Alys always kept a lamp, his head spinning at the same time.

He felt miserable.

Quickly he lit the lamp and sat up, finding something dropping into his lap as he did so.

He picked it up. What was this? A necklace? *Aa*, yes. But not any necklace. He held it up to the light. This was the same one he had once given to Alys. *Tsa?* What was the meaning of this?

He glanced toward *Makoyi*, toward Wolf. He didn't even put the question into words.

Makoyi nudged him yet again.

"What is it?" he asked, tying the jewelry around his own neck.

Makoyi whined and ran away, toward the place where the cave emptied into the Claytons' root çellar. Back again, nudging him up.

Moon Wolf rubbed his eyes and looked around him. Something was missing. What?

Again *Makoyi* ran away, toward the root cellar, then back.

"You want me to go out into the fort? Why? You know something, don't you, old friend? *Haiya,* I will follow you." Moon Wolf came up onto his knees and reached behind him for the headdress. His hands met with nothing.

He brought the light to that area, shed it all around.

Gone. "*Tsa,* what is happening?"

Makoyi howled.

Urgency filled Moon Wolf. There had to be only one explanation.

Trouble, with Alys involved in it. And *Makoyi* knew.

Gathering up his gun, his bow and arrows, and his knife, Moon Wolf followed *Makoyi*'s trail, trying at the same time to shake off his lethargy. Quickly, he jogged toward that part of the cave where it met the Clayton root cellar. He bounded up the ladder in a few jumps, pushing back the cellar's false bottom, while both he and *Makoyi* burst upwards. In a matter of seconds the two figures emerged into the fort's twilighted landscape, only to be met with the sound of gunshots.

But the shots were not directed at him. They exploded off in the distance.

Haiya! Alys. Was she in trouble? It couldn't, it shouldn't be, yet . . .

His gut twisting with premonition, Moon Wolf hesitated no longer than a mere moment. Besides, *Makoyi* was already leading the way, and Moon Wolf bolted after him.

It didn't take long to find her, crouched down beneath a wagon for cover and, as he had suspected, his headdress fixed atop her head. The sight of her in danger gave him renewed purpose, and he pushed forward, a single swipe of his knife taking down one of the seizers in his way.

Makoyi struggled with the next closest soldier. Moon Wolf left the animal to finish the job, rushing himself to the next. Another swipe of the knife ceased that resistance, the element of surprise catching the trooper off guard.

"Wolf Shadow," he heard her call.

He didn't answer, there wasn't time. Shots still fired from the other side of the wagon. He, too, took shelter beneath the wagon, placing his body between hers and the gunfire.

Still, he spoke no words.

Quickly he surveyed the enemy. There were only three of them left, but soon there would be more as the others in the fort awakened to the sound of fighting. He had to act—now.

Wolf whined from close by.

"We have only one chance," he directed his words over the gunshots. "We must push this wagon onto its side . . . after the next shot." He studied her briefly. Relieved that she appeared to be unharmed, he was able to smile encouragement at her. Later would come the lecture she so deserved. Another shot fired. "Now!"

In one fluid motion, the two of them sprang up, as though they had planned this action all along. Lending it all their effort, they pushed the wagon up and over. Within seconds, the contents of the wagon spilled over in front of the soldiers, giving the two fugitives the cover they needed to escape.

Moon Wolf didn't hesitate. Pulling Alys with him, he sped back in the direction of the cellar, Wolf hanging back to howl out their success.

"*Makoyi*, now. *Oki*, come on!"

A shot fired, followed by a screech. Wolf!

Moon Wolf pushed Alys on forward, while he sprinted back toward the wagon in time to witness the animal fall. Something akin to rage took form within him, but there was no time to act on it. Not now. Picking the animal up and turning around, Moon Wolf hurled himself back toward Alys, who, he discovered, had hesitated, waiting for them at the entrance to her cellar.

He handed her the animal and pointed to the cellar. "Go!"

"But—"

"Go now!" His voice brooked no argument, and she gave none further, as she pulled up the cellar doors and hurried to safety, *Makoyi* tucked gently within her grasp.

Moon Wolf sighed with relief, and, turning, rushed back toward the seizers' fight.

He was no more than a few buildings away from the place when a friend stepped out of the shadows, pushing a buffalo robe into his arms. Moon Wolf acknowledged the man, accepting the article and pulling the robe around his shoulders.

"I did not know what she was intending," his friend offered by way of explanation, handing over a bottle of whiskey. "I had heard that she was making inquiries about Wolf Shadow and was asking strange questions, but we did not know that she was a friend. No one gave her information. She is the one who has helped you?"

"She is." Moon Wolf took a swig of the awful stuff, so that the stench of it was on his breath. Then he spit it out, pouring a little more of it over his body.

"And she is the woman who has been with you day and night for this past full moon?"

"*Aa,* yes, she is that and we have been together, but not in the way you might be thinking." Another swig, which he just as quickly spit out. "She is a woman, yes, but there is nothing intimate between us. She is a friend. That is all."

There was the hint of a smile in the other man's voice

as he muttered, "You are quick to assert that, my friend. Maybe a little too quick?"

"*Haiya*," Moon Wolf snorted, handing back the bottle, "do not put meaning into my words that I do not intend."

"As you say," the man agreed, though the teasing quality did not abate. He tucked the bottle away. "I regret that I did not take her inquiries seriously."

"Think no more of it. It is not your fault," Moon Wolf answered. "She is strong spirited."

"You are not angry with me, then?"

"*Saa,* no, why should I be? That woman is as easy to manage as the wind, I think." Moon Wolf cast a brief glimpse around him. "Were you able to cover our tracks?"

"Only the ones leading to the cellar. The others, closer to the fight, are still there. The seizers are watching that place. Be careful, my friend."

Moon Wolf nodded before pulling the robe up and over his head. He said, "Let us hope that the soldiers are still so groggy from sleep that they will not wonder what a drunken Indian is doing still up and awake at this early hour of the morning."

His friend signaled agreement and, with a quick pat to Moon Wolf's shoulders, faded back into the shadows.

Moon Wolf watched him for a moment before, taking a deep breath, he began to sing his courage song in the best drunken voice he could muster. Perfecting his stagger so that he epitomized the image of a drunken idiot, he sauntered unsteadily back in the direction of the all too recent fight.

"Well, if it isn't ole Moon Wolf," Lieutenant Warrington's voice alerted Moon Wolf to the man's close presence. "Where've you been, you old drunk?"

Moon Wolf halted for an instant in his wobbling act and pulled the robe down from around his head. He had been erasing the tracks they had left behind and hoped that his disguise had once more masked the truth of his identity. He pasted an inane smile on his face, turned, swaying at the same time, and uttered, "Mor-r-re whisk-ee," slurring the words.

"No more for you, you good-for-nothing rotten bag of fleas."

Moon Wolf deliberately rolled his eyes until they bulged, then hiccupped. "This one not—hiccup—flea-bitten, not drunk either."

"I wouldn't take any bets on it." The lieutenant paused. "Did you see what happened here tonight?"

Moon Wolf staggered forward, clutching onto the lieutenant. "Mor-r-re whisk-ee."

"No more." The lieutenant disengaged Moon Wolf's hands from upon him, none too gently. He made a face. "Whew, you smell worse than a skunk in heat. I think you've already had more than your fair share of liquor for the night. You were supposed to be watching here and listening. And you had better be doing that or I won't be giving you any more of the brew. Have you news for me?"

Moon Wolf didn't answer at once. Instead he kept on singing.

The lieutenant tried again. "You good-for-nothing var-mint, what news have you?"

"Mo-r-re whisk-ee."

"Not until you tell me what you have heard."

More singing followed the demand, and the lieutenant began to lose all patience. But then, just as the man made to turn away, Moon Wolf volunteered, "There are those—hiccup—who say the Wolf Shadow was killed."

"Killed?" The lieutenant stomped back. "Killed, you say? Why you no good old bummer of an Injun. You're crazier than a loon. If he was killed, what do you call this tonight?"

Moon Wolf staggered forward. "Information must be . . . not good."

"Pshaw! Not good, you say. Is that all you can tell me? Now, what use are you to me if you can't get me the details I need?"

"Much good is this one . . . heap big good."

Lieutenant Warrington snorted, "I wouldn't take bets on that either. Now, no more whiskey tonight, do you hear? There'll be none for you at all until you tell me what I need to know."

Moon Wolf teetered unstably. "No more whis-kee? But you promised you would get the white man's drink for me—hiccup. Said you nothing of these . . . details you needed."

"Details? . . ." The lieutenant made a face. "I need to find myself another Injun is what I need to do. You're turning out to be nothing but a no-account dirty critter, and a drunk." The lieutenant turned away and began to stroll off in the opposite direction.

"Don't need another," Moon Wolf called after him. "This one good."

"Good for nothing."

"You tell this one what you need to know," Moon Wolf staggered after him, adding another hiccup for good measure. "This one will get it. Besides, know . . . that all others are afraid . . . to be cursed, they are . . ."

Lieutenant Warrington stopped, and shook his head before he turned around. "All right, then," he said. "See if you can manage to get it right this time. I need to know the identity of this Wolf Shadow, not his state of health, nor any other trivial facts about him. I need you to discover how the trickster gets into and out of the fort without leaving a single trace. Who helps him? Who are his friends? D'ya hear me? That's what I need to know, not, not . . . and no more whiskey until I get what I want."

Moon Wolf deliberately bulged his eyes. "But what you ask is impossible. They say he is a ghost. How can I? . . ."

"That is your problem, not mine. And he is not a ghost."

"But—"

"If you can't do it, I promise you that I will find myself another Injun, curse or no curse, and damn you and your whiskey."

Moon Wolf remained silent, swaying slightly.

"Good," the lieutenant asserted. "I guess we understand one another well enough." And with that said, the man stomped off, back toward the barracks, anger marking his every step.

Moon Wolf watched for a moment before turning away. Hiding a grin with the easy stoicism of his race, he pulled the robe back up around his head, continuing to erase all signs of his and the new "Wolf Shadow's" tracks.

Chapter 8

"Is he still alive?" He crouched down beside her, where she squatted over his pet, and extended his hand to stroke the wolf.

"Yes," she responded, watching that hand and his long fingers in fascination, "the bullet didn't hit any of his vital organs. See?" She bent over and pulled away the bandage she had set to the animal's wound, pointing to where the bullet had grazed its chest.

Moon Wolf drew in his breath, the sound of it resembling a hiss. He asked, "Will he live?"

"I'm fairly certain of it. There's a lot of blood, but I believe it's only a surface wound. I will go home shortly and get the herbs we will need to heal it. But if I am right, your wolf should be up and about again in a few weeks." With a jerk, she raised her head and sniffed the air around her, asking after a few moments, "Moon Wolf, have you been drinking?"

He didn't answer, merely stared back at her until at last he stood. Grabbing the lantern, which he had set off to the side, he signaled her to stand, too, and follow him.

She did as he asked, bringing another lantern with her.

They had gone only a short distance, their figures casting two large shadows on the cavern walls, when Moon Wolf suddenly stopped and rounded on her. "What is it that you do?" he demanded.

"What do you mean, what do I do? I am trying to save the wolf's life."

"That is not what I mean and you know it. What did you mean to do tonight at the fort?"

She swung the lantern to her side, set it down, and crossed her arms over her chest, her own shadow flickering against the walls. She said, "I might ask you the same."

Moon Wolf ignored her. "Did I give you permission to act as me?"

"Did I give you permission to get out of your bed?"

"Since when do I need such a thing? I am well and have been up and hunting for several suns now. I am capable of fighting my own battles."

"I beg to differ."

"What sort of lies are these that you tell me? Can you deny that I have been hunting every day?"

She held her ground. "I would deny that you are well enough to go up against the soldiers."

"I am well enough and I am recovered."

"I didn't think so at the time and I still have my reservations about it now."

He scowled at her. "Do not bicker with me. It only causes us to leave the point, which is that you are not to go about disguised as me again. Do you not realize the danger you brought onto yourself tonight?"

"It is the same danger that you face whenever you go into the fort. Why should you have all the adventure?"

"Adventure? Is that what you think this is, why I do what I do? Do you not realize that I have no other life than this? Do you think I would not rather be with the rest of my tribe, listening to the old men talk of the long ago days, smoking my pipe and watching my children grow fat from lack of want?"

She swallowed, only one thing he had mentioned holding her attention. "You have children?"

"That is not the issue."

She backed up, unaware that his shadow loomed over hers. She asked, not caring if it concerned the subject at hand or not, "How many children do you have?"

She could sense his anger, yet still his answer was polite as he offered, "I have no children and we leave the point I am trying to make."

"And your wife?"

His frown deepened. "Do I look the sort of man to be married?"

"Yes," she returned. She could very well imagine it. From the recesses of her memory, she recalled just how well equipped this man was for such a role.

He made a sound deep in his throat, perhaps to vent his frustration, before he uttered, "If I were married, I would be with her now, helping her during the period of the white man's terrible injustices to our people."

"Then you are not married?"

His brows narrowed. "*Saa*, no, I am not married."

She let out her breath, unaware until she did so that she had been holding it. She couldn't quite bring herself to look at him as she came away from the wall and asked, "Why ... why are you not married?" She risked a brief glimpse up at him to find him looking momentarily puzzled.

It was a fleeting impression, however, for he quickly swept all emotion from his countenance, pointing out, "I am not seeking a wife so do not put these thoughts into your mind, if it is a husband you are soliciting and the reason you ask me these questions. You will not find a husband in me for I have no time for such a pleasant thing. But again, we leave the reason why we are even now talking, which is your recklessness tonight."

"It was not reckless," she defended. "And I am not seeking a—"

"You could have been killed."

"But I was not."

"No thanks to your own lack of planning. Did you go there with no strategy in mind as to what to do if the soldiers attacked?"

"Strategy? I didn't know I was supposed to have a plan."

"Did you not? Then you should know better than to go out alone, with no one to help you if you should get into trouble. If it hadn't been for *Makoyi* awakening me, I hate to think what might have been."

"*Makoyi*? You mean Wolf? The wolf awakened you?"

He nodded. "And led me to you."

"I didn't know . . ." She glanced toward the wolf. "I didn't realize that animals could be so . . . so . . ."

"Human? So capable of feeling? What do you think? That an animal does not experience loyalty and emotion, just as you and I feel these things?"

"Of course I know that animals do, must have feelings . . . it's only that I . . . I owe the wolf a debt of gratitude, then."

"Make him well. That will be enough."

She nodded. "I will."

"Hear me well, Little Brave Woman. Never again are you to go into the fort without at least two escape routes well planned. Nor should you let yourself be led into a trap."

"A trap? That wasn't what this was tonight, was it?"

"I believe it might have been." His face showed none

of the concern she heard in his voice as he continued, "How did you learn of this bull train?"

"I overheard some men talking."

He paused a beat. "Why did you not tell me about this?"

She backed away from him, straightening up. "I knew you would only try to stop it and I didn't think that you were ready for that yet."

He withdrew from her, too, and appeared to be lost in his own thoughts, barely listening to her, until, at last, he said, "They were talking to set up a trap, I believe. Did they see you listening? I should never have asked you to do my work for me. You must be careful in the future. You do not want suspicion thrown onto you."

"I do not think anyone would suspect that I am helping the Wolf Shadow. I have been back here such a short time." She frowned. "What makes you think it might have been a trap?"

"Because there was no whiskey on that shipment and I think that the wagon was there only to lure the Wolf Shadow into the open and capture him . . . which they almost did."

She gave him an incredulous look. "How do you know that those wagons had no whiskey?"

"I went back to the scene of the fight that I might cover our tracks."

"You what? Are you crazy? You could have been captured . . . you should have been. Why were you not? . . ."

He shrugged.

She thought for a moment, while several unanswered questions, like pieces of a puzzle, started to fall into place. She stated, almost to herself, "You use some sort of disguise when you go into the fort, don't you? That's how you can go into it and out of it as easily as you do. That's it, isn't it? I should have realized this before now." She scrutinized his appearance. "What is it you pretend to be?" She sniffed at the air. "A drunk?"

He lifted a single eyebrow at her, his only response.

"I'm right, aren't I? You pretend to be a drunken Indian, don't you? And I wager that you have other people helping you in the fort, too. That's how you can mastermind several routes of escape. And that's why no one has been able to catch you." Her glance up at him was full of respect.

His expression, however, didn't change, nor did he utter a word.

"Although if that is the case," she continued, "why did none of the Indians I approached in the fort help me? In truth, most of them seemed antagonistic toward the Wolf Shadow."

"Because," he spoke at last, "no one knows you and no one understood that you were a friend. You are white. Did you think others would trust you so easily?"

She shrugged. "I guess not."

"*Haiya*," he said inspecting her up and down, his gaze lingering over that area of her body where her breasts should have been in evidence. Under his intense regard, her knees went a little weak, while a sensation like white-hot lightning careened down her nervous system. She had never felt more like collapsing. But she didn't. She stood before him, shoulders pressed back, listening as he continued, "It seems that like the wily fox, you are very clever and quick of mind, yet it occurs to me that, once again, we leave the purpose of our talk. I can only wonder, do you distract me purposely?"

Her answer, a simple one, was a mischievous grin.

He shook his head. "Now hear me well. You are not to masquerade as the Wolf Shadow again."

"Fine. I won't."

He relaxed.

"As long as you promise me that until you are completely recovered, you are not to become the Wolf Shadow, either."

"*Haiya,* you are impossible. This is what I do. What gives you the right to dictate my actions to me?"

She raised her chin. "The right of any nurse. Besides, I am not trying to tyrannize you. I am only trying to cure you."

"Then beware the cure." A hint of humor tainted the hard quality of his words, though he paused for a moment. "What is this 'tyrannize'?"

"I . . . well I guess it means to try to run other people's lives and not necessarily for their own good."

"*Aa,* yes, this is a good word, this *tyrannize,* and describes exactly what you are trying to do."

"I am not."

He held up his hand. "We will not argue this any further. Do not make me repeat this again. You will not go about disguised as the Wolf Shadow again. I have spoken."

"Fine," she said. "I will devise my own disguise."

"You will do no such thing."

"And who will stop me?"

"*Haiya,* you would test the patience of Sun," he uttered before he moved forward so swiftly that she didn't have time to react. He swept her into his arms. "It is I who would stop you."

She didn't resist. Indeed, such a thing would have been the last thought in her mind. The clean, though earthy, scent of him assailed her, and she stared intently up into his dark, dark eyes, his lips so very close to her own. She dared to ask, "And how would you do it?"

In the space of a moment, he captured her mouth with his own, his answer to her, and she rejoiced, her own lips hungrily seeking out the sweet-salty taste of him. Was this what she had been awaiting all these long weeks? Was this where the long hours of teasing had taken them?

Indeed, her head spun, her body felt light, and excitement, sexual and thrilling, washed through her. It was as though an emotional reservoir had been let loose within her. Never, she realized, never would a kiss such as this stop her from trying to protect him. In truth, it made her all the more determined.

It did occur to her that perhaps, because she acted as a nurse, she should follow some code of ethics and pull away from him. But as his arms swept her even closer to him, with the rock-solid contours of his body outlined against her, she ceased to think at all.

Ah, sweet heaven. She felt herself melt.

All at once he drew back from her, staring down intently at her. Briefly, his fingers came up to brush over her cheeks once, again; his eyes alternately adoring, then angry. He asked, "Alas, Little Brave Woman, is this a madness with us?"

She couldn't answer.

"Do you feel it, too?"

"Hmmm," she nodded, unable to voice a single word.

He groaned. "I don't need this right now," he protested, even while his lips assailed hers again, kissing her, then holding her tightly to him, rubbing his cheek against hers. "Do you understand that, Alys?" he asked, his voice heavy with dissent. "I don't need this." But even as he spoke, his lips, his tongue, played havoc with her.

"I must see you," he admitted contrarily, breaking off the kiss and pulling her in closer. He ran his hands up and down her spine as though he might ease the yearning between them with his touch alone. He said, "My memory is not so long that I desire to use only it to bring the naked image of you back to mind. I must look upon you again, now, and"—he tugged on the shirt—"without this."

She didn't think to deny him. She couldn't. Coherent thought had deserted her, her body now under his command, and she let him ease the buckskin shirt up and over her head, the chilly touch of the cave's cool air only adding to her awakening. His fingers, however, met with the layers upon layers of linen she had used to wrap her breasts.

Clearly frustrated, he drew back, but only a little. "What is this?" he asked, fingering the material, his tone half amused, half tormented.

She grinned up at him. "I did not think it right that the Wolf Shadow should have breasts. I thought it might spoil his reputation."

"It might at that," he uttered, his voice a mere whisper. "But perhaps the seizers would not have fired upon you had they seen or been aware of these." His hands cupped the material where her soft mounds should have been.

"Perhaps not."

"Then you must promise me that if you decide to do such a reckless thing again, you will not wrap these. If you must fight, and I am prevented from stopping you, promise me that you will go as yourself, as a woman. In that way will your safety be assured. Do you so promise?"

She nodded, looking up at him, her eyes meeting the haunting euphoria in his.

"Not that I have relented," he persisted, his hands beginning the task of unwinding the cloth.

"I understand." She held up her arms, giving him full access to her, while the yards and yards of material began to curl and tumble to her feet.

"I think I knew, all those years ago," he mumbled, his eyes dark with desire, his hands full of the cloth, "that you and I were destined to be together. It is why I gave you the necklace and asked you to accompany me. But you denied me."

"Though I do not deny you now."

"No," he admitted, the last of the material falling away, harmlessly hitting the ground, "you do not." He stared at her, at all the bareness revealed for the space of a second before his hands came up to massage her through the thin layer of her chemise. "But I think if I had known back then what a beauty you would become when you had grown, I would have stolen you away, no matter your protest."

Her stomach twisted as though in agony at such a declaration, although it would have been inaccurate to label what she felt pain. She fell against him, gladly giving herself to him.

His voice husky, his hands shaking slightly, he declared, "I think I died a little when I saw the seizers firing at you."

"I think I did, too."

"It would have been a great loss if their aim had been a little better. I am grateful for the inaccuracy of their training."

"As I am, too."

"What is this thing that you wear?"

"This?" She stared down at herself, at the newest shade of apricot underclothing. "You mean my chemise?"

"It is too many clothes; let us remove it." And as she smiled her encouragement at him, he tore into the delicate garment as though beneath it waited a feast—and perhaps one did. Quickly mastering the art of the hook and eye, and pushing the chemise off her and to the side, he left her standing before him in only knee-high moccasins.

As a man might pause for a moment to admire a banquet laid out before him, so did his gaze relish over her nakedness, allowing her to become more than a little aware of his own desire, so clearly outlined there within the tight fit of her father's trousers.

Alys suddenly felt the uneven odds of their various states of dress—or, rather, undress. She wished to see him, too.

With delight, she reached over to pull at his shirt,

snatching it off him with his complete cooperation. Her eyes noted the necklace he wore, one she had left for him, but she said nothing. Next to his trousers.

His hands were upon her flesh now, his fingers seeking out her curves, her breasts, the femininity of that, her most secret realm. Her knees buckled under her, and she found herself unable to finish the task of undoing his trousers without his assistance.

Her hand reached out to him again and she whispered, "I cannot control the urge to touch you, Moon Wolf. What is happening to me? Can you tell me what is wrong?"

"Shhh. It is nothing wrong. It is desire, that is all."

"Desire? But is it always so . . . intense? . . ."

"*Saa,* no, I do not believe so. What we share is a coming together of spirit, I think, a nourishing of the soul, as well as passion. I can feel you, the essence of who you are and in this moment, I can see the beauty and simplicity of you. Can you feel it in me, too?"

She nodded.

"*Aa,* I have heard of this before, have known men who speak of this thing, but never have I experienced it. *Saa,* there is nothing wrong. There is a great deal that is right."

"Is that why I want more? More of what? And why can't I stop myself from wanting to touch you?"

He groaned, his eyes closing.

"I think, Moon Wolf, that resisting you when I was younger was not so wise a thing. I should have gone with you and taken your offer of marriage all those years ago. If I had, do you think we would have experienced this passion long before now?"

"I think that is possible," he responded, his voice no more than a hoarse whisper.

"Has it always been this way between us, unacknowledged, do you think?"

He nodded, his head against her own, his breathing quick and shallow.

"And do you think it will be like this still, when we have been long married and are growing old together?"

He caught his breath and held it while several moments swept by, followed by a deadly silence. At last he uttered, "Married? . . ." It was almost a whisper. "Old age? I think that . . ." He didn't finish. His hands slowed in their exploration of her, and his body went suddenly rigid. He backed away slightly. Had she been at all experienced, she might have taken heed of the brusque change in him, but she had never been in love before, had never been with a man. And even when he took a short step back, away from her, she didn't register his transformation.

More startled than concerned, particularly since she stood nude before him, she took a shaky step forward, trusting him to wrap her back in his arms. After all, this was a time of great import for her; the moment when she would give herself fully to the man she loved.

That he remained before her, his hands to his side, his stance tense, escaped her notice, at least for the moment.

"Alys, Little Brave Woman, we must talk."

"Talk? We are talking." She reached out her hand for him.

He ignored her and glanced away. "Alys?"

"What?"

"I must think." He stepped back, even farther away; she tread forward. He shook his head, frowning. "Do not consider that this is something that I wish to do, but it must be done and you are not making it easy for me."

"What are you talking about? Easy for you . . . to what?"

He flashed her a scowl. "We must stop this."

"Stop?"

She didn't need his quick glance to know what he meant.

She tilted her head to the side. "Why?"

"Because you need to allow me to think . . . more clearly. I must remember again the words of my grandfather, who instructed me that when a woman is in the heat of passion, I must reason for the two of us. A woman pushed too far can too easily be toppled, leaving her ruined. It is not a wise thing to do to a good woman." He cast a brief glimpse down at her. "And you are a good woman."

"I should hope so, though I do not feel so proper right now."

"But you are a very good woman and what I was about to do is best done only to one's wife, which you are not. It is for this reason that we must stop. We must refrain from becoming . . . physical with one another."

She closed her eyes and sighed. "I see." She paused. "And this is because we are not married?"

He nodded.

"Well, if it is merely the lack of a marriage certificate that makes you desire to stop, perhaps arrangements could be made . . . if you are willing . . ."

Her words trailed off as she watched an invisible mask drop down over his features, his look all at once deadly stoic.

His dark eyes captured hers, though it did her little good to stare back at him. She could detect nothing. And he became so still that she wondered if he continued to breathe. In response, she uttered no sound, though she did shiver as the lethal silence spread around them, the water dripping in the cave somewhere far away the only sound in an otherwise silent universe.

At last he spoke. "I do not know what this certificate is but I know that it would do us no good."

She caught her breath, watching as he bent to pick up the shirt he had so recently removed from her. He didn't look up at her, either, not even when he uttered, "Have you considered what the consequences would be if I were to get you with child?"

A child? She hadn't thought of it. But now that he mentioned it, the idea gave her mood a certain buoyancy. That is, until she glimpsed his expression.

Then, with a single glance, she plummeted, trembling with a premonition.

"It would be an Indian child," he was continuing. "Can you tell me how a child such as this would be viewed by the white man? And how you would be as well?"

She lifted her chin, dismayed that she had started to shake. "Do you honestly think that I care about such pettiness?" Her voice quivered.

But he appeared oblivious to it. He sent her a heated look. "I think that you should. I know you are a strong and a good woman, but you must regard for a moment the other life that you might carry if we were to . . . continue as we were."

"But—"

"Know that I am not in a position to marry. I may never be."

There it was, she thought, his intention clearly stated. She tossed her head and straightened her spine, as though his simple words hadn't affected her. But her bravado was fleeting; within herself and in secret, she withdrew.

"My life is too unstable," he continued to speak, apparently unaware of the changes taking place within her. "I cannot permit a wife into my life. It would be unfair to her; from one day to the next I do not know if I will be alive. Such is the direction I have chosen to take my life. I do it willingly for my people. But it is a life that does not permit the presence of a woman, or a child." He stood up at last, tossing the borrowed shirt at her, which she caught in midair. "What would happen," he asked, "if I were to get you with child and then die? You alone would have to bear the brunt of the talk and the prejudice that would surround you. Do you think I would wish this upon you, upon a child of my own making?"

She shook back her head, thrusting her arms into the shirt with vigor. And, pulling the material up and over her head, then down her body, she felt a little better, at least a little less vulnerable. Enough so that she could point out, though perhaps only in an attempt to spare her dignity, "I have not asked you to marry me, nor to get me pregnant."

He smiled, a temperate half smile. "Not in words."

She froze, mortified. "You misunderstand my intention. I only mentioned that you had once offered to marry me. I did not mean that I was seeking that sort of thing from you now."

"Were you not?" He grinned again. "It does not matter. I would not take you as a man does a woman he loves unless we were married. One does not linger over a good woman without justification." His eyes darkened, if that were possible, with an emotion that was silent and defeating at the same time. He said, "Do not think that I would not like to have you in the way of a wife. I would like it very much; it is only that I cannot. I am Indian. You are white. Perhaps we should seek a mate, when the time is right, from within our own people."

Stunned even further, Alys could do little more than stare at him, barely able to utter, "You . . . you are prejudiced."

He shrugged. "I could be."

She backed away from him, but even embarrassment couldn't keep her from asking, "Then while you were ill and were teasing me, and now here today, how you touched me, the things you said to me; have you only been pretending your affection?" Mortified, she couldn't help the sob that escaped from her throat.

He moaned, and at last his gaze came up to study her. It was only then that he looked at her, really looked at her. She would never know with certainty what he saw, but, as though suddenly beside himself, he closed the distance between them.

He took her in his arms, preciously folding her back into his embrace, murmuring, "Alys, my good Little Brave Woman, you misunderstand," he explained, mumbling into her hair. "I know that what I am saying is not easy to bear. But do you honestly think I could pretend such eagerness with you? Hear me now and do not mistake me again. It is because I care deeply for you that I am trying to show you the respect you deserve. It has been wrong of me to tease you these past few weeks. I knew it even when I was doing it; knew it was a path I should not take with you, particularly since it is you who always comes to my rescue. But it cannot now be helped. I can, however, keep myself from making a worse mistake."

Her chin trembled. "What do you mean, worse mistake?"

"Making love to you would be a terrible mistake on my part."

Alys gulped. Whatever gladness his speech had at first inspired died a quick and silent death.

She felt foolish, uncertain, and particularly childish all at the same time. How could she have misinterpreted him so completely? She went rigid, although, contrarily, her knees began to quiver.

"You are shaking."

She couldn't respond.

"I know that this is hard to accept, if you will try to think as I do, you will see that as you grow older, you will be happy that I was strong at this time of your life. After all, would you have me treat you as one would an unfaithful wife? You," he pushed his hands through her hair, "whose delicate care has saved my life not once, but twice."

With all her will, she stepped away from him, out of his reach, and said, "But you saved my life tonight and so we are even." Her composure was shattered, and she turned her back on him that he might not witness her humiliation.

"That is not the same thing," he said as though those simple words would explain it all. "Tonight was my duty."

Duty? Was that all she was?

She whispered, not even glancing over her shoulder, "As it was mine, to save yours."

"No, not duty. What you did came from the heart, a very good heart. One I will not spoil."

She heard his breathing behind her, could feel the nearness of him by the tingling sensation upon her skin.

And then the worst thing happened. She sobbed. She couldn't help it.

She didn't want to cry, didn't want him to witness the weakness in her. But she couldn't help it, and her shoulders shook with the force of her feeling.

Maybe he would leave. She desperately hoped that he would, that he would allow her enough time to collect herself.

But he didn't. All at once, he closed what little distance still remained between them and took her in his arms, though her back was still toward him. He proffered, "I do not mean to hurt you."

"You do not." Her voice trembled with the lie.

"*Haiya*, this is not easy for me, either."

An unwanted tear fell down her cheek, but she tried to hide it, bending her head forward and letting her hair fall over her face. She couldn't speak, and it didn't matter that she told herself to be strong, that she understood why he was doing what he was doing. She did.

Such things, however, did not matter. She felt mute. So she nodded as though to say, "I know."

"*Haiya,*" he uttered again, his hands beginning to assuage her, roaming up and down her, massaging over her stomach, while the hard imprint of his masculinity pressed up against her back. He murmured into her hair. "Do not feel bad."

"I—I don't," she lied again. "Please," her voice trembled, while another whimper escaped her throat. "Please go," she managed to say. "I will be fine. Ju-just leave."

He should have gone while he had the chance. He should have just walked away. But he didn't. Instead, he tried to console her, saying, "It was wise of you to go your own way all those years ago, I think. Our worlds are too far apart."

She nodded. Another lie.

"We cannot belong to each other. You know that, do you not?" But his touch on her told her that these, his words, might not be true.

She moaned, and she tried to nod again, but she couldn't even manage that. And she knew that if he wouldn't, she should be the one to leave.

To her credit, she tried to do it; tried to force herself to pull out of his embrace and walk away, but she couldn't find the strength. Not right now. Instead, she did her best to keep her wits about her.

She shook her head, as though that action might give her courage. And when she spoke, her voice was no more than a whisper. "But we already do belong to each other."

She cringed. Had she really said that? What was wrong with her?

He, however, agreed. "*Aa,* yes, you are right," he said. "We do belong to each other, but in spirit only, I think. You must know, however, that I am not talking about that.

I am speaking of the physical act of love. We must not do that, despite—"

"Moon Wolf, please," she protested, finding her voice at last and keeping it steady for all that she trembled. "You must stop this. You talk about the act of love being the worst thing you could do with me and yet you continue to hold me. Please, speak plainly with both your body and your tongue, for you are confusing me."

He groaned. "I know," he said. "I know. I am confusing myself, too. Try to understand that I am attempting to keep your own good in mind . . . despite myself." He said the words clearly, although his hands didn't relent in their touch.

She swallowed before she dared to point out, "Then you must cease what you are doing."

"*Aa,* yes," he agreed, though his actions further rebutted him. "I must stop."

She nodded. "Please."

He did try, albeit, being a bit more successful than she had been earlier. He let her go and stepped back, while she squared her shoulders and lifted her head.

She took a deep breath, saying, "I must see to the wolf," and took a jittery step forward, only to have her knees give out beneath her. She fell forward.

At once, he was there beside her, holding her up, turning her around to face him, his hands rubbing her back to give her comfort. He muttered, "The last thing I want is to see you hurt."

She agreed, nodding, although she could barely think. He had pulled her in close, his lips above her ear, kissing it, kissing her, rubbing his face into her hair, inhaling deeply as though he were memorizing the very scent of her.

He said, "Know that I would only hurt you if I take you as my own."

"Yes."

"I don't want this."

"Neither do I," she said, but she didn't mean it. She wondered if he did.

He pulled up her shirt, his hands coming at once to her breasts, while she melted. He said, "Know that I will not allow you to masquerade as the Wolf Shadow again."

"I know."

"Know that I am not certain where we will live together."

She nodded.

"Know, too, that I will not plant my seed in you even though I take you for my own."

What did that mean? She wasn't certain, but she nodded all the same.

"We will do the honorable thing."

"Yes." The shirt was quickly lost.

"And know that I do not pretend affection for you, have never done so." The words caught in his throat. "Any fondness you have seen from me, have experienced from me, is real . . . very real."

"Moon Wolf."

"Do not say my name like that unless you agree to take me, too. Do you not know what it does to me to hear your voice filled with? . . ."

Take him? As husband? Dare she believe this is what he spoke of? ". . . Moon Wolf."

That was all it took. He swept her off her feet, pressing her into his arms as gently as a man with his strength could, and carried her to his bed of softened blankets and downy pillow, there within the cave.

Laying her down upon it, he began to make a feast of her, his lips showering kisses over her body, suckling her breasts, down further to her belly button, over her stomach, down further and further.

"Moon Wolf! What is it you do to me?"

"I am making love to you as a man should to a woman as virtuous and as good as you, a woman who is to become that man's wife."

"But—"

"Shh. You will enjoy it. And it will make you my wife without . . ." He didn't finish.

His lips had moved downward until they'd found her most secret spot. And though she knew she ought to murmur some word of protest, she remained silent. Soon, where his lips kissed, his tongue followed, and quickly he discovered her most private, ultra moist recess.

She whimpered, never having experienced the exhilarating sensation of such raw sexuality. Heady emotion flooded through her, while blood pumped fast and strong within her, seeming to center itself around her naval, and she could no more have pulled away from Moon Wolf at this moment than she could have grown wings and flown from this cave.

She arched her back, aware of a strange fulfillment washing over her. So, she thought to herself, this was love; this, the ultimate of physical expression between two people.

She wondered briefly if she could create the same sort of desire within him if she were to reciprocate? The thought was wickedly stimulative.

But even that consideration dissipated as the frenzy of first discovery began to overwhelm her. A need had begun to build up, down there where he held her, its demand consuming and overpowering her. She thought she might scream with the passion of it.

She did scream, after all, and as she did so, she felt herself spiraling upward, out of her body, free and disentangled from all things physical, at least for a moment.

No wonder, she concluded, two people made a habit of

loving one another if this were the result. No doubt this explained why songs and tributes, down through the ages, had been written toward the object of one's affection.

One's lover; one's husband.

She smiled leisurely at the thought, at last content. And on this most wonderful insight into humanity, she drifted lightly back to earth.

Chapter 9

He welcomed the cold spray of the water upon his heated flesh. He had fled, practically flown, the distance up to this waterfall. And it hadn't mattered what his sweet Alys had thought of his actions.

He had to think, and think clearly, without the sweetened fragrance of her to disturb him. For he had now committed more problems than he could easily solve; big problems.

What had he done? He had gone and married her, that's what he'd done; going so far as to make love to her, although he had yet to feel the release of his own passion from that union. He threw himself farther into the icy water.

He, who had no need for a wife. He, who knew not from one day to the next if he would live. He, who had no right to marry at all, now had.

He stood silently beneath the falls. And, as he had predicted, as his ardor began to cool, so, too, did his reasoning return.

He had been consumed by passion, by love, too. These were his excuses. But now?

Had she understood that they were married? She had mentioned something of a . . . certificate, whatever that was, which was needed in the white man's world. Was it possible that she could not be married without one?

He would have to ask her, not that it would make any difference to him. He had committed himself to her. He would not back out of it now.

It was not as if he would never have desired to marry her. If his circumstances were different, if he had certainty of his future, he would have been greatly pleased to have her, particularly if he were white, or, failing that, if she were of his tribe.

But it was not the way of things. She was what she was. While he was the Wolf Shadow . . . his life was not his own. It might never be. He had committed himself to this purpose years ago . . .

It had happened in Moon Wolf's eighteenth year, in the season when the leaves change color. Many of the warriors, seeing what was happening to the people, had begun attacking the bull trains that traveled over the whiskey trail. Charging down upon the trains, destroying their kegs of liquor, and taking any other goods carried on those schooners, the warriors had kept the intoxicating brew from causing too much harm.

But then the bullies had come, guarding the whiskey trains, disregarding the rights of the Blackfeet and killing any Indian on sight, be they man, woman or child. Too many lives had been lost, and the warriors had been given no choice but to stop the assaults or to attack only those few trains that were either very small or not so heavily guarded.

As a result, whiskey had begun to flow too freely; too

many men were getting drunk, having too many arguments, the end always being the same: innocent people were killed. That winter so many lives were lost that even the old men could not remember a time when the grieving wails of the women had been heard so long or so incessantly.

And so it was that in this time period, it happened. A Black Robe staying with the people had asked Moon Wolf and two friends to deliver to Fort Benton a message requesting food and blankets.

He and his friends had been joyous.

"I bet I can drink more whiskey than you," Lone Owl, brother of Moon Wolf's more-than-friend, bragged.

"No, it is I who will show both my friends how to drink and how to have many great visions," Charging Boy responded.

Moon Wolf grinned, but remained silent. After witnessing so many deaths from the white man's firewater, he had no wish to imbibe.

They entered the fort easily enough, their weapons confiscated as was usual whenever an Indian penetrated the inner sanctum of the white man's shelter; there was no need to be alarmed.

They tread through the fort much as they had on other occasions.

"We should go first to the general store and deliver this message for the Black Robe," Charging Boy said. "Then when we have the white man's money in our hand from completing this task, we will go to the traders and ask for the white man's drink. What say you?"

Lone Owl agreed, while Moon Wolf again remained silent, voicing no argument.

Suddenly Moon Wolf heard an explosion, only to witness Charging Boy fall to the ground, a bullet through the head.

Another explosion quickly followed, as Moon Wolf

grabbed Lone Owl and pulled him into the shelter of a building.

There they huddled together, Moon Wolf recognizing the terror in his friend's eyes.

"We must find a place to hide," Moon Wolf said. "I know of such a place. After the next shot is fired, follow me."

Lone Owl signed agreement, and they waited. Yet no more shots came.

"Perhaps the white men have grown tired of watching for us," Lone Owl said. "Let us sneak from here and escape to your place now."

"No. It is not safe yet. They are expecting us to do exactly that. They cannot see us here; they would have been firing on us, if they could. We will wait."

Crouched in the shadows, filled with panic, suddenly they heard footsteps off to their left, then to their right.

Moon Wolf shot his friend a look of concern, signing that they were going to have to run. He pointed in a general direction and signed again for his friend to stay close to him. On signal, they burst from their hiding place, sprinting across the open streets as fast as they could.

Explosions sounded everywhere. Moon Wolf ran and ran, without stopping.

Up ahead loomed a row of bushes. He sprinted for them and dove into them head first, expecting to hear his friend do the same.

It never happened. Looking back, Moon Wolf spied Lone Owl sitting in the dirt several yards away, clutching his leg. On the verge of running back to rescue his friend, Moon Wolf froze when several white men ran over to the boy and shot him five times through the head. The other white men whooped and hollered and laughed.

Moon Wolf would never forget it, nor would he ever forgive.

He had escaped, hiding out until dark and then fleeing through the tunnels.

He had returned to his people and, his heart heavy, had demanded revenge. But the chiefs would not let him, nor would they allow Moon Wolf's more-than-friend, Never Laughs, to honor his brother's death through retaliation. The chiefs had given their word to their Indian agent to seek justice only in the white man's way, and no amount of talking would convince these wise old men that their sense of honor, their oaths of allegiance, fell on deaf ears.

Yet treachery, once practiced, does not breed honesty. And so the chiefs had gone to the white man's forts, had demanded the white man's justice. All to no effect.

No white man was ever arrested or punished. It was then that Moon Wolf realized that the white man had only one code of justice, and it did not encompass Indian rights or freedom.

Knowing this, Moon Wolf decided that he would have his revenge. Along with Never Laughs, he devised a plan, the two of them never once telling another soul what it entailed.

"There are caves beneath the fort where I can hide,"
Moon Wolf suggested to Never Laughs as the two friends
sat around a solitary campfire, talking and scheming into
the early hours of the morning.

"Caves?"

"Aa, yes, I discovered them long ago during the time
when the white man demanded our children go to the
fort."

"And they lead outside the fort?"

"Aa, yes," Moon Wolf responded, "into the hills. I could
use these caverns as a way to play hit and run with the
seizers. I could hide in them where I cannot be discov-
ered."

"I think you dream, my friend," countered Never Laughs. *"Perhaps the seizers are not so keen as to be able to track you, but have you noticed that these blue coats lure our own, one by one, into being slaves for them? They ask our own people to scout for them, and all for this thing they call money. Saa, no, I think it would not work. Not when there are Indian scouts who are the slaves of these soldiers."*

Moon Wolf thought for a moment, his eyes suddenly bright. *"Unless,"* he suggested, *"you were there—as chief of the Indian scouts. You, who are the best tracker in our camp."*

Never Laughs looked doubtful at first.

"It would be a good thing," Moon Wolf went on to explain. *"If you are there to cover my tracks, I would be able to annoy the white man where it hurts him most. Together we can destroy this liquor trade while helping our people at the same time."*

"Humph!" came the reply.

"But first you must become chief of scouts," continued Moon Wolf, *"you must become the one among them who is 'trusted.' Do you think you can do this?"*

Never Laughs had grinned at this and had applied as scout to the military within a fortnight.

A few days later, Moon Wolf had discovered *Makoyi.* And the rest had become history . . .

Cold water splashing in his face reminded him of where he was and, plunging his head under the falling water, Moon Wolf came back to the present. It had all been so long ago, yet those events had shaped his future.

He thought back to Alys's accusation that he was prejudiced. Perhaps he was, but with good reason.

When he had told her that she should marry someone

from her own race, he had been quite serious. She would fare better that way, as would her children. Did that mean he was prejudiced?

Maybe.

Why, he wondered, was she not? It was something that he would have to ask her.

Considering who he was, considering who she was and her own way of life, he knew it was irresponsible of him to have gone as far as to kiss her. He should never have started down that path. Nor should he have teased her so readily in the beginning.

He bemoaned such thoughts, however, and reminded himself that such lines of contemplation were useless. As the wise men often counselled, what was done was done. It could not be changed. But the present, the future . . . ah, now that was something that one could determine.

The future. He came back full circle. What was he to do about her, about their marriage?

It was not as if he could avoid her. He had pledged himself to her. Besides, even without that commitment, he had to remind himself that he owed her a great deal. She had nursed him to health, was probably even now tending to *Makoyi*.

Perhaps it would not be so bad. He had offered for her already, once in the past, and it hadn't mattered to him then that she was white. That she had denied him had been a wise decision on her part—at least so he had thought.

He wondered where they would live if he were to survive his mission. Certainly not at Fort Benton. Not with the memories that place held for him.

Would the reservation be any better? Without doubt his almost mother and sister would rejoice to have her. But would Alys thrive there? She, with her white man's need for fancy clothes and elegant ways; a woman who had never known adversity or hunger? She wouldn't survive the first small adversity, he feared.

And, as he had pointed out to her earlier, so too did he lecture himself: what if he succeeded in getting her with child, only to die soon after? It was a thought he could not ignore. Where would she go? There would be no society that would welcome her. And it would not matter that he had married her.

He had to do something, think of something. But what?

He had told her the truth, as much as he was able, and as he understood it. It was a fact that he did not think he would be a good husband because of all these things; it was also true that he adored her, relished her, despite the color of her skin.

What he hadn't finished saying was that since she had returned, he no longer looked upon his own death as the ultimate sacrifice for Lone Owl, for Charging Boy, and for his people. Since she had come into his life, breathing the power of her spirit within him, he had begun to think more seriously of continuing to live, perhaps of happiness.

But this, too, was a path he could not travel, at least not right away. He *was* the Wolf Shadow. So much depended on him. Fathers, mothers, even the elders of the tribe relied on him to bring about a condition where their children could have a chance to grow up, free men and free women.

However, he digressed.

Of one thing he was certain. He could not get Alys pregnant. With his life hanging so delicately, with so much uncertainty for the future, this was not an act he could sanction.

Yet how could he avoid it?

He could leave here, put the caves behind him, that way carefully avoiding her and the enticement she offered. But even as he thought it, he knew he couldn't do it.

He sighed. He had no ready solution, except this one: he could not plant his seed within her, even if he made love to her over and over again. How he would keep himself from doing this, he was uncertain. But he would do it, somehow.

Fantastic as it was, the thought caused him to feel better, realizing that in this, he had a solution, if a dubious one. If he could do it . . .

Her freedom would be his gift to her. Then if he died, she would be unfettered by her past, able to marry another, and to live the life that perhaps she was meant to live—with one of her own kind, a white man.

That this thought made his insides churn, that it set a rage to burning within him, he ignored. He would withhold that anger. After all, he could think of no other solution.

But the image of a white man with his beautiful Alys would not easily go away, and he cringed. Was that really the best solution?

Perhaps she was right, he considered; perhaps he was, after all, prejudiced.

Was that what the long years of doing battle with the whites had gained him? Only loathing and hatred?

Yet, was there any other way to deal with these strange beings, these pale faces? If there was an alternative, he had yet to discover it.

But again, he digressed.

He turned around and faced back into the caves, tossing his head as droplets of water sprayed over him, pushing his hair away from his face. It was a good time to make resolutions, a good time for decisions.

He took a deep breath. *Aa*, yes, he had married her. He would be her husband in every way save one: he would hold himself from her and give her no children. If he had to, he would keep her attention diverted away from marriage and the marriage bed. For his own peace of mind, he must do this.

With this conclusion firmly planted in his mind and with a plan of action clearly decided, he stepped out, away from the water, and drew on his clothes.

Chapter 10

───◦◦◦◦───

She had welcomed him back with a smile, which was perhaps why his question took her so much by surprise.

She had found him watching her, arms crossed over his chest, a brooding expression on his face. How long he had stood there before her, staring at her, with his look so melancholy, she did not know.

He asked her again, "Why are you not prejudiced?"

It was an odd question considering their most recently shared intimacy. How could he think of prejudices at a time like this? His voice had been deep, though, as he had spoken to her, slightly husky, too, still mirroring a passion that she had little idea how to fulfill.

She grimaced at the thought of his fulfillment. Now, there was a topic she would like to discuss, since she was more than aware that he had not met with satisfaction.

She chanced a glance at him as he squatted down in front of her. Nervous and self-conscious, she hesitated to say anything to him, and she quickly looked away, back toward the wolf.

Having just finished applying an herbal compound to the animal's wound, she was glad to see that the wolf at last was drifting off to sleep. She sat back, letting herself examine her handiwork as though she were witnessing not a bandage but a work of art, so closely did she inspect it.

However, she could not long deny the inevitable, and after several more lapses into silence, she found the courage to answer, picking her words well. "I don't know exactly why I'm not prejudiced, perhaps because of my mother. But," she lifted her eyes, stealing a surreptitious look at him, "don't you think there is something else more pressing that we should discuss?"

His features became completely unreadable as he lapsed into silence.

She should say something else about it—quickly, before she lost courage—but how did one talk about these things? She sighed. He could give her a little more encouragement.

He didn't, however. He sat before her, unspeaking, waiting patiently.

She peeked at him once more before venturing, "Moon Wolf, I would ask you something."

"Humph." He didn't budge an inch, saying only, "I am listening."

Taking in a quick gulp of air in the hopes that it would give her courage, she asked, "That isn't all there is to love-making, is it?"

He drew back as though surprised. "Are you not satisfied?"

"Oh, yes, yes, I am," she reassured him. "It's not that. It's only that I'm wondering . . ." Again, she swept up her eyelashes. ". . . are you?"

"Am I what?"

"Are you . . . satisfied?"

"Do you mean, am I happy to have you as my wife? I am."

She sent him another curious look, not convinced.

"There are many things we will have to discuss," he was saying, "many parts of our lives that we will have to reconsider, now that we are committed to one another. We have much time to do this, however."

She nodded. "Earlier today, before we ah . . ." She cleared her throat. "Earlier today, you said something about . . . marriage?"

"*Aa*, yes, it is this that is on your mind. It is true that I have taken you for my wife. Did you think I would bed you without that?"

"I . . . I wasn't . . . no, of course not."

"Why do you ask? In my village a man marries a woman in one way alone, with intimacy. Is this not how it is done in your culture?"

She shook her head. "No."

"Do you need this cer-ti-fi-cate that you have spoken of?"

She nodded. "That and a preacher to seal the pact."

"*Aa*, yes. Then it is probably true that we are married by my customs, but perhaps not by yours."

"Yes."

He contemplated this in silence. "Would the white man marry us within his own practice?"

She regarded him through lowered lashes. Did she dare tell him the truth? Of course she had little choice. "I do not think we could find such a man here in the west," she said.

He nodded. "It is as I would have thought."

She waited a few moments, then continued, "Moon Wolf, I . . ." She felt the beginnings of a flush on her face. Thank goodness for the cave's poor lighting. "I . . . ," she began again. "There is something else that I would discuss with you."

He raised an eyebrow. "Besides our commitment to one another?"

"Yes, I . . . what I mean to say is, what I need to know is . . . about the act . . . of love." There, she'd said it.

And he looked stunned.

But at least she had his attention. "I was thinking that . . ."—she flashed him a quick smile—"well, I've been wondering, not about our marriage, but while you were taking your shower . . . I was musing over it and it seems to me that you should have also been . . . satisfied, shouldn't you?"

He sat back, clearly stumped, though any initial surprise she glimpsed in his expression was quickly masked. His next words were spoken with care. "I know of few people, even when married, who discuss these things." He raised his chin. "However, you are wise to ask me. For I will tell you now that I *was* gratified . . . greatly."

She breathed out a sigh of relief. "Were you?"

"*Aa soka'pii,* yes, good," he said, his right hand signaling out in sign language the words that he spoke.

"But I thought that when two people made love, the man also reaches a certain . . . ah, release . . . and you did not do that . . . and . . . you were really pleasured?"

"*Aa,* yes, it is so." He held his head so high and sat so erect that she was reminded of this man's tremendous pride as he continued, "Though you are correct in observing that I did not reach complete . . . satisfaction."

"Oh," she raised her eyes to his, "that was what I meant."

"Humph!" He nodded quickly.

"Then . . ." She spoke with immense reluctance, not knowing exactly how to phrase these next words. But she would not stop now. After taking a deep breath, she asked,

"Then shouldn't you and I . . . shouldn't we . . . ah . . . continue?"

"It is not necessary." A long pause followed his words before he suddenly gave her a sharp glance. "This concerns you?"

She nodded. "Yes."

He acknowledged her with another nod, a stoic calm settling across his features. He said, "Do not worry. My passion is relieved for now."

"Is it? How?"

He smiled without humor. "A bath under a cold waterfall is a good thing sometimes."

"Oh." She digested this in absolute wonder. "And so you . . . ah . . . are no longer in need of . . ."

He nodded. "For now."

She fell silent, wondering how she was ever going to broach this next subject.

"But we leave the point," he noted, "which is my first question to you. I will ask it again, why are you not prejudiced?"

She thought for a moment, then countered, "Why *are* you?"

He drew back, the light from the lantern next to him casting shadows upon his face, illuminating only one side. It reminded her of a half moon, and it gave him an odd, phantomlike appearance.

He had crouched down to squat in front of her. Now, he shifted his position and came to sit in front of her crosslegged, there on their blanketed carpet in the cave.

He lifted his eyes to hers and sat slightly forward, over Wolf, as he asked of her, "Is it your wish that I answer your question before you take up mine?"

She nodded.

"Very well," he agreed and leaned back, only to lapse into silence, his attention obviously inward.

She waited, noticing little things about him . . . his hair, free of braids, hanging loose and wet over his shoulders; his eyes, dark and unfathomable, staring off into nothing, his look somber. He seemed slightly heavier now than when they had made love, though it appeared to be more a graveness of spirit, not of actual weight. Was something troubling him?

There was an intoxicating scent about him, too, a fragrance that was part mint, part sage, and part prairie grass, as well as all rugged male. Mixed with the earthy scents of the cave and the wolf, the aroma held her captivated.

There was no mistaking the enticing, sexual quality of this man, either. But there was something about him, a unique characteristic that was hard to pinpoint but that had always drawn her to him.

It was not simply that he was handsome; he was, without being greatly aware of it. But that was not what drew her to him. There was something else about him . . . a beauty . . . an ethereal trait that she would have been hard pressed to express in words. It was as though he thrived, not only in this, our physical universe, but in some other world as well: perhaps a universe of beauty.

She gazed down to watch his hands as they petted the wolf. The dusky color of those hands, though only a few shades darker than her own, seemed a pretty contrast against the more whitened color of his nails. His fingers were long, graceful, and watching their movement, she could not help but remember how those hands had felt against her skin.

No body hair marred his figure, either, she was quick to observe; not on his fingers, nor on his arms or chest. Even his chin remained smooth, despite the lack of a razor. She noted again the chain about his neck, the same one she had returned to him, but she hadn't the courage to ask about it, wondering why he simply did not return it to her.

He took his time responding to her question before finally replying, "You must allow me some moments in which to think before I answer you. You have brought up something that I must give careful consideration. I am not certain why I am prejudiced, if I am. Perhaps you could answer my question first."

She gulped. "Very well."

He asked again, "I have observed that you appear to have no prejudice. You and your mother are the only white people I know who are not. Why?"

She didn't know how to respond to such a question without sounding either righteous or indignant. But, after some thought, she replied, "I only know that being prejudiced makes little sense. Perhaps, too, I am not trying to take something away from the Indians." Her own fingers came up to stroke the wolf.

"Take something away? You mean the land?"

She agreed. "That, and the furs, the horses, even your art."

"Art?"

"Your robes and blankets, things your women make. They sell quite well in the east."

"Humph. I did not know that. And what, do you think, should the Indian do about this?"

She shrugged. "I don't know. I truly don't. Perhaps what you are already doing?"

"Humph!" Moon Wolf had bent down over his pet as though he listened for its heartbeat, and Alys was struck at once by the look of her husband's pitch black locks, coarse and wet, against the gray-brown fur of the wolf. She reached out to touch a droplet of water where it fell from a single tress of his hair, the feel of the liquid cold and invigorating against her hand.

He raised his head in reaction to her, his eyes staring

straight into hers, his look for a moment full of carnal interest. He quickly turned his gaze away.

She tilted her head and studied him. He had to be the most handsome man of her acquaintance. Her gaze roamed over him lazily, as though she might have several years in which to examine him.

She smiled then, leisurely, before saying, "Maybe I also feel no prejudice because my mother raised me differently than other children. From the beginning of my life, I remember the scorn my mother showed to the townspeople who lived here at Fort Benton, the care she displayed to the Indian maids who served her and others. She, more than anyone I know, hated prejudice."

"Your mother is a good woman. Almost as good as her daughter."

"Hmmm." She raised her eyes to his, only to find him watching her. She ventured, "And now it's your turn to answer the same question."

He caught her eye. "*Oki,* come," he commanded, then motioned toward her with his right hand as he stood up, his movement so graceful she knew she would never be able to duplicate it. "Let us leave Wolf," he explained, "and allow him to sleep without us talking over him."

"Yes," she agreed and stood up, following Moon Wolf.

He led her to his own blanket, where he at once sat down, cross-legged, pulling back the blanket and lifting out an object that looked to be very much like a pipe.

With a beauty of grace and some ceremony, he stuffed tobacco into its pot, held it up, and lit it, slowly brushing the smoke in toward his head. Then he offered it to her.

She almost choked. "You want me to smoke?"

He nodded.

"Even though I am only a woman."

He gave her a puzzling glance. "Only? Why do you say that?"

"I don't really have a reason. It's just that I thought that your women do not sit in council, nor do they smoke, and so—"

He paused significantly, letting her words trail away before he began, "Let me tell you a story that my grandfather once told me, so that you will understand the Indian a little better.

"Once, a long time ago," he continued, not waiting for her reply, "Old Man, or *Napi,* ruled the world. But it was a very boring world. Men stayed with men; women with women. Men went to war with each other, but they had no clothes and no lodges in which to rest. They ate raw meat and had no comforts.

"Now, the women had many beautiful things and great lodges, but no one to provide for them or to give them protection.

"And so it happened that *Napi,* seeing this, bargained with the women, taking the wisest and most intelligent woman as his own. All the other men did the same and soon, all was in great harmony.

"It was only when this happened that our men began to develop compassion and valor. But a man only kept his heart so long as he had nurtured and stayed with his woman. My people have a saying, *mat'-ah-kwi tam-ap-i-ni-po-ke-mi-o-sin,* 'Not found is happiness without woman.'

"It has been the way of the people since that time to honor our women and to uphold and protect their place in our society. And as you know, we have flourished, at least until recently."

Alys sat for a moment in silence before whispering, "That's a beautiful story."

"*Aa,* yes, so it is. So now you know that it is the woman who nurtures the zest and the very life of our people. While a man may fight and die, so long as our women are strong, so long as they live and are allowed to create the art and beauty that is naturally theirs, our people will grow and thrive. For theirs is the life-blood of our people, our very heart." He finished in silence.

A long moment followed. "That is a very beautiful way of putting it." She smiled at him. "Thank you."

He nodded, then held the pipe out to her again. This time she took it, bringing it to her lips. Hesitatingly, she drew in the smoke and sent him a speculative gaze, seemingly all right for a moment. But her composure couldn't last. All at once, a look of pure revulsion crossed her face, then a fit of coughing.

He merely observed her calmly, commenting, "You have not smoked before."

She shook her head, one hand going to her throat, the other offering the pipe back to him.

He nodded and, taking the object into his hands, balanced the stem of it over his legs. He said, "Know that the smoke from the pipe is sacred. It calls upon the ancient ones above us to take part in our council. Know that whatever we say here must be the truth. Do you agree?"

She nodded acceptance.

He didn't speak at once, but having started, he spoke slowly and deliberately. "It is hard for me to think well of the white man and so, as you have pointed out, maybe that makes me prejudiced. I see that he takes our land by treachery, I see that he sells my people into slavery for the mere price of a drink, and I see that he degrades our women in ways foreign to an Indian mind. You ask me if I am prejudiced. I will tell you true that I have not seen much about him that is good." He looked at her, passing the pipe back to her.

She accepted the sacred item into her hands, carefully avoiding inhaling any more smoke. Observing him, she held it in the same manner as he, and only then did she begin. "I understand what you say. But there are other people, other whites, that are not like these people here in the fort. Besides, I am white. If you would hate all whites, would that not extend to me, too?"

She gave him back the pipe.

His look swept over her slim body before he responded, "You are white in flesh alone. Your heart is Indian."

She sighed. "Take a good look, Moon Wolf. I am not Indian."

He gave her a stern look before at last capitulating, saying, "It is true."

"There are many white people who would be ashamed if they knew what is happening here to the Indians," she continued. "I am not alone in my way of thinking. But most of these people live far from here, to the east. They are not people you are likely to encounter in the west." She glanced over to him.

"Why do they not come here and stop their own brothers, then, these other white men, if these people truly do not approve?"

She shrugged. "Most cannot make the journey here. They have their own work, their own families to attend to. It is not an inexpensive thing to do—to make this trip. Besides, just as the red man wars with his own kind, so, too, does the white man argue with his brothers."

He nodded.

"Most people have to trust our government to do the right thing."

"Humph!" he sneered. "The white man's government. Is this the same power that tries to put the Indian on reservations, that takes away his freedom, that sells him cheap whiskey and spoiled food?"

She caught her breath, the hatred in his words so distinct. Of course, it was easy to empathize with his concern, and he did have justification for the way he felt. Still . . .

"I understand, Moon Wolf," she said sincerely, "but tell me true. Are all Indians honest and just? Can you tell me that there is no Indian any place that has never committed a wrong to you or to your family?"

He remained silent.

"Do not do it, Moon Wolf. Do not, yourself, become as prejudiced and as hateful as some of the white men here in this fort. Because if you do," she proffered, her voice soft, "you will have learned too well the wrong lesson. You will have begun to hate. And when that happens, well, they couldn't have done a better job on you than if they'd painted you white and plucked the feathers from your head, because you will have become just like them."

He signed acquiescence. "What you say is good, but it is innocent, too; you have been gone from here for a long time. Hear me, my wife, no amount of talk will bring back the dead, nor put an end to the injustices being done to my people. I cannot abide by it. And I will never stop my resistance until these wrongs no longer fill our land."

She tilted her head toward him and frowned. "But do you need to hate all white men in order to have your triumph?"

"You do not know all of the injustices done to my people."

"No, I don't."

"Humph. If you did know of these things, you might not ask me these questions."

She sighed. "You are right. But you must also know I speak the truth, too. Once you begin to hate, you have become just like the white man. Is that what you want?"

"Humph," was again his reply. He folded his arms over his chest. "I will think on it. That is what I will do. I will think. And now, I have spoken . . ."

Chapter 11

～～⌒◯◯⌒～～

Sitting up a little straighter, Moon Wolf took hold of his pipe and flicked the ashes onto the floor, signalling with his hands for her to take note of what he did. "Do you see what I do here?"

"Yes."

"This is how a council should end. When the ashes are discarded, the evening is finished and one's friends go home. And so it is with ours, too. Our talk is finished."

"Good," she said, "except that . . ." She stopped and cast a look around the caves, at their familiarity, hoping these walls might give her courage.

He gave her a level look.

"There is one other thing that I would ask you."

He nodded, but otherwise remained silent.

She cleared her throat and sent up a silent prayer before she began, "I would know . . ." Her voice cracked. "I would have you teach me, please . . . the . . . ah . . ." She stared down at the floor, up, then glanced all around. "The best ways to . . . to . . ."

He examined her curiously, patiently waiting.

"To please a man," she finished in one quick sentence, casting her eyes down at the same time. She held her breath, more than a little mortified at herself. But she had to know.

He, on the other hand, became even more serious, a shrouded mask stealing down over his features, effectively concealing his thoughts. He frowned at her as he asked, "You do not know how to do this already?"

She shook her head.

He sighed, deeply; very, very deeply. At length, he asked, "Do not the women in your culture prepare you for these things?"

"No, it is not something one discusses at all, except with one's . . . husband."

"Humph! Then it is good that you have asked me."

She waited.

"But I will not, I cannot speak of it."

"Why not?"

He paused, his silence meant to be her answer. At length, however, he said, "You are making this very difficult for me."

"Making what difficult for you?"

He groaned, his eyes begging her for understanding. "You ask me to do something that I cannot do," he said. "You ask me to discuss something that will only end in one way. I do not want to hurt you."

"But it seems to me that if you don't do this, then you will be hurting me."

"*Haiya!*" He groaned. "No harm will come to you at all. Why are you so persistent about this?"

"Because . . ." Why was she? She sat back, momentarily baffled. "Because," she began again, "I fear that if I don't, *I* will hurt you."

He raised his chin, the look in his eyes showing her that

he clearly disagreed with her. He said, "I assure you that no harm will come to me."

"And I am afraid," she went on as though he hadn't spoken, "that if I let this pass, a barrier will be erected between us that will be harder and harder to break down. So I am asking this of you. Please, Moon Wolf, you are my husband. Teach me."

He groaned, a very masculine, seductive sound. She could even feel the heat of his gaze as he glanced at her. He commented, "You must not speak to me in this way. Do you have any idea the kind of effect this has on me? Do you tease me?"

If only she were. She didn't answer, just stared at him, her own eyes drinking in the sensuality of him.

He shifted. "We should not again indulge ourselves in the weaknesses of the flesh." But even as he spoke, she could feel him relenting.

He shifted his weight until, looking decidedly uncomfortable, he stared off, away from her.

"Moon Wolf," she touched his arm, "I need to know how to please you. I fear that I did not do that very well during our first time together."

He brought his gaze back to her, the tortured look in his stare so intent that she thought she might burn up under the heat of it. Up and down her face his eyes wandered, down further still, to her bosom, until all at once, he uttered, the words sounding as though they were torn from his throat, "You say these things to me and I fear you would test the last of my reserve. I should keep my distance from you, should set you free. Yet, even as I know this, even as I think it and say it, look at me and what I do. I am as unable to keep from touching you as I am to keep myself from breathing."

As though to prove it, he drew her to him, his touch firm and insistent as he pulled her over his lap and into his embrace. "You must tell me to stop," he muttered, but his lips came down on hers in a kiss that shook her to the tips of her toes. "Tell me now," he pleaded again, but she could not have spoken at this moment had she wished to do so. And she did not so desire.

Her stomach dropped, twisted, and she buried her face in his neck, content for the moment. For she sensed, no matter his obvious frustration with himself, he complimented her, and she responded with every bit of femininity she had. In truth, she arched herself further into his embrace.

"*Aa,* you are innocent, much too innocent. And I should let you go free."

"Yet we are married," she commented. "You have every right to—"

"Sh-h-h. Do not tell me these things."

"But if we are married . . ."

A deep groan escaped him, the sound pure seduction. "The fault is mine."

"What fault?"

He straightened his spine, jerking his head to the left before he answered, "Just because we are married does not mean our problems no longer exist. All that I have told you is still true. We might be married, might love one another more than any other two people alive, but the dilemma of where we will live, where we will raise our children—if I live—still remain."

"But—"

"Yet, even as I know this," he continued, "I cannot stop touching you." He shoved up her top as he spoke, his fingers spreading over her breasts.

"Moon Wolf, you must know that I want this as much as you."

He nodded. "*Aa,* I know. And that knowledge is my enemy, I think. I am the one who is supposed to be composed, the one able to think no matter the strength of our passion. Yet, do you know how easy it would be for me to . . ."

A soft whimper left her lips, followed by a hoarse growl from him. She uttered, "Please."

Perhaps it was her voice that proved to be his undoing, maybe her plea; suddenly he tumbled her back onto his blanketed bed, pulling her shirt off with ease, up and over her head. She reached out toward him, tugging on his pants.

But his stomach muscles contracted to hold her hands in place. His pants remained where they were, at least for the moment.

She whimpered, "Don't you want me to love you?"

He made a sound that was half desire, half frustration. "You must know that I have wanted to make love to you since the first moment I saw you again."

"From the very first moment?"

"*Aa,* from then."

"Then I don't understand."

He threw back his head and gave her a look, his eyes piercing hers with a hunger that shattered her self-control. Surely, he must want her as she wanted him. Surely.

He said, "I cannot have you. Please try to understand, if I touch you in the way of passion, I would ruin you for any other man."

That statement gave her pause. "What did you say?"

He drew a deep breath. "You came here into my life, knowing that my life could end at any time."

"As could anyone's."

"But look at the difference. Look at what I have chosen to do with my life. Since it could end in an instant, I would ensure that you would be cared for when I am gone."

"But, Moon Wolf, you are not gone."

"That does not matter. My life could end tomorrow."

"Mine could, too. I don't think you are being sensible about this thing. Another man is not the answer."

"It is the only way . . . if I am gone. Surely you can understand this."

She turned around until she faced him, coming up at the same time onto her knees, unembarrassed by the fullness of her breasts, extended out toward him, within his reach. She said, "No, I don't understand. I don't want anyone else. And I might never want anyone else."

"But I must secure your future."

"Fine." She inched forward until her breasts were a mere hairsbreadth away from him. She could almost feel the nervousness within him. She commented, "I think you are thinking so much in the future, that you forget that there is a great deal of pleasure in the present."

"I do not forget," he said, even while he began a light massage upon her, the action sending tiny flickers of sensation coursing though her. She curled herself into his arms.

He moaned, "I do not need this right now."

"Yet we are joined as husband and wife."

He groaned and threw back his head. "All right," he said, "I will make love to you. Still, you must understand that I will not make love to you in a way that could get you with child."

"Fine," she responded, arching her back into him invitingly. She asked, "Even if I desire it?"

"Even then. You are still innocent, you are not looking at the far-reaching consequences of this, I think."

She decided not to reason with him; he appeared to be beyond all that. Instead, glancing up at him, she pleaded, "Please, this is something that a husband and wife should experience together."

But he ignored her as though she hadn't spoken, going on to say, "You deserve a man who will love you all your life, one who will treasure you and take care of you and be there for you every morning and every evening that you should live. This is what you should have. Not one who can promise you no tomorrow."

With her back still arched so enticingly, she placed her hands on his stomach, letting them slide down to his trousers. "Who said I want all those promises? And who are you to protect me?"

"I should be like a brother to you more than a husband," he responded. "In that way I can look out for you and take care of you."

She backed up slightly. "A brother? Moon Wolf, are you trying to tell me that you care for me only in the way of . . . a sister?"

He winced. "Perhaps a brother was not the right comparison. Maybe I should have said—"

She didn't wait for him to finish. "If that is true, then did you only marry me because of your sense of responsibility for me?"

"*Saa*, no. We have been through this before. I only said brother because it is how I *should* feel, not how I *do* feel."

However, Alys could not be so easily comforted. "But you said—"

"Enough!" A growl sounded deep in his throat, and though he might have been hesitant at first, he did not fail to pull her in close to him. That he also rose up onto his knees before her, letting her feel the entire length of his masculinity, gave her some comfort.

Still . . .

She sighed while he began to shower her with kiss after kiss, one hand rubbing over the rosy tips of her breasts, the other pulling her in toward him. He kissed her lips, her eyes, her throat, whispering, when he could at last come up for breath, "Does this look to you to be the offerings of a man who feels the same kind of affection that he might for a sister?"

"But Moon Wolf, I would know if you—"

"Sh-h-h." He drew her even closer, if that was possible, knee to knee, chest to chest, the exotic feel of his desire engraved upon her. Again, she tugged on his trousers. But he didn't pay her any attention. Leaving off, he pressed his face into her hair, inhaling deeply. "Know that I care for you," he murmured, "have always done so from the first moment that you saved me and my sister. It was a bad likeness, that is all. I do not think of you as a sister. I never have. That was my point. Now, no more of this talk." His lips sought out hers again, raining kiss after kiss upon her—her cheeks, her neck, her breasts.

And she moaned, caught up in the marvel of him. She was his, he was hers, and it didn't matter if she had a marriage certificate to prove it.

Reaching out, she tugged on those trousers, unbuttoning them at last, managing to pull them down until the full length of him fell against her. Her knees went weak without her being consciously aware of it. He held on to her.

She whispered, "You are big, my husband. But you will show me how this is done?"

He sighed against her mouth. "I will teach you, some-day."

"And will you fit, I wonder?"

"Your body has been made for this. But enough of this. I will not plant my—"

"Oh, Moon Wolf," she cried, unwilling to let him finish, "teach me well." And as the incredible intoxication of him engulfed her, she came to a realization: she would hold on to this man, no matter what the future held.

It didn't matter what he said; it didn't matter that he tried so gallantly to save her from himself. His actions alone spoke more readily than any words could have. He wanted her, too.

What she was doing was good, she thought. So very, very good. And as she surrendered herself to him, letting the warmth of their mutual fervor wash over her, she vowed that she would make this man change his mind.

Alys was no fool. She knew the treasure that she held.

He might try to walk away from her after this—for her own good, as he put it—but she would never let him go. Not ever. He had said he was committed to her.

She aimed to keep it that way.

Chapter 12

❦❦❦❦❦

"You say that he married you?"

Alys nodded as she stood at the foot of her mother's bed.

"He's always been such a kind man. I liked him from the first moment I met him."

"Then you're not upset that I . . . that he and I . . ."

"Land sakes, child, why would I be upset? You should know me better'n that."

Alys rushed forward to hug her mother. "Of course I do, it's only that I couldn't be certain that you would be happy about a marriage between us."

"Better him than that horrible Lieutenant Warrington who keeps coming around here."

"Yes, Mama, I agree. So very much better. Mama, how did you ever meet Moon Wolf? Neither of you have told me."

Ma Clayton leaned back against her pillows, the look in her eyes dreamy as she said, "One day while I was working in the caves, I heard a strange sound down in one of the tunnels. I followed it, which led me to him. Almost blew his head clean off, that day. But something stopped me. And that wolf of his bared his teeth at me, snarling so much, I was afraid I was going to have to shoot him, too. Talked me into putting down my gun, even with that wolf staring at me. That's when I knew I liked him.

"Explained to me right off who he was and what he was using the caves for. Told him I'd help him as best I could. And so I did for a while, but then I took ill and he's been on his own this past year."

"Mama, I didn't know that you'd been helping Moon Wolf. What else don't I know about you?"

"There's probably quite a bit, child, probably quite a bit, indeed."

"So tell me more, how did you help him?"

Ma Clayton gazed upward. "Them were exciting times, Alys," she said. "Right exciting times. I'd listen for news of those bull trains, I'd try to find out what supplies they had on them, when they were planning to leave."

"Well, that explains why one time he asked me to glean some information for him."

"That's right. Of course I did all this before he perfected his disguise. Now, he can go almost anywhere in the fort with complete impunity. But it wasn't always like that."

"You must miss the excitement."

Her mother grinned. "Why, I believe I do. But you didn't come here to discuss the first time I met Moon Wolf. I think we had better talk about your problems. Let me understand you completely. Are you telling me that the marriage has not been consummated?"

"I don't think so." Alys looked away.

"You don't think so." Old Ma Clayton set her daughter away from her, giving Alys a sharp glance at the same time. "I think we had better have a long talk."

Alys sighed. "Mama, there's no need. I've told you all there is to tell."

Her mother sent her a shrewd look. "All?"

Alys pulled a face. "Perhaps not *all*."

"Well, it seems to me that you'd better tell me all of it. Ain't seen you quite this huffy in a long spell."

Alys could feel herself flushing. "Mama, I don't think I could tell you about the more . . . more graphic . . . after all, you are my mother—"

"And who else are you gonna tell?" Ma Clayton grimaced. "I can see we should've had this talk long ago. Guess it's as hard for me to broach the subject as it is for you. Reckon, too, that I haven't been looking at you as full grown, and I'm deeply sorry about that. Now, tell it to me straight—all of it."

Alys frowned, breathed deeply, shifted her position once, then again, finally managing to say, in a small voice, "Moon Wolf married us, yes . . ." She glanced up quickly. "Not that we have a certificate or anything."

"Couldn't get one here, near as I can tell. Don't make no difference, though. Not to the Indians. Now, stop looking so flustered and tell me the whole story."

Another deep sigh. "He doesn't want to get me pregnant. Because his life is constantly in danger, he is afraid that if he is not there to protect me, that his child and I would be ridiculed, both here and with his own people. Reckon he figures that if he were there with me, we could live with his people."

Ma Clayton nodded thoughtfully. "Indian people don't carry such a powerful hatred as do the white people in these parts. Don't know why. Seems to me they have more reason." She shrugged. "Don't matter, though. Go on with your story."

"Well, he couldn't commit the act that would . . . well, that is to say . . . we couldn't . . ."

"Indians marry in only one way—don't rightly see how you could have avoided that one."

Alys stared straight down at the floor. "We *didn't* get around it, at least not completely."

"Now you've gone and lost me again. Did the man make love to you or not?"

Alys chanced a swift glance up at her mother. "Sort of."

Ma Clayton lifted her eyebrows. "He is capable of it, isn't he?"

"Yes, Mama, he is."

"Then land sakes, child, what's the problem?"

He . . . he didn't violate me."

"I'm right glad to hear that, but I don't need to know what he didn't do. What *did* he do?"

"I'm getting around to that." She squared off her shoulders and took a steadying breath. "He used . . . ah . . . other means to gain satisfaction for me without actually joining the two of us in body."

"Hmmm. Now how could he have? . . ." Her mother's face brightened. "Had you laid out like a banquet, did he?"

"Mama!"

"Goodness, child, there's nothing wrong with what he did. Don't mind saying he's being real gentleman-like. But that's not the problem, is it?"

"No, it's not." Alys felt the blood coursing through her, swift and fast; felt also the dark red stain of embarrassment spreading down onto her chest, her arms. She raised her eyes briefly to meet her mother's, saying, "That was the wonderful part."

"Well, can't say as that surprises me none. I was once young and impulsive, too."

"Mama!" Alys felt herself burning up with humiliation. Still, she had come this far. "But that's all we've done. Nothing more. He gives me satisfaction and then leaves me to run off to that darned waterfall, staying away from me for hours on end."

"Hmmm."

"And no matter how worked up I get him—I have attempted to flirt with him—he won't go any farther."

"Right stubborn young man."

"He is that."

Ma Clayton's eyes sparkled briefly before she offered, "Now, I don't have a mind to making you feel uncomfortable, but I don't rightly see what the problem is, child."

"Mama, he gets no satisfaction from our union . . . only me."

"Can't say as I've ever heard of that before, and especially from a newly wedded husband. Man must have a will of stone." She grinned, then, and, sitting forward in a conspiratorial fashion, said, "There is something you can do about it, though, if you've a mind to."

Alys pouted, "I told you, I've already tried to seduce him. It always ends the same way."

"Dad-blame it, child, I'm not talking about simple seduction. What I'm thinking of is more than that. Now, if you're of a mind to have him, I think this might do the trick."

Alys blinked twice. "You know of something I could do?"

Ma Clayton winked. "Sure as fire."

Alys slowly smiled, the expression completely wicked. And bringing her head in closer to her mother's, she commented, "Then what are we waiting for?"

"I don't know, child. Don't rightly know. Now here's what you've got to go and do . . ."

Moon Wolf trod back toward the cave, carefully avoiding the slippery rocks and the moss-filled crevices. On his shoulders, he carried the meat of a buffalo calf that he had run down and slaughtered. He had been happy to find it, too, needing the activity to keep his mind from other pleasant, yet forbidden things.

Little Brave Woman. His Alys.

He grimaced.

Just how much of her sensuality he could take he was uncertain, but he congratulated himself on his control.

The fact that his body was healed—which allowed him to spend less and less time with her—helped, of course. But he would not always be able to ignore her. He only prayed that when that day came and he could no longer offer resistance, he would have long since put the Wolf Shadow to rest.

In the meantime . . .

Makoyi trotted along beside him, and Moon Wolf glanced down at his companion. "You cannot possibly be hungry," he complained to the animal. "I thought you'd had enough buffalo this day to last you a full moon."

Makoyi paid him no notice, except to raise his tail a little higher and dart a yellow-eyed look at his master. He trotted on ahead.

It was late afternoon, the sun still bright despite the fact that it had already started its descent in the western sky. The air hung warm and heavy with moisture from the waterfall up ahead.

Perhaps it was the waterfall and its noise that were to account for the mistake. Perhaps not. No matter—Moon Wolf should have been more aware that someone awaited him. His senses should have alerted him; they did not.

But maybe he should not have blamed himself too much. After all, since he had first learned of the caves, he had never encountered another soul in this place.

High hills, canyons, and large valleys hid the caverns from all sides; the waterfall, as well, made the caves inconspicuous. Perhaps Indians had once known about this area, but, no mistake, they came here no more.

He felt good and might have started singing his war song had he not so suddenly come upon her.

She lay there in the sun, next to the pool of water . . . stretched out naked. He stopped perfectly still and stared for a very long time, any hint at rationality deserting him in an instant.

Had she seen him?

Quickly, not wishing to be caught, he ducked down behind a bush, peeking out in secret to inspect her.

Her long brown hair fell gently over her shoulders and to the side, the ends dipping down into the water, where the strands rippled as though they kept time with the rhythm of the water.

She had bent one leg at the knee, the further one from him, the other laid out straight, so that her femininity was not hidden from him.

He felt himself responding to the sight of her, too, and knew he should announce his presence, leave, or simply ignore her and enter the cave.

He did none of those. Crouched down, he was as incapable of movement as he was of changing the color of his skin.

Her back was slightly arched, pressing her full breasts outward and up at an enticing angle. And her head tilted back as though she were in communion with Sun.

One arm lay outstretched, her hand lazily dipping into the water, her other held high above her head.

Had he ever seen a sight so beautiful? *Haiya,* he did not think so.

Suddenly, she brought one of her arms up to shield her eyes and glanced over toward the bush where he hid.

Perhaps he had stared too long, knowing that a human could feel the attention of another upon him. Deciding he had been discovered, he stood up.

He caught her glance and stared at her, noting that her eyes watched him with a keen and observant curiosity.

She asked, after a time, "What do you have there?"

"Where?" he asked, looking down at himself to see if he were once again embarrassing himself. He chided himself. *"Aa,"* he gazed over his shoulder, "you mean this buffalo meat here?"

She smiled, and he caught her look of predatory delight. He tensed slightly. What was she about this day?

He did not think he could take much more of her flirting. Not now. Not at this moment. Perhaps he should turn around and walk the other way.

Still, when she called out, "Come closer," he did exactly as she asked.

"Why don't you put the meat in the cool water here beside me so that it will keep for a little while? That way you could come here and keep me company."

Again, as though she held rein over his determination, he paced toward her. Then, bending down, he placed the meat in the shallow water beside her.

He squatted close to her head, and looking down at her, he asked, "Have you been swimming?"

"Not yet. I've been waiting for you."

He scrutinized her face, searching out, there within her eyes, a hint of her purpose. He feared she intended something that would bode ill for his resolves.

She continued, "I thought you might like to go swimming with me today."

He bent further toward her. "A good idea. But we must first see to the meat."

She smiled lazily at him. "It'll keep where it is, at least for the short amount of time we will be here at the pool."

He slid his gaze downward, over the rest of her, from her face to the very tips of her toes, stopping at each and every curve along the way, a hunger beginning to build

within him. *"Ha',"* he observed, "I think you might have
more on your mind this day than a simple swim."

Her smile was oh, so seductive and so very, very be-
witching. She said, "What makes you think so?"

He shook his head, wondering if she knew to what
lengths he went to ensure that she remained pure? Did she
realize the self-control that it took him to keep himself
from her?

She might not, he answered his own question. She was
still so very innocent, and he had yet to show her the ways
of how to please a man.

The thought of that, of how she might pleasure him,
however, and how she might very well go about it, caused
a thin film of sweat to break out on his upper lip and he
tried to suppress the instantaneous thirst that such thoughts
provoked.

Perhaps a cold bath in these waters might cool his desires—and perhaps hers, too.

He stood up, not even bothering to hide the evidence of
his fascination with her. Soon, the frosty waters would
have their way with him, and he would be able to regain
his dignity. He gave her a brief glance, his eyes recklessly
ransacking her nude form, as he would permit only his
eyes to do. He mentioned, "I do not swim in any clothes."

She gave him that smile again and said, "I know."

And he practically took her in his arms right then.

But he didn't. Instead he shook off his moccasins and
shed her father's borrowed pants, making a clean dive into
the water. He surfaced a moment later, relishing in the
refreshing temperature of the water, relying on it to soothe
and take away the heat of his desire.

But he had thought too soon.

She turned over to watch him, coming up slightly to rest
her weight on her elbows, her hands holding her head. And
he was presented with the all too inviting image of her

rounded buttocks, her soft breasts, only slightly hidden behind her arms, seeming to beckon him. She held one leg bent, her foot in the air, waving back and forth. Again, that smile of hers hit him as if it alone had the power to control him.

And perhaps it did. His body jolted in reaction. He felt as if he'd been struck by a single source of lightning, so intense was the craving within him. Worse, his masculine parts throbbed as though alive with a will of their own.

He moaned. How could he possibly take such seduction from her? He should have ignored her, that's what he should have done. But that wasn't possible, either.

However, he might be able to play at her own game. He gave her an expectant glance. "Am I the only one who will enjoy these waters this day? I thought you wanted to go swimming."

She rose, coming up onto her knees in front of him, and he practically moaned his appreciation.

She pushed back her shoulders and shook her head, letting her hair fall down over her breasts, practically hiding them, but not completely, and he noted each and every sway of them. She said, "I do. I am."

Suddenly she shifted position to sit back on one leg, while bending her other one at the knee. Very effectively, he was presented with a view of a great deal of her femininity.

Such did not pass by without his notice, either.

Gulping silently, he decided he had better determine her exact game. He noted, very directly, "I think that you flirt with me."

Again, that smile came to her lips, her eyes inviting. She countered, "Do you only think so?"

He let out his breath in a noisy rush of air. If she was this intent upon her own seduction, who was he to keep it from her?

He groaned. He was the one who would, that was who. He did not think he could take more of their lovemaking without gaining his own satisfaction from it. It was beginning to have an ill effect on him, manifested in certain parts of his very sore body.

Yes, he should have ignored her.

"Moon Wolf," she said to him, "I think I should make love to you as your wife."

He nodded agreement. "You have that right."

"Then why do you deny me?"

"You know why. It might relieve my pain of the moment, but it would bring me more suffering shortly, not knowing that you would be well cared for in the future. Please, you must remind me of this."

She licked her lips. "I know a way to give you the pleasure that is any wife's right to give her husband without compromising you."

Now she really had his attention. He raised an eyebrow. "Of what do you speak?"

Again, her tongue flicked across her lips. She suggested, "Come out of the water and I will show you. I promise that you will be happy with me."

Did he dare trust her? Truth be told, he had little choice. He was practically her slave at this moment, bending to almost any whim she desired.

He put one foot forward, and she sat up on her knees, her bottom wiggling so slightly that it was barely perceivable. But he noticed it. What man wouldn't have?

He took another step forward, although he did think to ask, "What have you in mind?"

"I will not speak of it yet."

He did think to wonder where she had learned these ways. It was a certainty that he had not taught them to her. He could barely be around her without the rigors of his body making themselves known.

"I have been speaking with my mother." She answered his unspoken question just as though he'd asked it. "Come here, Moon Wolf."

He took another step forward, warning her at the same time, "I will not violate you. No matter what you do, I will stop it before it goes that far."

"I will not ask you to, I promise you," she said. Then she added, "In the white man's wedding ceremony, there is a line that reads, 'With my body, I thee worship.' I think that I would like to amend it to, 'With my lips, I thee worship.' " Again that oh, so seductive smile lit her face, and his body responded, all out of control. "Does that give you an idea?"

Eagerness, hunger, and excitement filled him all at once. Still he did think to observe, "And your mother told you about this?"

"She did."

He shook his head. *"Mat'-ah-kwi tam-ap-i-ni-po-ke-mi-o-sin,"* he said, "not found is happiness without woman, or perhaps I might also add without mother-in-law."

Alys grinned at him. She intended to prove, too, just how right he was.

Chapter 13

◦─────◦◯◯◦─────◦

Moon Wolf had no choice. He went to her. How
could he not? At this moment, the strength of his
desire for her, their own mutual passion, held him completely captive.

In one fluid dive, he shot toward her, at once bridging
the distance between them. Supported on his elbows, he
drew himself out of the water and, coming up onto his
knees, swept her into his arms. He held her, just held her,
his touch upon her gentle, rocking her back and forth as
though he might never let go. That this might communicate
the overwhelming power of his feeling for her did not dis-
hearten him as perhaps it should have if he were to keep
good his resolve. The intensity of his mood and his complete adoration of her fed his desire like fuel, and he could
not have stopped had he willed it, which he did not.

At once her honey-sweetened scent encircled him and,
as though existing in a life of its own, it enveloped him
in its silky cocoon. He breathed in unsteadily, and the refreshing fragrance of her stirred him to his soul. His in-

tention to keep her pure, practically virginal, almost evaporated under such an onslaught—almost . . .

His strength of will was such, however, that he continued to hold on to a part of his reserve—just . . .

"Little Brave Woman," he muttered hotly against her hair, "it is in my heart to protect and nurture you, but I fear that you need shelter from no one else but me."

She arched her neck and his lips at once caressed those oh, so vulnerable spots, glorying in the sound of her high-pitched moan as she responded to his ministration. She did manage to utter, her words softly spoken, "But you do protect and nurture me, my husband."

"*Saa*, no, I fear my own passion."

"It is my intent to fulfill that passion. I would have you experience all that I have, all that you have given me."

He groaned. "I fear your intent."

He had knelt in front of her, the position forcing her onto her knees against him. She now bent to smother kisses over his own neck, to those same sensitive spots he had discovered on her; down further, to his chest, to his own nipples, voicing, between kisses, "There is no need to fear me."

He could feel her quivering within his arms, her response so swift, the thought did occur to him that he might burst with the need to take her. "Alys, I cannot abide this," he confessed. "I worry that you will send me up in smoke, and perhaps yourself, too."

He could feel her smile, there on his chest, before she murmured, her voice husky, "I hope so."

He grunted. "Please, I must keep you pure."

"I will not do anything you will not like and I vow to abide by your protests. I will not do anything to cause you alarm. I promise this. Please, trust me."

She had already brought her kisses to his stomach, the touch of her lips on him, the fleeting caress of her hair, creating havoc within him and upon a more centralized area, greatly sensitized; her name escaped his lips once more, but whether in protest or in encouragement, he was beyond contemplating.

And when her kisses found that place most tender to him, most masculine of all, he surrendered himself to her, completely, utterly.

It did occur to him to wonder at old Ma Clayton, realizing the debt he would owe the woman and her experience; for he, himself would never have thought to teach this sort of lovemaking to his wholesome, sweet Alys. But even that thought was quickly lost as conscious thought deserted him, overtaken momentarily by the thrill of his own passion and desire.

He met his release quickly, mayhap too quickly, but he gave such little thought. The buildup to this had been so intense, so powerful, that it had to be expected. And as he spilled the essence of his seed, he spiraled up high, up into the late afternoon sky, his spirit soaring. Physically, he held Alys in his arms, her own slim body trembling.

And, as they knelt there, embraced, he realized that if he'd had any doubts about his feelings for this brave and heroic woman, such qualms had fled. As the gray sky does to the golden rays of the sun, all uncertainty was vanquished, leaving him feeling brighter.

Moreover, he realized that for all his life, all his existence, he had committed himself to her, not only in this life but spiritually and forever. And though he could not visualize the full significance or the complete implications of such a pledge, at least not right this moment, it did not detract the least from the power of his commitment.

He had dedicated himself to her, for all eternity.

Several hours later Moon Wolf lounged within the cave, awaiting Aly's return. He was thinking. He sat cross-legged upon his blanket, his pipe at his knees, his knife within ready reach and his trusted pet at his side.

No longer influenced by the whims of momentary passion, his thoughts had become clearer, and he had concluded that he could not allow Alys to stay with him. Truth be told, if he'd had any inclination in the past to keep her from his side, it was doubly so now. He had finally realized that he loved her, deeply. He probably always had, thus explaining the incredible lengths he had gone to in order to protect her.

Although to another such an enlightenment might be used as cause to hold on more firmly, not so Moon Wolf.

He would not, could not allow this woman to ruin her life. And he saw himself as a catalyst to doing just that.

He could not deny that the old ways, the glorious ways of the free and independent Indian were on the brink of extinction, perhaps never to return. It wasn't a pleasant thought, but it was one that demanded his acknowledgment. Also, like the buffalo, Moon Wolf could not deny that the red man's numbers decreased daily. Whether by disease, by gunshot, or by the evils of the white man's spirit water, the red man's power upon this land, which he had once held undisputed, had deteriorated, leaving only devastation of the land, of the Indian people.

Moon Wolf no longer knew with any certainty what the future held. And though he might himself be doomed to an early death because of this, he did not wish this upon Alys, would not sanction such a thing for his wife.

It remained a fact that she was white, and because of this, she could still secure a bright future if he could hold himself in check long enough to disentangle himself from her.

And so it was with such purpose that he awaited her now.

But, as though aware that he might have disruptive

thoughts, she had excused herself and had disappeared soon after their lovemaking, not to return, not even to give him supper. And though he was more than capable of providing for himself—he had, after all, brought home meat— he had become accustomed to Alys's bringing him food.

Patiently, as was his training, he sat within the cave, his thoughts in chaos, *Makoyi* at his feet.

Looking down, he addressed the animal. "Where do you think she is?"

Makoyi lifted his eyes to his master, seemed to chide him for such foolishness, then rested his head back on his paws.

"I think I had better pay a visit to the fort this night."

Again, a warning look from *Makoyi.*

"What thinks you, *Makoyi?* Why do you frown at me? If not for her, I need to be going there to give the lieutenant all the 'information' I have collected on the Wolf Shadow. I have business in the fort, after all."

Wolf didn't even deem to look up this time. He closed his eyes.

"I think you are right and I should go."

Makoyi pulled back his ears, wiggling them as if he hadn't heard correctly.

"You stay here and sleep. If you come into the fort with me, it will look bad. Many people know you. But they do not relate the drunken Moon Wolf with the Wolf Shadow."

No response from the animal, although there was clearly another pout.

"What say you?" Moon Wolf scrutinized the animal more closely. "Is this about that young female pup we saw today in the wood?"

Makoyi raised his ears.

"Humph," said Moon Wolf. "I saw the look you gave her, and I noted the answering gleam in her eye."

The wolf continued to pout.

"Fine, then go ahead and go to her," he voiced to the wolf, waving his arm. "If I am going to seek out my own lady love, I see no reason to hold you here. It is spring, the urge is strong within you, too. Just do not forget to return in the morning."

Makoyi raised his head and stared at his master, as though he comprehended each and every word.

"There is the scent of the human being on you, though, old friend. She will smell this on you and might not pay any attention to you. Do you still wish to go?"

In response, the wolf started off toward the cave's entrance, but he returned in a moment, placing his paws on his master's shoulders and licking his face.

Moon Wolf laughed and petted the animal gently before *Makoyi* came back down on all fours, turning and cantering off in the direction of the waterfalls, looking back only once. And Moon Wolf, watching him, shook his head.

They were a pair, the two of them, moping after their women, following them wherever they went.

Was there no hope for them?

He found her at a dance.

A dance. Why had she not come to him and explained what she intended? And there he had been, waiting for her.

He watched her as she frolicked, coupled with another man, spinning this way and that, stepping around the dance floor. His gut wrenched, and despite what he had told her about his wanting her to marry a white man, despite his own desire that she be freed from *him*, seeing her like this, in the arms of another man, gave him pause for consideration.

Especially when that man was Lieutenant Warrington.

Lieutenant Warrington. Could she not feel, did she not notice the snakelike qualities of this man?

He supposed that she might not. Many women were blind to the more deceitful qualities of men, especially when a particular man was handsome of face. But then, there seemed something insubstantial about a woman who judged a man based on physical image alone.

Irritated, Moon Wolf pulled his robe up and over his head, leaving himself a mere crack through which to see. He peeked through the thin glass of the white man's window.

The strange music from the fiddles, the twang of the guitar strings, and the buzz from a harmonica hung lightly in the air, their pitch high-toned in comparison to the accompaniment of the more baritone singing. No drumming accompanied the music, either, which seemed odd to the Indian ear, although the sound of the stomping feet from inside kept up a simple rhythm. Laughter and the hum of the many voices drifted out through the window, too, their words hitting upon his ears without meaning, his attention centered on her and her alone.

He had come here looking for her; he had found her. Now, he should leave.

But he knew he wouldn't.

He watched her smile at the lieutenant, and though Moon Wolf recognized her look as that of one held more captive than attentive, he clenched his jaw. He scrutinized her as well he could for signs of her mood, as she allowed her hand to be held, her waist to be encompassed. It didn't matter to Moon Wolf, either, that he realized that this was simply the way the dance was performed. *He* did not like it.

He did note that she held her arms rigid against her partner, as though she held him at a distance, and when the lieutenant didn't watch her or speak to her, she frowned, a clear sign she was not enjoying herself.

Still, as she strutted around and around the room, dancing the lively steps that Moon Wolf had once heard referred to as a jig, Moon Wolf came to a sudden realization: he wished to proclaim to the world that this woman was *his,* not the property of this lieutenant. And it didn't matter the antagonism such an announcement would create.

But he knew he would not, he could not do it. Such would serve no good purpose.

But he should do something. What?

Not certain exactly where his thoughts were taking him, but unable to stand by and watch any longer, he sauntered into the hall, bypassing the guards who had perhaps imbibed too much on this evening, for they barely noticed him.

He held himself back from the dancing couple, fading in unnoticed against the walls. At least for the moment.

Almost all the females in the place were Indian, though a strict division had taken place on the dance floor, the few white women holding themselves as far away from the Indians as possible.

All the men dancing, the traders, the merchants, the military, were white; while the male Indians had been relegated to the sidelines.

Moon Wolf joined the latter.

The volume of the music had increased, the shuffling of feet and the murmur of voices had become louder, too, and the air felt stifling for all that the doors remained open. Still, Moon Wolf held his robe up and over his head, hiding his face and watching his wife.

She glanced his way once, a question on her face. Had she recognized his robe? Perhaps his particular gait? Or did she simply feel the intensity of his gaze upon her?

The music played out a happy melody while the dancers stamped their feet, the women twirled in circles before their men, and the people on the sidelines clapped.

Soon the music stopped and, with Alys already wrapped

in his arms, the lieutenant pulled her closer toward him.

Rage swept through Moon Wolf, and without thinking, without even waiting to see his woman's response, which was perhaps a counter to the lieutenant's move, Moon Wolf acted, pushing himself away from the wall, positioning himself beside the couple.

With a deliberate stagger, he bumped into Lieutenant Warrington, sending the man sprawling onto the floor.

"Humph, Lou-ten-tant," Moon Wolf slurred his words. "Let this one help you up." He bent down to assist the lieutenant to his feet, to brush the dirt off him, with none too gentle a hand.

Lieutenant Warrington stood, refusing any help. Pushing Moon Wolf away, the officer slapped out at him; Moon Wolf, as though unable to fully comprehend, countered each strike, "trying" at the same time to aid the man to his feet, making quite a show of it. But amid all the confusion, Moon Wolf "inadvertently" stumbled back into the man once again, pushing the officer back onto the floor and landing conveniently on top of him. Again, amidst a tug of war of hands and arms, Moon Wolf managed to pull a few punches in most strategic places.

"This one comes to you ... with heap big knowledge ..." Moon Wolf slurred his words and repeated the whole process, only this time, in brushing the man's uniform, he "accidentally" bumped into the lieutenant's sword, causing the tip of it to hit the poor fellow in his cushioned backside.

"Stop it, you fool." Lieutenant Warrington tried to disentangle himself from the Indian, resulting in a skirmish that served to produce the same effect as before: the lieutenant ended up on the floor.

Moon Wolf jerked the lieutenant roughly to his feet, bumped into him and, as only a drunken man could do, clutched his cape, and "unexpectedly" ripped it.

"Oops, Lou-ten-tent. You have torn your cape," Moon Wolf observed.

"You clumsy oaf!" Lieutenant Warrington jerked himself away and turned toward Alys, who was hiding her expression—at least her lips—behind her fan.

But her eyes danced with merriment. The lieutenant couldn't have missed it.

"If you would excuse me, Miss Clayton," the officer's words were clipped. "I am sorry, but I must see to my uniform."

She inclined her head. "By all means."

With a curt nod to her, the lieutenant spun around on his heel and should have left forthwith. However, a misplaced moccasined foot had been left in his way, and the unfortunate man tripped over it, falling flat on his face.

A trill of feminine laughter sailed through the air, while the lieutenant, red-faced, squared off against the swaggering and "drunken" figure of Moon Wolf.

"You are the sorriest excuse for a human being that I have ever seen."

Mumbling his words, Moon Wolf responded, "But this one has . . . information for . . . more whiskey   "

Lieutenant Warrington hissed out another oath and, sweeping what was left of his cape over his shoulder, stomped from the hall. Curious looks and giggles followed him.

Meanwhile, the music, which had been stopped all this time, started up again, and people were once more taking to the dance floor.

Alys sent a puzzled glance toward Moon Wolf, who motioned her outside with a quick dart of his eyes. He then stumbled and staggered his way to the exit, looking, to all the onlookers, the epitome of a once proud warrior, turned drunk. And, singing his courage song in his best falsetto voice, he made his way toward the back of the building, there to meet his lady love.

Or so he hoped.

Chapter 14

"You must be careful. Lieutenant Warrington is a dangerous man. You should not anger him unnecessarily."

Her whispered words fell into a rhythm with the sighings of the wind as she waited for his reply, her back to him, as though she stood alone, out here in the night.

She reclined near the shadows of a building; he hidden by them completely, she more obvious to any onlookers. Above her splashed the light of a million stars, illuminating her dress and her features in an iridescent glow; below her, the firm feel of the dry prairie grass cushioned her feet, though her step felt light against it. In the distance, the river rushed by, its current reminding her of the hushed murmur of a whisper, the quiet sound accompanied only by the mournful howls of the wolves and the wind as it swept across the prairie.

Her hair stirred against her neck, but whether from the wind or from a gentle caress, she could not tell. Nor would she turn to determine it. No one must see her; no one must be alerted to what she did, that she stood here in the shadows . . . with him . . .

At last he proffered, "*Aa,* yes, the lieutenant is a dangerous man. It is good that you see this."

"Nor is he an honest man," she replied. "What dealings do you have with him and what were you talking about—having information for him?"

Moon Wolf paused for an instant and then said, "He pays the drunken Moon Wolf to gather all the information that he can on the notorious Wolf Shadow, that the lieutenant might find out who this scoundrel is and hang the man."

"Moon Wolf, no! This is a dangerous game you are playing."

"So it is and yet I have been playing it for some time now."

Alys drew in her breath. "It cannot go on. Sometime he will discover your true identity and then you will be . . ."

"Did I not tell you that my life is forfeit? Did I not explain to you that this is the reason I would make a bad husband? But this is also a thing I must do if I am to be of any help to my people."

Another long pause. This time, her own. "I see," she said at last, and she did. However, that didn't mean she liked it.

After some time, he mentioned, "I was waiting in the caves for you to return."

She didn't answer.

Again, he hesitated. "You did not come back to me."

"There wasn't time," she whispered all at once, "the lieutenant was waiting for me at my house and I had no choice but to accompany him."

"You could have been busy. If my memory is correct, you were."

"What? And have him grow suspicious of me and follow me to the caves? I think not."

"You did not have to dance with him."

She snorted. "A simple dance means nothing."

"And yet it looked like very much to me."

She widened her eyes, though she did not turn around to look at him as she voiced, "Moon Wolf, are you jealous?"

He gave no answer, though at length he said, "I did not like seeing you with another man—and especially the lieutenant. I am hoping that I will not have to see that again. If you are to marry another in the future, and I hope that you will, I pray I will be gone by then."

"It is possible I might not marry again."

"And yet, you should. I know this."

She glanced over her shoulder.

"Do not look this way!"

She faced back around, though she did comment, "Perhaps you should stop trying to marry me off to another and enjoy our time together."

"Perhaps."

More silence, until she asked, "Where is the wolf? Does he wait for us in the caves?"

"He has gone to seek a mate." A hint of humor tinged Moon Wolf's voice.

"Your pet? To seek a mate? Will he return?"

Moon Wolf reached out a finger to trail a line of sensation over her neck, causing her heartbeat to race, her stomach to lurch and a moan to escape her lips. He commented, his breath hot on her neck, "I do not think he will be greatly successful. The human scent is too strongly imbedded in his fur. I believe that this alone will keep the females away from him. At least for now."

"And in the future?"

"The wolf mates with another but once and for his entire

lifetime. It is not something I can stop. I only hope that if he does leave me to make a home with a wife, he will not trust other human beings and try to become close to them. He does not understand to fear them."

She nodded.

His fingers grew more insistent, and he muttered, "I shouldn't . . . I know it, but I want you . . . again."

Her stomach dropped.

"I did not like seeing you with another. If I could, I would pronounce you mine before the rest of the world."

"If I could, I would let you. I do not understand entirely why you do not do this."

"Do you not? Look around you. Who here would welcome you if we announced ourselves married?"

She remained silent.

"We have been through this before. Our hearts are as one, but the color of our skin sets us apart. I must think, not of myself, but of you, of your acceptance within my own tribe, with your people; I must think of our unborn child and what life would hold for he who would be not wholly Indian, or white. But most of all, if I live, and if I am to hold on to you, I must find a place for us to live. A place where we can prosper without fear of prejudice. Do you know of such a place?"

She couldn't answer. She knew of no such haven—not even back east.

She smiled, just a little. "I don't suppose we could bring a child up in the caves?"

He grinned too. "*Saa,* no, I do not believe so. All men and women, all children, too, need the camaraderie of their own kind. One cannot live alone for long without the mind being taken away by the Above Ones."

"Do you mean 'being taken' as in crazy?"

"*Aa,* yes, it is so. Look here to me. Even the Wolf

Shadow has friends within the village that help him, and he always has *Makoyi*."

She became silent, reflecting for a moment. "Perhaps it is up to us, then," she said, "to create this kind of place. Not only for ourselves, but for others like us."

"Perhaps."

"It has to start somewhere."

"How wise you are." His lips followed where his fingers had led him. He nibbled her skin, his breath hot against her, sending chills along her nerve endings. Murmuring, he said, "But we must cease this talk. We are not safe here. Someone could see us. Hostile eyes might find us, and I would not know it. Better it is if we return to the caves."

"Is that advisable? Will the lieutenant not be looking for you and the 'information' you have for him?"

"I will see him tomorrow."

She hesitated. Finally, though, she proffered, "And you think this is prudent?"

"He will not expect me tonight."

"Then I will return home at once," she said.

"Home?" he asked. "To the caves?"

She arched her neck against his silken caress. "To the caves."

He set her slightly away from him, then murmured, "You must go now. I cannot take you there at this moment and we must not be seen together."

He dropped his hands from her, and she stepped forward. Without turning around, she beseeched, "Do not be long." With that said, she stepped away, hurrying back in the same direction from which she had come.

Lost in the shadows, Moon Wolf contemplated her every movement with admiration, a slight grin on his face. So much was he taken by her that he became temporarily oblivious to the other eyes that observed him. He started to step forward, instantly jerking back as he sensed another's attention upon him. Noiselessly, he sank back into the shadows.

He let the blanket fall from his head and glanced around him; nothing. He listened carefully, barely breathing; he heard nothing.

Yet, someone was out there. He *felt* it.

A tiny rustle sounded off to his right; footfalls, barely discernable, fading away. It had to be an Indian, one man alone. No white man that he knew of could remain so silent.

But was the Indian friend or foe?

Foe, most likely, or the man would have presented himself. Who could it be? Moon Wolf knew the Indians in the fort personally, called most of them friend; none would spy on him.

Who was this, then?

Gathering his robe about him, Moon Wolf hunched down, moving forward silently, each step carefully placed. Instead of the hunted, he would become the hunter; his safety, and perhaps Little Brave Woman's, depended on it.

He skulked after the intruder, following his tracks like a hound when the sound of the man's steps were no longer audible.

He pursued the man round one building, and another, finally coming to the end of the trail; the berthing of Lieutenant Warrington.

"Humph!" Moon Wolf muttered softly to himself. Lieutenant Warrington.

Circling the quarters cautiously, for it might be guarded, Moon Wolf traced the man to the entrance. And there he waited, his senses attuned to the slightest of movements, the faintest of sounds. Finally, satisfied that no one else watched this place, Moon Wolf stole toward the window closest to the two figures inside, and, crouching down, listened.

The voices were low, barely audible. Still, of one thing he became certain: no Indian accent was this. This . . . this scout was a white man. A white man spying on an Indian?

Perhaps the man was a white hunter, those who had taken to the habit of lodging with the red man. Such might account for the man's ability to sneak upon a person and remain unnoticed.

But these speculations answered none of Moon Wolf's questions: Why was the white hunter here? And on whom had he been spying? Little Brave Woman, or himself?

What was the lieutenant's involvement in this? What were these two attempting?

"I don't believe you," came the jarring voice of the lieutenant. Moon Wolf listened carefully.

"I seen the calico out there in the moonlight, Cap'n," replied the white hunter.

"Don't get too familiar, Jake. It's Lieutenant Warrington to you." The lieutenant took a shot of something, whiskey most likely, for he grimaced before he asked, "And who was the man with her? What outfit is he with?"

"I don't rightly know, Cap'n," the man emphasized the word. "Couldn't see the man's face, standin' in the shadows an' all, though I did smell whiskey on 'im."

"I hire you for your information, man, not your ignorance. Why didn't you wait until he had stepped out of the shadows?"

"I did, Cap'n. He faded back into them shadows, though, like he knew someone was watching 'im. And when I checked 'em, he was gone."

The lieutenant paused a moment. "I see. And where did she go?"

"Back to her home, I believe, Cap'n. It's what she said she was doin'."

Moon Wolf heard steps stomping one way, back again, over and over. "So," it was Lieutenant Warrington speaking, "she is having a secret tryst with someone else. That would explain why she is rarely at her home when I have gone to call on her."

"Seems likely, Cap'n."

"How could she do this to me? Me? Why, I have gone out of my way to be tolerant of her, even when she has been much too inquisitive. And I have done my best to coax her into affection for me." A long pause followed. "But there is a certain amount of distaste in her eyes whenever she thinks I am not watching. Distaste? Why, the harlot. Who does she think she is?" More steps, going away, coming back. "Why, I'll tell you this, if it weren't for her mother's wealth and that prime property that Miss Clayton will eventually inherit, I'd spurn her for less'n that . . ."

"Beg pardon, Cap'n, but you ain't got her yet."

"But I will, my good man." Another long pause. "I will."

"She's a right pretty calico, Cap'n. That's fer sure. Hard ta believe you ain't got a hankerin' fer her alone, only fer her money. But then, never could get a grip on you tenderfoots from the States."

"Watch it, Jake. I'm a terrible man to cross."

No response from Jake.

"Now, I want you to watch her. That's all. Put a watch on her day and night until we discover who this bullwacker is that she thinks is better'n me. That's what I'm paying you for, not your opinions or your . . ." The lieutenant's voice changed, becoming slyer. "I must say, if he is a soldier, a transfer might very well be in order . . ."

"And if'n he ain't, Cap'n?"

The lieutenant didn't answer all at once. "You just watch her, Jake. Find out who this man is and let me worry about the rest. But when I finally get her—and I will get her—I'll . . ."

Moon Wolf didn't wait to hear more. He didn't need to.

Alys had unwittingly drawn attack upon her person, simply by not being romantically inclined toward the lieutenant. And what had he meant by saying when he finally got her? What sinister plan had he devised for her?

No mistake, Little Brave Woman would have to be more careful than ever. She could no longer afford the luxury of coming and going from house to cellar on a whim.

Moon Wolf jerked his head to the left and frowned. His Alys would have to remain in the house, here in the fort, in order to draw the attacks away from her. At least she would need to do this until he rendered the danger from the lieutenant harmless.

Taking a moment, he said a silent prayer of thanks to the Above Ones, to his ancestors. At least he had been warned.

"Tell me about your pet wolf," she entreated, "and how he came to be with you."

Moon Wolf drew his right arm under his head, his left acting as a cushion for her, Alys's body snuggled in close to his. They reclined in the open, on a grassy knoll close to, but away from, the spray of the falls. Wrapped in a buffalo robe, they were shielded from the cool, though refreshing, mountain air. Above them, and spread out in all directions, lay a canopy of stars, all of which twinkled and shone with a hazy light.

Had he ever looked more handsome? She didn't think so. His dark hair had entwined with her own, and strands lay across her arm like silk. The fragrance of his skin, clean and fresh-smelling, combining with the scent of the grasses, the trees and the pureness of the invigorating mountain air, was intoxicating. The potpourri sent her head spinning slightly, causing her to think of other things, perhaps more pleasant things, that they could be doing with one another rather than simply lying here.

She breathed in deeply and closed her eyes, wondering if she would remember these things about him always. Enamored, she made a mental note never to forget.

She had come to this spot earlier in the evening to await him, and, preferring the open air to the dark dankness of the caves, she had lain down here.

She had been asleep when he had first come to her. But once he had crawled in next to her and had taken her in his arms, her sleepiness had evaporated, as though it had never existed.

Now they lay awake, together, awaiting only the return of *Makoyi*.

After much thought, Moon Wolf asked gently, "So it is the story of *Makoyi* that you wish to hear?"

She nodded.

"It is a sad story in the beginning. Are you certain you wish to know it?"

She snuggled her head more deeply into the crook of his arm, sighing at the same time. "Perhaps not the gory details," she muttered, "but I have been wondering how he came to be with you, and to be so tame, too."

"Aa," Moon Wolf took a deep breath, "so I will tell you of it. It happened a few years ago when I was hunting buffalo. Out on the north plain, I could find no signs of the buffalo. But I did run across two different sets of tracks, one of an antelope, the other of the white man. Because game had become scarce and I had no sign of buffalo, I followed the tracks of the antelope, but soon lost them in a rocky area.

"It was then that I heard the cry of a young one. It was the wail of a wolf, but it was like that of a baby. I thought to investigate.

"What I found was a pitiful sight. A lone wolf pup sat beside its parents, who had been caught in the awful traps of the white man. The necks and legs of the parents had been broken by the traps and the pup sat alone, moaning its loss.

"There it sat, a fluffy-tailed, fuzzy little thing, all weak with hunger and grief. It trembled as I approached it, but it did not bite me when I picked it up by the neck. It shook even more when I put it in my arms and tried to hide its head under my arm. It was a male pup.

"I decided then to take pity upon it and to take it home and feed it and see if it might someday make a companion for me. I have never been sorry for that decision. *Makoyi* has been my constant companion since that day, and many is the time when he has saved my life; sometimes by scenting danger before I am aware of it, sometimes by guarding me and helping me fight when I upset the caravans of the whiskey traders."

She offered, "And he saved my life, too."

Moon Wolf nodded. "Then, too."

"And you say he has gone to find a mate tonight?"

"*Aa*, yes, I believe that he has." Moon Wolf gathered her in closer to him. "A wolf is different from a dog in many ways, and one of those is in the manner of courtship. A male dog will never know his offspring. Not so the wolf. A wolf pairs off and stays with his mate all his life. He is a good father. He hunts for his young, he will stay with the pups, too, allowing the mother to hunt and to run around and regain her strength. He is a strong-hearted animal, this wolf of the plains, and he loves deeply those to whom he gives his affection, that love lasting his whole life. He never forgets."

"And he loves you."

"*Aa*, yes, and now you, too."

"What will happen if he finds a mate?"

Moon Wolf paused before he replied, "I am uncertain. The wolf is a good hunter. Never does he or his family starve. And *Makoyi* enjoys the adventure of the Wolf Shadow as he might enjoy the thrill of the chase. I taught him many things when he was young: to help round up my horses, to chase down wounded game, even to carry a pack and to sneak along with me when hunting. He has proven himself to be a brother and a friend many times. But the mating instinct is strong with him, and if he finds a mate, it will be his duty to protect and nurture her and their young."

"Then we might not see him again?"

"Perhaps. But the human scent is strong with him. For now, we are safe from him leaving us, I believe."

"I hope so."

Moon Wolf relaxed, and as though he might have all the time in the world, stretched out his legs, which had been crossed at the ankles. At length, he began, "There is something else that we need to discuss, I think."

"Oh?" she asked. "And what is that?"

Another slight pause. "There was a white hunter watching us from the shadows tonight as we stood beneath the moon. I heard him after you left and followed him to the lieutenant's house."

Alys gasped, then frowned. "Lieutenant Warrington's house?"

"*Aa,* yes, that is right."

"Then Lieutenant Warrington knows about us?"

"*Saa,* no, the white hunter did not see who I was. All he knows is that you are having a lover's liaison with someone. I do not believe that either of them suspect that man to be a red man. So in that we are safe. But you are in danger. After tonight I do not think it would be wise for you to come here to the caves."

"But—"

"Lieutenant Warrington has asked this white hunter to watch you. If that man sees you coming and going from your cellar and staying there for great lengths of time, he will become suspicious. He might even try to follow you into the caves."

"But why? Why would Lieutenant Warrington want me followed? Why would it upset him if I did have a love interest?"

A long hesitation followed her question, and when he did at last answer her, Moon Wolf spoke slowly, as though he chose every word. "The lieutenant has been trying to court you, this I overheard."

"But I have never given him any reason to believe that I might fancy him."

"He needs no enticement from you, this Lieutenant Warrington. For I believe that his purpose lies more toward your wealth and your property than it does—"

"But I have no wealth of my own."

"*Saa?* Do you not? And your mother, does she not have this wealth?"

"Well, yes, she does. My father was, after all, a miner and a founding father of the town and left us quite well off."

"Then I believe it is this that draws the lieutenant to you."

Stunned, she became silent, but for only a second. "Why have I never thought of it? Of course, that would explain his uncompromising interest in me, when I am so reluctant to be in his company. It is to be thanked, then, that he does not know about my family's other wealth, for then . . ." Her words trailed away.

Moon Wolf frowned, but she did not finish the thought, nor did she enlighten him. As though she had only paused a beat, she continued, "I don't see why I should stop coming to the caves just because of Lieutenant Warrington.

These are my caves. Mine and my mother's. I have been going there, using them all my life."

"And they shall continue to be your caves," he reminded her, "but you must not enter them until the danger is past."

"You cannot glibly ask me to do this. It would be as though to cut off a part of me. Besides, it would mean that I would not see you, either."

"Yet it must be done. Perhaps that is for the best."

"What do you mean?" she asked, frowning.

He gave a faint shrug. "I still believe that you should try to find one from your own culture who might protect you if I am no longer here."

"But you are here and I do not believe we should discuss that kind of thing any further."

"Perhaps," he stated simply, offering no argument. "But still, you must do it. You must stay away from the caves. For if you do not, you might lead the white hunter to suspect something here. You do not want to arouse his suspicion that you are aiding the Wolf Shadow with your secret place. More than your wealth would be at risk then."

What could she say to such uncompromising logic? Very little, really.

She asked, "Then if I don't come to the caves, when will I see you?"

"Until this white hunter leaves and there is no longer any suspicion of you, we will not meet."

"Not at all?"

"*Saa,* no, we cannot risk it."

"That seems rather extreme, don't you think? You could visit my mother from time to time, couldn't you? Then we could see one another."

His body went tense. He said, "I cannot. I am not in the habit of visiting her, at least not when others can see me. To start doing so now would throw suspicion onto you, perhaps onto her, too."

She sighed, unwilling to debate the point with him. At length she asked, "And the Wolf Shadow? How will you be able to play the part of the Wolf Shadow if the house, and with that, the cellar, are under constant watch?"

"I do not know. Not yet. I do not mind the risk, but I will not endanger either you or your mother."

Alys smiled. "Maybe I could become the masked devil from time to time."

He gave her a sharp look. "*Saa*, no, you will not. Think what would happen if this man sees you dressed like the Wolf Shadow, going into and out of your house? And you must know that this white hunter will see this. He will observe your movements at all times of the day."

"Even when he is sleeping?"

"It is possible he will enlist others to help him."

She moaned, hesitating. "So will the drunken Moon Wolf disappear from the fort, too?"

"He will have to, at least for now."

"But isn't that dangerous? Isn't Lieutenant Warrington expecting to hear something from Moon Wolf tomorrow?"

Moon Wolf shrugged. "My people often appear or disappear into and out of the fort without warning. It matters not what he thinks. This must be done."

"Then you, too, must be careful," she cautioned, thinking to induce him into being more mindful of his own safety. However, he didn't seem to notice, and she continued, "I will miss you. Surely we can meet at some given places."

"*Saa*, no. We cannot. We cannot risk discovery of me, of you, of your caves, or of you and me together."

She groaned. Of course he spoke with wisdom, but really . . . not meeting at all?

"You are not, per chance, happy about this, are you?"

"*Saa*, no, why would I be happy?"

Something nagged her on to observe, "Because you

keep trying to pawn me off onto some poor unsuspecting soul—for my own good."

"*Aa*, yes, I understand you now," he grinned at her. "Alas, such would seem to fit into my plans, would it not, except that I would not wish you to be put in danger, not ever, and I do not believe that I wish to see you with another man while I am still alive. I am trying to think of your future."

"And what of yours? What of your future?"

"I do not believe that I have one."

"I see," she said and paused, choosing her next words carefully. "So will you find it hard to be away from me?"

"*Aa*, yes," he answered at once. "I will find my thoughts turning to you often, I fear."

"Good," she said. "That is as it should be."

She could feel his tender smile against her cheek. He said, "That I can promise you. I will keep you close to me in thought."

She became silent, though at length she commented, "I do not like it."

He nodded, answering, "Nor do I."

She rolled over until she lay on her back, her gaze centered upon the star-littered midnight sky. She voiced, "And when the white hunter finds nothing? That I have no lover?"

"Then let us hope that the lieutenant will no longer feel threatened and will stop the constant watch over you, although it is almost certain that, if the lieutenant is after your wealth, he might become even more persistent in his pursuit of you."

Alys nodded, muttering uneasily, "Yes, I believe you could be right."

She rolled her head one way, then the other, her thoughts uneasy. There had to be something she could do, something the both of them had overlooked.

A star twinkled in the night, another shot across the sky. If only there were someone, some young gent in town that she could turn to—

An idea suddenly took hold of her. It might work. No, she daren't.

But the idea would not be put aside. She trembled slightly with the excitement of it, while an unexpected warmth rushed through her. She had a plan; something she could do.

Of course, she had better not tell Moon Wolf. It was almost certain he would object, even if he did keep trying to hock her off to the nearest bidder.

But then, what husband would not disapprove of her scheme? And with this last thought, she turned over in order that she might make her man more comfortable .

Chapter 15

She opened her violet-and-lace-trimmed parasol and rested the handle on her left shoulder, shielding herself from the noonday sun. She wore an elegant dress of violet silk, adorned with scalloped ruffles and tied with black ribbon.

Her overskirt, a lighter shade of violet faille, was trimmed in the same lace as her parasol, and around her waist she wore a skirt, which favored a polonaise, longer in front with the whole of it finished in back with a pleated silk scarf hanging down and tied with black ribbons. A white chip bonnet sat tilted back upon her head, while her chignon had been braided and pulled up with only a few curls left loose at her nape.

She looked the epitome of fashion and as far removed from the Wolf Shadow, and from the western plains, as possible.

Now she only had to begin her plan.

She had already picked the man she would seek to help her, and she saw him now, standing by himself at the far end of the street. Bobby Thompson. Perfect.

She examined him, from the top of his beaver-fur stove-pipe hat to the very tips of his plain brogans. That his pantaloons were wrinkled and fit too loosely, that his waistcoat emphasized his rounded belly, and that his coat showed too much of the dust from the street didn't bother Alys. His was a kind face.

She strolled up to him, noting that he stood barely eye level with her. Still, she gave him a smile that was more than a little provocative.

Bobby glanced up at her, raised his hat, and had just uttered, "Good morning, Miss Alys," when he caught her eye.

He looked away, but glanced back quickly, perhaps only to ensure he had, in truth, observed the gleam in her eye. Immediately he gulped, sending her another second, more startled, glimpse. He cleared his throat nervously.

But she only grinned back at him before inquiring, flirtation coloring her every word, "Excuse me, Bobby, but I seem to have lost my necklace down the street and cannot find it. Would you be so kind as to help me?"

His mouth practically gaped open. Not even a fool could have missed the warmth in her voice. "Of course, Miss Alys, of course I'll help you." He tripped over his own shoes as he made to move forward. Carefully righting himself, he glanced up at her shyly. "Could you lead me to the place?"

"Certainly," she agreed, smiling adoringly at him.

She took his arm, as though he had offered it to her, and, turning in unison, they strolled back down the wooden planks of the sidewalk. "It is so kind of you to come to my aid, Bobby," she proffered, flashing him another of those smiles and batting her eyelashes at him. "I don't know what I would have done if I hadn't happened upon you here in town."

His face colored until the pink staining his cheeks became a bright red. However, he managed to utter, "I . . . I'm certain someone else would'a come to your rescue, Miss Alys."

"But maybe not quite so speedily. I so appreciate this. Ah, here it is." She stopped and bent down, pointing in between the slabs. "Do you see it?"

Bobby bent forward, too, coming down onto his knees. Unfortunately he slipped and knocked into her, sending her falling straight onto her rump and whacking her hat off at the same time. It went flying.

She caught her breath.

"Oh, I'm sorry, Miss Alys, I didn't mean to bump into you like that." He had already jumped to his feet and had taken off, chasing after her hat.

She grimaced. "Not to worry, Bobby," she called after him. "I have many petticoats to cushion my fall."

He retrieved the hat in reasonable time, although it no longer resembled anything to do with headgear. She sighed when he handed it to her.

"Come here, Bobby, do you see the necklace?"

He bent down again, this time very carefully.

"Why, yes, Miss Alys, I do."

"Fine, fine," she answered. "And do you think you could get it for me?"

"I am pretty certain I can, Miss Alys. Yes indeed, I believe that I can."

She smiled at him, though the gesture held more grimace than pleasure. She had lost the necklace quite purposefully, placing it beneath the boards herself, in such a way as to make it easy to obtain. Bobby, putting his fingers through the planks of wood, maneuvered it until he had the thing in his grasp, pulling it back through the wood, the necklace thankfully all in one piece.

She let her breath out, unaware until she did so that she had been holding it.

"Here," Bobby said to her, drawing the gold chain up and giving it a quick once-over. He handed it to her. "It looks to be good as new."

"Why, thank you ever so much, Bobby," she said, appearing, she hoped, to be genuinely surprised and pleased. She continued, "I don't know how I can ever repay you for your kindness. The necklace means a great deal to me. It belonged to my grandmother, you know."

Bobby gave her a shaky smile, the fullness of his cheeks trembling with the action. He said, "No, Miss Alys, I didn't. But I reckon I'm glad I was able to help." He righted himself with some difficulty and got to his feet, but, as though remembering her, reached down a hand to help her up, too.

She ignored the slip in manners, saying, "You must come to dinner, Bobby, as a reward. Please say that you will."

"Why, Miss Alys, that's right neighborly of you." Bobby practically beamed at her. "Why, I'd be pleasured, Miss Alys. Real pleasured, indeed."

Alys could barely contain her own sense of accomplishment. Her plan was working like a charm. She suggested, "Say tonight? At six?"

Bobby held his hat in his hand, turning it over and over until it more resembled an animal than a hat. He agreed. "Six will be fine. I'll be there."

Alys smiled. "I'll be looking forward to it."

She turned, then, to begin her trek home, but called back over her shoulder, "Six o'clock tonight. Don't be late."

Bobby grinned back at her. "I won't."

"What were you about today?" Moon Wolf caught her as soon as she opened the cellar doors. Her purpose had been to retrieve a few jars of jam; however, she was just as happy to come face to face with Moon Wolf. He had clearly been anticipating her, and without awaiting her reply, went on, "First you flirt with Lieutenant Warrington and now the owner of the general store. Do you purposely do this in order to offer my mind up to the Above Ones? Perhaps I should just declare to these white people that you are my wife and take on the world and what they will do to us because of it."

"Perhaps you should."

He gave her a silencing look. "We have been through this before. I will not have you ruin your life because of me."

"Maybe I should be the judge of how I could ruin it."

He shook his head, smiling blandly. "We leave the point. What were you about today?"

"How did you see me?"

He hesitated. And though she could sense his irritation with her, he asked in a kindly voice, "Do you always answer your questions with another well-chosen one?"

She grinned at him, baiting him. "Do you?"

She heard his slight chuckle, saw him shake his head, and, despite the darkness of the cellar, noted the tender mirth in his eyes. She leaned in toward him. "Moon Wolf, it is dark in here, we have only a few more moments together. Could we not spend it in a more amicable way?"

"We could. You will tell me what you were doing today with the storekeeper and then we can share those few stolen moments."

She pouted, "Do I have to account to you for everything that I do?"

"I am your husband," he pointed out, his hand coming up to touch her lips, where she frowned, his caress soft, loving. He said, "We should have no secrets from one another."

"Are you jealous?"

"A little, perhaps."

"There is no need to be."

"I know that, too," he admitted, "but even if there were a reason to be suspicious, I would listen to you quietly and try to understand you. A man should not become overly angry with his wife, even under the greatest provocation. No good ever comes of it. Now tell me, what were you trying to do today?"

She sighed. She did not want to share her plan with Moon Wolf, certain that he would object to it and try to stop her. Still, with the touch of his gentle gaze upon her, she found herself weakening. "I . . . I . . ." She caught herself. "I lost my necklace and asked Bobby to help me retrieve it."

"That is not what it looked like to me."

"And where were you? I don't remember seeing you."

"Were you looking for me?" he countered. "From where I stood, you did not appear to notice anything else around you except that merchant."

"How could you be jealous of Bobby?"

"Very easily, I think."

"Well, ease your mind, Moon Wolf. I am not romantically interested in Bobby Thompson."

"He is coming to have dinner with you tonight?"

She nodded.

"And you asked him to do this?"

"Yes," she admitted.

"Why?"

She chanced a quick glance up at him. "To thank him for helping me find my necklace."

He gave her a shrewd look. "A necklace that you placed very deliberately below the boards."

Did nothing escape this man's attention? She raised her chin, but said nothing.

"What do you do, Little Brave Woman?"

"Nothing," she insisted. "I am simply being neighborly."

"I think it is more than that. I think you are planning something."

"Do you? Then you are wrong."

"You lie, too, I think."

She tilted her head back at a more defiant angle, remaining otherwise silent and oblivious to the cunning gleam in his eye.

"Let me take care of this latest problem that we have with the lieutenant, Little Brave Woman," he said. "Go you about your duties as usual and leave the rest to me."

She struck a pose. "And never see you again?"

"*Aa*, so you are planning something."

She gazed at him from beneath the shadow of her lashes. "And if I were?"

"Do not do it. The lieutenant, the people who watch you, are dangerous. Do not do anything to bring grief upon yourself. Let me take care of this. You must learn to be patient."

"Why?" she countered, throwing back her head. "Why must I be patient? I am already like a prisoner in my own home."

He visibly flinched and became silent; noticeably and suddenly withdrawn. He dropped his hand from her and took a step away from her.

His withdrawal was so instantaneous, so unexpected that she reached forward as though to bring him back. She asked, "Is something the matter?"

"It is nothing," he said, "but you are right. You should go now. You must not be here long and draw attention to yourself or to your cellar."

She hesitated. He hadn't answered her question. She asked again, "Did I say something to offend you?"

He jerked his head swiftly to the left. "Words do not

hurt a person. If there was offense, it is my problem, not yours."

"Then what is it?"

He shook his head. "It is a bad thing when a man cannot mask his reactions from his wife. I have been too long gone from my people, I think, and like the white man, I begin to show my feelings so that all can see them. It is not a good thing."

"Moon Wolf, please . . ."

He hesitated, preoccupied. At length, he said, "I will tell you this once, but I must have your word that you will not show pity for me or for what I say, for I do not want it."

She nodded. What, for land sakes, had she said? She uttered, "I promise."

He inhaled deeply, then began, "Long before my grand-father's grandfather, my people roamed this land, free. Always my people have been independent in this, our homeland. We fought for our home, too, and many times we were successful, but our fighting was not enough. No matter the fights won, the white man's diseases came and took many of us away, too many of us, and we became weak, always weaker, when the white man became always stronger.

"And now," he continued, "look at what we have become. With the arrival of the white man, with his cattle and his treaties, our home has become a white man's prison, and we Indians the prisoners in it, though the bars are invisible, drawn on the maps of the white man's creation."

It was now her turn to remain silent.

He continued, "You sounded very much like my people when you said that you felt like a prisoner in your own home. I have heard those same words often, but from the lips of my people. And it made me fearful for a moment that our cause, yours and mine, might have the same outcome as that of my people."

Her heart wrenched for him, for those close to him, perhaps for the two of them, too. But what could she say? No mere words would heal these wounds. She said, "I . . . I'm sorry."

"There is no need to be. How could you have known? And it is not pity that I feel for my people. Never pity."

"But—"

"Pity is for the weak, for the old people and for the feeble. This I do not wish upon my people. For those I love, I would see them again strong and happy . . . free."

She nodded. "Yes, I understand."

"Know, too, that I do not intend you to be as a prisoner for long. I have a plan."

"Do you?" Her eyes grew wide, and she took a step forward. "What is it?"

"There is not the time to tell you now, for you must go soon. Know only that I have one. But before you go, you must tell me why it is that you flirted today with the storekeeper."

She gave him a shy glance. "I . . . I cannot. There is not the time and I must go, you know I must." She spun around.

He caught her. "You do remember that you are a married woman, do you not?"

"Am I?" she countered recklessly. "I don't believe our marriage has been consummated in the traditional sense. As you put it, I am still virginal, at least in body."

This was clearly not the response he had expected. "Do not play with me, Little Brave Woman, for as long as I live, you are my woman."

"I know," she said, "and I will not forget. I vow this to you. Now I must go."

"Humph," he said. "Do not forget tonight in all things that you do that you are my wife."

"I won't."

"I will be watching."

"But there is no need," she said in a rush.

"Humph," was again his quick response. "I think perhaps there might be."

"I have no more time to stand here arguing with you." She stepped around him to grab a couple of jars of jam. "Just you remember, if you do come tonight, that my bedroom is the second one on the left."

Moon Wolf chuckled, his only response to her suggestion, and before she could become consumed with embarrassment, she fled up the narrow cellar stairs.

Moon Wolf, crouching behind a bush, watched her from the shadows of the house where she stood near a window. He had easily stolen to this spot in the quiet of the night, once he had observed the posted sentry through a crack in the cellar doors. The hour had become late, and the lackey had at last grown tired. And, as the man had sat back for a nap, Moon Wolf had escaped.

Looking at her now, Moon Wolf knew a moment of pure panic. She was beautiful, so very beautiful. And she had invited another man to be with her tonight.

How could a man, who was any man at all, resist her? But worse, how could he ever attempt to hold on to such a person? She, with her exquisite taste in clothes and her white man's ways?

He had observed in the past that each time he saw her, she wore a different gown. He was not disappointed with that observation now. Her dress tonight looked as though it had been spun from the clouds, so fragile and vaporous was its material. With every step, she seemed to float, as though she were taking a walk amongst the clouds.

He chided himself. Women were such delicate creatures, having need of such things; for the frills and luxuries of life. Luxuries he could not supply, he reminded himself.

It was not a matter of whether she would stay with him despite his poverty. Her integrity had never been in question. No, the question was rather, If he lived, how could he make her happy without these things? Was such a deed possible?

Certainly she had denied that she needed beautiful things, but a man had to live by his own instinct, and he could not envision this charming creature being happy amongst his own people, living the simple life.

Nor could he be content within the confines of her society. His beliefs were such that, as it was in the old days, so it was still: only the weak or the men who had become too much like women desired material wealth.

"I have something to ask of you, Bobby." Moon Wolf stopped his line of reasoning to listen to her.

He could not hear Bobby's reply, but as though she were drawn to the man who crouched down in the shadows, Alys stepped closer to the window.

"I am in some trouble," she said, speaking to the man behind her, though she faced the window.

"I reckon I'd do most anything to help you, Miss Alys," the gentleman said. "What is it you need? Money? I've been in a good spell now for a while, and I reckon I could loan you whatever you need off the reel."

"It's not money I'd be needing, Bobby." She spun around to face him. "Do not be alarmed, but I fear it is you that I need . . ."

The young man actually jumped backward, so taken aback was he. Moon Wolf, himself, stood up, oblivious that he was now fully exposed.

"Let me explain," she went on, obviously not immune to Bobby's reaction. "I . . . I am having some trouble with a persistent suitor, and it is my desire to discourage him."

"Miss Alys, you had only to say so, and I—"

"It is not you that I am speaking of, Bobby. In truth, I am looking to you for my salvation."

Moon Wolf gritted his teeth.

"Why, Miss Alys," Bobby was saying, "you know I would do most anything for you, but—"

"I am hoping that you will. For you see, Bobby, it is my desire to become . . . engaged to you. . . ."

"Miss Alys!"

For a moment, Moon Wolf could not move. *"Engaged to you."* The words echoed over and over in Moon Wolf's ears. *"Engaged to you."*

She was already seeking one to take the place of her husband?

Moon Wolf didn't wait to hear more. Creeping away, not even bothering to determine if he were being watched, he stepped out of the shadows.

And so caught up was Alys in the success of her plan, she didn't hear the rustle of the bush outside the window, nor was she aware of the emotional explosion taking place under her very nose.

And when a skirmish took place between two men, one white, one Indian, outside her home, she remained unaware of it, at least for the moment.

Chapter 16

"**E**ngaged?" This time Bobby took three steps backwards. Three big steps. He twirled his hat in his hands. "Why, Miss Alys, th-this is unexpected . . . and I . . . I . . ."

"Not a real engagement, Bobby, only a betrothal to discourage this particular suitor. As soon as the suitor withdraws, you will be free, and I . . . I am willing to pay you for your trouble." Her voice held a note of hope.

Bobby's face, in the meantime, had become a bright shade of red. He said, "I . . . don't rightly think I could take money from you, Miss Alys."

"But I understand that I am putting you into an awkward situation and so I am willing to—"

"It's not that, Miss Alys. I'm willing to help you with most anything, but . . . and you don't need to feel obligated."

"But I would," Alys pressed her point. "I know this is an imposition."

"I . . . I . . . couldn't—"

212

"Is it because of your mother?"

"My mother?"

Alys nodded. "Yes, I know she might be upset, you being her only boy and all. But perhaps you could explain it to her and then she wouldn't—"

"It's not my mother." The hat in the little man's hands twirled even faster.

"Then—"

"Miss Alys, excuse me, but it's just that I don't think that I . . . I . . . that I'm . . . in love with you."

She sighed. "I know that." Her voice held a patience she was far from feeling. "That's why the engagement would not be a real one. It would only be something to discourage this—"

"But if I become engaged to you, then I'll never get her . . ."

Alys stopped absolutely still, as though suspended. She lifted her head, her chin jutting forward as she repeated, "Her?"

"Abigail Flint."

"Abigail Flint? The young girl in the store?"

Bobby nodded.

"You're in love with that girl?"

Bobby's eyes looked momentarily dreamy. "Ever since the first day she walked into my store. She's as pretty as a picture and as sweet as a drink of water on a hot day."

Alys spun around, away from Bobby, retracing her steps toward the window. She said, "But she's the daughter of one of the richest, most influential people in the territory, and she's only here for a few more months."

"I love her," Bobby reiterated, "and I couldn't think of marrying anyone but her."

"I see," Alys said slowly. "Then I guess I will have to help you to get her."

"And so you see I couldn't possibly think of entering

into an agreement which . . . wh-what was that, Miss Alys?"

Alys whipped around to face Bobby. "Then I will have to help you court her, won't I?"

"C-court her? Y-you would do that for me?"

Alys nodded. "Yes, I would, provided that you are willing to also help me with this unwanted suitor."

The man glanced over to his left, to his right, looking much like a cornered raccoon.

At last, however, he glanced at Alys, down at the floor, back at Alys. After some time he said, "Then I reckon we got ourselves a deal, Miss Alys." He moved forward, stealing slowly toward her until he at last grinned. "Or should I say partner?"

Alys smiled, accepting his handshake in the spirit in which it was given. She said, "Yes, Mister Bobby Thompson, I think we have ourselves a deal."

She stood at the French window of her bedroom, waiting for him. She knew he was out there.

Where was he? She had invited him here. What kept him?

She had donned her white nightdress. The light silk of the material was very thin, very scandalous, but it was the perfect complement for what might be her true "wedding night," if he ever decided to grant her an audience.

She needed to speak to him, to let him know her plans. Now that she had Bobby's agreement, she should explain the mock engagement to Moon Wolf before he found out about it from someone else—and without her reasons for doing it.

She faced outward as a warm wind whispered through the chiffon of the curtains, pushing back her hair, outlining her figure against the light touch of her gown. Still, she didn't move.

Something grazed a strand of her hair. She shook her head but didn't turn around, her attention outward, into the night.

A finger trailed over the nape of her neck.

Gasping, she spun around.

"Do not worry," came a familiar baritone voice. "It is your husband."

"Moon Wolf, you frightened me." One hand at her throat, the other on her heart, she stared at the man who was her husband, even though the shadows hid his figure. "How did you get in here? I had expected you to come, if you were coming, through the window."

"I did," he agreed. "But not by your window. Were you expecting someone else, perhaps?"

"Of course not," she replied at once. Now what had he meant by that?

He commented, "You stand here where others might see you and this thing you wear is very thin, I think. Do you try to entice someone else to you?"

She felt taken aback for a moment. What, for land sakes, was wrong with the man? "I am trying to entice no one but you, my husband."

"Humph," was his only reply, and Alys noticed for the first time that there was a difference about him this night. The space around him radiated with intensity, so much so that it felt as if it, the very atmosphere, were in motion.

No, she must be imagining it.

He said, "Perhaps I have been a fool to try to keep you virginal."

"Perhaps you have," she agreed unwittingly.

"Maybe you are not so maidenly after all."

"What?" She drew her head back from him so that she might gaze into his countenance. "What are you talking about?"

"Many days ago, by the creek, you played the seductress

well, perhaps too well, my wife. Why I did not notice this from the beginning, I do not know. You say it was your mother who taught you to do those things?"

"Of course, who else?"

He grinned, but it was not a gesture of humor. He repeated, "Who else, indeed." One arm wrapped around her waist, he pulled her forward, enfolding her against him and bringing his buffalo robe around her to keep her in place.

"Moon Wolf." She pushed against him. "Is something wrong?"

"What could be wrong, my wife?" He gathered her back into his arms, the scent of his robe, of his skin heavy upon her senses. She swam in the wonder of it. He continued, "You asked me to come to you tonight, I am here. Not even the guards posted outside your window could keep me from you."

She tilted her head, glancing at him suspiciously. "I don't know," she said, "but you are not acting quite like yourself."

"And how should a husband act toward his wife?"

"Please, Moon Wolf, what is the matter?"

"Nothing," he said, "only that I think it is time we consummated our marriage."

With those golden words, her doubts fled, and she practically beamed up at him. "Truly?"

He nodded. "Truly."

"No more hesitation? No more worrying about a child and what might happen to it?"

He shook his head gently. "No more."

"Oh, Moon Wolf." She flopped herself into his arms, surrendering. "Take me."

He complied easily enough and picked her up off her feet, drawing her toward the bed, while the moonbeams flooded in through the open window, outlining the white of her nightgown.

She remarked, "I have waited for this all my life."

"Have you?" He smiled at her, and in her own happiness, she failed to note the strained quality about him.

Her only response was to grin at him and pull him closer to her. "Moon Wolf, you will be gentle, won't you?"

"Always," he said, as he laid her none too tenderly on the bed, his fingers coming to the tie of her gown and the row of buttons under it.

His fingers quickly pulled the tie loose, though they stumbled over the buttons. Obviously frustrated, he pulled at the material until it gave under the pressure.

"Moon Wolf!" Her words might have scolded, but in her eyes lay pure invitation. She whispered to him, "Are you so anxious?"

"Always, my wife. I would see all of you."

She smiled at him. "And so you shall." Sitting up, she shrugged off the nightgown, leaving her body bathed in the pearly glow from the moon.

She heard his indrawn breath. "I do not think I will ever become used to the sight of you like this," he said. "Promise me that when we are together and alone, you will wear as little clothing as possible."

Drugged by the passion in his voice and immune to any danger, she agreed, "I promise."

"And you will not forget, not ever, that I am the man in your life. The only man."

"Never."

He flopped down next to her, losing the buffalo robe that had hid his own body from hers. She noted, in turn, that he wore very little beneath it—her father's pants, his moccasins, and the white shell necklace.

"Moon Wolf, please," she begged. "Love me. Do not hold back," she whispered.

"I will," he murmured, "I promise. I will love you until

the sun comes up to begin a new day and I promise you that you will be my wife in fact."

She drew her hands over his chest, down to his flat stomach, on downward, her gaze following where her hands led. Briefly she brought her glance back to stare up at him. "I love you," she said.

Her words seemed to be his undoing. He groaned and, pulling off his pants, settled himself on top of her. He muttered, "Remember me, Little Brave Woman, that is all I ask. Remember me to our children."

She smiled and pulled his body down closer to hers, ready for whatever he held in store for her. "How could I ever forget you? But I won't need to remember you to our children, for you see, you will be there, too."

With that said, she began to nibble on his neck. And lost to all but the wonder of him, she didn't hear his tortured reply . . . "But as what?"

She would remember him to their children, but as what . . . ?

His agonizing words hung heavy in the air, at least to his own ears. Even if he survived this time in his life, in what capacity did she envision him? As her husband?

And what of the replacement she encouraged?

He grimaced. He loved her; he'd come here tonight to consummate their marriage, not lovingly but in anger. But he had not been able to do it. Not when his heart was filled with her.

Her skin, beneath his embrace, felt like the softest of elkskin, her hair like the airy touch of a warm wind, the silken strands falling over his arm. The heightened scent of her urged him to love her deeply, forever, and her lips tasted sweeter than the ripest berries in spring.

No more holding back, he confirmed to himself. He would give her the full extent of his love, fulfilling the pleasure she had sought from him from the beginning. And the consequences? Need he think of them, when she already encouraged his successor?

He pressed kisses down her face, toward her neck, down further, over her breasts. He felt her response, too, gloried in the way her body arched into his.

Au, yes, he would give her great pleasure this night, and he hoped that she would never forget it, nor him. In truth, he would ensure that she would not.

Down further still, he kissed his way to her stomach, the tangy taste of her skin driving him slightly mad for more; more of her, more of what he knew lay nestled there between her legs.

She opened up for him readily, and he moaned, hungrily accepting the gift she offered him.

He tasted her once, twice, briefly lifting his head to say, *"Kitsikakomimmo."*

And somehow, though he knew she didn't understand, she must have gleaned the intention from his words, for she arched her back, opening to him even more.

He built her up then, taking her higher and higher, more than aware when she met her release, letting her drift slowly downward before he began the same ascent again. Over and over, not just once or twice, he brought her to the height of ecstasy, until he could no longer stand the pressure building within him, and, rising up onto his forearms, he lay over her, yet above her.

Gazing down into her eyes, he repeated again, *"Kitsikakomimmo."*

She reached up and touched his cheek. "I love you, too." Her words were soft, so very genuine, he could almost believe her . . . almost.

Aware of the direction of his thoughts, he asked, his voice husky with passion, "Are you ready for me?"

"I think so."

He would be considerate, he determined. This night might have brought him uncertainties about her, but there was no doubt within him now as to what he felt for her.

He loved her, and she, him. That was all that mattered. Not race, not prejudice, not culture, not even her past. They loved. It was that simple.

Slowly, yet with surety, he joined his body with hers, lingeringly, the warmth of her silken recess encompassing him as though he were being gradually wrapped in a co-coon. He felt the evidence of her maidenhood and knew a moment of surprise, since he had been certain, after what he had overheard tonight, of its lack.

He ceased that line of thought almost at once, however, and gloried in the discovery, then pushed upward.

She gasped, but he kissed away her protest and whispered, "It will hurt but a moment."

She nodded, her hands reaching down to cup his buttocks and push him, if possible, ever upward.

She asserted, "I would have all of you."

He groaned in response, and after some moments began to move with her. Still, he asked, "Does it hurt?"

"Very little."

"You must tell me."

He saw her grin. "I am fine."

Like honeyed nectar, the perfume of her engulfed him, the magic of her spirit inspired him, and soon he was driving within her, over and over, faster and faster, she keeping an even pace with him.

He heard her gentle groans, soft and high-pitched, the sound almost sending him over the edge. And as he drove within her, he felt the power between them building, building until she began to trip over the edge, her muscles contracting around him.

It was more than he could take and still remain immune. He let himself go all at once, spilling his seed within her, rejoicing in the sensation of being one with her, if only for a moment.

He floated for a moment, above his body, above hers, the essence of who and what she was staying with him as though neither one of them could afford to leave the other, not even in spirit.

And as her hands ran up and down his back, he uttered again, *"Kitsikakomimmo,"* and fell immediately into an exhausted sleep, his wife, his love, still wrapped firmly within his arms.

Chapter 17

◦～◦◯◦～◦

The tinkle of laughter, the clamor of feminine voices, and the clinking of teacups and saucers combined to fill the Clayton parlor. Two young women sat before her, dressed in the very best Dolly Varden walking suits, one adorned in a green foulard polonaise overskirt and the other in peach silk. Each young lady sat clutching a cup and saucer in their hands and gazed in rapt attention at Alys.

As she had expected, the announcement of her engagement to Bobby Thompson had become the talk of the town, thus allowing the rather limited social circle in Fort Benton to seek her out.

"Tell us, Alys." It was Emma speaking, the governor's daughter, the pretty blond who appeared to have very little on her mind except fashion and climbing the rather limited social ladder. "Tell us, what made you decide to marry Bobby?" She gave Alys a brief, forced smile, as though she were trying to veil some hidden intention. "Truth to tell," the young lady continued, "you two seem quite ill matched."

"Do you really think so?" Alys countered. She cast a swift glance at the other young lady, Abigail Flint, who sat directly to her right. The two young women, Abigail and Emma, had called upon Alys late in the afternoon, clearly more than a little curious about the announcement of her engagement.

Under more normal circumstances, Alys would never have sanctioned the two women in her own home, but things had changed. She had to remember Bobby, her commitment and her pledge to him. She said, "Then I suppose you have never heard about the royalty on Bobby's side of the family."

"Royalty?" Emma seemed to choke for a moment. "Surely you jest. If there were royalty in his family, do you think we wouldn't have heard of it before now?"

"Ah," Alys gave her challenger a conspirational wink. "That's just it. Bobby doesn't speak of it much because it's too painful. But truth is, his mother was a countess."

"A countess?"

"Emma, please, keep your voice down." This came from an elderly matron who had accompanied the two women.

Alys continued in a voice barely above a whisper, "Bobby doesn't wish to speak of it because his mother chose to marry a commoner. At the time, her family disowned her, and she and her husband sought to lose themselves here in the west. But that is all behind them now, the rest of the family is wanting to make it up to Bobby. Did you know that we have an invitation to Austria at the end of this month?"

"Austria." This came from the winsome Abigail. "I have always wanted to visit the Continent. You must be excited no end."

"Oh," said Alys, "I am." She straightened away from the back of her chair, delight etched in her eyes as she continued, "But that's not the only thing that makes Bobby such a handsome matrimonial match."

"No?" Emma, replied disbelief coloring her tone.

Alys sat forward, lowering her voice at the same time. "Have you ever been kissed by a man who really knows how to kiss?" Alys added a note of enchantment to her voice. "Have you ever been held by a man who you know will never desert you? Who you know will stand by you all your life?"

"You are not speaking of the same Bobby Thompson that we know, are you?" Emma said, Abigail remaining conspicuously quiet.

"That I am, ladies," said Alys. "That I am."

"Oh, my dear, I feel I must protest," Emma giggled slightly, fanning herself furiously with a free hand. "Kissing Bobby Thompson? Really, banish the thought."

"His kisses are divine," Alys improvised, "heavenly really, and he makes me feel like a princess."

"Bobby Thompson?" This from Abigail.

Alys nodded. "I feel like I walk on air whenever he is around me."

"Well," said Emma, "this is certainly a side of Bobby that none of the rest of us have ever seen."

"And thank goodness that you never have, otherwise I might have all of you as competition." She gave Abigail a brisk glance, repeating Emma's words. "Banish the thought."

Gunfire sounded from outside, causing all three women to jump.

"What was that?" Alys was the first one to speak, sitting up a little straighter and staring out the window.

"I don't know," said Emma, "but I'm certain it's not something I want to be a part of. You don't suppose it's that Wolf Shadow again. The man is becoming quite a menace."

Alys grew morosely silent. She rose, pacing toward the window, her guests forgotten for the moment.

She hoped it was nothing to do with the Wolf Shadow, although lately Moon Wolf and Makoyi had been taking too many chances—even challenging the soldiers during the daylight hours. What was wrong with the man?

If she didn't know him as well she did, she might be led to believe that he was trying to cause his own demise. What was more, she hadn't seen him or talked to him since that night in her bedroom almost a week ago.

It was practically more than she could stand. She dared not seek him out in the cellar; he did not come to her. It was a situation she would have to change, but how?

She voiced, almost to herself, "I certainly hope it is not the Wolf Shadow."

"Heaven forbid. As I said before, the man is a menace." Emma's cold voice penetrated Alys's meanderings.

Alys swung around to face her guests. "Do you think so? Do you really think the man is a menace?" she asked.

"What do you mean, Alys? Of course he is, destroying the merchandise on the bull trains. I would think, you being engaged to Bobby and all, that you would be more concerned about it."

Alys glanced back at the pretty blond. "Those shipments have nothing to do with Bobby. They originate with the government and go through the Indian agent. Trading with the Indians is not like it used to be in the old days when the Indians bartered directly with the general store. The government now controls what gets sent to them, what gets bought from them and anything else that pertains to them. Heaven only knows what would happen if the government agent were at all apathetic to their cause."

"My father says the Indians need to be exterminated from this land," Abigail asserted.

Alys sent the woman a sharp glance.

"That way," the young Abigail continued, apparently unaware of the onset of friction in the room, "civilized man can use the land for profit and for his own benefit. Why, my daddy says it's the only way this state will ever be admitted to the Union."

"Humph," replied Alys. "Thank goodness not everyone shares your father's opinion on that."

"What do you mean, Miss Alys?"

"I'm sorry, Abigail, but your father makes it sound like the Indians are nothing more than animals."

"What do you mean? They are little more than animals, aren't they?"

Alys gave Abigail a tolerant smile. "Hardly."

"Well," Emma volunteered, "I guess we will have to allow that you feel the way you do, seeing as how your mother always was a bit eccentric—"

"Please, do leave my mother out of this. It has nothing to do with her. No, it appears to me that we, as the newcomers here, are doing no more than stealing land from the Indians. But we don't seem to stop at that. Not only do we want the Indians' land, we seem to desire to change him into our own image."

"Really, Alys! How vulgar of you," Emma declared.

"It's easy to pretend the Indians are animals," Alys continued on as though Emma had not spoken. "It then makes it all right to commit all manner of evil upon them, doesn't it? It seems a harder, although a much more humane route, to admit that the Indians, too, are human, just like ourselves, and to try to find a solution that benefits both cultures."

Both women sat stunned. Alys could see it upon their faces.

Emma was the first to speak. "I think that perhaps your viewpoint is too radical for this town," She picked up her fan and straightened it out with a flick of her wrist. "And I do believe that if you persist in this outlook you might find yourself ostracized by the very best people."

Alys smiled. "Ah, the very best, you say?"

"I do."

Alys sighed. "Tell me, ladies. Will you risk taking a challenge?"

Both young women glanced at one another.

Alys carried on, "If you can catch him some night, look again at the figure of the Wolf Shadow, if you dare, that is. And when you do, then you will have to tell me true if you have ever seen a man or an animal as handsome or as well built as the man we call the Wolf Shadow."

Emma and Abigail exchanged a more wide-eyed gape, both ladies coming to sit up perhaps a little straighter than was necessary. Emma commented, "Why would you notice such a thing?"

Alys turned her back on her visitors, choosing to stare, instead, into the early evening. "Who wouldn't? In truth, young Emma, your comment makes me wonder about you."

"Whatever do you mean?"

"You do prefer the male gender, do you not?"

Her question was met by the loudest of gasps. "Why, I never."

"That's what worries me about you," came Alys's rejoinder.

As though her chair had suddenly been set afire, Emma jolted to her feet. Chin out, nose in the air, she commented, "I did not come here to be insulted."

"No, I suppose you expected to give out ridicule, not receive any."

"Really, I refuse to stay here one more instant and endure your—"

"Hush, Emma," Abigail commanded. "We are here as guests of Miss Alys and you have done little this evening but insult her. If you cannot keep a civil tongue in your mouth, then I suggest you leave here with all due haste." And while Emma clucked, young Abigail turned back toward her hostess. "Thank you so much for the tea and the chat. It has been enlightening seeing you and talking to you. I hope that you will excuse Emma's impudence and will not hold it against her. I, for one, will communicate your opinion to my father. It is certainly a fresh outlook."

Alys nodded toward her.

"I also hope that you will come and visit me soon where we can . . . talk some more of your trip to the Continent."

"Of course I will. Thank you for dropping by to see me." Alys inclined her head toward them. "Now, please, our maid will see you to the door."

And with that said, Alys turned her back on the two women and their chaperon, retracing her steps to the window, the click of the door signaling their departure.

Alys's thoughts immediately turned to Moon Wolf. Was he out there, she wondered, challenging the soldiers? And if he was, why was he doing it, fighting them in the light of day? What did he hope to accomplish with such recklessness?

But most of all, and where her thoughts really were leading, was simply this: why had he not sought her out this past week?

She thought back briefly to the night they had shared. It had been wonderful. It had been perfect. But, if she really thought about it, Moon Wolf had been acting strangely then, too.

Was something wrong?

Well, standing here at her window certainly accomplished nothing. She had best leave the house and go and determine what the commotion was all about. If it were the Wolf Shadow doing something, she would do what she could to help him.

This decided, she turned away and hurried toward the door.

Her stomach fell, her heart stopped for a moment, then it raced on, thumping wildly, as though it might never stop.

She gazed on at the fight as though in a dream.

What did he do? In one part of the fort, a fire blazed—the Bureau of Indian Affairs's storage building—while farther away another fire twisted through the army barracks. Soldiers and civilians alike tore from one part of the fort to another, weapons forgotten as each man and each woman made ready lines for water. Shortly, she heard the reverberation of shots fired from even farther away, from the stables. Soon frenzied horses raced through the streets.

Alys didn't see him. She couldn't find *Makoyi,* either. But she didn't need to; she knew the Wolf Shadow was responsible for this. He had become reckless this past week, starting skirmishes, battling the soldiers single-handedly.

Why? Why had he taken to fighting in the light of day? Did he not know that such a confrontation would be difficult to win? Especially since he could not fade into the shadows?

Her eyes scanned the horizon for a glimpse of him. Nothing out there until . . . There, off in the distance, barely discernable, raced a figure . . . a man with a wolf by his side. Up, up he climbed to the top of a mound, *Makoyi* by his side.

Briefly, *Makoyi* howled, and Moon Wolf cried out his war whoop before the two disappeared down the other side, their figures lost within a group of Indians that had appeared from out of nowhere. No shots followed their trail, the townsfolk remaining too busy putting out the fires.

An explosion ripped through the air as ammunition caught fire. Efforts to put out the blaze doubled. Lieutenant Warrington rushed past her, issuing orders.

Lieutenant Warrington? An idea suddenly flashed. Was it possible her home might not be so heavily guarded at the moment? Could she take this opportunity to steal into the caves?

She had to try. She had to speak with Moon Wolf and discover his plans. She had never seen him so reckless as he had been this past week. If he continued taking so many chances . . . she didn't want to finish the thought.

Turning away from the throng of people, she picked up her skirts and hurried back toward her home, fighting the crowd that pushed her in the opposite direction. It took a few minutes for her to free herself, a few more to ensure no one watched her, and then, lifting her skirts once more, she ran as quickly as she could toward the back of the fort.

Where was he?

She had been waiting for what seemed like hours. Was he still using the caverns?

She had expected him to be here when she arrived. But she had figured incorrectly.

She remained seated on the blankets of his bed, alone.

What was that? Some rocks hitting the cavern floor? Or was it Moon Wolf?

Footsteps sounded off in the distance, coming down the ladder.

She breathed out a sigh of relief, and, standing, rushed forward to meet him even before he'd had the opportunity to take more than a few steps.

"Ah," she began, unable to stem the flow of sarcasm in

her tone, "the great Wolf Shadow has fooled the soldiers yet again . . . this time."

His head came up with her words, but it was the only reaction she obtained from him. He barely acknowledged her presence, though his eyes scanned her form up and down.

She couldn't help feeling that he should have taken her in his arms right then. He should have kissed her until her fears evaporated. It was what she wanted, needed. He did neither, however, saying only, "You should not be here."

She raised her lantern that she might see his face better. She responded, "And you should not be fighting the soldiers during the day. What are you thinking?"

He ignored this last comment and made to move around her. She stepped in his way. "Please, Moon Wolf, tell me. What are you doing? Why are you starting to attack the fort during the daylight hours?"

"A real wife would not question the wisdom of her husband."

"What is that supposed to mean? A real wife? And I think I have every right to wonder and question you about your plans."

He didn't answer her, merely met her questions with a quick jerk of his head before he made to move around her again. This time she stepped aside.

Luckily *Makoyi* did not share his master's curtness. Whining, he came to stand before her. Coming up onto his hind legs, he pressed his paws onto her shoulders, his nose in her face. She laughed and petted the creature. "I'm glad to see that someone here is happy to see me." She darted a quick look at Moon Wolf, accepting *Makoyi*'s wet kisses at the same time.

Moon Wolf hardly spared a glance for the two of them before calling to his pet.

Makoyi obeyed his master, coming down on all fours, and trotted off.

She pressed on. "Where have you been this past week? Why have you not come to see me? And why are you attacking the soldiers in the light of day?"

He had taken off his headdress to place it beside his bed. Next he started to remove the black paint from his face. He didn't answer her, seemingly intent on ignoring her.

She glanced over his body, noting blood on his legs and arms. She asked, "Are you hurt?"

Another shrug. "Some scratches, perhaps. It is nothing. I will go and wash them and they will be fine."

"Still I would have you sit before me that I might see them for myself."

He didn't appear to object to this, but she approached him with a good deal of hesitation.

She touched his arm above a minor cut. He jerked in reaction and shivered, as though her touch had set off a minor explosion within him. She glanced up at him quickly to catch his look, but found that he had already masked whatever he had been feeling.

She cleared her throat nervously and began, "I have become worried about you and I would speak to you about it. But you have not visited me so that I could tell you all that I feel."

"Humph."

She gulped. He could make this easier for her.

She volunteered, "I have missed you and have looked for you every night. Why have you not come to me?"

Again, that jerk of his head, a gesture that had to be a purely Native American display. Still, he didn't speak.

She touched a cut on his leg, watching that limb twist out of her reach. She raised her eyes to his, uttering, "I do not think you are as immune to me as you would like me to believe."

He said, "Perhaps I am not. But one cannot always control the urges of the body."

Reeling from the curt comment, she drew back from him. What, for the love of God, was wrong with the man? He practically gushed antagonism . . . for her.

She tried again. "Are you not going to share your plans with me? Would you have me worry?"

He drew back from her and came up onto his feet. She took note that he was indeed not as invulnerable as he might like her to believe. He said, "I cannot sit here and talk with you now. I must go to the falls and wash these wounds."

"I could bring you some warm water and do it for you."

"You could not. You might have come here without incident this once, for there is great commotion within the seizer's fort, but it cannot be repeated. You must leave now."

"I will not."

She watched his body become tense. It was the only indication of his reaction. He said, "I will not have you followed here."

"I do not believe that I was seen coming here."

"Still I cannot take the chance. You must go."

"I will not leave here until I talk to you. This might be the only chance I have to do so. I will not let it pass."

He didn't argue the point with her, stating only, "Then you will have to wait for me to return from the falls."

"Why?" she asked at once. "I will go there with you."

"You will not." He frowned at her. "If you wish to discuss something with me, you must wait for me here. I will not speak to you at the falls, I promise you this."

"But—"

She didn't finish. He had already turned away from her,

was already sauntering down the tunnel that would lead him to the waterfall, the tension about him clearly stating that he would brook no argument.

And she didn't need his "Do not follow me" to remind her that he did not wish to speak with her.

As his figure dimmed to a silhouette, she let out her breath and prepared herself for a long wait. It appeared she had little choice.

Chapter 18

⁓᭙᭠᭙⁓

He never returned. Darn the man.

She should have followed him to the falls despite his protest. She should have demanded the audience he seemed so reluctant to give her.

She made her way to the end of the tunnel now, but she knew he would not be there. He clearly did not wish to speak to her, was all too obviously avoiding her.

Why? What had she done?

She arrived at the falls in time to witness the rise of the full, orange moon in the eastern sky and spared a few moments to admire it. Too soon, she shivered under the cool spray from the water.

"What is wrong?" she asked of no one in particular, perhaps of the moon. Something was. Something was desperately wrong. But what?

And what did Moon Wolf plan next? His schemes no longer seemed to center around the supply wagons, but rather upon a war of hit-and-run with the soldiers, a dangerous game. One hard to outwit.

What could she do but sit and watch . . . and hope . . .

Darn the man. What was wrong with him?

Disgusted with herself for caring so much, yet more displeased with him for refusing to communicate, she made her way back through the tunnels, back toward his bed; back to where he had left his headdress. Coming down onto the floor, she picked up the figure-head and fingered the piece absentmindedly.

"The Wolf Shadow," she whispered to herself, "alone defying the United States cavalry. Alone . . ."

Or perhaps not.

An idea came to her. A wickedly, wonderful idea.

She only needed to talk to a few people, gather together a few things, and she could perhaps put a plan into action. Hopefully a plan that would ensure the safety of her man.

Hopefully . . .

Two days later three prairie schooners sat conspicuously within the fort, due to leave soon, the wagons filled to overflowing with whiskey. Guards were posted around the wagons; some lay hidden within the shadows, while others were staked out on the roofs. Clearly, all were expecting a visit from the Wolf Shadow. The situation looked to be more of a trap than any attempt at shipping.

What could she do?

Moon Wolf would not rest until he had stopped the shipment. It would be perfect for him, since he seemed intent to risk his very life.

But tonight he would have help, aid in the form of an ally he would not expect.

She, too, waited in the shadows.

She had escaped her own home, noting that the guards posted around her house seldom bothered to watch her closely. More intent upon their card games than on keeping vigil, the guards allowed her a fair amount of freedom.

Perhaps, though, they were relaxed as a result of her recently announced engagement; perhaps, too, there had proved to be little for them to see.

Whatever the cause, she had easily escaped their notice.

Now she waited, perched like the soldiers in the shadows, but with a different purpose from those men Moon Wolf called the seizers.

The hour became late and she yawned, pinching herself and fluttering her eyes to keep them open. She must keep alert; she would not fail her man.

It was close to daybreak, in the darkness before dawn, when she rocked herself awake. She had sensed something. Was it the Wolf Shadow?

She glanced around her yet saw nothing. But it was dark, much too dark. Then, *swish,* the sound of an arrow whizzed through the early morning air.

One wagon went up in flames, the next, and finally the third. But no one scuffled to put out the flames. Instead, lanterns in hand, the soldiers raced toward the place where the arrows had originated.

Alys followed.

"There he goes!" someone shouted. "Do ya see 'im?"

"Shoot 'im!"

A shot followed. Then a wail of pain.

"What the blazes? You idiot! You've hit one of us!"

"Sorry Cap'n."

Alys sunk back into the shadows.

"Dad blame it, you're the sorriest excuse for a . . ."

Alys didn't wait to hear more. Men were already gaining on the Wolf Shadow.

She had no time to lose. Gulping back her fear, she climbed to the top of a building, a wolf headdress, which she had sewn together, sitting atop her head, though her figure, beneath her borrowed dress, loomed obviously female.

She screamed at the top of her lungs, "Here I am, you oafs! See if you can catch me!" And she clamored over the side of the building.

"What the . . . who was that?" It was a soldier speaking.

"Don't know," came the reply. "Looked female. First time I've ever 'eard 'im speak. Is the Shadow female?"

"Follow her!"

"Yes, Cap'n."

"And if you find her, shoot her!"

"You 'eard the Cap'n! Find her and shoot her!"

Alys plunged into the shadows, cautioning herself to remain steady. She had planned every detail in advance.

She tore off the headdress, revealing her nightcap. Next the buckskin dress, up and over her head, leaving her standing in her linen nightdress. Then off with the moccasins, uncovering her own silken slippers. She folded the extra items hurriedly—even the headdress, which she had made out of nothing but fur—and stuck them into a pouch beneath her dress.

Then as casually as possible she stepped away from the shadows and into the crowd of people, which had all gathered in the town's center. Not the least out of place, since all stood in their nightclothes, she joined in with the talk.

"What was that?" she asked someone next to her. "Did you say the Wolf Shadow was female?"

"'Pears so."

"No, it's someone else who's come to help him," came another reply. "Couldn't be no female."

"And why not?" she asked, feigning surprise. "Seems to me a woman could do just as good a job as a man. Did anyone catch the Wolf Shadow this time?"

"Catch him? Can't rightly figure out who the Wolf Shadow is now."

Alys smiled. And no one paid her any attention when she gradually drifted off toward her home, pleased as pudding with herself. She had successfully diverted the soldiers away from the real Wolf Shadow.

Now all she had to do was anticipate all his moves.

She grinned to herself. If it all went as easily as this, it should be a piece of cake.

Of course she hadn't reckoned on Wolf Shadow discovering her surprise so soon, nor had she anticipated his reaction to it. Or perhaps, in the back of her mind, she had—had counted on it all along.

Whatever the reason, she now had his undivided attention.

He had crept into her room, had been waiting for her when she returned just as the first rays of sun had stolen across the eastern sky.

At first he hadn't said a word and, believing herself to be alone, Alys had begun to unpack her pouch.

"*Aa*, yes," he said from a darkened corner of her room, "so the Wolf Shadow is, indeed, a woman."

She spun around toward his voice. "Moon Wolf!"

Still, he remained in the darkness. "Did you not promise me that you would not impersonate me again?"

"I did not."

"Humph! I thought you a better person than to lie."

"I am not lying. I did not impersonate you. I went as myself—a woman—just as you asked me to do."

She heard him draw a deep breath. "But as a female Wolf Shadow, I believe. Do not bother to deny it, I have already heard the stories."

She grinned inanely. "Then I won't deny it. But, please, try to remember, I did not promise you that I wouldn't try to help you again, only that I would go as myself if I did so, as a woman. I did that."

He stepped forward. "Why?" he asked. "Why did you

try to draw the gunfire to yourself? You could have been killed."

"But I wasn't." She hesitated, her face flushed, though the darkness thankfully hid it. At last, she countered, "Why are you?"

"Why am I what? Why am I trying to keep the bull trains away from my people? I thought we had been all through that."

"No, that is not what I mean and you know it." She took a step toward him. "Why are you taking such reckless chances?"

"This was no reckless chance tonight—on my part. I escaped easily, as you can see."

"I disagree. I saw many men chasing you and practically catching you. I became a diversion in order that you escape."

"I do not need your help, nor do I want it. You will not do it again."

"Try to stop me."

"You would defy your husband?"

"I would defy the man who calls himself my husband, yet who refuses to talk to me or even to visit me at night, when he is supposed to be performing his husbandly duties."

"*Aa,* so that is it. You are upset that I am not keeping you satisfied?"

She folded her arms over her chest and turned her back on him. Soft footsteps shuffled up close behind her, and she offered, over her shoulder, "You make it sound like a crime."

"Perhaps it is."

"What are you talking about? We are married."

"Are you?" came his instant argument. "I know that I am. I am not so certain about you."

She reeled under the insult. "How can you say such a thing?"

"Very easily, I think." A finger trailed along the sensitive skin at her nape.

She closed her eyes, letting the sweetness of his touch wash over her. Oh, how she had longed for this.

She spun around, coming instantly into his arms. "Hold me, Moon Wolf," she pleaded. "Just hold me."

His arms tightened around her. "I am."

"Moon Wolf, have you not missed me?"

He groaned, nestling his face in her hair. "Every day."

"Then why," she asked, whispering to him, "why haven't you come to me?"

"And spoil your plans? I would not do that."

"Spoil my . . . what are you talking about?"

"It does not matter. I understand why you do what you do, and I must admit that I approve."

She was lost. "What?"

"But we leave the point, which is your recklessness tonight."

"I was not reckless," she protested. She was more than aware that he tried to divert her attention, yet she felt unable to stop him. She elaborated, "I planned every detail. And I was successful."

"You will not do it again."

She looked up steadily into his eyes. "Moon Wolf, hear me well. I will continue to do it as long as you risk your life so dangerously."

He kept her gaze for several moments before at last, he sighed. "Arguing with you," he admitted, "is like talking to the wind. One only gets back the same question he puts to it. I already have a companion to help me. His name is *Makoyi* and he is my constant friend. I do not need your interference."

"Nevertheless," she held her ground, "you have it."

He let his hands drop from around her, while a raw, primitive groan escaped his throat. "You would do this no matter that I forbid it?"

His voice was hard, unemotional, carrying none of the frustration she witnessed in his countenance. He looked away from her, toward the corner of the room, before he turned observant eyes back to her.

She swallowed noisily, saying, "I will help you so long as you take the chances you have been taking."

He took a step back. "Then I would have you know what you are doing."

She nodded, however, as though slow in comprehension, she asked, "I beg your pardon?"

He didn't answer. He asked, instead, "Do you know how to use a gun?"

She nodded.

"Have you ever shot one?"

Another nod.

"And do you know how to hide so another cannot find you? How to master a horse?"

"I . . . I think so."

He grunted. "It is not a matter of thinking. You either can do these things or you cannot. And if you cannot, they can be learned."

Her eyes widened. "Oh," was all she admitted.

He turned toward her window. "You will come to the caverns today where I will begin the task of teaching you."

"But the guards, how will I—"

"They no longer watch you during the day, only in the evening."

"Oh," she said. "I didn't know. I thought that . . . how long have you known this?"

"For the past few days."

"And still you did not come to me?"

"I told you. I will not spoil your plans."

"What plans?"

He didn't answer, merely shrugged. "You will come to the caves when the sun is high in the sky. We will begin then." And with this said, he put a leg outside the window and jumped to the ground, as quick as that. Alys stood still. What in the dickens was wrong with the man?

Well, she would soon discover it. She would meet him at noon and she would not leave until she'd had a long talk with him.

She promised this to herself.

Chapter 19

⟨✦⟩

Was it possible that he had heard of her engagement? It might explain his odd behavior and his insistence on taking such daring chances this past week. Still, he couldn't believe that she, his wife, would tie herself to another man.

Or could he?

She'd not had the chance to explain her actions to him. And even if she had, wasn't it possible that he still might think the worst? Wasn't it why she hadn't told him her plans in the beginning?

Still, if he had already heard of it . . .

She needed to talk to Moon Wolf.

And so it was with great purpose that she stole into the caves at noon, intent upon having a private conversation with her husband. But he was nowhere to be found.

She cut a glance to the ceiling and sighed. She supposed he had already gone to the waterfall. Well, make no mistake, she would find him and get this squared away, no matter the consequences.

* * *

"Do you know how to handle an arrow?"

These, his first words to her, did not encourage her. She gave him a hesitant glance, saying, "I don't think so, but there is something I would—"

"Come you here, then, and I will teach you."

They stood outside, in an open meadow, downhill and to the right of the falls. Staked out in front of her were sticks standing straight up in the ground. And before her stood her husband, a hoop in his hand, the wind blowing back his hair.

She took the few steps necessary to close the distance between them, as Moon Wolf tossed her an arrow at the same time.

He continued, "This is the hoop and long arrow game."

"Oh." The wind caught her hair and the side of her dress, and she reached down to keep her skirts from blowing.

He pretended to take no notice, however, and went on to explain, "The game comes to us from the Kit Fox society, which is part of the All Comrades society. It is usually played by boys too young to travel or hunt with the men."

"Wonderful, but I—"

"Come," he pointed to a place next to him. "Stand here and I will show you how it is done."

She went. "But Moon Wolf," she protested, "I would have a few words with you first."

He gave her a scowl. "If you plan to go on raids with me, then I must first ensure that you can protect yourself."

"But I—"

"Later we will talk. Now, I want you to hold on to this arrow. Look you here at the wood. It is made from choke cherry and at this end is a deer antler which I have made into a point. If you choose to, you can decorate the other end of this in any fashion that you might desire. For now I have put a feather on it."

"Moon Wolf," she said, grasping hold of the arrow, but not giving it so much as a quick glimpse. "Moon Wolf, first I need to talk to you about a plan that I had devised to—"

"Are you to learn these skills or not?" he interrupted her. "If you do not master these, I cannot allow you to go on the raids, no matter your temperament or your arguments with me. If I must, I will tie you to your bed each and every time I go on a raid."

"Fine, I will do what you want," she said, "but I would talk to you first, before we start."

He came up to her then, taking the few steps necessary to place a hand on her shoulders. That the simple gesture sent a feeling of excitement racing over her skin she chose to ignore, at least for the moment.

He said, "I promise you that we will talk, but I would ask that you save whatever it is until after we have practiced. Can you agree to that?"

Put that way, how could she refuse? She nodded. "All right, then. But you must promise me that you will not leave me until we have had a chance to talk."

"I give you my word."

She squared her shoulders. "All right. What do I have to do?"

He held up a round hoop in front of her face. It was made of willow sticks pulled into a ring and wrapped in a hide. Colored beads decorated the inside of the thing. He said, "I am going to throw this hoop out in front of you, close at first, but then farther and farther away, and it is your duty to throw that arrow into the hoop."

"Oh, I see."

"Once you have mastered this skill, we will go on to the next. Are you ready?"

She nodded, and he rolled the hoop in front of her.

She tossed the arrow, missing the hoop by at least a foot.

"Try again," he encouraged, collecting up the hoop and rolling it again in front of her.

Once more, she missed it.

Again, he rolled the hoop, over and over. She never made the target, not even once.

Observing her, he said, "I think it is the way you are throwing the arrow. Have you never been taught how to throw?"

"I've not had a reason to learn," she said.

He came up beside her on the left. "Here, watch me." He reached over her to take the arrow, his fingers brushing against her hand and her stomach at the same time. A shock of raw feeling burst through her with the simple gesture, but she remained silent, merely changing her stance in reaction. He continued, "This is a long arrow, much like a lance, and must be thrown from over the shoulder. Notice how the hand holds the arrow cocked until the last moment, and then the wrist is flicked. Do you see?" He demonstrated.

She nodded. "I think so. Let me try it again."

He let go of the arrow, his arm brushing against her stomach, and almost, but not quite, touching her breasts.

Still, she pretended immunity. She put the arrow up over her shoulder, giving him a swift look at the same time. "Are you going to roll the hoop?"

"I think that we will first learn how to throw the arrow."

"Do you think I will need this skill, when I have a gun that I will be using instead of the arrow?"

"It will not be a waste. Learning how to throw correctly will serve you well, I think. Besides, we cannot practice with a gun, for I do not wish the noise to draw others to us. It is the eye we are training, for the object of the game is to throw the arrow through the hoop. It is a skill you can use with a gun, too, for it teaches you to hit a moving target."

She gave him a brief nod. "Okay, if you say so. Here we go." She threw the arrow, imitating him as best she could.

"That was better," he said, retrieving the arrow for her. "Try again."

Over and over she practiced, though still without much success.

He came up to her. "Watch for a moment." He took the arrow from her. "The arm needs to go back over the shoulder farther." He demonstrated once before handing over the arrow to her.

She took it from him, poised the arrow over her shoulder, and practically melted into the ground when his arms came around her, his right arm holding hers, imitating the correct motion. His body was close to hers, too close, and she felt herself wanting to merge her body with his.

She let him take her arm through the correct movements, all the while snuggling in as close as possible to him, the evidence of his masculinity, though unaroused, pushing into her side. Timidly, she stole a glance up at him.

He glared back at her, his look tolerant, not in the least erotic, although there was a huskiness in his voice when he asked, "Do you think you have it yet?"

He took a step back.

Now, truth was, she might have had the action down perfectly. But, even if she had, she wouldn't have admitted it.

She sent him a look of what she hoped was innocence, saying, "I'm not certain yet. Could you show me again?" She placed the arrow above her shoulder, and he stepped in toward her, though he sent her a knowing look, one that might have said he wasn't fooled by her in the least.

However, he didn't protest. "Hold it this way." He took the necessary step to put his arm around her. He held her arm captive. "At the last minute," he said, "flick your wrist thusly." He had her release the arrow. "Do you see?" This last was whispered into her ear so huskily, that she actually moaned. Momentarily, she glanced up at him, making a mental note that his eye had not followed the arrow's progress in the least.

She turned in his embrace. "Moon Wolf," she said, "I have something to say to you."

"I know." His lips came to her neck, where he began to nibble.

She threw back her head that he might have better access. "Moon Wolf," she murmured, "I have missed you."

"I know," he uttered again between kisses.

And while she had his attention, she added, "There is no one but you. Surely you must know that. Is your impatience with me because you have somehow heard of my engagement?"

"I have not been impatient with you."

"I think that you have, almost to the point of antagonism. Is it that you have heard of the engagement?" She put the question to him again.

"It is not important," he said, though his body stiffened beneath her touch.

Still, she felt heartened. He had exhibited no surprise at her crude delivery of the truth. He must have received word of it. That would explain much.

"No," she agreed with him after only a moment's hesitation, "it is not important. The engagement is a sham. It is not real. I only did it in order to discourage the lieutenant. Bobby Thompson is in love with another, and I am helping him to get the woman of his dreams. It is how I am returning his favor to me. There is no more to it than that."

"Humph!" was Moon Wolf's only response, though he had resumed caressing her, bending to her neck as though she were a flower and he, a bee.

"You do believe me, do you not?"

"Why would I not?" His fingers touched the base of her neck, there massaging while he leaned back from her slightly. He raised an eyebrow. "If this was all there was to it, why did you not take me into your confidence or seek to enlighten me in some way?"

"There has not been time. I could not come to the caves and you did not come to me."

His fingers toyed with the braid in her hair, reaching up to take the pins from it and let the length of it fall into his hands. He gazed steadily into her eyes. "I think," he said, "that there was a night we spent together when you could have told me."

She turned her face away from him. It was true. She could have confessed then. But she hadn't. She said, "I was afraid to. I was certain you would not approve."

"I would not."

"I did not want to be a prisoner in my own home. Nor did I wish to wait to see you. And I did not want you ordering me not to do what I thought was best."

"I would have listened to you, patiently, like I am now."

"And then told me to stop what I had already set into motion."

He blinked. It was the only hint of emotion on his countenance. He said, "Yet you did not come to me once the plans were set. This you could have done."

"I could not. You forbid me to come to the caves."

He sighed, saying after a moment, "Perhaps you are right. Still, I cannot help but think that you might have sent word to me somehow. You must have known that I would discover this."

"I never thought that you would. You are so disconnected from the fort's society."

"And yet I saw a man coming and going from your house freely. What did you think I would do?"

"I didn't think. And I guess I was a little afraid to tell you."

He nodded. "So I understand."

"And now? What will you do with me now?"

"I think that I will ensure that you know how to throw this arrow through the hoop." He withdrew his embrace from her and picked up the hoop.

Darn! He was so hard to read. What was he thinking? He hadn't smiled at her, hadn't raised his voice, hadn't even voiced much disagreement.

She trembled and asked, "Are you wishing you hadn't married me?"

He didn't look at her as he admitted, "I have had much time this week in which to ponder the facts of our marriage, and it came to me that you are not truly married to me, I think."

She gasped.

He must have heard it, too, for he gave her a swift glance, though he looked quickly away. "Do not believe," he said, "that this makes my commitment to you any less. It is only that we do not have this certificate from your culture that is needed to make you fully mine within the eyes of your own people."

"But I could care less about such a thing."

He raised a hand as if to ask her permission to continue. "So," he said, "I have come to understand that in my society, we are husband and wife. In yours, we have only a short liaison, I fear."

She snorted. "It doesn't matter if we are married by the customs of my society or not. We are joined together by our hearts, aren't we?"

She looked to him for confirmation. She received none.

She tried again, "It is the only thing that matters, isn't it, that we love one another?"

He raised one eyebrow, saying only, "Is it?"

She didn't answer, the quick flash of her eyes, her defense.

He stepped toward her. "It changes nothing from me to you, but it could leave you free, if you desire it."

She, too, stepped forward. "But I don't desire it."

"I would admit that I am glad to hear that the engagement is not real. I had begun to think that you might be one of those women who cannot live without several men."

Her eyes widened.

"I am glad to discover that you are not. For, even thinking it might be true, it made no difference in my feelings for you."

She took another delicate step forward. "Didn't it?"

"*Saa,* no, it did not."

"And now?"

He grinned, the first smile she had seen from him in a very long time. He said, "I think we might never finish this game." He came up beside her. "Come you here now and let us try to finish." His arms came around her, to her throwing arm. "Do you see that stick in the ground there, the one with the feathers on top of it?"

She nodded, sending him a shy smile.

"This is a game our youngsters play called make the stick jump. If you are able to hit the stick, it will jump. Here, try it and see."

She threw the arrow, his skill and brawn guiding her small lance. Sure enough, she hit the stick, making it jump out of the ground.

"I did it." She grinned up at him.

He returned the gesture, smiling at her, only this time, when he looked at her, she found admiration, perhaps even understanding, in his glance. He said, "Yes, you did. I think this lesson is over for the day." His fingers had already gone to the buttons at the front of her dress. He commented, "You wear many clothes."

"It is the custom. This dress is actually a very simple calico."

"Still, it, like many of your others, is very hard to remove."

"Perhaps," she suggested, "that is its purpose."

"Perhaps," he agreed before he bent his head to hers.

His lips touched hers gently at first, barely an impression at all.

But the prairie wind blew at them, imprinting his body on hers, as though the breeze conspired along with him to provide an excuse to bring his head down even further.

"You are so beautiful," he muttered before his lips closed over hers yet again. "Tell me, does he kiss you like this?"

"Who?"

"Your intended."

"He doesn't kiss me at all."

Moon Wolf ignored her, running his fingers over her cheek. "Aa, so if he does not kiss you, does he touch you like this?"

She groaned. "You know very well that he does not."

"I do not know anything that happens when he is with you. You must tell me."

"I told you, the engagement is a sham."

"Aa, yes, so I understand. If he does not kiss you and does not touch you, does he pull you close to him, like this?"

"Moon Wolf, cease this. You know well that he does none of these things. Do you purposely tease me?"

"Me?" he asked, none too innocently. "Why would I try

to tease you with thoughts of another man . . . the man you are to marry—"

"Stop it, Moon Wolf, you know now that it is not a real engagement."

"Do I? I think I must make certain of it. You are the one who became engaged. I only try to figure out how this man won your heart."

She stole a quick glimpse of him, meeting the delightful sparkle in his eye. She asked, "Won my heart? You know darned well that my heart belongs only to you."

"Do I? I am not so certain. Perhaps I had better make sure of it by kissing you here." His lips found a vulnerable spot on her neck. "Or maybe here." He kissed her eyes. "Or perhaps you like to be kissed like this." His lips touched hers lightly, softly, but only for a moment before he deepened the embrace, his tongue invading her mouth, one time, again.

She moaned in response, the sound lost to the breeze. But he obviously heard her, for he groaned, too, their sighs mingling together and becoming a part of the music of the wind, the birds, the thunder of the falls. And as his tongue swept again into her mouth, she felt herself transported.

The wind wrapped around them, throwing them into a tight embrace, and they fell to their knees before one another.

"*Kitsikakomimmo,*" he murmured to her, while with his hands he undressed her. "I would see all of you again."

"Yes," she answered, stripping the material of the dress to her waist, the top of her petticoat and chemise following in their turn.

"Do I dare ask if he touched you like this?"

"Moon Wolf, you know that he—" She didn't finish. She couldn't. One of his hands had come up to her breasts, the other stroked her cheek while his gaze adored her.

Downward his fingers caressed, over her neck, making a silken path to her stomach.

"Moon Wolf," she thought to whisper, "we are in an open meadow. Should we not seek shelter?"

"There is no danger here. I have seen neither red nor white man here on this mountain. We are safe, I think."

"But to make love in the open, where we could be seen?"

"By the Above Ones? I would have all of creation, whether god or creature, know that you are mine, that we love. There is nothing to be ashamed of, and no one, save ourselves, is here, I promise you."

With such a declaration, her heart leapt into her throat.

She pulled at his shirt, and he shrugged out of it with ease. "At least," she said, "both of us are now bare to the waist."

"But you will soon be naked all over," he promised, his hands moving smoothly down the length of her back to the buttons of her dress and petticoat.

"As will you be, too," she said, bending her head to run a delicate tongue over his male nipples.

He drew in his breath.

"Do you like that?"

He merely nodded. The wind whipped her hair back from her face, while it blew his forward, the touch of those strands on her cheek like that of a caress. She said, "I love you, Moon Wolf. I think I have done so from the day I first saw you. Even my time in the east did not diminish my feelings for you."

"Yet I have nothing to offer you, not land, not security, not even a family life."

Her hands were at his chest, massaging him, while his fingers released the buttons at her back.

She asked, "Does that bother you?"

"It is one thing to love you, to make love to you, this I

can do, I will do. It is another task to find a place where we can live our lives in happiness."

"I know, but—"

"It does not make me love you less." He slid the dress off her hips, complete with her petticoat and chemise, down to her knees. He said, "You will have to step out of it."

"Yes," she said and arose, no sooner kicking the dress away than he pulled her back to him, his face on her stomach, his hands lightly touching her most private areas.

She arched her back, letting the breeze whisper over her skin and ruffle her hair. Maybe there was no place for them, maybe what they attempted was impossible. Still, they would have this moment. And neither the wind, the land, nor the forces of nature bore a harsh word for them this day.

Perhaps that's where they belonged: to the land, to each other, in love.

And as he gradually drew her down to him, settling her over him, she knew their life would be together, no matter the prejudice, no matter the trials they might have to endure. Living without one another would hold no happiness.

They had to find some place, some sanctuary where no one would judge them, or their children.

It was out there. She knew it.

But where?

Chapter 20

> "Seizer Chief, come give me a drink.
> Seizer Chief, come give me a drink.
> Hey, hey, hey.
> Bear Chief, your children are crying.
> Bear Chief, your children are crying.
> Hey, hey, hey.
> Young warriors, they are all of them drunk.
> Young warriors, they are all of them—"

"What in tarnation?" Lieutenant Warrington interrupted the song and emerged from his home, taking up a quick stance outside. He looked up toward the roof, the dim starlight silhouetting the darkened figure of a man. "What are you doing up there, you drunken varmint, singing on my roof in the middle of the night?"

Moon Wolf let his robe fall from around his head, answering slowly, "Comes this one here to give you infor mation on the villain Wolf Shadow. Have heap big knowledge."

257

Lieutenant Warrington shook his head. "Can't it wait until morning?"

"Look around you, Lou-ten-tent. Morning has already come."

"Of all the dad-blamed, stupid . . . it's pitch black out here, you no-account scalawag. Go away." The lieutenant started walking back into the house. "And shut up."

"Seizer Chief, come give me a drink, hey, hey, hey. Seizer Chief, give me a drink, I will tell you what I know."

The lieutenant rushed back out. "Shut up, I said." A pistol shot split through the air, the bullet barely missing Moon Wolf.

Moon Wolf didn't budge, didn't even jump. Without raising his voice, he observed, "If you shoot me, then you will never learn what I know."

"Maybe I don't care. Maybe it's been so long since you've given me useful information that I doubt you have any now."

Moon Wolf ignored him, singing again, *"Seizer Chief gives me whiskey. Seizer Chief gives me drink, hey, hey, hey."*

"Damned savages!" The lieutenant stomped back into his house, still muttering, yet he returned within minutes, none too patiently. This time he carried a rifle. Undiplomatically, he demanded, "What do you know about the Wolf Shadow?"

Moon Wolf didn't respond, except to continue singing, *"Come, Seizer Chief, give me more whiskey. Come, Seizer Chief, quiet your enemies."*

"Tell me, you drunken idiot or I'll fill you full of—"

"Perhaps the Seizer Chief will take pity on this one and give him more whiskey that he better spend the rest of the night. Then, after a good sleep, this one might tell the Seizer Chief where this menace, the Wolf Shadow, comes from."

"You have discovered his hiding place after all this time?"

"Maybe. Maybe not."

"Ah, I don't believe you. You're crazier than a loon."

Moon Wolf shrugged and, after a moment, broke out again in song. *"Come, Seizer Chief, come give me more whiskey. My ancestors await. Come, Seizer Chief, come give me more whiskey."*

"Shut up."

"When Sun rises, this one will quit."

"Shut up now." The lieutenant pushed the rifle into his shoulder, taking aim.

Moon Wolf observed him, ignored him. *"Come, Bear Chief, come quiet your children. Your ancestors await. Come, Bear Chief, come quiet—"*

A single shot flew by Moon Wolf, another followed.

Moon Wolf didn't flinch, didn't even raise an eyebrow as he continued, *"Come warriors, come and rise again. Your ancestors await. Come warriors, come and rise again."*

"Shut up, you drunken fool." One more shot whizzed past Moon Wolf.

"Hey, hey, hey. Your ancestors await." He lay down.

By now, a crowd of four other men and a few of the traders' Indian wives had gathered around the lieutenant. "Go ahead and kill the varmint, Cap'n."

Moon Wolf recognized that voice. It belonged to Jake Berry, the man assigned to watch over Little Brave Woman's house. Beneath the brilliance of the starlight overhead, Moon Wolf grinned, in private and in secret. Perfect. His ruse had worked.

He had needed some way to get Alys back into her home without arousing suspicion about where she had been. He could have devised a simpler diversion, he sup-

posed, but he also had business with the lieutenant. Best
he get that piece of nastiness behind him.

"Ah, he ain't worth it, Jake," the lieutenant replied. "Go
home, everybody, it's just a drunken Injun. Nothing to see
here. Jake, you come inside with me, I need to talk to you
before you go."

"Young warriors, take not to the drink," Moon Wolf
continued to sing. *"Young warriors, take not to the drink,
hey, hey, hey."*

The two men disappeared into the house, the others returning to their homes.

Moon Wolf stared up into the sky. Little Brave Woman
would have made it to her own house by now, where she
would slip up to her room and quietly disrobe. Shifting,
he envisioned every gentle curve of her figure as though
it were being slowly unveiled to him now.

Unfortunately, it didn't take a great deal of imagination
to visualize how she looked, since he had committed every
slight variation of her body to memory. Much too soon,
lust stirred within him.

He ignored it.

It had become more and more obvious to him, in these
last few days, that his original plan for his sweet Alys
must, of necessity, be put to rest. He had found certain
paradise with her. He could not let her go to another, even
if that man were a white man. Not now. Not ever.

Ha, there appeared to be only one solution for him: he
must find a place where he and his Little Brave Woman
could live in relative peace, without the prejudice of the
white man's world, and to a lesser extent, that of the red
man's, also, spreading around them.

He was not without ideas on how to accomplish this.
But first he must put an end to the whiskey smuggling and
to the need for the Wolf Shadow.

And to that end he now sought out Lieutenant Warrington. Though there was little to recommend the man—not honor, not valor, not even honesty—there was one thing the lieutenant had that Moon Wolf did not: the knowledge of who was behind this.

Aa, yes, Moon Wolf had at last discovered the answer to Little Brave Woman's question from so many weeks ago: he was not prejudiced.

Amongst all tribes there are the good people and the bad. Just as the red man had borne a few unpleasant souls, so, too, had the white man. No, not *all* white men were bad. He had the evidence of this truth all around him, and he admitted his error in assigning the characteristics of a few to the whole.

However, that did not negate the fact that the bad in this white society seemed to dominate the good, at least out here in his own country.

No, by his own observation it appeared that these few treacherous folk who profited from this kind of trade cloaked themselves in invisibility, their means of operation being disloyalty, covert hostility, and underhanded dealings. What Moon Wolf needed to know now was who they were—who was behind these bad things; who sanctioned and surreptitiously supported this whiskey smuggling?

Of one thing Moon Wolf was certain: Lieutenant Warrington was not one of those privileged few. His was a bully's heart, hired by cowards who themselves dared not show their face. What sort of man hired another to do his killing or his stealing for him, who never dared to show the true colors of his face to the light of Sun?

Weaklings, most certainly, but worse. These people had not the decency to challenge another in open warfare. Instead, they pretended to have land, never asking the permission of its original occupants; they posted their fences without council, and, when the Indian objected, devised a way to call the Indian a thief.

When the white man had first come to this land, those precious few had been friendly toward the Indian. Although there had been some treachery, it had not been so widespread. So it was that from those first few, the Indian mind had not been alerted to the intrinsic danger.

Even later, when there had been more reason to doubt, no one had appreciated the threat. Loathing duplicity and dishonesty, it had never occurred to the Indian to doubt the sincerity of these pale-faced people—not until it was too late.

But who would have known? No red man could have anticipated his ultimate demise. It would have been too fantastic to be believed.

Yet, if one looked, no longer would he see the beaver swimming in the rivers; no longer did the mountain lion and the wolf roam as freely as they once had. Even the huge buffalo herds were disappearing.

Had any medicine man predicted this, he would have been laughed from the village. And perhaps it had been this, the unbelievability of it all, that had given this new white man the upper hand.

Moon Wolf sighed. He disgressed.

Lieutenant Warrington had information. Moon Wolf determined to discover it. And to this end he sought council with the man, even if it meant giving a little of himself . . . very little . . .

As promised, Moon Wolf continued to sing his drinking songs until at last the sun peeked out above the horizon, there in the eastern sky. He sent a prayer to the Above Ones, asking them to take pity on him and to help him in this, his given task. For a moment he basked in the newly forming rays of the sun.

Then, quickly and silently, he arose and, leaning over the side of the roof, jumped to the ground.

He would see Lieutenant Warrington.

*   *   *

Moon Wolf trod to the wooden door and, opening it, staggered inside.

"Where is the Seizer Chief?" he demanded of no one in particular, his articulation slightly slurred.

"I am in here," the lieutenant called from an adjoining room. "Come in."

Moon Wolf became alert. There was no hint of frustration in the lieutenant's voice. In truth, the man's utterance held a note of satisfaction.

Pulling his buffalo robe up over one shoulder in the style of a Roman toga, Moon Wolf paced into the room, his robe hiding one .44 Winchester and one knife. He did not wish to fight the lieutenant—rather, he would obtain what knowledge he could from him—but he was not reckless enough to go before him unprepared.

"What news have you for me, Moon Wolf?" The lieutenant didn't even look up, intent upon some papers strewn over his desk.

Moon Wolf slowly strode forward, giving the room a quick glance, which, although done swiftly, noted everything in the surroundings; only one entrance with the possible exception of the two windows, one placed at his back, the other at his right side. Two guns sat loaded and ready upon the lieutenant's desk, another one in his belt, along with a knife and a sword, located strategically by the lieutenant's right hand.

Dirt and grime streaked across the lieutenant's desk, while papers scattered here and there from the breeze blowing in through the open window. Moon Wolf turned a sneer at the disarray.

Lieutenant Warrington's face looked pompous, condescending, and Moon Wolf made a mental note to be careful. This man hid something; something vital to Moon Wolf.

"*Ok-yi,*" he greeted the lieutenant. "We will counsel."

"Fine," the lieutenant replied. "Tell me what you know."

Moon Wolf shifted his weight, asking, "Do you wish this one to speak without inviting me to sit and partake of a council pipe?"

"I have no need for such things. I would have the details alone and be done with it."

"But this one has need of the council pipe," Moon Wolf persisted. "How else can you—and I—know that we speak the truth to one another?"

Lieutenant Warrington looked up from his papers at last, a brief flash of frustration crossing his face. "I have tolerated your insolence and insubordination too many times in the past, Moon Wolf, because I know that you do valuable service for me. I have been kind to you to a fault, plying you with the necessary whiskey that you seek. But come now. Surely you know that I am your friend, that I would hardly tell you lies."

Moon Wolf became instantly alert. Only those with hostile designs ever felt the need to broadcast their "friendship." True friends remained merely that, rarely, if ever, feeling the need to proclaim their benign intentions.

It was only then that Moon Wolf realized the lieutenant meant to deliver this Indian's immediate demise. *Aa*, yes, now Moon Wolf understood the lieutenant's complacency. This seizer chief would have what information Moon Wolf had, then put him to a quick, sure death.

Out of the corner of his eye, Moon Wolf picked up a movement at the window to his right. Someone waited there; someone with a cocked pistol.

Moon Wolf straightened up and grinned. "*Aa*," he said, "the lou-ten-tent speaks great 'truth' when he says he is surely this one's friend; so the seizer chief will undoubtedly indulge his 'friend,' as comrades will often do for one another. Let us, as companions then, oblige a goodwill smoke before our council. Is it not little enough to ask?"

Caught in his own lie, the lieutenant frowned but had little choice. At last, he nodded, albeit reluctantly.

Moon Wolf produced a council pipe from the folds of his robe, then sat on the floor, cross-legged, gesturing to a spot next to him—a site that placed the lieutenant between the Indian and the window.

"Come here now," said Moon Wolf, "and sit with me. We will smoke and talk to one another as our fathers have done in the past."

He gave the lieutenant no choice, making it understood that without the smoke, there would be no powwow. The lieutenant rose and came around the desk, squatting down—although with great hesitation—next to Moon Wolf.

"*Ok'yi napi,*" Moon Wolf began. Taking hold of the pipe, he raised it first to Sun, the chief; then to Wind-maker, *Ai-so-pwom-stan;* to Thunder, *Sis-tse-kom;* to Lightning, *Puh-pom,* and to the earth and Above Ones. Lastly, he took a puff before handing the pipe to the lieutenant. Moon Wolf commented, "Know that what we say here must be the truth, lest the forces of nature conspire to harm us, one and all."

The lieutenant took the pipe, inhaled a quick puff, and handed it back to Moon Wolf.

"So it is," said Moon Wolf. "I will tell you what I have learned, but only after you answer a question of mine."

"What is this, you scoundrel? Do you think me an idiot? I have not agreed to share information with you, only to obtain yours—for whiskey. That is our agreement."

Moon Wolf nodded, nonplused. Placing the pipe on his knees, he began, "There is another who has joined the Wolf Shadow."

The lieutenant nodded. "We had suspected that after the last raid. Do you know who it is?"

"I have learned one thing."

"What is that?"

"It is said that this Wolf Shadow and his companion now know who is behind the whiskey shipments and, instead of making more raids upon your bull and whiskey trains, they have become intent on hunting down the man who does this and then killing him."

The lieutenant remained silent, Moon Wolf observing the man from beneath heavy eyelids.

Moon Wolf continued, "I have heard talk that they will not rest until they find him."

"Ha, I'd like them to try to locate him here."

With stoic indifference, Moon Wolf took note of the statement. He continued, "*Haiya,* but there are more than the one man they seek and they will hunt the others down, too, there where they live in Helena . . . those also in Fort Buford . . . and there on the white man's cattle ranch at Big Spring Creek."

With seemingly unobservant eyes, Moon Wolf attended to every tiny fluctuation in the lieutenant's breathing. He took careful regard of each reaction, too, noting that the only significant response had been when Moon Wolf had mentioned Helena. At that time the lieutenant's breathing had become slightly labored, his skin tone changing from a pale yellow to a slight shade of red.

Obviously the men Moon Wolf sought were in Helena.

He continued, "The Wolf Shadow and his partner now know that these men they seek run the trading post." No reaction from the lieutenant. "The place where the white man keeps his treasures." Again no reaction. "And the place where the white men go to grab the Indian land."

Minute muscle flicks leapt across the lieutenant's cheek, his skin tone changing once more to a dull red.

Aa, thought Moon Wolf, the ones he sought had to do with the land and its disbursement.

He continued, "The Wolf Shadow also knows that one of their names is he who is one of your guards, Jake Berry." Very little reaction. "Also he who deals out the land to the white men on the scraps of paper." A bit more reaction in the lieutenant's face. "Know they too, that there are men in the far-off place in the east that control the land and the people here that seek to claim it." A tiny tic fluctuated in the lieutenant's eye. "The bandits will seek these men out and expose them to the white man's government. It is what they intend to do before they kill these people and all those who associate with them."

"Now, see here, Moon Wolf, I think your sources are misinformed."

"Yet it is as I tell you."

Behind Lieutenant Warrington's seemingly complacent facade, the pupils of his eyes dilated, darting from one object in the room to the next. Moon Wolf, however, met the man's stare straight on; the lieutenant, on the other hand, was barely able to hold Moon Wolf's gaze. The officer's voice appeared calm, however, as he observed, "You have done the right thing, Moon Wolf, in bringing me this information on the threat to our people. I thank you for that. But there is one thing you still have not obtained for me."

Moon Wolf remained silent.

"I still do not know the identity of this man they call the Wolf Shadow."

Moon Wolf nodded. "It is because he is more shadow or spirit than man. But I will keep searching."

"Then," said Lieutenant Warrington, "in this you have failed me yet again."

"Aa, but I have given you much information this day. As you said, I have done well, yes?"

"No, you have not . . . not entirely. And I think it is time to put our association to an end. I grow tired of our skirmishes and twisted talk. It is obvious that you cannot be the kind of spy that the military needs."

Moon Wolf acknowledged the man with a nod. "So be it, lou-ten-tent."

"What? No argument?" The lieutenant emitted a jeering laugh.

"None from this one," Moon Wolf said, taking hold of his pipe and emptying the ashes on the floor. Then, placing the object back into his robe, he commented, "Our council is at an end, as is our alliance. I will arise now and do as you wish, never to return."

Moon Wolf stood up, half of his attention on the lieutenant, half on the window at his right. *Aa,* there it was, the barrel of a gun, a partial view of a head, an eye. Suddenly Moon Wolf grabbed hold of the lieutenant, placing the officer between himself and the window.

It took Lieutenant Warrington several moments to appreciate what was happening before he screamed, "Don't shoot!"

But the request came too late. The shot was fired, straight into the lieutenant's arm, followed by another one from Moon Wolf, out the window.

A pained groan came from outside.

"Why you two-bit bastard," the lieutenant spit out as he grabbed hold of his arm, rushing to the window and looking out. "You've shot me. You idiots. I'm surrounded by idiots."

"Perhaps," said Moon Wolf, having followed the lieutenant to the window, there to espy Jake Berry, sitting up and holding his arm, which bled profusely. "Perhaps there are more simpletons here than those that surround you." And with this said, Moon Wolf grinned at the lieutenant, took hold of his arm, and jerked the man over to his desk, slamming him against it and stating, his face no more than a hairsbreadth away, "I think that you will live, Lieutenant, as will your bully out there, although I believe it is more than the both of you deserve. Know you, that the Above Ones have seen your treachery in our council. You tried to trick me into an early death. Now, I will assure you that your treason will not be looked upon with favor, and I fear that great disaster will befall you. If you treasure your life at all, I would pray, Lieutenant Warrington . . . I would pray very hard."

And with nothing more to be said, Moon Wolf let himself out of the house.

Chapter 21

She hid beneath a bush in a low coulee, just outside their cave and below the waterfall, awaiting him. This sport of "hide and seek" was among her favorite of all their "games," perhaps because it required the least amount of effort on her part.

All she had to do was find a good place to hide and wait for him to locate her—if he could. Actually, he always did, following her tracks as though he were part hound. Still, there were a few times when she had fooled him, and once it had taken him hours to find her. Her reward for her skill had been many pleasurable hours, spent in his arms, a circumstance which had repeated itself over and over.

She sighed. These last few weeks had been amongst the most enjoyable in her life. The days had been consumed with activity, as Moon Wolf had insisted she practice her skills; the evenings had been spent in one another's arms.

Never could she remember being happier or more at peace.

She was also pleased to observe that Moon Wolf no longer risked his life by making daylight raids into the fort. In truth, since that time, many weeks ago, when she had confessed the facts of her "engagement," Moon Wolf had committed no raids at all. Instead, he spent his days tutoring her in the art of Indian resistance.

At first she had thought that he might renege on his promise to teach her the ways of a warrior, but his instruction had been thorough. She supposed that she had reckoned without comprehending the sense of honor possessed by the Native American. Once pledged, an Indian would do almost anything to keep his word.

And so he had trained her in the arts of plains warfare, teaching her little by little the ways of the prairie. She had mastered the ability to throw a lance through a hoop and to make a stick jump by throwing a long arrow at it. In addition, she could cast arrows quickly and accurately at a target, and she'd begun to learn the basics of the sign language that all the Indian tribes used.

Alas, at first her muscles had ached, since he had made her practice intensely, every day. But eventually, as her body had adjusted to the physical challenge, she had noticed her strength beginning to build.

"Animals made the first paths," he had told her one day as he had taken her on an outing, pointing out different trails through the prairie. Up until then she realized, she had never been aware of them.

She had looked at him strangely. "How do you mean?"

He had pointed to the sky as they'd stomped across the plains that stretched out from their mountainside. "Watch the birds from one season to another as they make their journeys north and south," he said. "Watch them carefully and observe that they appear to follow a path that neither you nor I can see." He'd grinned at her and had taken her hand in his as he'd gone on to explain, "Even the fish in the creeks and rivers follow a trail to their breeding beds. If one will observe them and carefully mark them from one year to another, he will see this."

She had nodded. "I didn't know that."

"It is an important fact to realize. Many of the paths that the red man and the white man walk were once animal trails. Animals are natural trailblazers, for it is they who make the best path toward water. Remember this if ever you lose your way on the prairie. Follow the path of the elk or the buffalo, for they will always lead you to water and to food."

"I will remember," she'd said, smiling at him.

"You must also learn to observe small things. Often one's life depends on it. Trails can become 'blind,' meaning that they will lead into rocks or streams where it is difficult to follow, but if you can learn to observe little things, you can find your way. Once, when I was a little boy, I remember following a trail that abruptly ended. It was dark and I could not follow it any farther. It had been a good, worn path that suddenly ended in rocks. Bending down, however, I found that the soil had changed from one that was mostly sand to one that was clay. Observing this, I was able to find the path of sand over the rocks, though it was faint. Small things, remember that. One must be alert to the tiniest change, even to the birds that sing. If all is quiet, with neither the song of a bird or that of an animal, beware. An enemy is close by."

And so it had gone, week after week, day after day, until a few days ago, when Moon Wolf had told her that they were soon to have an adventure.

"There is a whiskey shipment that is leaving the fort," he had informed her. "It will be crossing over to Fort Whoop-Up. We will stop it from reaching the medicine line if we are able."

She had nodded. "Do you think I'm ready?"

He'd smiled at her. "I know that you are. But come, we must make our plans, for that shipment will be well guarded."

And so they had.

She heard the rustle of footsteps beside her . . . it had to be Moon Wolf, searching for her. Forcing herself to think of nothing, she sat still, barely daring to breathe.

The soft flicker of her hair against her back, a gentle graze of a finger across the nape of her neck alerted her to the fact that she had been found. She let out her breath.

"Seems to me," she said on a sigh, "that you find me much too easily in these games of ours. I really am not providing you with ample chase, am I?"

A mere few steps brought him around her until he faced her. Squatting down, Moon Wolf reached out to comb his fingers through her hair, his attention seemingly caught on the way the auburn waves reflected the sun. He commented, "I think that you have led me on a terrific chase. Is it not true that I had to wait many years to make you my wife? And after I asked you so grandly—"

"I think that you are speaking of another pursuit, my husband. Is your attention not on our game of hide and seek?"

"Not on our game?" His tone practically dripped innocence as he continued, "With you here beside me, and nothing to do but bask in the sun and enjoy one another's company? How could my attention be distracted from our game?"

"I do not know," she responded with amusement, reaching out a hand to trail a finger over the hard muscle of his buckskin-clad thigh. "But I fear you have other things on your mind besides my education."

He bent to her, his face a scant fraction of an inch away from hers. "Other things?" he asked guilelessly, kissing her. "You must tell me what these things are, for I do not know them." He voiced the lie easily, kissing her yet again, his lips lingering over hers.

"Hmmm." She opened her mouth to say more, but didn't have the chance to articulate a single word. He took immediate advantage and set upon her, his tongue invading her mouth. In sensual delight, she threw her arms around his neck, pulling him toward her and forgetting whatever it was she had been about to say. Nothing was more important than this.

He had taken off his shirt and placed it behind her, his shirt becoming her pillow, and she spared a moment to gaze up at him as he eased her onto the ground. The sun had caught the blue-black highlights in his straight, dark hair, making the locks shine like a midnight sky under a full moon. As he removed her blouse, one of those long locks, warm from the sun, caressed her bosom as though it, too, were alive and capable of loving her. He smelled of the mint leaves he had been chewing, of the earth, and of the clean mountain air. And she thought she had never witnessed anything more potent or more beautiful than this man, her husband.

How she loved him.

She made a delicate path down the bareness of his chest with one finger and had the pleasure of witnessing how the sudden arousal to passion changed the harshness of his features to the more muted qualities of desire. He drew in his breath and growled at her . . . gently.

Oh, how handsome he was. She felt her heart burst with the strength of her feeling.

"I love you, my husband," she confessed and watched as a smile lit up his face, the gesture so full of tenderness for her that she glowed. Had she ever been this happy? Never, she answered her own question.

Oh, she thought again, how she loved this man of hers.

He removed her dress, her chemise, and her underthings

with care and set them aside, his gaze lingering over her with concentrated interest as he stood to remove his trousers.

"And I love you, my wife." He then knelt before her, and she couldn't help but admire the look of him, the strength of his potency inspiring her to an even higher degree of longing . . . and loving. He added, leaning over her and tracing a finger down a path over her bosom, "There is only one thing I would ask of you, Little Brave Woman."

She reached out a hand to caress his cheek and, adoration coloring her voice, she asked, "What is that?"

"Please," he stopped, his throat working as though he were having difficulty swallowing. "Please remember me to our children."

"Always, my husband," she promised. "But I keep telling you, there will be little need, for you will be with me. This I know, my husband. This I know."

He groaned, and, bringing his lips again to hers, kissed her over and over as though, while he might like to believe her, he still had his own doubts. At last, with a sigh, she made the overture to join her body to his, and with their bodies so intimately placed, she sealed her devotion to him with the strength of her knowledge.

And for a moment, perhaps a moment alone, she knew he believed her.

As she lay in the prairie grass, the sun bore down on her back, providing a welcome warmth against the chill of the early morning air. Close by her a bird sang, another answered, while an eagle flew high overhead. It was a good sign.

Next to her, Moon Wolf stretched out on a hill overlooking the whiskey trail. The pure scent of the earth and the grasses surrounded her, their clean fragrance a gentle reminder of the task before them. Behind her a smokeless fire burned low to the ground, and she prayed that the wind would not betray their presence to the enemy.

Beside her, Moon Wolf was completely still, the wolf headdress and black paint hiding most of his features. Even his body bore the markings of paint, she noted. She reached out to touch him, to give him encouragement, her fingers coming away with the black, oily substance, which she rubbed on the grass. *Makoyi* lay to his other side, the animal every now and again getting up to sniff at the rocks.

Looking back toward the trail, she absentmindedly adjusted her own softer version of the wolf headdress and sank down as far as possible into the cover of the grass.

This was the path taken by the whiskey laden wagons, Moon Wolf had told her. Horses, not oxen, pulled these wagons and flew as fast as possible across the prairie and over the medicine line into Canada, thus avoiding any law-abiding citizen who might try to stop them. Few people knew of this route, the oxen-pulled schooners traveling the other, more direct, path into Canada.

Because those were filled with food, clothing, and other common trade items, they were rarely, if ever, raided. However, it was that route which the military heavily guarded.

The whiskey train must have felt secure on this afternoon, for the horses traveled at a walk, advancing slowly up an incline. That didn't upset Alys, however. The slower the vehicles, the easier the raid.

Moon Wolf glanced at her, signaling her to stay where she was, while he scooted backward, down the hill, *Makoyi* beside him. Reaching the ground at a place hidden from the four wagons, he turned and ran to another hill, one slightly ahead of the wagons.

He kept within eyesight of her, and soon, reaching the

place where he had decided to make his stand, he signalled her again.

On cue, she scooted back down, out of sight, to the campfire that Moon Wolf had built earlier in the morning. Taking a few bullets from the saddlebags she carried over her shoulder, she threw the slugs onto the fire. Turning, she ran as fast as she could toward another hill, one that would put her to the rear of the wagon train. She crouched behind a big boulder.

It didn't take long for the bullets to explode.

Down below, horses whinnied and reared at the sudden noise, trying desperately to bolt. But the scouts and drivers, by their very brawn, reined them in.

Soon a party of four men assembled. After some talk, they directed their mounts toward the place where the shots had been fired, leaving the drivers and the others with the freighters to keep control of the horses.

Into this confusion, Moon Wolf jumped, vaulting from rock to rock, each leap gaining him a better position, one closer to the train. At last, he was safely in range, with no one but Alys the wiser.

She, too, emerged from her hiding place and ran quickly to the next spot, according to plan. She was barely in position when . . . *Swish!*

A firelit arrow from Moon Wolf's bow struck one of the wagons, followed by another arrow, two more, all in quick succession until all four wagons went up in flames. Panic ensued. The horses reared, fleeing in terror, their drivers no longer able to restrain them.

Shouting and screams to order could be heard, but it didn't matter. Chaos spread all around them.

"Water, water, form a line to water," the command rang out over the prairie. A bugle sounded, while the four men from the posse rushed back to the train, each one springing from his mount and hurrying toward the emergency.

Under cover, Moon Wolf and his pet raced back up the rocks, darting up the hill, down again, until they could sprint toward the place where Alys waited, holding the horses in check.

"Hurry," he cried out as he approached her, "soon the whiskey traders and the seizers will leave the wagons to come and find our trail."

He jumped onto his mount and leading her horse, they rode to the highest hill, where, in plain view of the wagons, he let out his war cry. Their horses reared, *Makoyi* howled, and just as quickly they were gone, back down the hill, sending their mounts in a dash across the prairie, toward yet another safe refuge.

All this had been part of their plan, even to the pursuit that would follow. But these three "bandits" would be back again, under the cover of darkness. The fire had halted the whiskey train for a time, perhaps doing some damage, but the schooners would soon resume their course toward the medicine line if nothing more were done.

No, tonight the Wolf Shadow and his cohorts would have to finish the job, ensuring that this whiskey train never reached Fort Whoop-Up, at least not with its terrible cargo intact.

Doubling back in the evening, they found a buffalo herd two or three miles from the valley where the whiskey train had entrenched itself for the night. Earlier, both Moon Wolf and Alys had observed the caravan, noting that the prairie schooners had suffered fire damage mostly to the wagons themselves and their canvas covering, the contents of the wagons seemingly undamaged.

The schooners had now formed a sort of corral, as was the usual custom. It made disabling them harder, for the train would be guarded with firepower from within.

Sitting atop a nearby butte, the three of them—Alys,

Moon Wolf, and *Makoyi*—basked beneath the soft glow of a golden sunset, the last rays of day turning the burnished prairie to the tawny color of white gold. High above them flew an eagle, while below them grazed a vast herd of buffalo. In truth, little more could be seen below them except the buffalo. The coulees, the valleys, even the flat prairie were alive with the creatures.

Thus, the three of them sat, contemplating what they might do next, but mostly doing no more than gazing about them, at the wonder of nature—at the mountains in the distance, the plains all around them, the herd of buffalo quietly grazing. How beautiful it was . . . , and occasionally Moon Wolf would utter, "*I-tam-ap-i*," meaning happiness or being perfectly content.

At length, after the sun broadcast its departure from the sky, filling the heavens with screaming pinks and hot reds, Moon Wolf turned to Alys, saying, "This herd gives me an idea."

She gazed back at him, raising an eyebrow.

"*Aa*, yes," he said, "I think that the buffalo down there might be able to damage that caravan, in a way the fire could not."

Alys, lazily observing the rise of the full moon in the eastern sky, looked down upon the land to the west of them, which at the moment looked black almost to the horizon, covered as it was by the vast buffalo herd.

"How would you do it?" she asked.

He jerked his head to the left. "If I approach that herd and start into it as though I am about to kill some of them, I believe that I can make them stampede and, as you can see, that caravan would be in their path."

"Moon Wolf," she touched his arm, "is that wise? Look at that herd. It is immense and there is only one of you. Besides, the buffalo might run in an opposite direction and leave the caravan unharmed."

He acknowledged her with a nod. "That is true. No one can tell for sure where the buffalo might run. But still it might work, and it would be easy to do. Come," he said, getting to his feet. "I will paint myself and my pony for this raid while I tell you more of my plan."

"But I'm not sure I approve—"

"Come . . ."

Moon Wolf stood before her, his body nude except for breechcloth and moccasins. Black stripes streaked across the whole of his body, while plastered on his face was a look of grim determination. No amount of pleading had changed his mind about this.

"Would you have me stay here for fear that something might go wrong?" he had asked her when her appeals had begun in earnest. "If other people were to learn of this, that I even listened to you, they might tell you to start fitting me with dresses."

She shook her head. "I don't think so, for I would tell no one of it," she had countered.

But he would not be held back, nor, it appeared, could he be reasoned with. He said, "You will stay here with *Makoyi* while I ride into this herd and drive the buffalo toward the whiskey train."

"So you have told me several times," she acknowledged, "but what I don't understand is why, if you are determined to go down there and there is nothing I can do to make you stay, why must I remain here?"

"Would you have me put you in great danger?"

"Why not? You are putting your own life in jeopardy."

"That is different. I am a man; I am expected to do what I must in order that I secure the safety of others. But with the run of the buffalo, anything is possible. I have been trained, since the day I could sit a horse, to ride into the buffalo herds and select out the finest of them. It is something I have done often. You, however, are not so experienced. And so you will wait here, as will *Makoyi*."

Alys didn't reply, setting her lips, instead, into a straight line. She was certain that while Moon Wolf spoke with a great deal of wisdom and had, of course, her best interests at heart, his ordering her about and telling her what she could and could not do did not sit well with her. She persisted, "I would go with you, all the same."

He grimaced before he drew in a deep breath, proffering, "I would ask that you not do this. I will need someone to wait here in case I am not successful. Also, if you do not stay here, *Makoyi* will go with me and I would rather he stay here. He might set the buffalo to running in the wrong direction."

"But—"

Moon Wolf held up a hand. "I will need all my cunning about me this night in order to get this herd into that camp. I would prefer not to worry about you, too."

Good, simple logic. What argument could she give him against it?

She could think of none at the moment, and so it appeared, at least temporarily, that she had no choice but to agree. She muttered a curt, "All right."

In return he gave her a sympathetic grin. "Do not look so sad," he encouraged, "this is as it must be." He drew level to his horse and jumped on it, while she arose and came to stand beside him, taking his hand into her own.

She said, "You will be alert to any danger?"

"*Aa*, this I can promise you. But come, this is not a time for sadness. If we are successful this night, this whiskey train will not make it north of the medicine line. It is a good thing."

"Yes," she agreed, smiling up at him shyly. "It is a good thing."

He leaned down to her, placing his cheek against her

own and, running his fingers softly over her skin as though he were wiping off the paint left there, he reassured, "Do not worry. I have ridden into the buffalo herd many times."

"I know, but—"

"Come, if we succeed in removing the whiskey sneakers from our land, we will be able to live together in peace. This is something worth having, is that not right?"

"Yes, but—"

"Little Brave Woman, listen to me. I promise you now, before the Above Ones, that if I am successful this night, I will not rest until I find a place for us; a place where we can live our lives without the prejudice that surrounds us. There must be a place such as this and if necessary, I will spend my life finding it. This I promise you."

She gave him a weak smile and glanced up at him, then away, before saying, "That was very beautifully said, Moon Wolf, and I accept your vow. I know it was spoken from your heart. And though I understand you well, I would still come with you."

"Not tonight," he insisted. "You know what to do if I do not return?"

Resigned, she bobbed her head. "I do."

He kissed her then, a slow, lingering caress. One she would have liked to continue. But he drew away much too soon and said, "Know that I have always loved you."

"And I, you."

He straightened up in his seat and, with a quick jerk of his knees, set his pony into motion, guiding it down the butte, leaving Alys behind and, along with the wolf, watching.

"I don't know about you, *Makoyi*," she muttered under her breath as she watched her man ride away, "but I have a bad feeling about this. I wish we'd never found this herd."

Makoyi sat up on his haunches and looked wise for the

space of a moment, finally whining and putting his head down on his paws.

Moon Wolf had barely been gone a few minutes before she saw him charge into the herd, splitting the buffalo apart and driving a few thousand of them straight down upon the valley . . . and the whiskey train.

She watched him with something akin to awe. The darkened edges of night had finally fallen around them; the full moon, having already arisen, painted the landscape in shadows, while it, like a luculent globe, remained the single source of light.

She could barely see, yet she remained aware of when the buffalo started into a run. Slowly at first, but then with more and more vigor as they sensed the danger, the buffalo began to bolt in the general direction of the caravan. Never had she witnessed so close at hand the vigorous power of these shaggy and ill-shaped beasts. The sound of their thundering hooves as they picked up speed was deafening, while the force of their weight caused the ground around her to quake.

And there, in the thick of it, rode Moon Wolf, guiding his trained mount in and out of the herd, rousing them on into a more dashing run.

That the men in the whiskey train would hear the approach was without doubt. But this, too, had been anticipated. It had not been a part of Moon Wolf's plan to kill these white men, simply to disable their wagons.

Alys held her breath. She could no longer make out the figure of Moon Wolf. She sat up quickly, brought out her saddlebags, and fumbled in it until she produced a pair of binoculars.

Focusing on the spot where she had last seen him, she stared, and stared.

Where was he? Was he all right?

She changed her focus to the head of the pack. Assur-

edly, there he was, out to the side of the herd, driving it
forward.

She watched for several long moments, not letting Moon
Wolf out of her view.

Soon, she noticed that the forerunners of the herd had
reached the outskirts of the encampment. She could barely
make it out from where she sat, but that didn't stop her
from her self-imposed vigil.

Onward those buffalo loped, onward toward the camp,
until finally they spread out upon it and began threading
their way through it, winding around the whiskey schooners much like a stream of water might around an island.

Suddenly a shot fired, the noise sending the herd into
confusion. Some of the animals tried to stop, bunching up
and causing one of the caravan wagons to fall over. Soon
another wagon collapsed.

Makoyi arose and, pacing back and forth for several seconds, came to sit down upon a ledge, where he ruffed the
hair on his neck and immediately began to howl.

At the same time, an awful feeling took hold of her.
Where had that shot come from? Surely not from Moon
Wolf, for he carried no gun.

Who then? What an irresponsible thing to do, to fire a
shot into a herd already frightened.

Premonition struck. Someone had been shooting at
Moon Wolf. She knew it. Had they made their mark?

No. Please, dear Lord, no, she prayed.

Jumping up, she sent a quick look to *Makoyi,* who was
howling all out of control. She said, "Quit it, we are going
to go and find him. But I will need your help to guide me
to him, for there is still a herd of buffalo between me and
Moon Wolf."

Makoyi stopped his howling to stare at her, and she continued, "If the shot occurred close to the bull wagons, there
might be other problems, too. For there will be those who

will want to kill our man. Still, we must go and find him and hope for the best."

With her words, the wolf came up onto his feet and began pacing back and forth, whining and glancing alternately at her, back at the buffalo, to her again. She spoke to the animal anew. "Yes, we need to get to Moon Wolf. You are going to have to guide me, *Makoyi*, for I do not know how to find him."

Makoyi gave a yelp as though he understood every word and trotted off, coming back and looking at her, trotting off again.

Alys ran to her pony and mounted, cautioning the wolf, "Do not run so fast that we cannot keep up with you."

Makoyi was already away, however, and Alys, leaning down to her pony, prayed, "Let him be alive. Just let him be alive."

Alys was to learn that her mount was indeed one of those special ponies trained for the buffalo run. He seemed to know exactly what to do.

Alys, however, was not so ready for him. He darted into the buffalo herd with an abandon that had her closing her eyes before she gained the courage to take control and guide him back away from the main rush of the buffalo, keeping her pony close on *Makoyi*'s trail.

"Find him, Wolf," she encouraged as the animal again came into sight.

So far they had stayed to the same side of the herd as Moon Wolf had. What if they needed to get through to the other side? What if Moon Wolf had ridden off in that direction? How would she do it?

It would have been impossible. The buffalo still charged through the valley, following their leader wherever he might take them.

Makoyi suddenly ran ahead, out of sight, quickly reappearing, then running ahead again, doubling back.

"Have you found him, Wolf?" Alys pressed her mount on.

Suddenly *Makoyi* ran a little farther away, sat down, and howled.

Had he found Moon Wolf?

Alys dismounted, being well to the side of the buffalo, and, on foot, ran as fast as she could toward the spot.

Sure enough, Moon Wolf lay on the ground in front of her, the tall grasses all but hiding him. Was he unconscious? He made no movement, nor could she detect the rise and fall of his chest. Either he had passed out or . . . dear Lord, no, he couldn't be dead . . .

She rushed to him, putting one hand to his wrist, the other to where his pulse should be at his neck.

She let out a deep sigh. He lived. At least for now.

Where was he hurt? His well-trained mount still stood beside him, munching the grass as though only awaiting his master's recovery and order. Oh, how she wished that pony could talk and tell her what had happened. She didn't dare move Moon Wolf for fear of causing him more damage. Still, she could not attend to any injuries here, not with the pounding of buffalo hooves all around her.

Or could she? She had to try.

She began to inspect him with her fingertips, starting at his head, checking for any bumps or gashes. She could find little, but that could mean anything.

She moved her hands down further. Had he broken something? She felt along the back of his neck. No reaction from him. Unlikely that was broken.

Down further, to each arm, his chest. Still nothing.

She expanded her search down further, to his stomach, down each leg, to his calves, on downward, until at last he winced.

His ankle. Had he broken it?

If that's all that was wrong, why was he passed out? Oh, how she wished at this moment that she were a doctor.

Tears of frustration welled up in her eyes. She had to do something, quickly. But what?

It was dark, and she could not see well enough to know what was around her, nor could she hear very well. The herd of buffalo, not more than a few hundred yards away, still stampeded. Worse still was the knowledge that somebody had shot at Moon Wolf. That person might search for him.

What should she do?

With some difficulty, she rolled Moon Wolf onto his side, feeling down his backside for any injuries. She could find none. At least whoever had shot at him had missed his mark.

What had happened, then, to cause his fall?

She might never know. But of one thing she was certain: she had to get him out of here. Now.

How?

His horse still awaited him, *Makoyi* whined and howled next to him, refusing to be quiet even when Alys tried to make him stop. Would the others from the whiskey train hear the wolf and come to investigate?

If he hadn't been shot and she could feel no evidence of an injury to his head, it might be all right for her to move him. She had to take the chance. They could not stay here.

She could probably get him to his horse, but what then? How would she get him up on it?

She glanced at the horse, at the wolf, back to Moon Wolf. An idea took hold, and she jumped up quickly, running to her own horse and grabbing a rope.

If she could tie this around *Makoyi*, perhaps the two of them, she and the wolf, could raise Moon Wolf up onto his pony. She had to try.

"Come here, *Makoyi*. I will need your help to rescue your friend."

To her relief, the wolf did not protest when she tied the rope around him; she repeated the procedure upon Moon Wolf.

Now for the hard part.

Using every ounce of her strength and then some, she took Moon Wolf's weight upon her own and, with difficulty, dragged him toward his horse.

"Easy, boy," she comforted the horse. "You will need to stand still while I get your master onto your back. Do not betray me."

The animal pawed at the ground.

"*Makoyi*, go to the other side of the horse." She motioned to the animal. Quickly she threw a blanket over the horse and stretched the rope over the animal's back.

"Pull, *Makoyi*, pull, fella." She wished she knew the Blackfoot word for pull, but it seemed to make no difference. *Makoyi* knew what was needed. Backing up and pulling on the rope with his teeth, the wolf struggled. She added her strength to the effort, pushing Moon Wolf up and onto the horse.

Finally he lay over the horse's back.

"Good, boy," she comforted the wolf. Could she get Moon Wolf into a sitting position on the horse? She tried to move him again, all to no effect. It was just as well. He might fall from that position.

She heard movement in the grass and held her breath, awaiting discovery. But the stir turned out to be no more than a buffalo calf, which the wolf quickly chased away.

She had to get out of here.

There was nothing for it. She would have to leave Moon Wolf dangling on the horse for the moment. It couldn't be helped. At least he wouldn't fall from there if she were careful and if she walked the animals out of the clearing.

Coming around to the horse's other side, she untied the rope from around the wolf and reached down to pet him. "I could not have done this without you, *Makoyi*. We must now get him out of here and into a hiding place so that I can come back and erase our tracks. You must lead me to a place. Do you understand?"

Again, the animal whined and, lifting his tail, trotted off in the opposite direction of the buffalo.

Alys grabbed both of the horses' reins and slowly, so as not to injure Moon Wolf further, followed the wolf, praising the powers that be that Moon Wolf surrounded himself with creatures so very, very wise.

Chapter 22

*M*akoyi led them into a wooded area close to the water. Alys busied herself with finding a well-hidden spot, finally settling on one close to some rocks and tucked away beneath some pine boughs and bushes. Returning to the horses, she brought out a blanket from her own mount and spread it on the ground in preparation for her last task—pulling Moon Wolf from his pony and settling him onto the ground.

She managed to take his weight on her own and drag him toward her blanket, easing him onto it and making him as comfortable as possible. Next, she returned to the horses to take their burdens from them and tether them.

Makoyi had disappeared on some self-appointed task with which Alys could little concern herself. She knew the animal would return; she also realized that she could not stay here with Moon Wolf. She had to go back the way they had come and erase all signs of their tracks. Someone would search for them sooner or later.

"Guard him," she told the horses and, taking up a few pine branches, began her trek back toward the buffalo herd.

Having successfully erased their tracks, she returned to camp. She still did not know the outcome of Moon Wolf's daring attempt, for she had been unwilling to go too close to the whiskey train.

Now she found that *Makoyi* had caught a couple of rabbits and had brought them back to the camp. She smiled at the animal. At least they would not starve.

"Thank you, *Makoyi*. After I see to your master's injuries, I will cook these rabbits and we will have a feast."

Makoyi whined and trotted off to a spot a few feet away from her. He lay down, head on his paws.

Alys turned her attention back to Moon Wolf. "What have you done to yourself that you do not awaken?" Except for his foot, she could still find little sign of injury.

Well, she would wrap that ankle with some of the material from their blankets and then build a fire. Luckily she was well versed in how to start a fire in the wilderness, a result once again of her mother's unorthodox education.

Wolves began to howl in the distance, *Makoyi* answering their calls and looking to her as though seeking her approval.

She pointed out to the beast, "I cannot go out there, *Makoyi*. Please stay here. With Moon Wolf injured, I may need you to hunt for us again."

But *Makoyi* could not be stilled. The wolves' howls lured him, and he paced back and forth, now and then stopping to return the summons.

It was close to morning when the wolf finally left. Alys did not protest. What could she say? What could she do? The animal had become more than a pet; it was possible that she and Moon Wolf would not be alive if not for

Makoyi. And because of this she could not deny *Makoyi* the right to live his own life, with his own kind.

She called out to him as he left the camp, however, "Just make sure, if you are going courting, that she comes from a good family, *Makoyi,* before you pair off with her."

The wolf glanced back at her once and then, with his tail straight up, trotted away.

Alys busied herself with the fire.

Something wet touched his brow.

He moaned. His head hurt with a pain made worse when he tried to open his eyes.

Perhaps he would just keep them closed. He muttered, *"Tsaahtai'kayi."*

"I don't understand you, Moon Wolf."

English. Someone spoke to him in the white man's language with the white man's accent.

"What happened to you?"

He knew that voice. Little Brave Woman. His wife. *Aa,* memory came flooding back to him.

He uttered, "Alys?"

A hand squeezed his own. "I am here," he heard her say.

Still, without opening his eyes, he asked, "What happened?"

"I don't know exactly," she said. "You charged the buffalo herd, do you remember that?"

"Aa." He kept his head still, since even the simplest of movements sent it throbbing.

"There was a shot."

"Aa, yes, the shot. When that happened, the buffalo turned all at once."

"You went down somehow, do you remember?"

"A buffalo fell into my pony and tripped him, sending

me flying from his back. I must have hit my head as I fell. It is all I remember."

"That would explain why you have been unconscious, then. *Makoyi* led me to you and helped me to raise you onto your pony, who stood by you all the time you were out. *Makoyi* brought me here, too, and even hunted for us."

"*Aa*, a good warrior is *Makoyi*."

"Yes. He has gone for now."

"Gone?"

"Yes. The wolves were howling and he could not resist going to them. I can only hope that, as you once said, our scent is so strong on him that he will not be lured away from us."

"*Aa*, yes, we must keep that hope," he said, adding, "I am going to try to open my eyes."

"Don't. There is no need right now. Rest some more; we are safe here for the time being."

Still, he opened his eyes all the same, squinting and muttering to himself as he came up onto his elbows. "Where are we?"

"We are in a wood that *Makoyi* led us to. There is a creek nearby, and we are well hidden. I also went back and did my best to cover our tracks. Why do you not try to recover your strength? Then, when you are better, we can go back to the fort."

"The whisky train," he said, ignoring her plea that he rest, "what happened to it?"

"I don't know exactly. After the shot fired, I saw two wagons fall, but I did not wait to see more. It became a more urgent task for me to find you."

He lay back. "Then I will have to go north beyond the medicine line as soon as I am recovered to find out about it. I cannot allow that shipment to reach my people."

She nodded. "I understand. If that is what you must do,

so be it. But please, for now, rest and build your strength."

As though now he agreed completely, he grinned at her and did exactly as she asked.

Four days later they rode into the Indian encampment that lay stretched out around Fort Whoop-Up which lay to the north, above the Canadian border.

Having sprained his ankle, Moon Wolf could barely walk without a limp, yet he insisted on going into the fort immediately. He refused her accompaniment, saying that there were too many bad things that happened there and he would not take her into it.

He had left her with his sister, Butterfly Woman, the same girl Alys had met so long ago. Alys was happy to see her again. Unfortunately, their mutual delight was dampened by the fact that neither young woman could communicate to the other.

"How have you been?" Alys asked her.

The young woman smiled at her, but shook her head. *"Tsa k-a:nist-a-opii-hpa?"*

It was Alys's turn to shake her head. There followed a companionable silence, the two women exchanging more smiles at one another. But soon Alys began to fret.

What if something happened to Moon Wolf? If bad things took place in that fort, did it not follow that bad things might happen to him, too?

She tried to start up a conversation with Moon Wolf's sister, to ask her about it, perhaps using sign language. But unfortunately, Alys's command of that language was also limited.

At last, she came to a decision: she would not stay here in the relative safety of Butterfly Woman's lodge while Moon Wolf went off into the fort alone. And so to this end, as soon as she could, without seeming to be rude, she excused herself and meandered into the camp's pony herd, seeking out the mount that Moon Wolf had given her.

Little did she realize that Moon Wolf's sister had followed her, bringing with her a blanket, as well as a supply of dried meat and a knife encased in a beautiful beaded buckskin sheath. After gaining Alys's attention, the young woman tied the knife onto Alys's belt and by hand signals, told Alys that the knife was now hers. Together, the two women began to saddle the pony.

Soon, the pony had a blanket over its back and a rawhide rope in his mouth. While the two women stood together, the young Indian trying to communicate something by means of sign language, her right hand over her heart, followed by a quick action to her right side as though she were throwing something away.

Alys merely shook her head. With only a rudimentary understanding of sign language, she could not communicate fully. She regretted now that she hadn't taken the time to learn more.

"*Sstonnat,*" the young woman tried again. Then suddenly she said, "Da-ger . . . bad . . . hearts," pointing in the direction of the fort.

Alys leaned down toward her and said, "I know there is danger. I will be careful."

Another series of signs followed, Butterfly Woman's hand coming over her eyes, fingers extended, backs of the hand out. This particular sign would have communicated in any language.

Alys said, "I will do my best not to look around me." She grasped her sister-in-law's hand.

Butterfly Woman nodded. "*Ihtsisoo, innaihtsiiyi.*"

But Alys didn't understand the words. She gave her sister-in-law a smile of appreciation and, after a touch of their hands, Alys gave her pony a quick kick. Whereupon she set out for the fort to rescue her man.

*   *   *

She could see the ill-reputed fort up ahead of her, noticing that it was one of the most well fortified forts she
had ever seen. A stockade of massive squared logs, Fort
Whoop-Up was well equipped with corner bastions for defense, bars in the windows, and loopholes every so often
along the bulky walls for firearms.

Only one window—and it was barred—in the weighty
oak gate operated as the trade center, and it appeared to
her that no Indian was permitted past that gate. Lines had
formed outside the window, while someone closer up to it
argued with the gatekeeper.

To her left, several men fought with one another; to her
right, a skirmish had ensued while one woman stood between two men and another woman postured farther away,
crying. In the distance guns blared, drums beat out a fast,
though steady, rhythm, and people shouted, sometimes taking a shot at one another.

The environment did little to encourage Alys, but she
would not use this as an excuse to return to her sister-in-
law's lodge; not until she had found Moon Wolf would
she be satisfied. Luckily, she still wore the feminine version of the Wolf Shadow disguise—a buckskin dress and
moccasins. In this way, at least, because she dressed like
an Indian she would not bring undue attention to herself.

She approached the gate with more than a little appre-
hension. Would she be admitted to the fort if she unveiled
her true self? Did she even want that, not knowing what
might await her there? Perhaps a more important question
would be, would Moon Wolf have gone there?

The chances were that he had not, since it did not appear
that any Indian was permitted within the inner sanctuary
of that gate.

She would have liked to have sat still, weighing her
choices, but any decision she would have made was
quickly taken from her as a throng of people suddenly

appeared at her back and pushed her forward and onward, closer and closer to the fort.

The people disbursed and from out of nowhere, an intoxicated man suddenly appeared before her. Pouncing on the neck of her horse, he grabbed the reins from her. At first she thought he meant to steal the horse, but then he spoke.

"Where're ya goin', girly?"

The words were English! She looked up suddenly. It was a white man, and his intent appeared to be not upon apprehending of her horse but on her.

She stated, calmly at first, "Let me go," making a grab to regain the reins.

It didn't work. The man only seized hold of her hands. "Ah, I gots me an English-speakin' Injun. Come here, you pretty squaw, and set your harlot ways onta me."

Alys was at once indignant. "I am no squaw," she informed him, "nor am I a harlot, my good man. Now let go of my horse." She tried to squirm out of his grasp.

Instead of letting up, however, the man moved in closer, doubling his grip on the pony . . . and on her. "Don't like being called a squaw, do you? Must be a 'breed of some sort. And I'm guessin' that I'll be the one to be the judge of whether or not you're a good whore. But you're already eating your way into me heart, young calico. I sure does like a fight."

Alys breathed in deeply, trying to keep her wits about her. What could she do? As of yet, the man's hold on her didn't seem too great, and he was drunk. Maybe she could evade him. She suggested in a matter-of-fact voice, "If it's a fight you're wanting, go pick on someone else," whereupon she jerked away quickly, trying to free herself.

It didn't work. He only held on harder.

"Why should I go lookin' for someone else?" came the drunken answer. "Seems to me I'm doin' you a favor. Not

too often does a white man—th' great Jake Berry at that—
take a favor to one of you redskins."

Jake Berry? Why did that name sound familiar? Surely
this couldn't be the same Jake connected with Lieutenant
Warrington. But if he was, what was he doing here?

Her hands still trapped in his grasp, she kicked out at
the man instead. A mistake. He grabbed her foot along
with her hands, making her double over. Then he pulled
. . . hard. For a drunken idiot, the man had incredible
strength. She yelled again, "Let me go!"

"I likes 'em a little wild. Come here to your new papa."
Another sharp pull and he sent her tumbling from the
horse.

She screamed, not that it would help her cause. No one
would notice. Yelling, shouting, and crying sounded all
around her; her own howl only adding to the general din.

The man unexpectedly let go of the horse to pull at the
bodice of her dress, effectively countering her efforts to
push his hands away. Unable to help herself, she screamed
again.

"Stop it," she howled. "I am a white woman."

But her words, instead of gaining her freedom, only
served to give the man courage. He even laughed. "I gots
me a feisty one as well as a pretty good liar, you 'breed."

"I am no liar."

He laughed. "Sure you're not. Come here, you calico."

Dear Lord, this couldn't be happening to her. Was the
man bent upon rape? If he was, there didn't seem to be a
thing she could do about it, for she could not match his
strength.

Then the worst happened. He ripped her dress down the
front, while wave after wave of raw terror washed through
her. One scream followed another as though drawn from
her throat involuntarily, the sound of it so awful that one
might have thought she were being murdered. And perhaps, for a woman, it was close to the same thing.

The man picked her up, her efforts to free herself ineffective. She cried out at the top of her lungs, "Dear God, help me!"

"Let her go!" a familiar male voice demanded—in English.

Jake Berry's grip on her did not diminish, however. He spared only a swift glance up at her defender. "I found her, Moon Wolf, go find your own woman."

Moon Wolf didn't bat an eye. He declared, "How is it that you come among us, here at this trading place and do not know the woman, Jake Berry? And you, a trapper? Have you not yet learned that this woman that you hold against her will is my wife?"

"I ain't holdin' her against no will. She's only playin'. And if'n she's your wife, why ain't she back there in the women's quarters, instead of out here where th' women are fast and cheap?"

"None of our women are cheap," came the answer, which merely elicited a hoot from the white man.

Moon Wolf persisted, "Since when did our women have to stay in certain places in order to be safe from men trying to force themselves? Since when can they not roam where they wish without fear of rape?"

"Since I come into your camp and say so, that's when."

"Then perhaps it is Jake Berry who is at fault and Jake Berry who should be killed before he dirties more of our women."

The man loosened his grip on Alys, allowing her to disentangle herself from him. Clutching the shattered ends of her dress around her, she fled toward Moon Wolf, putting him between herself and the white man. She gasped, her breathing coming in short spurts, while tears fell down her cheeks. She gulped unsteadily for air, her composure shattered.

But the danger was not past. Her man stood between

her and certain hell. And it was *she* who had put her husband's life in danger by not staying where he had told her.

Jake Berry demanded, "Get outa my way, Moon Wolf."

Moon Wolf held his ground. "Here I will stay. This is my woman. You cannot have her without going through me."

An evil laugh split through the air before Jake Berry spoke the words, "Fair enough."

It all happened so quickly that Alys had no chance to feel fear. A revolver was drawn, a shot was fired, Moon Wolf pushed Alys to the ground and dodged, throwing a knife through the air. Immediately, she heard a gasp and a thump, and looking around, watched as Jake Berry fell to the ground, the knife through his heart.

Alys collapsed onto the ground behind Moon Wolf, sobbing. Nothing, not all of her Wild West training, nor her more staid education in the east, could have prepared her for such a confrontation. She had felt, had been, so helpless.

Moon Wolf picked her up in his arms and, taking hold of the reins of her pony, began walking her toward the lodge of his sister.

He whispered into her ear, "It is over. He is dead, never to bother you again."

She could only nod, still sobbing.

"Sh-h-h. It will be fine now."

"I'm so . . . so very sorry," she cried.

"For what? What did you do wrong?"

"I came a-after you when you had ordered me to stay away."

"And when have you ever listened to me and what I tell you to do? The fault, if there is one, is mine for bringing you here. Or maybe the fault is this fort and the whiskey. This is what it does to my people. Never, not ever, in an Indian encampment, before the white man came to us with his drink, were our women assaulted in our own camp. But now, look at us. All those around us are so drunk, no one even notices the abuse, let alone stands by to protect their women. It is the liquor that is the cause. It is the liquor that I fight, that I will continue to fight so long as I exist."

They had reached his sister's lodge, and Moon Wolf entered it after scratching at the entryway. He took Alys to the women's section of the lodge and set her down on the warmth of a buffalo robe.

It was well known in a Blackfoot camp that after a certain age, a man was not supposed to address his sister, at least not directly. However, casting aside conventions in light of the present situation, Moon Wolf found himself asking, "Have you water to drink that you might give it to my wife?"

"Aa, kyai-yo." His sister rushed to bring something to him. *"Tsa anistapiiwaatsiksi?* What happened?"

"A white man called Jake Berry, who came here to guard a whiskey shipment, tried to force himself upon my wife. She is still frightened, I think. I ask of my sister that she take care of my wife, to guard her and not let her go out again until she is well. I must go, for there are things I must still attend to. I would have these things done and leave here as soon as possible."

"Kyai'-yo, soka'piiwa, it is good. You go," his sister said, nodding and coming down on her knees before Alys.

With a brief nod, Moon Wolf arose and slipped quietly out of the lodge while his sister spoke these words to Alys, *"Nit-ik-oht-yaahs-i'taki k-ikaa-o'too-hs-yi,* I am glad you have arrived." Whereupon she took Alys into her arms, much as one might a small child.

And while Alys tried to compose herself, the gracious woman began to sing a song, the melody tender and in a strange, minor key.

> *Kitsikakomimmokoo*
>   (you are loved),
> *Nitanistoo'pa* (I said it),
> *Soka'piiwa* (it is good).
> *Nitanistoo'pa* (I said it),
> *Soka'piiwa* (it is good).
> *Kitsikakomimmokoo*
>   (you are loved).

Then daintily, soothingly, as though Alys had merely had a bad nightmare, Butterfly Woman rocked Alys back and forth, over and over until at last the worst of the fear had passed.

"The redcoats are coming."

Moon Wolf awakened her with these words.

"What?" She stirred beneath the warmth of the buffalo robe and gazed around her, disoriented. Ah, yes. She was in the lodge of Moon Wolf's sister, Butterfly Woman. She yawned and asked of Moon Wolf, "Have you even been to bed yet?"

"*Saa*, no, and I will not. We must prepare to leave at once. I know this might be hard for you, especially after what happened today, but it cannot be helped. My sister is already up and is starting to pack so that she and her family may leave here quickly."

"But why? Why must we go now? What time is it?"

"The last brother is pointing toward the ground."

Alys paused for a moment, recalling what Moon Wolf had told her about the night sky. She groaned. "But that means it's still the middle of the night."

"It matters not; we must go," he urged, pulling down the buffalo robe and rubbing her arms.

"Hmmm," she murmured. "That feels good."

"Then turn over. I will rub your back. But you must

promise me that after I do this, you will arise and pack our things."

She obediently turned over, muttering, "But we brought very little with us."

"Then it will be easy," he said, beginning to massage her back, starting at the neck.

"Tell me why we have to leave," she asked as she brought a hand around to scratch an itch.

He scooted that hand away. "I will do that," he said, and did so, proceeding to scratch her entire back, leaving out, however, an awfully big section in the middle. He said, "Scouts have returned to tell us that the redcoats of the Queen Mother are coming here to arrest these American traders. The whiskey sneakers do not know of this yet because we caught their scouts before they could warn them."

"Hmmm," she responded. "Is that good?"

"It is very good, it means that the whiskey sneakers won't be able to hide their liquor, and that the redcoats—"

"Moon Wolf," she interrupted, "you are ignoring a part of my back. Could you scratch it in the middle?"

"How careless of me," he said, but she detected a note of teasing in his voice. He proceeded to scratch her, still ignoring the middle.

She brought a hand around to do it herself, but he immediately captured it. "I will do this for you."

She laughed, "Then do the middle, too."

"You mean like this?" He scratched the middle-upper section of her back.

"A little lower."

"Here?"

"No, that's too low. Moon Wolf, I think you tease me."

"Tease you? How can you say that? Am I not doing all that you ask of me?"

She groaned. "No, you are not. Here, I'll do it myself."

Again he caught her hand. "*Saa,* no, I will do this for you."

She moaned. "Then do it, scratch the middle."

He scratched over to the left, then the right. "Do you mean like this?"

"Men," she muttered. "Stop it, Moon Wolf."

He laughed and scratched the middle up and down until she was satisfied. "Come," he said, "you must arise and get dressed."

"Hmmm." She rolled over, the buffalo robe already pulled down toward her waist. "Tell me more."

But Moon Wolf was looking at her, his glance falling heavily onto her breasts, an odd expression in his eye. At some length he brought his gaze up to meet with her own. He grinned. "It seems so long since I have seen you like this, that like a child, I cannot help looking."

"I am not stopping you."

His eyes narrowed. "Yet you should. We must leave here at once."

She drew her arms under her head, so as to draw even more attention to her chest.

A gleam came into his eye. She should have sensed what was coming next, but she didn't.

He tickled her.

And she gave an involuntary screech.

"Sh-h-h."

"Then don't tickle me," she whispered.

He grinned at her. "Come on, we have much to do. We will let the redcoats deal with these traders. Maybe they will take away their liquor. It is said that this is their purpose."

"Good." She rolled over, and he tickled her again, this time with his hand over her mouth.

"Moon Wolf!"

He laughed. "Come, I am anxious to go. There is a

rumor that a new lawman has come to Fort Benton."

"A lawman? You mean a sheriff?"

Moon Wolf nodded. "Some of our people have just come from there and say that he has already arrested some of the whiskey sneakers and that he has destroyed some of their supply."

"He has?" She sat up sparing no more than a moment to wonder if it had been her series of letters which had brought the law to Fort Benton. She said, "Then this is good."

"It could be very good. If this man is honest and is true, it could mean that . . . *haiya,* I think we will talk of that later."

She had arisen, was standing nude in front of him.

"*Ok yi,* come here."

It wasn't in her to fight him; she surrendered at once, falling against him, his lips at her belly as he knelt before her. "Hmmm," she let out a low moan. "Has your sister already left?"

"*Saa,* no. She will return soon."

Alys shrugged. "Too bad."

She could feel his lips on her stomach, his tongue tracing the outline of her belly button. She asked, "Your work here is done, then?"

"The liquor shipments did not arrive," he murmured. "Our attack on the whiskey train worked well." He drew back from her. "But come, I do not wish to be here when the redcoats arrive. There will be much confusion and someone could get hurt. And we have no more need to be here. Get dressed and let us go. Perhaps we can find a safe spot where we could stop on the way back to the fort."

"Perhaps we could," she agreed. "Or maybe I should say, I think we'd better."

He laughed, a warm, beautiful sound that had her sighing.

She became suddenly serious and said, "I did not thank you for what you did for me today."

He shrugged. "I need no thanks to protect my woman."

"All the same," she insisted, "I would have you know that I am beholden to you."

"Beholden?"

"Yes, beholden. In your debt."

He drew away from her and looked up to her, whispering, "Never, not ever are you 'beholden' to me."

"But—"

"Is not your life my own? Do I not protect you now as I would protect myself and all whom I love?"

With his words, his sincerity, a tear threatened to spill over, onto her cheek, and she shook back her head to keep it away. He was such a good man.

He rose up onto his feet before her and, putting a finger indulgently under her chin, lifted her head up until her eyes met his. He commented, "Is not our path now the same?"

She compressed her lips together, as though the action might hold back that darned tear. "Moon Wolf, I—"

"Know that I would protect you as though it is through you that I breathe," he said, putting his arms around her and pulling her against him. "Believe me. From now, until I cease to exist upon our mother, the earth, you, your spirit and your life force are here in my heart, forever."

He placed his hand over her heart, then his, and, reaching for the back of his neck, he released the single shell chain necklace that he wore. With both hands, he placed it around her neck, saying, "Once, long ago, I gave you this necklace that I might honor you. Now, again I give it to you that you might always be reminded of my love. This which I feel for you will never die. And now, you know it."

The threatened tear fell, and with a sob, she threw herself into his embrace, her arms coming around his neck to hug him. "I love you, Moon Wolf," she said. "I love you so very, very much. I am glad to have the necklace once more. I had wondered about it, why you did not give it back to me when I left it with you."

He shrugged. "I thought you no longer wanted it."

"Never," she shook her head. "That was the first night I pretended to be the Wolf Shadow. I only left it with you so that, if something happened to me, you would remember me, too."

He breathed in deeply. "Know always that I do not need, have never needed, such a reminder to keep you forever with me."

"Oh, Moon Wolf." She held her hand over her heart, the universal sign for love. She said, "You, too, are in my heart. I love you."

In reply, he pulled her into his arms, repeating in her ear over and over, "*Kitsikakomimmo, kitsikakomimmo, kitsikakomimmo . . .*"

And together, in one another's arms, they cried.

"This is a beautiful spot," Alys commented as she sat down next to a clear mountain stream. She and Moon Wolf had stopped beneath a shelter of aspens and pine trees, which grew profusely on this mountainside. They had both of them hobbled their ponies and had paused to rest as they pushed their way back to Fort Benton. "Tell me," she continued, "is there danger of meeting bears here?"

"There is always that danger. But do not worry. I have seen no evidence of bears here, and it is getting close to that time of year when the bears will be searching for a place to spend the winter."

"I am glad to hear that."

He acknowledged her with a brief tilt of his head. "I wonder," Moon Wolf pondered, "if it might be a mountaintop like this where we could secure a place for us? It is far enough away from the white men's prejudice that it might function as the perfect setting for us, but alas, it is also too far away from my own people, I fear. Too soon, we would be coveting the company of others."

She nodded. "And I would miss my mother."

He sighed and leaned back against the trunk of a cottonwood. Picking up a blade of grass, he began to chew on it. "There must be someplace," he contemplated, "somewhere here in this country where we will be welcome. Where is it, I wonder?"

She leaned back against the tree trunk as well, her head nestled in the crook of Moon Wolf's neck. "I don't know, my husband. But I think it is important that we discover this place, for there will be others like us, I believe. Others who wish to love one another despite the strict conventions of society. Perhaps we can light the way for them."

"Perhaps," he agreed, "but for now, I worry only about us. We must progress step by step. If there are others, we will lead them by our example. But first we must find a place where we are safe."

"We will have to keep searching, then."

Again, he inclined his head, pulling her in closer to him. "I think we will make camp here tonight."

"Yes," she agreed and closed her eyes.

Several moments passed before he observed, "Are you going to sleep so soon?"

"Hmmm, no," she replied, though her eyes remained closed. "But it has been a long journey."

He chuckled and, releasing his arms around her, came up onto his haunches, squatting down beside her. "You stay here and rest. I will get our things and prepare our camp."

She sighed her pleasure at his suggestion and fell asleep at once, her dreams filled with the prospect of a home on a beautiful mountainside, her darkly handsome husband by her side.

A full moon had climbed high in the eastern sky by the time she awoke. She pulled the buffalo robe more firmly around her as she sat up and took stock of where she was.

Moon Wolf sat across from her, stoking the gentle blaze he had made. She allowed herself the delight of studying him unawares. He had released his hair from his braids, the locks falling down his back and around his shoulders. Moonlight played over his features, casting shadows over his cheeks and making him appear more phantom at the moment than real person. Light from the fire showed off the fullness of his lips, and she concentrated on those, remembering the way they felt against her own.

She drew in a deep breath of the fresh, cool air and sighed. Oh, how she wished he would kiss her.

As though she had spoken her thoughts aloud, he raised his head, his eyes searing into hers. He said, his voice hushed, "You are beautiful as you sit here before me in the moonlight."

She sat up then and moved forward until she came closer to the fire. "And you, my husband," she observed, "are handsome beyond compare."

That seemed to gladden him, for he smiled. "I think that you compliment me," he said.

"No," she disagreed. "I speak the truth as I see it. Only the truth, my love."

"Come you here." He motioned to a spot next to him.

And she went, no questions asked.

She fell into his arms at once, the musky scent of him, combining with pure mountain air, an intoxication.

One of his hands came up to thread his fingers through her hair, though all the while he leaned her back against the robes he had placed next to him. "It has been too long, my wife, since we have sealed the pledge of our love with our bodies. Too long, I fear, we have been plotting the ruin of the whiskey trains without giving ourselves that pleasure which is ours, as man and wife, to take."

"Are you only now becoming aware of this?"

He grinned. "Have I been so unattentive?"

"Hardly," she replied, "although I have discovered myself studying you lately with great intent, I am afraid."

His fingers came up to run over her cheeks, while with his eyes, he revered her. A half smile lit his face, and he leaned down toward her, placing a sweet kiss next to the pulse beat at her neck.

She moaned and squirmed.

He acknowledged the sudden desire in her by placing a stream of kisses to her neck, her cheeks, her eyes. He nibbled on an earlobe, while his hand moved lower and lower, over the delicate skin of her neck, to her breasts.

And where his fingers pressed, his lips followed, a sensual growl sounding in his throat. "You are like a vision come true," he murmured between nibbles. "I think I knew, when we first met, all those years ago, that our paths were to be as one. Even then, when you were so very, very young, I desired to kiss you. Did I ever tell you that?"

She wiggled beneath the pleasure of his touch, and smiled. "No, you did not. And I think you have been remiss in keeping this to yourself until now."

"We were both so young, yet I found the desire to kiss you strong within me."

"And now?"

He issued a low growl and nuzzled her stomach, his fingers fast at work releasing the snaps which held the clothing in place. Soon there was nothing but her skin beneath his lips and, unable to keep still, she fidgeted under the erotic rush he made upon her.

"Moon Wolf," she pleaded, "love me."

"I am."

But she could not lay there so inert. And so, instead of meekly accepting his ministrations, she raised up onto one forearm and pushed at him with her other hand until he lay beneath her.

"I think," she suggested, "that I would like to love you."

Though he did not utter a word, his look alone urged her to continue.

First she removed his shirt, and while her gaze feasted on him, she brought her own breasts to his, touching him tip to tip.

He groaned and closed his eyes.

"Do you like that?" she asked in a whisper as she massaged him, chest to chest.

He drew in his breath. "I like it very much, I think."

She came up to trace her tongue over the delicate skin of a warm, male nipple. "Do you only think so?" she teased.

"Know, I should have said," he acknowledged. "I know I like it . . . very much."

With her tongue, she traced a path downward, the rasp of his breath telling her better than words could that she pleased him.

She pulled off the breechcloth that hid the evidence of his desire and scooted downward until the warmth of her caress encompassed even the swollen part of him.

Again, he moaned, and the sound of his passionate response sent a shot of delight through her.

But she had no more than begun to love him when he raised up onto one arm, gazing intently down at her. He muttered, "And now it is my turn."

"Is it?"

He simply nodded and, taking her in his arms, drew her down, his own lips rejoicing over the softened mounds of her breasts. On downward, he continued to kiss, over her belly button, to that secret moist recess between her legs.

"Hmmm," he whispered, "you are so beautiful. I cannot get enough of you. And you taste like a fresh breath of air . . ." The rest was lost beneath his lips as he began to pay sensual tribute to her.

And Alys, arching her back, lay down, spreading her legs around him, opening to him, as only a woman in love can do.

She met her climax almost at once, and pausing only a beat, he joined his body with hers.

She whimpered in ecstasy, her body attuned to his as she lay beneath him. He pushed upward, giving her the desire she yearned for, and she accompanied his every motion, rhythmically moving her hips with his as though they performed a dance of desire.

He shifted onto his side, his body still joined with hers, and came up onto his forearm, staring down at her. Belatedly, he smiled while his fingers roamed over her cheeks, her neck. "I think that we love well."

She could only nod, even now, the pleasure they were making with one another too much for her to trust in her voice.

And then, her gaze locked with his, she met with the liquid fire of her release, Moon Wolf watching her in wonder before he at last spilled his seed within her.

They lay entwined, their bodies moist from their exertion, their breathing unsteady. Wrapped in each other's arms, they drifted, each one content to simply bask in one another's space. And for a moment, as though one, they knew one another's thoughts, desires, and passions as though they were one's own. And how beautiful they each were.

Ah, yes, for a moment, if a moment only, they were as one, with no secrets between them. And in this instant,

Alys knew there would be a place for them—somewhere. If they could not find it, they would make it.

For together, united in cause, they were more than each one separately, more than anything that this universe could throw against them.

Yes, she thought, they would create a home for themselves and for others like them. It was a promise.

Chapter 23

～⌒○⌒～

Bobby Thompson strutted through the streets of Fort Benton, young Abigail Flint on one arm and the snobby Emma on the other. Although Alys had only arrived home late last evening, she had made a trip into town in order that she might visit with the sheriff to find out all she could about him.

Alys spared a quick glance at the odd sight of the threesome there on the street and turned away, only to spin back around, staring . . . and staring.

Goodness. Had Bobby gone through some sort of transformation?

His style of dress had certainly changed. These clothes were of the latest fashion, not some homespun wear that his mother might have produced. His suit, a British two-piece, was a brown striped wool affair and was topped by a single-breasted cutaway jacket; his trousers were narrow and in a matching striped wool, while a waistcoat of a gray patterned silk hugged his waistline. He wore a winged collared white shirt, blue silk necktie, and black boots, and on his head sat a black felt hat with a high flat-topped crown and a narrow curved brim. With a pair of gray gloves and a cane in one hand, he might have stepped off a fashion plate.

Also, where had that mustache come from, waxed at the ends so that it curled up? The last time Alys had seen him, he had been clean-shaven.

And what were Abigail and Emma doing with him? Hadn't they been of a mind, only a month ago, to ignore him?

Stunned, she brushed a hand over her eyes and looked again upon the little scene before her. "Well, I'll be . . ." she muttered under her breath.

Not wanting to be caught staring, however, she turned away, but it was too late. He had seen her.

"Miss Alys." It was Bobby calling to her. "Miss Alys, I'm real glad to see you back again." Pulling Emma and Abigail along with him, Bobby approached Alys. "Your mother told us how you'd gone to visiting relatives. She didn't rightly know when you'd be back, either." Bobby drew level with her as he spoke. "I sure was hoping it wasn't the *breakup* of our *engagement* that sent you packing . . ." His eyes pleaded with her for understanding.

Ah, so that was it. In her absence Bobby had called off their engagement. And in the process had attracted the two prettiest girls in the county. Well, good for him   and for her. One less problem to solve. Alys breathed out a sigh.

She didn't dare let her relief show too much, however, not in front of the girls. After all, Bobby had a reputation to uphold. She laid her hand on Bobby's gloved one and said, "Do forgive me, Bobby. One does not lose a fine man like you every day and . . ."—she pretended a sniffle—"I needed some time to myself. But," she added, "I understand that it would never have worked. You in England and on the Continent with your estranged, yet *titled* family, and me here, stuck in this remote western town. Please," she pleaded, "don't tell me again that you would stay with me in this terrible little town . . . no matter what might come. I wouldn't think of holding you back." She laid her hand on her forehead for good, dramatic measure.

Bobby looked more than a little startled at the news of his new and *titled* family, not to mention his intended trip to the Continent. She only hoped that he would not call her out for it.

"Yes, Miss Alys, well," he said. Taking his cue from her, he patted her hand. "I sure am glad to hear that you've recovered."

The two women at his side listened to the conversation with rapt attention. Said Emma, "You spoiled our surprise, Miss Alys. Why, only this morning Miss Abigail and I were saying that we should ask Bobby to invite us to go to the Continent next year."

"Do tell," purred Alys, summoning everything in her to keep the tone of her voice level. Truth to tell, she failed.

Abigail, however, flushed. She offered, "Please do forgive us, Miss Alys, but when we heard that your engagement to Bobby had ended, we could not help but seek him out and try to discover more about his heritage. I hope you will forgive our lack of manners in not waiting until you returned. That is, before we approached him."

Alys gave the girl a warm smile. *At least her heart was in the right place.* She patted the young girl's hand. "Please don't worry about me. I only desire that Bobby will be happy. I think he deserves it."

Bobby cleared his throat. "Yes, well, I was also hoping that you could come down to the store later so that you and me could catch up with . . . matters . . ."

"Yes," she agreed, "I would like that very much. Thank you, Bobby. Now, if you would be so kind, could you direct me to where I will find our new sheriff? I heard that he arrived in town while I was gone."

"The new sheriff?" This comment came from Emma.

Bobby looked important. "Hear tell that he took the office next door to the tavern. Reckon that suits him, since he's then at the right place at the right time, whenever he's needed, that is." Bobby gave her a look of concern. "What is it you're needing to see him about? We'd be happy to accompany you there."

What a lovely gentleman Bobby was. Alys gave her friend a smile before answering, "Why thank you, Bobby, but there really is no need. I have only a minor piece of business with him."

"Fine," said Bobby, "that's fine, then." He raised his hat in farewell, but before he left, with one girl still on each arm, he added, "Sure would like to see you stop by the store so that we can catch up on one another."

She grinned. "I promise I will."

"Then I reckon I'll be looking forward to it, Miss Alys," Bobby grinned back. "I'll look forward to it, indeed." And with that, he bent down to press a light kiss to her hand.

Charming, thought Alys. Absolutely charming.

The threesome turned away, Bobby leading. She watched the cut of their figures for the space of a moment before she, too, turned away, resuming her search.

So, the sheriff's office was on the other side of the tavern? As Bobby had said, how apt.

She set off in that direction.

"I demand that you help me find and arrest this fiend, this Wolf Shadow . . . now!"

"Sorry, Lieutenant Warrington," came a bored reply, "but I don't rightly know as I see this man has broken the law."

Alys, hearing the exchange, came to an instant halt half-way to the door of the sheriff's office.

"What do you call attacking the bull wagons that are doing no more than traveling into Canada to distribute food and clothing to the Indians, Sheriff?"

A long pause followed the question. "Ever wonder," the new lawman responded, his accent a slow drawl, "why an Indian would be attacking shipments of food and cloth-ing?"

"The man is insane, I tell you."

"Nope, I don't rightly think so," replied the sheriff matter-of-factly. "My theory is that this Wolf Shadow was attacking these 'supply' wagons 'cause wagons they car-ried whiskey, illegal trade that the U.S. government has forbidden."

"Are you suggesting—"

"I'd hate real bad to find out you was mixed up in all this, Lieutenant. And you with such a fine career ahead of you 'n all . . ." Sarcasm fairly stroked every word. "Now, see here. The United States government has sent me out here to enforce its liquor laws. And I aim to do exactly that. I'll see them properly enforced, too . . . even if I have to fight the United States Cavalry to do it."

"You can't possibly think that I, or the cavalry, are mixed up in whiskey trading?"

A long pause followed.

"Why, that's slander."

"Nope. I'd call it fact. Might I suggest, Lieutenant, that you start looking real fast for another post to fill . . . some-where else . . . if'n you aim to keep that 'good career' of yours intact 'n all."

"Is that a threat, Sheriff?"

"Nope, Lieutenant. It's a promise."

The lieutenant's voice raised up an entire octave as he uttered, "We'll see about that. Just you wait 'til the rest of

the town hears that you've taken up sides with an Indian!
And you, a white man!"

The sheriff paused a moment, and she could hear the
scrape of a chair across the wooden floor, followed by
the sheriff's quiet voice. "I side, when I side at all, with
the United States government . . . and don't you forget it,
Lieutenant. Now, the way I see it, if'n this Indian's helpin'
me to do my job, why I think I might give the man a
medal. Yep, Lieutenant, the more I think about it, the more
I like it. I might just do that . . ."

Alys could hear the slam of something against a wall.
And somewhere inside a pistol cocked.

"You aren't going to shoot me, are you, Sheriff?"

"I might."

"Of all the high-falutin', governmental hogwash. You
haven't heard the last from me, not by a long shot."

"Naw, don't suppose I have, Lieutenant, I don't suppose
I have. But you've heard the last from me. The next time
I come after you, I'll be comin' with a warrant."

"You have no proof of anything."

"Don't I?"

"Who's talked?"

Dead silence followed the question. At length, the sheriff muttered, "Why, Lieutenant, that's all I needed to
know."

Heavy footsteps sounded from inside, coming toward
the door. Alys dashed around the side of the building.

"I'll find out who's been spilling their guts and then
I'll—"

"The only man that's talked, Lieutenant, is you. Maybe
. . . Don't mind tellin' you, though, that if'n I find some
poor man dead, I'll come gunnin' for you, no questions
asked."

"You can't do that."

"Can't I? You got friends that're gonna stop me?"

Another deadly silence.

"Like I said, Lieutenant, I think you might be wise to find another position—somewhere else."

More footsteps sounded, then the slam of a door. Footsteps again, going away, echoing against the wooden planks of the sidewalk.

Meanwhile Alys leaned back, resting her head against the side of the building.

Imagine that. The government had heard her plea, had sent them an honest man . . . as sheriff. It was enough to renew one's faith.

And as relief, quick and sure, washed through her the more she thought about it, she so very, very slowly smiled.

She thought about leaving to go home, right then and there. Her purpose in seeing the sheriff had certainly been taken care of without her having to do a thing.

At length, however, she straightened away from the building and approached the sheriff's office. She didn't know what she would say or what she might do, but it didn't matter. The least she could do was thank the man.

Coming up to the door and turning the handle, she walked in. As she swept into the room, the sheriff came to his feet, the look on his face more than a little surprised.

She smiled at the man, a tall, gangling fellow who appeared to be in his early forties. She didn't pause or put on airs, though. Instead, she came right to the point. "I'm sorry to be bothering you, Sheriff, but I couldn't help overhearing your conversation with Lieutenant Warrington."

Swiping his hat from his head and holding it across his chest, he said, "Why, ma'am, I'm right sorry about that."

She nodded. "I thought you might like to know that I'm glad to hear that you are taking Lieutenant Warrington to task for his involvement in the whiskey trading. In fact, Sheriff, while I was outside, I thought that such honesty and bravery deserved a little credit. I know you're new in town and all, but if you'd like, my mother and I would be happy to have you and your family over for a home-cooked meal. Would you and your Mrs. like to come to our house for supper sometime soon?"

"Why, that would be right neighborly of you, ma'am. Right neighborly. I know my wife and daughter would be real happy about that."

Alys smiled. "I'm Alys Clayton. My mother and I live at the back of town. It's the big house. You can't miss it. Say tonight at six?"

"Six would be fine, ma'am. Just fine."

Again, Alys smiled and, letting herself out of the office, skipped all the way home.

Like a sick hound with his tail tucked between his legs, Lieutenant Warrington left the next day, the town fairly buzzing with the gossip.

But that wasn't the only little bit of good news. Torn down, all around town, were the posters that had advertised a bounty of two thousand dollars upon the capture of the Wolf Shadow. Not a single poster remained.

Alys burst with the good tidings the moment she met Moon Wolf within the caves.

His reaction, however, far from being the joyous one she had expected, proved to be thoughtful.

"What's the matter?" she asked, stepping up to him where he leaned against one of the cave's cold walls. "Aren't you happy about this? I think it is good."

He nodded, sparing her a quick glance. "*Aa*, yes, that it is. And yet, there is more to be done, I fear."

"What do you mean?"

"I do not believe that the lieutenant was the person be-hind the attacks upon the Indian people, and especially not upon the rights of my people to roam over this land. Once,

I questioned him about who it was that he worked for and tricked him into telling me that there were other men who supported him."

Alys remained silent for a moment. At length she volunteered, "You might be right, but it is not something we can do anything about right now. Come, Moon Wolf, let us at least rejoice in this major victory. Because as of tonight, you have been set free. No more have you the need to don the personage of the Wolf Shadow."

A long, silent moment followed her statement until at length Moon Wolf grinned. "You are right. This should be a time for rejoicing. And for tonight perhaps, my wife, I should forget the rest of our problems."

Alys grinned and scooted over to him, placing her arms around his neck. "Then perhaps we should seek out a preacher at once and get that certificate so that no one, not even the good folk from Fort Benton, could keep us apart."

He grinned. "Perhaps we should, if that is what you wish, although I do not believe that this will make our marriage in any way more acceptable to the people at Fort Benton. But maybe it is a start. Do you know of a person from within your town who would marry us?"

"Not right now, but give me time. I will find one," she responded. "I promise you this."

Drums beat out a cadence as the soft atmosphere of dusk fell all around her. The wide, barren plains in the distance, the mountains, and the flat-topped buttes all glowed red under the waning, yet spectacular, sunset. The odor of prairie grass and sage filled the mountain-fresh air, while the melancholy howl of the wolves in the distance seemed to protest the end of the day.

Yet her heart ached.

Where was he?

She knew he hadn't left her, would never leave her. But where was he?

Alys stood at the window of her home, looking out onto the prairie. From her position, she could barely make out the encampment of Indians, but it made no difference. She knew she wouldn't find him there.

Earlier in the day, she had stood at the north bastion of the fort, looking out over the Indian encampment, watching, observing.

She had looked for him. She hadn't found him.

She had noticed, however, the several bands of Blackfeet and Cree who had entrenched themselves around the fort; had noted, too, the colorful lodges stretching off before her, far into the distance.

It had been many years since the Indians had camped so close to Fort Benton, mainly because of the antagonism between the two peoples. But something had changed all that.

The Indians had arrived.

It must be a good thing, some of the kinder folks were saying. Relations between the two races might improve because of it, it had even been conjectured.

Perhaps, she thought. However, that didn't help her own cause. To date, she'd had no luck finding a preacher who would marry her . . . to an Indian. This complication didn't lessen her commitment to Moon Wolf, but it did bring up the ever-present question of where they would live.

More important to her now, however, was *where was Moon Wolf?*

Oddly enough, with his duties as the Wolf Shadow no longer required, Moon Wolf had barely been around this past week.

Always before, he would have been in the caves, an easy target for her to visit. But no longer did he treat the caves as though they were his home.

She had not even seen *Makoyi;* although Moon Wolf had mentioned that the animal had been absenting himself more and more from his master.

"Come to my encampment with me," Moon Wolf had encouraged her a few days ago. But she had declined, uncertain what would await her there.

Although it was so very wrong of her, she could not help but remember what had happened to her in Canada. Of course, this situation was different; there was almost no whiskey flowing between this fort and the Indians here, and certainly things would be different because of that. But no amount of reasoning would give her comfort.

Where was Moon Wolf?

She needed to see him, to touch him. She needed to be held in his arms. Why didn't he come to her?

Nothing had changed between them, she was certain of that. Yet, why had he gone? And where?

It was the uncertainty that was taking its toll on her, she was certain. Still . . .

Closing her eyes, she said a silent prayer before she withdrew from her vigil and turned away from the window.

She had made a decision: she would go to the caves. Even if he wasn't there, the caverns would make her feel better, their darkened tunnels and cool air comforting. Besides, his presence would always be there, always a reminder of their love. And perhaps it was a way to draw close to him in his absence.

She turned back into the room, stepping toward the entryway, where she kept her wrap.

"Alys, could I speak with you a moment?" her mother called from the sitting room.

"Certainly," Alys responded. "A moment, please."

Alys grabbed her shawl and threw it around her shoulders, then paced toward the other room.

"Mama, I think that I need to get something from the root cellar," she said before stepping fully into the room. "Would you excuse me until later this evening?"

"In a moment, dear. First, come here, would you please?"

Alys stepped around the corner, her head down. "What is it, Mama?"

"Alys . . ."

Alys raised her head, her eyes widening as her gaze met that of . . .

"Moon Wolf." Her words were part exclamation, part sigh. "What are you doing here?" *In my house?* she added to herself. Hadn't he once declared he would never openly come here for her?

She stared at him as though she had never seen him before. And perhaps she hadn't. It was Moon Wolf and yet . . . not.

Before her stood her husband, yes, but not the same man that she had become so accustomed to seeing these past few months. Before her stood a warrior, and, in truth, the man she loved. But never had she seen him look so well dressed . . . or so handsome. And despite herself, she gawked.

He stood proudly in his native garb, a white elkskin shirt draped down to his knees; long fringes, close to a foot long, hung under the arms of that shirt and at the bottom of each sleeve, trailing down over each of his wrists. On the chest of the shirt and at the shoulders had been patterned a large circular design of quillwork, the colors blue, white, and red. Leggings that fit his muscular legs so well they might have been a second skin fell to the ground ending with fringes, lagging upon the ground behind him. The same pattern of design in blue, white, and red quillwork ornamented each seam of those leggings, from the top to the bottom.

White moccasins encased his feet, quillwork and beads covering the leather completely.

He had pulled his hair into braids at each side of his head, although when he turned, she noted another braid hanging down his back. All three were tied separately with white buckskin.

Shell hairpipes, fixed together with beads, fell down from his center part, down over each braid. And over his shoulder he had slung a white goatskin robe, the garment depicting painted battle scenes. One of those battles, the prominent one facing her, included a figure wearing a wolf-shaped headdress.

"Alys," her mother said to her, "I'm not certain that you know Brother Mark. He has come to visit with the Blackfeet while they are here at the fort."

Alys gave her mother a considering glance, noticing for the first time the gentleman beside her, dressed all in black. Had the man been there all this time?

Alys nodded her head. "Brother Mark," she acknowledged.

"Brother Mark," her mother continued, "wants to go with Moon Wolf to the Indian encampment."

"He does?"

"Yes, it seems he takes great pleasure in talking with the Indians and singing their songs, hearing their tales and discussing religion with them. There is to be a big celebration at the Indian encampment tonight, a celebration to mark the end of the whiskey trade in Canada. I think that you and Moon Wolf should accompany him there."

"I am not certain that is a good idea, Mama. The last time I was in an Indian encampment—"

Ma Clayton didn't wait for her daughter to finish. "I'll be going with you, too."

"You will? But is that wise? How can you be safe there when even I won't go there?"

Her mother made a face. "Are you forgetting that I have often visited the Indians in the past? I still have friends there. Besides, the good reverend will be with us, plus we will be under the protection of Moon Wolf and his friends."

"But Mama, I still am uncertain that I approve—"

"She had a bad experience at our camp in Canada," Moon Wolf supplied. "It is only to be expected that she is fearful and so perhaps it would be better if—"

"Who said I was fearful?"

Moon Wolf raised an eyebrow.

"If my mother is going there, then I will, too."

"Good," said Ma Clayton. "I'm glad that that's settled. Now, how long will it take you to dress?"

"Dress? I am dressed."

Her mother looked her over critically. "So you are, but not as elegantly as Moon Wolf. Perhaps you could run upstairs and grab that gown that you have been working over these past few weeks. I think that would do."

"Do for what?"

"For the celebration, of course."

"But, Mama, I'm not sure that would be appropriate to wear on a visit with Moon Wolf's people and—"

"I think," Moon Wolf spoke up at last, approaching her on silent feet, "that your mother forgets to tell you that this is to be a special occasion."

"Is it?" She raised her chin.

He nodded. "We are celebrating."

"Are we?" She pushed back her shoulders and tilted her head, asking the question uppermost on her mind. "Where have you been?"

He took another step toward her, stopped, and frowned at her, saying, "I have had many . . . things that needed my attention."

"Oh," she turned her face away. "More than your wife,

I suppose." Darn, why had she said that? It made her sound like a fishwife. She strolled casually toward the open window in the room, putting her back to him before saying, "I'm sorry, but I think that you forgot to tell me anything about where you were going or how long you would be gone. I have worried."

He made a move toward her, halted, and said, "I am sorry."

She turned an uneasy glance upon him.

"I did not intend to be away so many days," he explained, giving her a lopsided grin. "And I am not used to having a wife who is anxious for me."

She squared her shoulders and faced back into the room, smiling slightly before she bit her lip. "All right," she offered easily enough, "I am glad you have returned."

He nodded once, and she glanced back toward her mother, asking, "What are we celebrating?"

"You will see, but you must go and get your things."

"I could simply change here."

"No," asserted her mother. "Dear, please go collect your things. Moon Wolf has offered to carry me to his village that I may partake in the ceremony."

"What is this ceremony?"

"You will see."

"But—"

"Alys," her mother urged, "hurry along now and do as you are asked, please, for there is something else that needs doing."

"Oh?" Alys crossed her arms and planted her feet.

"Now don't be giving me one of your looks. There is simply more that needs doing."

"More than what? Mama, what are you trying to tell me? I'm not leaving until you've told me all."

Ma Clayton sighed and looked temporarily baffled. Finally, she asked, "You haven't by any chance found more than just gold in those caves, have you?"

Stunned, Alys turned toward her mother, her glance taking in the reverend, and then Mrs. Clayton. "Mama," she said, "you told me never to breathe a word of our caves to anyone, not even to our pastor. And what do you mean, just gold?"

Her mother shrugged. "There is other treasure besides gold in those caves."

"There is?"

"I reckon I should have told you this long before. It's only that I've been so derned sick; but I'm beginning to feel better now and I've been thinking." Ma Clayton drew a deep breath. "Now it's true that there's gold in the caves, but I don't rightly know where the vein is, and I haven't particularly cared about it. But there's another treasure there, one I've never told you about because I couldn't be certain that your father had hidden it there and then I didn't want—"

"Mama, whoa! You're not making sense to me. Back up now. What treasure?"

"A deed, Alys. Your father left us a deed to some property."

Alys stood as though dazed. "A deed?"

"Yep, three hundred acres south of the Sun River were deeded to him in the forties."

"Three hundred acres?"

"That's right." Ma Clayton sat up straight, her eyes staring at a picture in front of her, but her mind obviously far removed from it and from this room. She continued, "Do you remember how I told you that your father had served in the Mexican war?"

Alys nodded.

"He was one of those thousands of men who trooped into Vera Cruz in March of forty-seven. What I didn't tell you, child, was that this land was deeded to him in partial payment for his services. Land in the Montana Territory. It was the reason we came out here to settle at all, for your father was not a fur-trading man."

"Then why don't we live on this land now instead of here in Fort Benton? You and I have never liked it here."

"Because," her mother explained, "in the beginning, back in the late forties, we settlers felt we needed the company of other people like ourselves, to fend off Indian attacks. Not that there's been any, mind you, but there were always stories. When your father helped to found this town, he also discovered the caves and a strain of gold within 'em. But this land was the property of the American Fur Company, it was not something he could buy. So we remained here, and in secret your father mined them caves."

"So," Alys uttered, "there is gold in those caverns, after all." She glanced around the room. "Did father register the deed for the acres at Sun River?"

"Nope, that's why we've got to find the deed. When we came here, there was no General Land Office. We was told that one would be established soon at Fort Union. And so your father put the deed into safe storage. I believe he hid it in the caves until such a time when he could go east and register the claim. He died before he made that trip, and before he was able to tell me where the deed was. When you were young, I told you we was looking for treasure, for gold. I did it to make it a game for you. And I suppose there might be gold there, but that never really mattered to me. All the time, I have been looking for this document."

"I see." Alys turned to glance briefly at the reverend. "And what does this have to do with Brother Mark?"

"Brother Mark needs a bit of land, just a little to set up a ministry for the Blackfeet. Although the land will be

officially yours—if'n we find that title to it—I had promised him that if he would come here and perform a duty
for me, I would grant him some land."

"Mrs. Clayton, there really is no need," the good reverend protested. "I would have come here with this fine
young man anyway."

Alys now turned her wide-eyed glare upon Moon Wolf.
"You went to fetch the reverend?"

He grinned at her. "I did."

"With what purpose in mind?" she asked.

"Alys, I needed to see the reverend," her mother took
over the conversation. "Moon Wolf did it for me and
for—"

"Maybe you should run and get your clothes," the good
reverend now said in turn.

"What is going on here? Is there some plan afoot between the three of you? What kind of celebration is this
that we're going to?"

"A dance," Moon Wolf said.

"A dance that requires me to wear my best dress?"

"Everyone there," said Moon Wolf, "will be clothed in
their best apparel. You would not want to go there without
your very best, would you?"

She cut him a glance. These three were up to something.
She knew it.

Was it possibly something to do with their marriage?
Was the good reverend here to? . . . No, she daren't hope
for it, lest it not happen.

Well, the sooner she went, the sooner she would find
out.

"Land sakes," she said, "I reckon that, seeing as how
everyone here seems to be waiting for me, I guess I'd
better go upstairs and get my things."

And at that, she lifted up the bottom of her skirt, turned,
and raced from the room on up the stairs. But not before

she heard Moon Wolf's question, "What does this deed look like?"

Alys didn't wait to hear the response. After all, it would be no more, no less than a simple piece of parchment . . .

Chapter 24

❝I know that you have hesitated to come into my camp," Moon Wolf caught her as she stepped from her room, her clothing put neatly into a box, since she would not wear a white dress through the muddy streets of Fort Benton. "But I promise you," he continued, "that tonight it will be safe. My sister has journeyed here to lead us with our celebration."

Alys smiled at him. "I'm sure it will be fine."

He, however, must have read her thoughts, for he said, "That fort in Canada was a bad place. Even the Indians would hesitate to go there. It was not a place I should have taken you."

"You had no choice," she defended him. "I accompanied you there of my own free will."

"Still," he said, "the smart ones kept away from there. This is different, however, this encampment around your home. There is to be an 'I saw' dance, there tonight."

"Ah, so that is the dance we are to attend. What is an 'I saw' dance?"

"It is a dance where the renowned of our warriors reenact their exploits on the warpath. You will like it, I think."

"I am sure that I will. Is your sister there now? In your camp?"

"*Aa,* yes, she is. She and her sisters-in-law have already erected a lodge for you and me. It is an honor that they give to us."

Alys grinned shyly. "Then I will go with you quite happily. I would love to see your sister again. But, tell me, why has she never come here to see you before now?"

"*Ha!* My sister carries bad memories of this place, I believe, and she has not been back since her time here so long ago. But she is making an exception now, for you and for me. They plan to pay tribute to us and our marriage and have prepared a feast for us."

Alys caught her breath. She hadn't expected that. "I am honored," she said, and meant it. "Is there anything that my mother and I should bring?"

He thought for a moment. "Besides the dress?"

She nodded.

"Perhaps some gifts. Some blankets, beads, maybe some flour and coffee, some sugar."

She touched his sleeve and asked, "Do you think they might like to come to my house and have a sit-down dinner here, instead?"

"I do not think so. They would worry that other white people would see them and make their lives more difficult, perhaps. They have prepared us a marriage lodge. It is better if we go to them, I believe."

"Then so we shall," she said and leaned up to give him a kiss.

He chuckled, and, taking hold of the box she held and putting it to the side, he swept her off her feet, holding her so close, she could feel every firm imprint of his body. He muttered, "It is true that I have been gone several days.

I am sorry that I distressed you. Know now that from the first day I saw you until this present day, you have always been in my heart. If I fail again to remind you of this, know always, my wife, that it is you who makes my heart happy. Please always remember this."

"It will be my pleasure," she giggled against his throat and hugged him so hard, her arms hurt. "I love you so very, very much."

The wind howled across the barren prairie, right up to the lodges, where it set the drying skins, which had been placed there earlier, under the sun, to waving back and forth. It also blew Alys's hair back, away from her face, but she didn't mind. The breeze was cool and refreshing, the kind of wind she had heard Moon Wolf refer to as a "medicine wind." With it came the rousing scents of dry prairie grass, smoke from the encampment's fires, and the pure fragrance of mountain air. All around her women sat in the open air, working over a new lodge, their talking and giggling reminding her of a circle of close and happy friends. Alys inhaled deeply and closed her eyes.

She sat outside the lodge that had been given to her, the tepee placed next to Moon Wolf's sister's for convenience and safety. Painted in bright hues of red dots and blue triangles, their tepee lay within the inner circle of relatives and friends. Aunts and uncles, cousins and Moon Wolf's almost mother had converged upon them, ready to feast and to honor the new couple. All seemed anxious to meet *her*.

Alys had already learned that Moon Wolf's own mother and father no longer lived—one the victim of smallpox, the other a casualty of alcohol.

Meanwhile her own mother reclined in the lodge of Moon Wolf's almost mother, the many female relatives gathering there to pamper and fuss over her—much to Ma Clayton's delight.

Butterfly Woman, *Aapani-aakii-wa,* suddenly appeared beside Alys and shooed her back inside the colorful lodge.

"Ann-wa   ann-wa-hka   k-oom-wa-hka?"   Butterfly Woman asked.

Alys, after taking her seat on a soft rug in the women's section of the lodge, could do little more than shake her head. She glanced all around her, noting that the tepee lining, so carefully erected, boasted a patterned design of blue and red. Scents of sage, fire, and leather reached her nostrils, the odor fragrant and pleasant, one she would associate forever with Moon Wolf, with this night.

Butterfly Woman tried again to communicate, this time in sign language, repeating the words, *"Ann-wa ann-wa-hka k-oom-wa-hka?"* Still, Alys could not understand, and she cast down her eyes.

"She asks where is your husband," a warm male voice translated from the direction of the tepee's entrance flap. Alys looked up to espy her husband, still dressed in his best clothing, standing beside the portal.

"Oh," murmured Alys.

"Nitao'too, I have arrived," he told his sister.

Butterfly Woman looked up, then quickly down. She asked, *"Tsima k-omoht-o'too-hpa?* Where have you come from?"

"K-ota's-iksi nit-ii-yIssksipist-a:-yi-aawa, I tied up your horses that they not run away when the drumming starts."

"Soka'piiwa. It is good."

Perhaps because their conversation would normally be taboo, Butterfly Woman didn't raise her eyes to her brother's as she said, *"Poohsap-oo-t. N-oko's-iksi ayaak-wa:sai'ni-wa. Nitaakahkayi.* Come here. My offspring are about to cry. I am going home now."

Moon Wolf nodded.

But before she left, Butterfly Woman turned back once and, catching Moon Wolf's eye, asked, *"Tsa niit-a'p-a o'taki-wuatsiksi?* Does your woman know what to do when the guests arrive?"

"Saa, sspommihtaa. I am certain she does not, but I will help her."

"Kit-siim-o k-aak-sta'! I forbid it," Butterfly Woman said in a rush. *"Kiisto sskai'stoto,* you would do something shocking. Soon they would start asking me to make dresses for you if you do this."

Moon Wolf simply grinned. "Then perhaps you will have to make that dress since I will help my wife get through this. She does not understand our ways."

Butterfly Woman hesitated. She said, *"Tsaahtao',* perhaps I will return so that the evening is a happy one for all involved."

"Soka'pii, it would be good, I think. *Akai-soka'pii,* it would be very good."

Soon the evening was upon them, and Alys learned quickly that it was her duty to set the meat and blood soup, which Butterfly Woman and the other female relatives had prepared, before all of their guests. With tin plates, which she had brought from her house, she plunged into her duties.

It was going well. Each person who had come to feast with them seemed happy to overlook her lack of knowledge of their ways, complimenting her instead on the fine meal.

It was toward evening, when the last of their guests had arrived, that a man entered and took his place next to Moon Wolf. Alys automatically placed a meal before him without glancing up.

"So," said an oddly familiar voice, "this is the mystery woman who has become as great a legend as her husband." The words had been spoken in English, and she looked up into the kindly eyes of the chief of scouts for the United States military.

She remembered having approached this man once, when she was seeking one of his own to pretend to be the Wolf Shadow.

"You? I remember you. I once asked you to pretend to be . . ." Her words trailed off as she glanced around her.

"Alas," he said, "it is true. You once invited me to pretend to be another and I refused. Looking back on it now, I wish that I had agreed. It would have saved you some grief, I think."

"That it would have. Then you are . . . my husband's friend?"

Moon Wolf interrupted. *"Nit-o-ke'-man,* my woman, this is my more-than-friend, *Kut-ai'-imi,* Never Laughs."

"More-than-friend?" She tilted her head toward Moon Wolf. "What is a more-than-friend?"

"Ha, I have not observed this particular sort of friendship in the white man's society, and so it is to be understood that you may not have heard of this before now. Let me explain it. In my village, when a boy is young, he and another boy close to his own age become friends, or blood brothers, and vow between them to remain friends all their lives, to share all that they might have, whether in joy or in sorrow, to die for one another if the need arises. There is no more honorable relationship amongst my people than this friendship. It is this relationship which is the most unselfish, the most giving and decent of any I have seen, in my camp and in yours also. Nowhere are the bonds so strong, except, of course, with one's wife and children."

"A more-than-friend," she repeated. "And Never Laughs is that? Our own chief of scouts?"

Grinning, Moon Wolf nodded.

"No wonder the military could never find you . . ."

Both Moon Wolf and Never Laughs were chuckling, however.

Said Never Laughs, "Yes, we have given our mutual enemies many a running battle. And it is with great honor that I have been a part of my friend's coups, for we have helped each other in many ways, even avoiding the white man's seven eleven—seventy-seven, those men who do not reason well with their . . . enemies."

"It is true, my friend, we have had many adventures together, but I think that our escapades here in Fort Benton could be at an end. You have heard of the redcoats invading the north country to throw the whiskey traders out?"

"*Aa,* yes. Word has come to us of this. It could be a good thing."

"If the redcoats are honorable, it could be. We will have to trust them and hope that they do not become the same kind of liars that the Americans have proved to be."

Moon Wolf's friend nodded.

"What have you to say about this new sheriff?"

"I do not know what to make of him," replied Never Laughs. "It is true that he has routed out some of the whiskey traders and has forced Lieutenant Warrington to leave, but I am not certain that he is friendly toward the Indian. We will have to wait and see."

"*Aa,*" Moon Wolf nodded. "*Soka'pii.*"

The two fell into companionable silence while dusk fell all about them. At length, Moon Wolf added, "I went to see this sheriff."

"*Aa,* yes," Never Laughs nodded. "This is a good thing."

"*Aa,* that it was. I wanted to see if this man's heart was in the right place."

"And what did you find?"

"His heart is true."

Never Laughs nodded. "I am glad to hear this. Did you tell him who you were, then?"

"*Aa,* that I did, that he might know me and understand why I did what I must for my people."

"You what?" Alys raised up onto her knees, her hand coming to her chest, as though she might have trouble breathing.

Moon Wolf's friend, however, merely uttered, "*Soka'pii.*"

"He gave me this." Moon Wolf held up a medal with the face of President Grant on it.

Alys gasped. "Then he didn't arrest you?"

"*Saa,* no. Why would he do this? He, himself, is here to destroy the whiskey trade. Why would he arrest me when he and I are of the same purpose?"

"But the merchants, the other people in this town could be furious with you and could catch you and—"

"I would not hide from them and I would seek to live with the truth of who and what I am. Now that the whiskey trade is finished in Canada and the sheriff is here, there is no longer a need for the secrecy."

"You did the right thing, my friend," Never Laughs commented. "You have remained true and honorable to yourself and to the people. It took courage to confront this new sheriff."

"*Aa, aa.*"

"But come now, I must leave you so that I might go and prepare myself for the 'I saw' dance."

Moon Wolf acknowledged the man with a brief nod. "You are right. I must prepare, too . . . and my wife also."

"*Aa, aa, aa. Soka'pii.*" With this said, Moon Wolf's friend arose and departed.

"What did you mean, and your wife?" Alys asked after Never Laughs had left.

Moon Wolf didn't answer. Instead, he urged, "Come, we must go quickly to the caves."

"Why? You didn't answer my question."

But Moon Wolf had already arisen, was already at the entryway, holding the flap open, when he said, "Come, I will explain."

"But Moon Wolf—"

He was already gone.

Goodness, how people did come and go here. Well, what choice did she have? Getting to her feet, she followed him.

Makoyi greeted them as soon as they entered the caves, rising up onto his hind legs and resting his front paws on Moon Wolf's shoulders. Moon Wolf laughed and petted the animal.

He said, "I am happy to see you, too, *Makoyi*. I was hoping that you would be here, for there is something that you must do this night."

"What is that?" Alys asked Moon Wolf.

But he did not answer her, merely smiled, until he offered, "You will see. You will be pleased, too, I think. Now, come gather your things and mine, too, that we might quickly return to the encampment. I need to get something from one of the other tunnels."

"And all this is for the dance?"

"It is."

"Where will the dance be held?" she asked.

"In the big council lodge of the *Mut'siks,* the Braves Society," Moon Wolf answered as he set *Makoyi* onto his feet and began treading away, toward another cavern. "The people will want us to count coup," Moon Wolf told her nonchalantly.

She turned to give him a wide-eyed stare. "Us?"

Moon Wolf looked back at her and grinned. "*Aa,* yes.

You and me. Come, we must hurry. You collect our things while I investigate this tunnel."

"Is there something there that you need?"

"Perhaps," he responded and was gone.

"What is this counting of coup?" she asked as he returned.

"When a warrior returns to his people," he explained, taking his things from her and leading the way toward the place where the caves met Alys's cellar, "that warrior will tell the people all that he did that was brave and that helped the people, that all in camp might know of it. It is a good thing. Our young people hear it and want to be like these warriors, and our braves are honored, never to be forgotten."

"But why these clothes?"

"Because a warrior will usually tell of his deed dressed as he was at that time. However, because tonight is special, you and I will not be expected to do this, though we must hold these things in our hands as we speak. It is why we have come to the cave. We must bring our things, these clothes, with us."

"I do not completely understand."

"You need only to hold these things in your hands."

"Yes, yes, I understand that. What I don't comprehend is why you tell *me* this? I am not a part of your tribe that I could count coup."

"*Aa*, yes, you are. Have you not saved my life many times? Have you not done many brave things for me and for my people? Many persons will wish to hear of your deeds and will want to honor you."

She digested this piece of information in silence. Still she thought to protest, "But Moon Wolf, I know nothing about this. I have never done it and I'm not certain I can do it."

"You will do fine. Simply tell the people what you did that was brave and helped to save my life—the life of *Makoyi*'s, too. But I must caution you, one must always tell the truth without adding or detracting from it. It must be the complete truth. I will go first so you can see what it is that we do."

"And you are sure they want to hear this from me?"

"I am certain. You are a hero to the people. There are many that will look up to you and try to be like you. You must tell it true, for you will set an example that our young people will try to follow. It is an honor, this thing that is being asked of you."

"But, Moon Wolf, I don't even speak your language."

"I will translate. You will do fine. I might caution you, however, that if you wish your caves to remain a secret, you should not mention them. It is up to you, for I will not tell of them."

She scowled, fretting, "I don't think I can do this."

"Do not worry. If you say something wrong, I will not translate it. Come, all are waiting."

The people had gathered around a campfire, in the center of their council lodge, leaving room in the center for their warriors. Ma Clayton and Brother Mark sat with Moon Wolf's other relatives amongst the crowd.

One by one, the warriors who were to count coup filed into the lodge. She had discovered also that for tonight only those who had helped the cause of the Wolf Shadow had been selected to speak.

War drums reverberated in the background. Beneath her dress, Alys's knees shook. Each of the warriors beside her had stripped down to breechcloth and moccasins, she and Moon Wolf being the only ones in full dress. It didn't help to calm her nerves. She felt alien. But she kept close to

Moon Wolf; she on one side of him, *Makoyi,* on the other.

First, to the accompaniment of the drums, Never Laughs stepped forward. Awful scars had been painted on his body, depicting his war injuries. Proudly, he told of his adventures with the Wolf Shadow.

When he stepped back, several other military scouts stood forward, each one telling of their part in the Wolf Shadow effort.

At last, it was Moon Wolf's turn to recount his stories. He did so in English and in Blackfeet, explaining that he would have his wife hear of his adventures from his own mouth, that she might share in his honor.

How the people shouted and called out their approval to hear of this!

"Haiya," he began, "I am going to tell you a story of the Wolf Shadow and how it all began. You do remember it, Society of Braves!"

"Aa, aa, yes, yes," came the braves' response.

"On a night many moons ago," he continued, "as I hid in the fort, I discovered a wagon full of kegs of whiskey ready to be shipped to our people. It was guarded by three men. This whiskey is a bad thing for our people. It makes warriors into fools and good people into bad. You know it, Blackfeet women and children."

"Aa, aa, yes, yes," confirmed the women and youngsters gathered there.

Moon Wolf resumed, "My wolf and I came upon these seizers and because they were more than us, we had to think of a way to misdirect their attention.

"I threw a stone in one direction, making great noise. One of these seizers went to investigate. Because the white man kills many of our women and children for every warrior of theirs that we kill, I spared that one's life and knocked him on the head so that he would not help his fellows. This left only two of the seizers. I fought with one of them and *Makoyi* fought with the other, ripping open his arm.

"This we did without a shot being fired. And then, because it was late and no other seizers were there, I emptied every barrel full of the whiskey.

"But soon more seizers came out to fight me. There were many of them and so I ran to a safe spot, covering my tracks as best I could.

"But *Makoyi* stayed behind and began howling, so much so that the seizers began to believe that it was a wolf spirit that had attacked them. You do remember it, scouts!"

"*Aa, aa,* yes, yes!"

"From then on, the Wolf Shadow went on to destroy many of the shipments of whiskey, always evading the seizers and their guns. Sometimes the scouts of the military covered my tracks, sometimes I did. But always we have worked together.

"And now Moon Wolf has spoken. Moon Wolf has spoken true. You do remember it, all Pikunis!"

Throughout his speech, the drums had given him soft accompaniment. But now that he had finished, they started into a wild clamor while the people shouted and cheered, "*Aa, aa,* yes, yes! *Soka'pii! Soka' piiwa!* Good, that is good!"

Suddenly, amidst all the noise, Moon Wolf turned to her. "It is now your turn," he said, giving her a nod of encouragement. He added, "They will love you. I promise you. You will do fine."

She cleared her throat as the roar of the crowd died down. A little timidly, she stepped forward, while the rhythm of the drums settled back down to a hushed accompaniment. She began, "I am Alys Clayton, or, as Moon Wolf calls me, Little Brave Woman." She paused to let Moon Wolf translate. "Long ago, when we were young, I

helped Moon Wolf and his sister escape from my village
when others there wished them harm and were searching
for them. I befriended them and led them to safety outside
the fort, thus allowing them to return to their people." Another pause as Moon Wolf continued to translate.

"Soon after, however, I was sent to school in the east
but when I returned," she continued, "I found Moon Wolf
injured one night after he had attacked the whiskey wagons. I nursed him back to health as you can see.

"Lastly, when Moon Wolf had gone down into a herd
of buffalo to try to stampede them into the whiskey camp,
someone had shot at him. With the wolf's help, I found
him and dragged him to safety, helping again to nurse him
to health. That is all."

Unlike Moon Wolf's narrative, there had been no poetic
rhyme or rhythm to her tale. Still, how the people did cheer
and the drummers throbbed out approval.

Grinning Alys started to sit down, but Moon Wolf gently touched her arm. He whispered, "There is one more
who must speak."

Alys glanced down the row of warriors. All here had
told of their adventures. Who was left?

All at once Moon Wolf turned to his pet, calling out,
"Makoyi." The wolf lifted up and set his paws onto Moon
Wolf's shoulders. Moon Wolf, however, turned the wolf
around toward the people, still holding it by its forepaws,
as he said, "You are about to count your coups, *Makoyi*,
that all may know of your bravery. I am going to turn you
around, for you must face them."

"Makoyi," Alys murmured to herself.

Meanwhile, the wolf whined.

"My people," Moon Wolf spoke first in Blackfeet, then
in English, "this one is of a tribe foreign to us but he is a
warrior true. He will count coups with you, but because
you might not understand him, I will translate for him.

"My name is *Makoyi* and my master is Moon Wolf. I have gone to war with my man many times and always I protect him. Once when a soldier tried to kill him with a gun, I attacked that man and saved my master. Another time I helped him . . ." Moon Wolf went on to recount many more such tales. "Recently," he continued, "when my master was weak and did not know that his wife had gone on the warpath for him, I awakened my master from a sound sleep, thinking that he should protect his wife. I led my master to where the enemy was shooting at his wife and I killed two of the enemy that my man could get his woman and flee. In doing this, I took a bullet into my chest and was sick for many days."

Shouts began, but Moon Wolf held up his hand. He said, "The next part I cannot translate for you because I was unconscious. My wife will tell of *Makoyi*'s next feat of bravery."

Moon Wolf turned to Alys.

Alys found, to her horror, that her voice was hoarse. Something about seeing the wolf count coup had touched her. Still, she came to stand beside the wolf, petting him and putting her arm around him as she proudly began, "My master left me with his wife while he sneaked down to a buffalo herd that stood above the camp of the whiskey traders. His wife became very excited when a shot was heard and I knew that my master was in trouble. The woman told me to take her to her husband because she did not know the way. I did this and we found my man injured." She paused while Moon Wolf translated.

"In order to get my man to safety," Alys continued, "I allowed the woman to tie a rope around me and push it up over my master's horse, where I pulled on the rope to raise our man up onto his mount. Then, because his woman did not know where to take my master, I led them to a wood by a stream where my master might recover. While

she nursed him, I hunted for them that they would not go
hungry. This I did because I love my master. There," she
concluded, Moon Wolf quickly translating, "I have said
it."

Oh, how the people did roar and roar! How the drums
did beat! While drums whanged out a cadence that did not
let up for several minutes, chants of all sorts joined the
throb of excitement, trilling, *"Makoyi! Makoyi, Makoyi!"*

Makoyi seemed to perceive what was happening, too,
for he ran, alternatingly chasing and then wagging his tail.
He jumped up onto Moon Wolf, placing his paws on his
shoulders, and tried to lick his face. Moon Wolf laughed
and petted the animal.

A dance soon followed the ceremony, with Moon Wolf,
Alys, and *Makoyi* the honored guests. Ma Clayton reclined
next to her daughter, the reverend next to Moon Wolf.

As they sat on the sidelines, watching the others, Moon
Wolf put his arm around Alys and, as he took her into his
arms, he whispered, "Though you have never seen an 'I
saw' dance before tonight, you did it very well. I knew
that you would. I am proud and honored to know that you
are my wife."

She smiled leisurely and put her head into the crook of
his shoulder. "And how wonderful that you had *Makoyi*
count coup, for he is a true warrior, no matter that he is
not human."

"Aa, yes, he is a warrior true."

She sent *Makoyi* a loving glance. The wolf, however,
appeared to be somewhat distressed. Off in the distance
could be heard the melancholy serenade of the wolves, and
Makoyi lifted his ears, stirring uneasily.

"His kind are calling to him again," Moon Wolf nodded
toward his pet. "I will tell him to stay here, but he might
go to them. And I will not stop him."

"Nor will I," she said, and, laughing, melted into the arms of her husband.

"Nor will I prevent this reverend, Kind Heart, from marrying us."

This statement was uttered so matter-of-factly, that it took her several minutes to respond. "What?" she asked.

But Moon Wolf did not glance at her, sat perfectly erect and showed her only one side of his profile as he said, "I think that Kind Heart should marry us so that both your people and mine will know that we are now one."

"Marry us?"

"I think that we should have the white man's certificate. Is it not this that you wish?"

"Well, yes, but I didn't mean to imply that I am anything else but married to you already."

"Still," he said, at last grinning down at her, "I think this is something I would like to do."

"Why, I can't believe it. I . . ." She leaned over Moon Wolf so that she could address the reverend. "Is it true? Are you here to marry us, Brother Mark?"

"Yes, I am," came the deeply resonant voice of the reverend. "I was fetched by this young man to do exactly that. This party was really the start of the ceremony, I believe. But your mother and this young man here wanted you to be surprised."

"Yes, well, that I am." She turned to her mother. "Then you've known all along?"

"Of course, dear."

"But tell me, Brother Mark, I have been searching and searching this town for a clergyman who would marry us, and I have found none that would do it. You do not mind, then, that Moon Wolf and I are not of the same . . ." She left the rest unsaid.

"My child, I am only happy that the two of you have chosen to do the right thing and are seeking to have His blessing upon you. I assure you that the Lord cares not whether your skin color is white or red. I only wish the other settlers in the territory had a heart so open. It would certainly be easier to help the tribes of Indians if the moral quality of white immigrants improved. But I would ask something of you before we go any further."

"What is that, Reverend?"

"Do you love this man?"

Alys grinned wholeheartedly. "That I do, Reverend. That I do."

"Then," he suggested, "I think we should have that wedding."

"Especially," volunteered Moon Wolf, "since I have found the deed that both mother and daughter have been seeking so desperately."

A shocked instant followed those carefully chosen words until mother and daughter blurted out all at once, "You what?"

"I found this paper long ago when I was exploring the caves," explained Moon Wolf. "Remember, Little Brave Woman, when I was telling you to observe the small things? That sometimes this could save your life?"

She nodded.

"This paper was hidden behind a rock that looked like it might have been part of the wall. But one rock was of granite, the other of schist. I became curious about this and looked behind the rock. This is what I found." He produced the document.

Neither woman could speak for several moments.

At last it was Alys who found her voice. "But this is wonderful," she said, her voice barely over a whisper. "I will go to the General Land Office tomorrow and register this claim."

"That is good," he said, "that is very good. Perhaps this land"—he waved at the document—"is that special place we had hoped to find. Perhaps, too, this will be the start of our two worlds coming together, for, have you noticed one other thing?"

Alys could do little more than shrug her shoulders.

"This property is on the land that has been ceded to my people. They will be our neighbors."

Alys stared at him for a moment before she suddenly broke out into laughter.

"It is wonderful," she said, "it is truly simply wonderful, my love."

A breeze flew down through the ears of the tepee and up into the entryway of the council lodge. It lifted her white veil, which her mother had brought for her, away from her face. She grinned slightly, not paying any attention to the words that Reverend Mark spoke. She sneaked a peek to her side, however, and caught Moon Wolf's glance back at her. She bestowed upon him a shy smile.

He readily returned the gesture and reached down to hold her hand. No matter that she wore white lace gloves— the feel of his firm grip upon her sent shivers racing up and down her spine.

Not a single space remained in the council lodge, as all within the encampment crowded in to witness the joining of these, their two heroes.

She had dressed quickly in Butterfly Woman's lodge, her mother and the other female relatives only too happy to help clothe her in the white satin gown she had brought with her. The dress, trimmed with Valenciennes lace, was one she had started making while still visiting in the east, although she had finished the garment at home. Though it was not specifically made to be a wedding dress, she was certain that when she looked back upon this day, that wouldn't make the slightest difference.

She closed her eyes as a feeling of well-being swept over her.

Although she knew Brother Mark by reputation only, it was clear that he was a man of integrity and honesty, the name given to him by the Blackfeet, "Kind Heart," summing it up better than she could have.

"Do you, Moon Wolf," the reverend was saying, "take this woman to be your lawfully wedded wife, to love, honor and trust her, to have and to hold her, in sickness and in health, and for richer or poorer, so long as you both shall live?"

Moon Wolf's voice rang out with clarity as he said, *"Waanisttsi,* I do."

At last the reverend turned to her. "And do you, Alys, take this man to be your lawfully wedded husband, to love, honor and trust him, to have and to hold him, in sickness and in health, and for richer or poorer, so long as you both shall live?"

She smiled. "I do."

"Then by the power invested in me by the Lord, our God, I now pronounce you husband and wife." He turned to Moon Wolf. "You may kiss the bride."

Grinning down at her, Moon Wolf raised the veil away and, placing a finger under her chin, lifted her head toward his, bringing his lips to hers so softly, so tenderly, that she whimpered, tears of happiness streaming from the corners of her eyes. He whispered, *"Kitsikakomimmo,"* as the crowd around them began to sing and shout.

But the two lovers didn't even hear. Gazing down at her, he wiped away her tears with the tip of his finger, rubbing the moisture so very carefully on his own cheek. He whispered, "And now, as it has been in the past, a part of you is a part of me—always . . ."

Recognizing these as the same words he had once spoken so very long ago, she threw herself into his arms, crying, "For always and always . . ."

Epilogue

They stood alone on the hill overlooking the river that flowed steadily through their land. Clear, clean water rushed beneath them, as though endowed with a life of its own. The sun, high in the sky, beat down upon them, and in the distance loomed the hills and snow-capped mountains they loved so much. A hawk, flying high overhead, squawked, and in the distance a wolf howled.

Neither person said a word; neither one had to.

Though so very different, these two people loved, and no one, save the power of God, could take that from them.

Closer now came the howl of a wolf, joined in by another. Soon, two wolves appeared on the far horizon, one trotting toward the two people on the hill.

"Makoyi," the man called, and the wolf whined over and over again until at last came another melancholy howl, joined shortly by another. The two people hugged one another to this, their serenade, their prairie song.

Life would go on. The people would survive.

But most of all, there would be love in abundance.

*   *   *

"They both lived to a very great age and always was their love for one another a thing of beauty and inspiration for all the people. They had many, many children and grandchildren, some living to this day. Some, who are sitting here beside me, are direct descendants from those two heroes.

"But, come, when I started this story, I told you that there was only one hero. Do you see now that there were three?"

"Yes, Grandfather," said the little girl sitting next to him, her small arms wrapped around his legs. "Besides Moon Wolf there was his pet, *Makoyi*. And Little Brave Woman was a woman of great courage. But Grandfather, how can she be a Blackfeet legend when she wasn't even Indian?"

The old man raised his chin, his eyes flickering with an emotion that was almost unreadable. At length, he uttered, "Oh, my granddaughter, but she was of our tribe. For you see, being Blackfeet is not just a matter of color of skin or the place where one is born. Being Blackfeet, my child, is also a condition of the heart. *Aa,* yes, a condition of the heart. Remember this. The white man's ways may come and go, but so long as you remember us, the true and moral ways of your people, you will always prosper.

"And now I have spoken."

The old man hung his head, the young child at his side taking his hand in her own small one.

She whispered, "I will remember, Grandfather. I will always remember . . ."

Glossary

Aa—the Blackfeet word for *yes*.

Almost Mother—with those tribes that practiced polygamy, this was another wife of the same father. Often an almost mother was also an aunt, for a man would try to marry sisters.

Blackfeet—the tribe of Indians who now live in northwestern Montana. Originally there were three tribes of Indians that comprised the Blackfoot Nation—the *Pikuni*, the *Kainah*, and the *Siksika*. They were three distinct tribes, which hunted together and intermarried and spoke the same language and became known to the trader generally as the Blackfoot or Blackfeet (used interchangeably). In reservation days, the southern *Pikuni*, or, as they are sometimes known, the *Piegan* (pronounced Pay-gan), began to be called the Blackfeet erroneously by the United States government. This left the *Siksika* in Canada (*Siksika* means Blackfoot in their own language) as the Blackfoot tribe which resides in Canada; the northern *Pikuni* reside also in Canada. This northern *Pikuni* tribe is often referred to as the *Pikuni* or *Piegan* tribe. What this means is that today, when we speak of the Blackfoot Nation, we speak of four different tribes—the Blackfeet in northern Montana (really the southern *Pikuni* or *Piegan*), the *Piegan* or *Pikuni* in Canada (the northern *Pikuni* or *Piegan*), the *Kainah*, or Blood tribe, in Canada, and the *Siksika*, or Blackfoot, in Canada.

Black Robe—a priest, usually a Jesuit, called a Black Robe because of their dress.

Bull Train—bulls pulled the freight of the wagons from one place to another. "Bulls are slow travellers, and these had a heavy load to haul. The quantity of weight of merchandise that could be stowed away in those old-time 'prairie schooners' were astonishing. Berry's train now consisted of four eight-yoke teams, drawing twelve wagons in all, loaded with fifty thousand pounds of provisions, alcohol, whisky, and trade goods. There were four bull-whackers, a night-herder who drove the 'cavayard'—extra bulls and some saddle horses . . ." (James Willard Schultz, *My Life as an Indian*)

Faille—on a lady's gown, a material made of silk, finely ribbed.

Kit Fox Society—all Indian tribes had different societies for men and for women. The Kit Fox Society, or the *Sin'-o-pah*, a society of the *Pikuni*, was part of the

All Comrades society. These were more or less secret societies and were ranked according to age. Their duties were mainly to enforce tribal law. Different dances and games were associated with each society.

Last Brother is pointing down—in the night sky. The Big Dipper makes a circle around the North Star every twenty-four hours. Of the seven stars in the Big Dipper, this is the last star in the handle. Pointing down would make the time very late evening or early morning.

Medicine Line—the division between the United States and Canada.

Paletot—a lady's cloak. It is usually fitted loose with a cape collar.

Percale—lady's fashion. A calico material that has been slightly glazed.

Polonaise—on a lady's gown, an overskirt resembling a coat in which the front is pulled back. It is worn over an underskirt.

Saa—the Blackfeet word for *no*.

Seven — Eleven — Seventy - Seven — the Vigilance Committee. Civilians who took the law into their own hands. "You don't know exactly who they are, but you may be sure that they are representative men who stand for law and order; they are more feared by criminals than are the courts and prisons of the

East, for they always hang a murderer or robber."
(James Willard Schultz, *My Life as an Indian*)

Seizers—what the Blackfeet Indians called the soldiers at this point in history.

Soka'pii—the Blackfeet word for *good*, usually accompanied by a hand motion for good. Holding the right hand level with the stomach, palm down, make a quick motion outward, saying *soka'pii* at the same time.

Walking Suit—in women's fashion, a dress or a costume very popular at this time in history. They are distinct from the visiting dress in that the visiting dress is made from more than one material.

Whiskey Sneakers—what the Indians called the white men who peddled whiskey to the Indians.

Appendix

~~~~~~ ◦◦◦◦ ~~~~~~

"As the winter wore on the buffalo herds drifted farther and farther away from the mountain, and we had to follow them or starve. We moved down to the mouth of Two Medicine Lodges River; then in Middle-Winter Moon (January), moved down on Bear River and camped in a bottom that Mountain Chief's band had just left, they going a little way farther down the river. It was an unhappy time: the whites had given us of their terrible white-scabs disease (smallpox), and some of our band were dying. And the buffalo herds remained so far out from the river that we had to go for a two or three days' hunt in order to get meat for our helpless ones. One evening I arranged to go on a hunt with a number of our band. We were to travel light, take only two lodges to accommodate us all; my mother and one of my sisters were to go with me to help with my kills. Came morning and I set out for my horses; could not find them on the plain. Sought them in the timbered bottoms of the valley; did not come upon them until late in the day. The hunting party had long since gone. I told my mother that we would join the next party of hunters to go out. We still had dried meat to last us for some days.

"On the following morning I found my horses in the timber well above camp and was nearing it with them when, suddenly, I ran into a multitude of white men: seizers. I was so astonished, so frightened, that I could not move. One of the seizers came and grasped my arm; spoke; tapped his lips with his fingers; I was not to speak, shout. He was a chief, this seizer, had strips of yellow metal on his shoulders, had a big knife, a five-shots pistol. He made me advance with him; all of the seizers were advancing. We came to the edge of the camp; close before us were the lodges. Off to our right were many more seizers looking down upon them. It was a cold day. The people were all in their lodges, many still in their beds. None knew that the seizers had come.

"A seizer chief up on the bank shouted something, and at once all of the seizers began shooting into the lodges. Chief Heavy Runner ran from his lodge toward the seizers on the bank. He was shouting to them and waving a paper writing that our agent had given him, a writing saying that he was a good and peaceful man, a friend of the whites. He had run but a few steps when he fell, his body pierced with bullets. Inside the lodges men were yelling; terribly frightened women and children, screaming—screaming from wounds, from pain as they died. I saw a few men and women, escaping from their lodges, shot down as they ran. Most terrible to hear of all was the crying of the little babies at their mothers' breasts. The seizers all advanced upon the lodges, my seizer still firmly holding my arm. They shot at the tops of the lodges; cut the bindings of the poles so the whole lodge would collapse upon the fire and begin to burn-burn and smother those within. I saw my lodge go down and burn. Within it my mother, my almost-mothers, my almost-sisters. Oh, how pitiful were their screamings as they died, and I there, powerless to help them!

"Soon all was silent in the camp, and the seizers advanced, began tearing down the lodges that still stood, shooting those within them who were still alive, and then trying to burn all that they tore down, burn the dead under the heaps of poles, lodge-skins, and lodge furnishings; but they did not burn well.

"At last my seizer released my arm and went about with his men looking at the smoking piles, talking, pointing, laughing, all of them. And finally the seizers rounded up all of our horses, drove them up the valley a little way, and made camp.

"I sat before the ruin of my lodge and felt sick. I wished that the seizers had killed me, too. In the center of the fallen lodge, where the poles had fallen upon the fire, it had burned a little, then died out. I could not pull up the lodge-skin and look under it. I could not bear to see my mother, my almost-mothers, my almost-sisters lying there, shot or smothered to death. When I went for my horses, I had not carried my many-shots gun. It was there in the ruin of the lodge. Well, there it would remain.

"From the timber, from the brush around about, a few old men, a few women and children came stealing out and joined me. Sadly we stared at our ruined camp; spoke but little; wept. Wailed wrinkled old Black Antelope: 'Why, oh, why had it to be that all of our warriors, our hunters, had to go out for buffalo at this time. But for that, some of the white seizers would also be lying here in death.'

" 'One was killed. I saw him fall,' I said.

" 'Ah. Only one seizer. And how many of us. Mostly women and children; newborn babies. Oh, how cruel, how

terribly cruel are the white men,' old Curlew Woman
wailed.

" 'Killed us off without reason for it; we who have done
nothing against the white,' said old Three Bears, and again
we wept.

"As we sat there, three men arrived from Mountain
Chief's camp below. They stared and stared at our fallen,
half-burned lodges, at our dead, lying here and there, and
could hardly believe what they saw. They rode over to us,
asked what had happened, and when we had told them of
the white seizers' sudden attack upon us, it was long before
they could speak. And then they said that we were to live
with them; they would take good care of us poor, bereaved
ones.

"Said old Three Bears: 'We had warning of this. That
white trader, Big Nose, told us that the whites were going
to revenge the killing of Four Bears by Owl Child. But
why didn't they seek him, kill him, instead of slaughtering
us here, we always friendly with the whites?'

"That Owl Child—he had killed my father, and now he
was the cause of my mother's and all my womenfolks'
lying dead under their half-burned lodges. Well, as soon
as possible, I would kill him, I vowed.

"That night the white seizers did not closely watch the
hundreds of horses that they had taken from us. We managed to get back about half of the great herd and drive
them down to Mountain Chief's camp. During the day our
buffalo hunters returned. With many horses loaded with
meat and hides, they came singing, laughing, down into
the valley, only to find their dear ones dead under their
ruined lodges. The white killers had gone, turned back
whence they came. As best we could we buried our dead—
a terrible, grieving task it was—and counted them: fifteen
men, ninety women, fifty children. Forty-four lodge and

lodge furnishings destroyed, and hundreds of our horses stolen. Haiya! Haiya!

"And to this day I deeply regret that I had no opportunity to fulfill my vow: even then Owl Child had the terrible white-scabs disease, and a few days later he died."

Bear Head finished his tale, and I was silent, and very, very sad. The murder of the three Pikunis, Heavy-Charging-in-the-Brush, Bear Child, and Rock-Old-Man, by the three white men at Fort Benton had caused no particular comment. But the killing of Malcolm Clark (Four Bears) was different. The newspapers and the residents of the territory were loud in denunciation of the outrage; as it was, no settler, no traveler, was safe from the Indians, they said. The commanding officers at Fort Shaw and Fort Ellis as well as the Secretary of War were called upon to punish severely the Indians, to make the country safe for the whites, above all to make reprisal on Mountain Chief's band, of which Owl Child was a member.

So was it that Major Eugene M. Baker of Fort Ellis was chosen to lead an expedition against the band. Early in January, 1870, he left Fort Ellis with four companies of the Second Cavalry. Arriving at Fort Shaw, he arranged to have fifty-five mounted men of the Thirteenth Infantry under Captain Higbee join his command; and Joseph Kipp, a Fort Shaw scout, was sent out to locate the band. He found it in a bottom of Marias River Valley due north of Goosebill Butte and, returning to the fort, so reported. On the following morning the expedition set out northward and that evening camped on Teton River, close under Priest's Butte. Two mornings later, looking down upon the camp on Marias River, scout Kipp at once said to Colonel Baker, "Colonel, that is not Mountain Chief's camp. It is the camp of Black Eagle and Heavy Runner, I know it by its differently painted lodges."

And he was right. Since he had been there a few days

previously, Mountain Chief's band had moved down the river about ten miles, and this band had come down and occupied the deserted campground.

Said Colonel Baker, "That makes no difference, one band or another of them; they are all Piegans and we will attack them." And then to one of his men: "Sergeant, stand behind this scout, and if he yells or makes a move, shoot him." And finally: "All ready men. Fire!"

I obtained later some more information about the massacre:

HISTORICAL SOCIETY OF MONTANA (seal)

David Hilger, Librarian
Room 106, Capitol

Helena, January 17, 1936

James Willard Schultz
Indian Field Service
Browning, Montana
Dear Mr. Schultz:

Answering your letter of Jan. 14 the information requested on the Baker Massacre is as follows:

Col. Philip R. De Trobriand was in command at Fort Shaw at the time, Major Eugene M. Baker was in command of the expedition and was chosen by General Sheridan because of his experience in the Indian warfare in Oregon. These are Sheridan's orders verbatim, "If the lives and property of citizens of Montana can best be protected by striking Mountain Chief's band, I want them struck. Tell Baker to strike them hard." Baker marched from Fort Ellis with four companies of the 2nd cavalry and was joined at Fort Shaw by 55 mounted men of the 13th infantry under Capt. Higbee. Joe Cobell and Joe Kipp were scouts with the soldiers on the expedition. On the morning of Jan. 23, 1870 they came upon the band of Piegans under Bear Chief and Big Horn on the Marias, 37 lodges. The camp was still asleep and many of the people were ill with smallpox. Baker's orders were "Open Fire; continue as long as there is any resistance." The official report from De Trobriand was 120 men killed, 53 women and children, 44 lodges destroyed, and 300 horses captured. The report from Vincent Collyer of the Board of Indian Commissioner was 173 killed: 15 fighting men (between 12 and 37 years of age) 90 women and 50 children under 12 years of age. This information came from Lieut. Pease, agent for the Blackfeet. One cavalry man was killed.

Am interested in the account of the killing of Malcolm Clarke and it is probably the true version. Am always glad to be of service to you at any time.

Very truly yours,
(signed)
(Mrs.) Anne McDonnell
Asst. Lib.

—On the Baker Massacre, James Willard Schultz, *Blackfeet and Buffalo: Memories of Life Among the Indians* (as told to Schultz by Bear Head), edited by Keith C. Seele, copyright ©1962, University of Oklahoma Press